JANUS
ISLAND

JANUS ISLAND

a novel by SLOAN WILSON

LITTLE, BROWN AND COMPANY · BOSTON · TORONTO

Published simultaneously in Canada
by Little, Brown & Company (Canada) Limited

PRINTED IN THE UNITED STATES OF AMERICA

The author wishes to acknowledge both
the enthusiasm and criticism of Robert
Hazel in preparing this manuscript.

*To Betty, who for four years has made
my life quite improbably pleasant*

JANUS
ISLAND

THE telephone in Ben Powers's hotel room rang at a little after ten in the morning. He had worked most of the night trying to complete a television script, and the bell dragged him from a deep sleep.

"Hello," he said irritably.

"Dads! Did I wake you up?"

It was his nineteen-year-old daughter calling from college, and the sound of her voice changed the tone of his.

"Laura!" he said. "How are you, baby? Is everything all right?"

"Yes," she said. "Oh, Dads! I feel so bad and so good!"

"That sounds serious. What do you feel bad about?"

"Would you mind terribly if I didn't go down to Janus Island with you? I mean, I know you'll hate me, I know you have been looking forward to it. I feel like such a bitch!"

"Of course I'll be a little disappointed, but I expect I'll survive," he replied evenly, determined not to sound hurt. "What's up?"

"Bill Murphy is going to Bermuda with his whole family, and at the last minute they asked me to go along! I talked to Muth about it, and so did Bill's mother. Muth says I can go!"

"That's nice," Ben said. "What are the financial arrangements?"

"I haven't spent my Christmas money yet, and all I have to pay is my passage. Some friends have given the Murphys the use of a whole house, and they'll put me up."

"Your Christmas money won't get you to Bermuda and back. I'll give you the money I was going to use for your ticket to Florida."

"Oh, Dads, you're a love! I had so looked forward to being with you, but I never expected this. Bill is such a wonderful guy, and . . ."

"I know," Ben said. "Believe it or not, you don't have to explain."

Over Christmas vacation he had met Bill Murphy, a big, intense-looking young man whose father had recently died. The pain and confusion in the boy's eyes had both touched and alarmed him. He was, Ben suspected, going through emotional storms which might be difficult for Laura to weather or avoid, but what good would fatherly warnings do?

"You're an angel, Dads," Laura said. "Look, we're com-

4

ing into La Guardia Saturday morning at eleven, and we're going to join his mother and his sisters at Kennedy at noon to catch the plane for Bermuda. You have to meet us! I'm dying to see you, and we can have an hour together."

"That will be fun," Ben said. "I'll be there!"

"Thank you, Dads, and this summer I promise, promise, promise I'll spend a lot of time with you. Could we go camping on Janus Island then?"

"Our old place will still be there," he said. "Goodbye, baby. I'll see you at La Guardia, Saturday at eleven."

"Right. Dads?"

"Yes?"

"Is everything all right with you?"

"Everything's hunky-dory!"

"Is the work going all right?"

"The work is going fine."

"Dads?"

"Yes?"

"Are you getting out at all? I worry about you, just sitting around that horrible little room."

"I get out quite a bit. This weekend I'm going out to Long Island to visit Nort and Nancy Clay. I was going to take you along. He's got some big scheme he wants to talk to me about."

"Oh, I wish I could go! Does he still have that fantastic house?"

"Yes indeed."

"Anyway, I'm glad you're keeping busy. Now I don't have to feel guilty about Bermuda any more."

"Good," he said. "See you Saturday, baby. Don't worry about a thing."

Hanging up, Ben lay down on his bed and stared out the window at a gray April sky above Manhattan. Of course, nineteen-year-old girls prefer to spend vacations with their young men rather than with their fathers, he thought. It was ridiculous to feel lonely and hurt. There is no crisis in a man's life bad enough to justify emotional dependence upon a daughter for long, he reflected, and it would be psychologically brutal to Laura, particularly after his divorce from her mother. One thing he didn't want to become was a self-pitying father begging his daughter for her attention and time.

Still, he wished he had not made so many preparations for this particular spring vacation with Laura. How shocking it was to realize how much he had begun to build his life around her since his divorce! One reason he had been working so hard to finish up his television script was that he knew she retained a childlike pride in any little show he wrote or produced. His decision to spend the weekend with Nort Clay and his wife had also been based on the assumption that Laura would be with him, because that big old house was for many reasons not a place he liked to visit alone.

Getting up, Ben put a pan of water on a hot plate to make coffee. After all, he told himself, there were many things to keep him busy, many things to look forward to. At forty-five, a man has no reason to think his life is done.

But the only thing Ben really found himself looking forward to as he went back to work on the text of his script was the prospect of seeing his daughter at the airport. He would bring some paper cups and a bottle of cold champagne, he decided. That would help keep the hour light and gay.

"Dads!" Laura said as she came into the crowded terminal and saw him. "Dads, what's that you've got in the basket?"

"A modest repast," he said. "We can have it in the taxi on the way to Kennedy if you don't have time."

"With champagne!" Laura said, peeking into the basket. "Oh, Dads! Only you would think of that!"

Close to tears, she threw her arms around him. Over her shoulder he saw Bill Murphy looking somewhat embarrassed.

"A trip to Bermuda is something to be celebrated," Ben said. "In some ways, I feel sorry for you kids. In my day we whooped it up on a boat for two days on the way there."

"It's good to see you, sir," Bill Murphy said. "I'll get our bags. I'll be right back."

"Let's go over there," Laura said, gesturing toward a waiting room. "I can't wait to taste that champagne!"

They sat on a couch of imitation green leather with chromium arms, and he opened the champagne with a satisfactory pop.

"You're looking great!" Laura said. "Do you know that when Bill first saw you with me last Christmas, he thought you were my brother?"

"Did he tell you that?"

"He sure did."

"That boy will go far!" Ben said, and handed her a paper cup of champagne.

As she sipped it, tilting up her delicate chin, he was stricken by her resemblance to her mother, not the rather heavy, hard-eyed woman he had divorced, but the gentle, slender girl he had married twenty-one years ago. Her eyes, those dark eyes, met his, and he let his glance fall.

"You haven't poured any for yourself," she said.

"I will now."

There was a surprisingly painful moment of silence during which he could not say anything he wanted to say. Don't let it happen to you, he was tempted to blurt out. Don't get married too young and have to spend the rest of your life trying to make up for the mistake. Be careful on those beaches in Bermuda; be careful of the hurt lonely look in your young man's eyes!

"In Bermuda, be careful of the motorbikes," he said. "They're awfully dangerous on those little crooked roads."

"I'll be careful," she replied.

"Do you have enough money for clothes? Have you got a spring outfit yet?"

"I have plenty of clothes," she said, her voice suddenly grown husky.

"There should be some caviar and some crackers in here," he said, rummaging in the basket.

His attempt at gaiety was not going to work, he saw. There were still too many echoes of painful memories when he and Laura met, still too much love without any good way to express it, too much worry and concern for each other without any way to give real help. To his horror Ben found he was hoping Bill Murphy would hurry back to break the tension, but that young man, in an attempt to be tactful, was having a beer at the bar.

"You're looking great!" Laura said again.

"You are too."

"I think you've been losing weight," she said.

"A little. And you've put a little on, most becomingly."

"Thank you," she said, and looked down.

There was another moment of silence while he spread out a paper napkin on his lap and dabbed caviar on crackers.

"Where are you staying in Bermuda?" he asked.

"Somerset, right near that little bridge."

"It's nice over there," he said, remembering how Rita, his former wife, had criticized him when he had had trouble getting a sailboat through that bridge.

"Have you heard from Benny?" she asked.

"No. Your brother is spending this vacation with your mother."

8

"Have you heard from Granny?"

"Not lately. I'm afraid I'm even worse than you when it comes to writing my mother."

"I know, I should do better," Laura said. "Has she been complaining?"

"I don't know, but you should keep in touch with us both. Have you heard from your brother lately?"

Before she could answer, Bill Murphy strode across the floor carrying two big suitcases.

"Excuse me, sir, but we better hurry, Laura," he said. "It looks like it's going to be hard to get a cab."

The idea of riding in a cab between them with his ridiculous picnic basket on his lap, trying to make conversation for a half-hour, suddenly appalled Ben.

"I don't want to hold you kids up," he said quickly. "Run along! Take the champagne with you, if you like."

"Thanks, sir!" Bill Murphy said, accepting the bottle with a nest of cups over the top. "I didn't mean to rush you, but my mother will go crazy if we're late!"

"Then be on time, lad!"

Hastily Ben gave his daughter a kiss on the cheek. For a moment she clung to him.

"Off with you both!" he said.

"Goodbye, Dads!" Laura said. "Thanks and goodbye!" Taking the champagne from Bill, she turned decisively and headed for the door without a backward glance. Picking up the bags, Bill followed her.

When they got outside the glass door, the young man gave the heavy suitcases to a porter with a baggage cart. Turning to Laura, he casually put his arm around her waist, and, walking that way, they were soon lost in the crowd.

Looking after them, Ben could not help feeling a certain sense of finality. Before long, after all, Laura would be getting married, if not to this young man, then to some other. Even if she didn't, she would have jobs or want to study in the summers. Never again could he legitimately expect her to play an important role in his life, or at least to spend much time with him.

"It takes a man to rear a good daughter, and a man to let her go," he remembered some character actor saying in a television play he had produced long ago. At the time it had seemed pretty corny. It still did, Ben told himself with a wry grin.

Abandoning the picnic basket beside a trash barrel, he went to the bar for a double bourbon. He would collect some fancy camping equipment for use on Janus Island. Wouldn't anything be better than his hotel room? He would spend the weekend at Nort's house, and then go down to Janus Island, his childhood home.

Finishing his bourbon, he squared his shoulders and walked out to get a bus back to his room in the old Central Hotel, which he still thought of, since his divorce, as his monastic cell.

CHAPTER 2

WHEN Ben got back to his room he stared with disgust at the half-unpacked suitcases which littered the floor, the empty beer cans in the corner, and the stack of unanswered mail on his desk. He should put things in order, but he felt too restless for housekeeping activities now. Pacing up and down between two footlockers, he wondered whether he should go to a matinee, drop in at the Harvard Club for a drink, invite some woman to have dinner with him, or try to finish the television script. None of these choices appealed to him in the least. The television script had already begun to appear ridiculous, as so many of them did to him now, and most of the women he knew had troubles as bad as his own, or worse, which they would want to tell him about. With this thought came a name of one who apparently did not: Penny Savodi.

He had met her at a cocktail party the week before, one of those noisy affairs with a hundred men and women jammed into a five-room apartment in the East Seventies. Most of them had been sleek, middle-aged, somewhat jaded people, and he had first noticed Penny Savodi because she was so refreshingly young and slender. In her late twenties, she had brown hair cut rather short, large brown eyes and a deeply tanned face that looked as though she had both laughed and cried a lot. She had worn a tweed skirt and a white cashmere sweater which emphasized a pretty little figure, like that of a fortunate college girl, and throughout the first hour of the party she had stood alone in a corner, by a window with big drapes, looking oddly like a child in hiding. He had talked to her about the difficulty of producing good television plays, which seemed to interest her. She had a nice lyrical laugh, and a flattering way of nodding approval while he spoke. Somewhere along the line he had asked her telephone number and had written it down, promising to call her soon.

The next morning this had seemed foolish to him. In the cold light of reason, it had seemed neither sensible nor kind for a forty-five-year-old man loaded down with troubles and debts to pursue a twenty-eight-year-old who seemed sensitive enough to be vulnerable and desirable enough to hurt a man badly if she decided to. She certainly did not seem the sort of woman he could take lightly, and with things as they were for Ben, he felt he was in no position to take on a serious involvement. So he had decided not to call.

The decision was no doubt sensible, Ben reflected now as he paced up and down his hotel room, but like so many sensible decisions that he had made recently, it seemed to result only in boredom and loneliness. Ben took out his wallet, found the girl's telephone number, and leaned to the phone.

"Hello?"

Somehow she made that one word sound rather forlorn, as though she didn't expect much from whoever might be calling.

"This is Ben Powers," he said. "Do you remember at the . . ."

"Of course I remember you, Ben," she said, her voice warming, and he was pleased.

"I'm glad," he said. "Penny, I'm at loose ends today, can't work, and on the spur of the moment I decided to see if you were busy. Have you had lunch yet?"

"As a matter of fact, I haven't. I enjoyed talking to you the other night, and I've been hoping you would call."

The frankness of this also pleased him, and he found his depression turning into exuberance.

"Wonderful!" he said. "Where can I pick you up?"

"Where do you want to have lunch?"

"How about Sardi's?"

"Fine! I love their crabmeat with cheese. I'll meet you there. It will save you coming all the way across town — the traffic is terrible today."

"Thank you," he said. "I'll be there as soon as I can."

Full of enthusiasm, Ben grabbed his chesterfield and walked rapidly to the elevator. The shabby corridor of the old hotel did not now seem to bother him so much.

The traffic was extremely bad that day, and he was impatient. It took half an hour to go from the West Eighties to 44th Street. When he finally walked into Sardi's, he found she was waiting for him, perched on a stool at the end of the bar.

"Hello," she said. "I'm glad you had this pleasant thought."

"So am I," Ben replied, and sat beside her. "It's a corny line, but you're even prettier than I remembered."

"With corny lines like that, you won't go far wrong."

She took a thin gold cigarette case from the bag on her lap, and when she snapped the bag shut, it slid from her knees to the floor. With somewhat self-conscious gallantry Ben leaned over to pick it up. He was a big man made clumsy by exuberance, and when he straightened up, his elbow hit the glass of beer she had ordered. He tried to catch it but succeeded only in spilling it in his lap.

"Oh, Lord!" he exclaimed, looking down at his dripping trousers. "This is always the way it goes!"

"I'm sorry!" Penny said, and getting up, went to the headwaiter. A moment later she came back with two big napkins.

"I guess I better go back to my place to change," he said with exasperation, mopping up the worst of the mess.

"Yes," Penny said.

The hatcheck girl seemed to take a long while to find his coat. Ben waited with a knot of people, holding a napkin nonchalantly draped in front of himself, feeling thoroughly absurd. For some reason he was afraid even to glance at Penny, and found himself examining the ceiling.

When he got his chesterfield on, he felt better, and turned toward her. Her lips were firmly set to suppress laughter, and her eyes were dancing.

"I'm sorry!" she said, and suddenly was unable to hold back her mirth.

Her laughter was catching. The hatcheck girl and Ben himself joined in, along with the headwaiter, and what had been an exasperatingly embarrassing moment turned into fun.

They were still laughing when they got into a taxi.

"I'm glad you're not angry at me," she said.

"Why should I be angry?"

"Not everybody likes being laughed at. The expression on your face when you stood there holding that napkin . . ."

She broke up again, and though he didn't really think it was all *that* funny, her merriment was irresistible.

"I can sponge those trousers off for you and press them if you have an iron," she said, after she had quieted down.

"Thank you," he replied. "I guess I ought to apologize beforehand for the state of my room. I wasn't expecting company."

Just how great the disorder of his room was he did not realize until he saw it through her eyes. When he opened the door, his four footlockers looked as though they had been dropped by his bed from a great height, disgorging socks, dirty shirts and shoes everywhere. Stacks of mail and crumpled pieces of typing paper littered his desk and the floor beneath it. Trousers and coats hung from the backs of both the armchair and the straight chair, and empty beer cans gleamed in the corner by the radiator.

"How long have you lived here?" she asked, and her face showed compassion as well as surprise.

"About a week . . . I've been traveling a lot. Well, I was in Mexico getting a divorce."

"I'm sorry."

She glanced at her toes.

"Sit down," he said. "I'll go into the bathroom and change my clothes."

When he came out wearing a rather rumpled blue serge suit, he saw that she was picking up a tangle of neckties that had spilled from one of the footlockers while he was rummaging for clean shirts.

"Do you mind if I pick up?" she asked. "It's sort of an instinct."

"An instinct I need, but do you really want to be bothered?"

"Yes," she said simply, and hung the neckties on a coat hanger in the closet.

Moving quickly, they put the room to rights in a surprisingly short time.

"Now where's the iron?" she asked.

"Let's forget it — I'll send those trousers to the cleaners. Let's go downstairs to the bar and have a drink."

"All right," she said.

The exhilaration he had felt earlier was building up instead of wearing off, and he found himself talking animatedly to her about Laura and her trip to Bermuda, and about his son, Benny, who was already taller than his father. The need to keep spouting words scared him a little — had he really been alone so long that he couldn't stop talking the ear off the first attractive young woman he met?

"I'm sorry to give you such a monologue," he said, checking himself. "I'm not really used to living alone. To tell you the truth, I hate it."

"Yes," she said, and gave a rather wry smile.

"I promise not to talk about myself any more."

"I'm bored by my own problems. Yours are much more interesting. Are you going to go on living in this fantastic old hotel?"

"No, it's a horrible place, but I've just been giving myself time to think. There are a lot of things I may want to do . . ."

They talked all afternoon and most of the night, and though he didn't drink a great deal, next morning he was curiously unable to remember what subjects they had discussed with such animation for so long. When he opened his eyes the next day he was surprised at the orderliness of his room. He remembered with pleasure taking Penny back to her apartment house in the East Sixties and giving her a rather fatherly kiss on the cheek before saying good night to her in the lobby. It had been a nice evening, the first one he had really enjoyed in a long, long while.

Glancing at his wristwatch, Ben saw it was almost noon. Nort Clay was expecting him for dinner that night, and if he wasn't going to go, he certainly should call now. Restlessly Ben turned over in his bed. The idea of visiting Nort alone appealed to him less and less. For years he and Rita had spent weekends with the Clays, and the guest rooms of that great old Long Island mansion were shadowed with memories, some bitter, some sweet, but none that he wanted to contemplate in solitude now. Not only that, but Nort and his wife had also been having a hard time. Though they usually did not fight in public, they considered Ben a member of the family. When they were alone with him, they kept darting poisonous glances at each other and exchanging thinly veiled insults which made Ben feel he was seeing some terribly painful old movie over and over again.

No, he did not want to go to the Clays' alone. Nancy would keep him up talking all night, psychoanalyzing herself, Nort, Rita, Ben and all their friends. If she was drinking, she would start a lot of sentimental reminiscences about their youth, when Ben had had a schoolboy crush on her, and anything could happen, but nothing good.

If Laura had been there, it would have been different. The Clays would have had other young people in, perhaps some of their own children, if they were home on vacation, and everyone would have been on his good behavior, the old disciplined by the young.

17

But Laura was in Bermuda by now. Probably she was running on the beach with that young Irishman, exploring the coral coves which had seemed so beautiful to him long ago. It was silly to worry about her, absurd to live in fear of all the perils confronting the young which he could do nothing about.

It was then that Ben had the thought of asking Penny, with whom he had just spent such a pleasant evening, to go with him to Nort's house. Of course, it was silly to assume that this girl would accept an invitation to a weekend on Long Island with a man she had known only a few hours, but she had seemed to like him, and if he explained the situation convincingly, she might go. Finding that the thought of driving out to Huntington with her brought back the exuberance he had felt the preceding night, he took the slip of paper on which he had written her telephone number from his wallet.

"Hello, Penny?" he said eagerly.

"Ben!" she said, sounding surprised, perhaps by the promptness of his call. "How are you?"

"Grateful and hopeful."

She laughed.

"I'm grateful too — I had a lovely time yesterday."

"So did I. That's why I'm hopeful that I can talk you into an invitation any sensible young woman would turn down out of hand."

"What is it?"

"I have a friend I've known ever since I can remember. Among other things, he is that strange phenomenon, a very rich man, the only very rich man I've known well, and Fitzgerald was right, you know — they are different. This one has a huge old house out on Long Island that looks as though it's the last survivor of the Fitzgerald era. He often has people out for the weekend, all very proper, all very well chaperoned in the old-fashioned way."

"Sounds interesting."

"He wants me to come out tonight and discuss some new project of his which he says is 'fantastic' — that's his word. Apparently he wants to involve me in it. Anyway, he asked me to come out for the weekend and I was going to bring my daughter. But as I told you, Laura went to Bermuda. For all sorts of reasons I hate to go alone. Will you come?"

"Yes," she said. "Or should I beat about the bush for a while before I say it?"

"That won't be necessary. I'll rent a car and pick you up at four-thirty."

"I'll meet you out in front of my building," she said. "It's impossible to find a parking place."

"Thanks. Penny?"

"Yes?"

"You make me feel good."

"I'm glad."

"See you at four-thirty," he said, and hung up.

It was ridiculous to feel so boyishly enthusiastic, he told himself as he took an armful of clothes from his closet to get them pressed, but the thought of the girl continued to excite him. All his life he had loved women the way some men love automobiles, horses, money or fame. Nothing he could imagine could be exciting if a good-looking woman was not part of it. As a matter of fact, Ben loved women so much that he had known surprisingly few of them — each woman in his life had engrossed him far too much and too long to admit much time for quantity. But now he was free, and was going to spend two days with a girl whose eyes could flash or mist in response to his words and who had a laugh like the lilt of a flute. And although he was making vows to avoid any cheap, unloving seduction, it was comforting to know that she had a really good body. And what was more important, this girl, he guessed or at least hoped, had emotions like his own, that could blaze up.

After a disastrous marriage, he wanted to have no more truck with women who were harder to ignite than damp paper.

As he was packing his bag Ben realized that he should call Nort and tell him that he was bringing Penny, not Laura. This might be difficult, for both Nort and Nancy would immediately be curious about the precise nature of the relationship. For many reasons Ben found himself enjoying the idea of showing up with such an attractive young woman. For one thing, he would be declaring himself without need of the pity which Nort and Nancy, with the smugness of the firmly if unhappily married, would lavish upon the newly divorced. If they were curious, fine. It would do them no harm.

Picking up the telephone, Ben called Nort's well-remembered number. In the old days it would have been answered by a butler, but Nort and Nancy liked privacy too much to have many servants around, or so they said. The telephone was answered by Nort's own deep "Hello!"

"It's Ben, Nort . . ."

"Ben, now damn it, don't tell me you can't come tonight!"

"Not at all. I plan to start driving out at about four-thirty."

"Great! I can't tell you how much I've been wanting to see you. This new project of mine is something I really think you're going to love!"

"Can't you give me some idea of what it's all about? You've got my curiosity all worked up."

"I know this will sound melodramatic to you, Ben, but I do a lot of business over the telephone, and nowadays a prudent man has to assume that his wires are tapped. If it's not competitors, it's the government. A lot of this new plan of mine depends on secrecy, at least for the time being."

"I understand," Ben said, although he did not. "Nort, I

called to say that my daughter Laura can't come. She's off to Bermuda."

"Christ, so are my kids. What is that place now, the mating island of the young?"

"I hope not. Anyway, I'd like to bring a young lady I just met recently. Penny Savodi is her name. Would that be all right with you and Nancy?"

"Sure, Ben," Nort replied, but his voice showed displeasure, disappointment at the thought of no long, involved private conversations, perhaps, or moral disapproval of what he might assume was a cynical liaison or a foolish escapade to soothe the anguish of divorce. "Sure, Ben!" he repeated, trying to make his voice more polite. "Bring her along."

"Thanks," Ben said. "We should get in about six if the traffic isn't too bad."

CHAPTER 3

AT four o'clock Ben rented a Ford and drove toward
Penny's apartment on East 63rd Street. She lived in a new
building at a fashionable address, and he found himself
wondering how she supported herself so well. He knew
almost nothing about her, Ben realized, possibly because
he had done most of the talking when he was with her. The
only fact he had learned about her work was that she wasn't
an actress. It was curious how reticent she was, he reflected

— she never said anything about herself unless asked a direct question, a fact which seemed both refreshing and mysterious.

"Have you just come back from Florida?" he had asked the night he had met her, when first trying to make conversation.

"No," she had said with a smile warm enough to rob brevity of rudeness.

"I was wondering where you got that beautiful tan."

"California."

"Are you an actress?" he had asked with some trepidation, for he had known few actresses who could take a man as seriously as themselves.

"No," she had said with another flash of that smile, but she had not gone on to volunteer any information. Instead she had asked him what he did, and that is how they had got started on a discussion of television.

As soon as he drew up in front of her building, Penny stepped out of the front door. She was wearing a widely flared camel's hair cape and a small fur cap. Often when he first caught a glimpse of a woman after thinking about her a great deal he was disappointed and ashamed of himself for pinning his own fantasies on quite an ordinary person, but this girl provided no anticlimax. It was not that she was a great beauty like so many actresses and models he had known — it was just that for him, at least, she had an air about her, a kind of stylish vitality that was immediately evident in the way she came walking rapidly out to meet him, her high heels clicking, the hem of her cape swirling, the eagerness of her movements and expression undiminished by any attempt at sophistication.

"Hi!" she said, jumping into the car. "You're right on time. I love men who get places when they say they will!"

"You have hit upon one of my few virtues."

"Nuts," she said. "Why are you so self-depreciating?"

23

"Am I?"

"Last night you spent hours telling me about all your failures and you didn't once mention any of your successes."

"That's funny," he said. "I couldn't remember what we talked about."

"Mostly it was about your failures, but I found it quite refreshing. So many men have told me about their successes."

"It sounds as though I was a dreadful bore," he said, turning downtown and heading for the Queens Midtown Tunnel.

"I found you funny and handsome and brilliant. Does that make you feel better?"

"It makes me feel marvelous."

"Good. I feel marvelous myself today and I want to share it."

When they entered the tunnel the noise of traffic made it impossible to talk, and he found himself bursting with questions he wanted to ask her. For instance, where in the world did this open, uninhibited woman come from? A student of diction, he had long prided himself on his ability to determine a person's origin from his speech, but her pleasant, unaffected speaking voice seemed to carry no regional or class overtones at all. That probably meant she too had studied diction, he realized. Had she had a foreign accent once?

Savodi — the name sounded Italian to him, but her appearance contradicted the stereotypes. Her hair was a deep chestnut brown, not black, and though her eyes seemed to him to be big brown Italian eyes, her skin was conspicuously fair, with a sprinkling of freckles.

"It's funny," he said as they came out of the tunnel. "I somehow feel that we're old friends, but I don't know anything about you at all. Do you mind if I ask you some questions?"

"Like what?"

"Where do you come from?"

"Where would you guess?"

"I've been trying and I can't. From your speech I would say it's not New York, not New England, certainly not the South, not the Middle West, and not California for long, despite your tan. So where?"

"Do you have to know? I rather enjoy being a woman of mystery."

"My curiosity is piqued."

"Then I'm way ahead."

"And what kind of work do you do? I've been trying to guess that too."

"What are your guesses?"

"Well, you said you aren't in television or any kind of acting. I don't think you're a researcher or a secretary. You're not tall or skinny enough to be a model . . ."

"So? What's my line?"

"Maybe fashion design, something like that."

"No," she said with a laugh.

"Must you keep me guessing?"

"No," she said seriously. "I don't want to make a stupid, coy little game of it."

"And I don't mean to pry."

"You're not prying. It's just that, well, I'm in a mood where I don't want to talk about myself. Have you ever been in a mood like that?"

"Never, I'm afraid."

"I don't mean I'm covering up any big glamorous past," she said. "It's just that — well, like you, I've experienced a few failures lately, and I don't feel like opening up the whole bag, not just this weekend. I'd like this to be a time when we enjoy the present and let the past alone."

"I can certainly understand that," he said.

"I don't want to seem as though I were hiding something sinister," she continued. "It's just that everybody I know seems intent on psychoanalyzing me lately, and I'm sick of it. I'm tired of my own past, and why I am the way I am, and all that. I'd like someone to just take me as he finds me, and let it go at that."

"I understand."

"It sounds silly not to tell you where I come from, but even when I answer that, it gets involved. Nothing about me is simple, I'll tell you that. I've lived all kinds of places. My parents moved all the time. Now there I am, getting started again!"

"No more questions," he said.

"And I've had all kinds of jobs — that's why I don't want to answer that one. Right now I'm unemployed and I'm not sure what I want to do. If we get started on that, you might just as well get out a pad and tell me to lie down on a couch."

"No more questions."

"Someday I'll want to talk to you about all of it, some-day when we know each other better. I too have this curious feeling that we're friends, and I have to keep reminding myself that in point of fact, we just met. For the last few months I've been an idiot, opening myself up to encyclopedia salesmen and anyone who would listen to me in bars. It's ridiculous, and I have to stop."

"The man who tries to sell me encyclopedias knows all about the sad story of my life," Ben said ruefully. "I just can't seem to get used to living alone."

"I know, I know about that."

There was a moment of silence broken only by the hum of tires on the highway.

"Ben?" she asked suddenly.

"Yes."

"Can I ask you something silly?"

"No."

She laughed.

"I'm going to do it anyway. Do you like the way I look?"

"No. I think you're very ugly."

"I know I'm sounding coy, but I have a reason for asking. By the way you look at me, I know you like the way I look, and for reasons of my own, I want to hear it in words. I need that."

"Yes, I like the way you look," he said seriously. "Your body is young and graceful, as though you were spun out of all the half-forgotten dreams of my youth. Your face is symmetrical, but more than that it is kind and warm and understanding. I am a man who falls in love very easily, and I have to be careful not to barge around hurting other people and myself. As you said, we don't really know each other. I have to keep telling myself not to let things get going too quickly. I've ridden rockets before, and I know that usually they go down as fast as they go up. But as for the way you look, it's good enough to make me keep asking myself how much of you is my fantasy and how much real."

"Thank you," she said, and with astonishment, he saw that she was on the verge of tears. "My need is met."

Turning her face away, she looked out the window.

"It's a crazy world," he said. "Most of the beautiful women I've met feel at heart that they're ugly. I don't know what people do to them to make them think that."

"Do you think you're handsome?"

"No."

"What have women done to you to make you feel that?"

"Now it's my turn to resist being psychoanalyzed," he said with a rueful laugh.

"That is your right, but someday I will want to know. I

27

think I could make you feel handsome, given enough time."

"I feel fairly dashing already."

She gave her clear, unforced laugh.

"We're both batty," she said.

"Maybe."

"But I feel happy, happier than I've felt in a long time."

Leaning her head back, she dozed. For about a half-hour he drove, too preoccupied with his own thoughts to notice the rows of suburban homes they passed, bleak in fields of gray snow.

"Ben?" she said suddenly.

"At your service."

"I think you should tell me a little more about the people we're going to visit. I don't even know their names."

"Clay. Norton and Nancy Clay."

"And they're very rich. What else? Where and when did you meet them?"

"This is strange," Ben said.

"What is?"

"All these simple questions we ask each other get so involved. If I start to tell you about the Clays, I'll end up telling you the entire story of my life."

"Just because I've decided to clam up for a while, I haven't lost my curiosity about you."

"All right, if you're game I am."

He paused, his mind reeling backward, trying to decide where to begin, where to grab hold of such a tangled mass of facts and emotions.

"It all started with Cornelius Clay, Nort's father," he said. "He went down and bought an island off the coast of Florida, back in about 1920."

"That's a promising beginning," Penny said.

"It was one of the Keys — originally it was just called Sand Cay, but that wasn't glamorous enough for old Corny

Clay. He had the name legally changed to Janus Island. I never really knew why."

Penny kept her eyes intently on his face.

"Old Corny Clay made his island into a kind of super-private winter resort. He built a big mansion there, and he gave his best friends lots so they could build."

"Was your father one of that set?"

"Not exactly. My father was an artist . . ."

It was strange, Ben thought, how much that simple sentence was still full of secret pain.

"My father is an artist," he had said with pride when he was a boy. Then later, "My father tried to be an artist . . ."

And still later, in the cruelty of young manhood, "My father was sort of a fake artist . . ."

"My father was an artist," he repeated again now with a slight stammer. "A painter, though he never became famous or anything like that. Corny's wife and most of the women on Janus Island were big for art in those days. Hell, they had to have something to talk about. Anyway, they encouraged artists to come down and spend the winter. They gave my father an apartment over a garage and finally a house."

"Sounds nice," Penny said.

"It became sort of a permanent arrangement, and they even asked us up to Huntington in the summers. I guess I was one reason for it. They got themselves so exclusive and so isolated they had to take special steps to provide play-mates for their kids. Anyway, Nort and I were brought up together, in a manner of speaking."

"It all sounds very feudal."

"Of course, when I got to be about sixteen I began to resent hell out of it," Ben continued. "Oh hell, it's a long story, full of all kinds of things I don't understand yet. Anyway, it had some odd twists and turns. All through my boyhood I was kind of a paid playmate for Nort. But then I went on to college, and Nort flunked out of prep school. During the war, I was an officer and he was an enlisted man. We were even on the same ship together for a while, because he requested that. It did something odd to both of us."

"I should think it would."

"Then after the war, he came back to live the life of a millionaire, and I was broke. Things kept going back and forth. Ten years later he was getting all desperate because he hadn't accomplished anything — he went through a fairly severe nervous breakdown. Every time I had anything on television he used to get furious and write me page after page of the most biting criticism."

"How does the contest stand now?"

"I don't know. I think he still envies me because I made a little bit of a reputation for myself — or more than that, because whatever I've done I've done on my own. I think I keep doing things that he wants to do. Like commanding a ship, and writing a play, and even getting a divorce. And I'm afraid I haven't been able to get over my old envy for him."

"The big money?"

"Of course — and more than that, the assurance, the manner that goes with it. No, it's worse than that. Damn it, he's upper class, really upper class, and I'm not. I guess I've never been man enough to get that out of my mind."

"Sounds like an intricate friendship. What's his wife like?"

"Oh hell, she's hard to describe. When I was fifteen years old I was madly in love with her, and now she sometimes makes me think she escaped from some house of horrors. She's just a sad, middle-aged woman with a difficult husband, I guess. There's a lot of pain in her life."

"Do you see these people often?"

"I used to, but lately I've hated to go to their house. They say they're against divorce, but they argue all the time. They argue about everything from politics to the dinner menu, and they always try to get me involved. I hope they behave themselves this weekend."

"And you said the rich are different?"

He laughed. A truck blared its horn and sped past — only to slow down on a hill ahead and bunch up the traffic.

"In the old days," Ben said, "old Corny Clay had an express cruiser and a seaplane to take him to Wall Street. No traffic for him. He used to make it in about fifteen minutes."

"Does your friend Nort have those things?"

"He has one of those executive jet planes, and a yacht, a big yawl. For a while there he made kind of a career of trying to win the Bermuda race."

"Did he ever make it?"

"No. Nort . . . Well, I think I'd better shut up. I'll be very interested to see what your conclusions will be. I know these people so well that it's very hard for me to see what they are at all."

When they got to Northern Boulevard, the traffic thinned, and Ben let the car purr along at fifty miles an hour. The territory around him was familiar now, for this area had not changed so drastically during the past twenty years. There at that turn was the restaurant where his son, little Ben, had had a tantrum when he was three years old, and ten miles farther on was a motel where he and Rita had had one of their attempted reconciliations after a fight.

"Are we there yet?" Laura, his daughter, had asked when a child, as soon as they hit this stretch of highway, and his son would echo in a singsong, "There yet, there yet, there yet?"

"You can start counting," Rita would say when they

31

were only a mile from the Clay house. "We'll be there before you count to a hundred."

If he had been undertaking this journey alone these memories would have been painful to Ben, but with Penny sitting beside him he found he could contemplate them without anguish, if not without regret.

"I'm glad you came with me," he said impulsively.

"Good. You were looking so sad . . ."

"This is all haunted land for me. I spent so many years here."

The Clays' big stone gateposts had not changed, and the serpentine driveway leading past the pond, the barn and the eight-car garage were precisely as he remembered them. In the gathering dusk, the estate looked endless.

"Lord!" Penny said. "I didn't know anything like this still existed!"

Over the rise of the hill the lights of the big house blazed, and involuntarily Ben found himself driving faster, as though the children counting in the back seat had reached ninety. Then they were in the big parking lot. A floodlight was snapped on as they stopped, and there was Nort, who apparently had been waiting by the window.

He was big, well over six feet, and broad-shouldered. It was strange, Ben thought, how he kept forgetting that, as though subconsciously he wanted to cut Nort down to a size that could be more easily handled. When they were boys, Nort had always been the bigger, and had won whenever they wrestled or boxed. Somehow it had seemed unfair that he should possess both riches and superior physical strength. The image of the proletarian was of the brute, and the aristocrat was supposed to be delicate, effete, but there Nort was, combining the best of two worlds and leaving Ben with both poverty and comparative bodily weakness.

Nort hadn't changed. He was still relatively slim. And as

he so often did, he was wearing brown loafers, white woolen socks, a faded pair of dungarees, and a plaid shirt, with two buttons open at the top to show his hairy chest.

"Ben!" he boomed in his deep voice. "By God, it's great to see you again!"

With his large left hand he gripped Ben's shoulder, and pounded him on the back with the other so hard that it hurt a little.

"Hi, Nort," Ben said in his slightly nasal tenor voice which he often tried to make lower. Enthusiasm was always hard for him to express, and as he pounded Nort's shoulder in retaliation, he felt ridiculous. Climbing out of the car, Penny stood smiling.

"Nort, this is Penny, Penny Savodi," Ben said.

Glancing at Penny for the first time, Nort gave a smile that registered no warmth whatsoever.

"I'm glad to meet you, Penny," he said, and Ben wondered whether he was imagining that the tone of Nort's voice was distinctly supercilious. Ben felt disappointed. Somehow he had expected his old friend to be as enthusiastic about Penny as he was.

"It's good of you to include me in your invitation," Penny said serenely.

She did not look as though the coldness of Nort's manner had hurt her.

"You're looking well, Ben!" Nort said, turning from Penny, and all the old heartiness returned to his voice. "Let's go inside. We can leave the bags until later."

I always have to be aware that I may be imagining him to be snobbish when in fact he simply has troubles of his own, Ben thought. Despite his polished manners, Nort had always been awkward in the presence of pretty women, few of whom he ever really trusted. Perhaps Nort had jumped to the conclusion that Penny was just some little show girl that Ben really had no business asking to his home at all. By

33

the way Nort stared at Penny when she took off her cape, Ben knew his diagnosis was correct. Penny was wearing a brown tweed skirt this time, with another cashmere sweater, this one a soft tan. If she had come from this part of Long Island, the sweater would be two sizes too large and would hang on her like a blanket, but Penny was obviously from somewhere else, and the sweater fitted perfectly. This was plainly disturbing to Nort, and his whole face registered disapproval.

With the poise of a person without pretense, Penny seemed wholly capable of handling the situation.

"Would you mind hanging this up for me?" she asked coolly, handing her cape to Nort.

"Of course," he said stiffly, and put the cape in the hall closet beside Ben's.

The living room, which was eighty feet long, gave a curious example of the old kept new, of time brought to a halt. All the baroque Victorian furniture and all the Italian antiques which Nort's father and grandfather had bought had been retained, but refurbished every year to keep them looking as though they had just come from the cabinet-maker. Even the head of a tiger which Nort's father had shot seventy years ago was, through some triumph of taxidermy, still as sleek as though it had just emerged from the jungle. The oil paintings of the Clay family showed grandmothers and great-grandmothers in period dress, but because Nort had an artist come in every year to keep them in good repair, the paint and the gold frames still looked brand-new.

"I like old things," Ben could remember Nort's father saying, "but I detest shabbiness."

When Ben, Penny and Nort entered the big room there was no one in it, and Ben's first impression was just what it had been when he had first seen it years and years ago, when it had looked to him like an elaborate museum which no one but the Clays and their chosen friends were allowed to visit. He saw Penny glancing from paintings to marble nymphs to stuffed animals with interest, but not, he guessed, with awe or real admiration. For the first time Ben realized that the big room was by modern standards nothing but a hodgepodge of objects which looked as though they had been stolen from a good nineteenth-century hotel.

"Nance!" Nort called. "Nance, they're here!"

Nancy was waiting somewhere in the wings, Ben was sure, preparing to make an entrance. There was a moment of silence, and then, sure enough, that voice, musical but strangely clipped, came from the top of the stairs which curved into the opposite end of the room.

"How good to see you, Ben!"

She walked down the stairs slowly, giving him time to cross the room toward her. It was like a stage bit, he thought, something that must have been practiced many times to get so right. Her brown hair was long, as it had been when she was a debutante, and she was wearing a blue dress of some knitted material that clung to her slender body and her improbably propped-up breasts. She was holding a long black cigarette holder tipped at a jaunty angle, and she had on a lot of purple eye shadow.

My God, she looks old, Ben thought with a curious stab of pity, loss and disbelief. No, it was worse than that, she looked like an old woman trying to be young and terribly sexy, and the result was a mess. How curious that she should have aged so much faster than her husband, who still seemed little older than a college boy!

"It's good to see you, Nance," he heard himself saying. "You look marvelous!"

"That of course is an outrageous lie, but an admirable one."

She kissed him on the cheek, and there was the odor of some powerful perfume mixed with strong tobacco. Turning toward Penny, who with Nort had followed Ben slowly, Nancy said, "Hello, dear, you must be the young lady Nort said Ben was going to bring."

It was marvelous, what Nancy could do with one sentence, Ben thought with amusement. There were so many ironies and insinuations echoing in every word that the whole room seemed to vibrate. And another strange thing was happening. Although Nancy had seemed pathetically old in the shock of first glance, her confidence in herself or the strength of her own illusion was catching, and she seemed to be transforming herself, right in front of his eyes, into the desirable woman she wanted to be.

"I am the young lady," Penny said, and the two women took each other in with measured precision.

"We can take your bags up later," Nort said, after he had introduced them. "Let's go into the library and have a drink."

"The young lady may like to wash up first, Nort," Nancy said. "Take her to the guesthouse. We'll give Ben the green room here."

This did not surprise Ben — unmarried couples were always nominally split up in this fashion when they visited the Clays, and since the guesthouse was secluded enough for midnight visits, no one had ever objected. Going to get Penny's suitcase, Nort ushered her out the front door.

"I guess there's no reason we can't have a drink now," Nancy said with elaborate casualness. "How have you been lately, Ben? How have you survived the battle?"

"Pretty well," Ben replied easily.

She was looking at him intently, as though she were a physician trying to diagnose a disease.

"What's this little girl you've got with you? Anything important in your life?"

"I don't know yet."

"When I say my prayers for you tonight I shall include a

brief request that you not jump from the frying pan into the fire."

"Don't worry about me."

"Ah, but I do. You can't live alone, can you, Ben?"

"Not for long."

"If you could only wait —"

Getting up abruptly, she went to a portable bar in the corner.

"Scotch?" she asked.

"Please."

At the back of the house a door slammed, and Nort came in alone.

"I'll show you to your room now if you like," he said, looking quickly from Ben to Nancy.

"Thank you," Ben replied. "I would like to wash up."

Washing was the least of it. What he wanted most of all was to get away from the amused, malicious eyes of his hostess for a few moments and compose himself. There was a strange kind of power in the overtones of Nancy's voice and in the sardonic glances which Nort kept shooting at him, a curious ability to destroy hope or idealism of any sort and replace it with their own cynicism. When Ben had arrived he had considered himself a happy man on the verge of a love affair with an interesting woman. Now suddenly he saw himself in the eyes of Nancy and Norton Clay — a divorced, middle-aged lecher running around with a much younger woman who was not of their set. In their eyes, he was a fool or worse. Amused contempt seemed to be their main reaction, contempt laced with false morality, intensified by envy, and only half hidden by conventional manners.

They walked down a long corridor with French windows through which one could see a spectacular view of Long Island Sound in the daytime, but on this moonless and starless evening, there was nothing but blackness. The door of the Green Room stood open, and when he first stepped inside Ben received something of a shock, because the oversize double bed, the prints of wood nymphs, the French Provincial furniture arranged around the edge of the huge beige rug all came back to him in a rush of memory more painful than he had expected, and more sad. This sense of sorrow about his past was something quite new. While he was living it, he thought, most of the time at least, that his marriage was a happy one, and that Rita was an unusually beautiful, kind and intelligent woman, or would be when she got over a few of her difficulties. When the marriage began to crack up, he started thinking of Rita as a bitch to end all bitches, the most evil woman in the world, and bitterness took the place of mourning. But now, in this new perspective, she appeared to him only a sad, somewhat broken person, and the memory of the nights they had spent in this big room was somehow as upsetting as the thought of two cripples trying to dance.

"Is there anything I can get you?" Nort asked.

"No, thanks. I'll be down in a minute."

Nort gave a rueful smile — perhaps he regretted having been rude.

"It seems like old times," he said, slapped Ben on the shoulder, and hurried off down the hall after closing the door behind him. There was a moment of intense silence. That was another thing Ben remembered about that house, the silence of heavily carpeted halls, thick walls, and people who rarely raised their voices even when they were being deadly.

Loosening his tie, Ben lay down on the bed. Out in the guesthouse Penny was probably combing her hair, and he wondered whether she was wondering whether he would try to visit her that night. Certainly he did not know her well enough to attempt anything of the sort yet — it would be stupid to risk confusing or scaring her. A night alone in this chamber of echoing memories was going to be difficult, but not really as bad as he had feared, if he kept his mind on the future.

After resting for ten minutes, Ben changed his shirt and walked downstairs. The living room was empty, and he went to the library. As he came through the door, the first person he saw was Penny, standing in the center of the room. She had changed into a low-cut black cocktail dress which was frankly designed as a showcase for her pretty little figure.

"*There* you are!" Nancy said.

She was sitting in a big leather chair with her arms clasped around her knees. Beside a stand holding a tray of cocktails stood Nort with a pitcher of martinis in his hand. He had rolled the sleeves of his plaid shirt almost to the shoulders, displaying the biceps of an athlete, and his shirt was now unbuttoned halfway to his belt. His handsome face was flushed, and Ben guessed that he had downed two or three drinks in the ten minutes he had been waiting.

"Sorry to take so long," Ben said, feeling that an apology was somehow demanded.

"That's quite all right," Nancy replied, picking up her long cigarette holder from a silver shell on the table beside her. "Doesn't your young lady look lovely?"

It was clever of Nancy, Ben thought, not to try to compete with Penny in the matter of beauty, but to assume the condescending air of a tolerant mother. While he slowly stirred the martinis, Nort kept glancing at Penny and looking away, his handsome face sullen.

"Yes, she does," Ben said.

"Are you drinking now, Ben?" Nort asked, abruptly changing the subject before Penny could acknowledge the compliments.

"A little."

"How about you, Penny?" Nort continued. "Do you

want to try one of these martinis, or would you like something else?"

His manner still contradicted the courtesy of his words.

"A little scotch if you have it," Penny said, sitting down on a long couch of maroon leather.

"Are you still a martini man, Ben?"

"I'll take scotch too, if you don't mind."

"I'll have a martini, Nort," Nancy said. "I'm damned if I want you to finish that whole pitcher by yourself."

"Nancy is the only woman in the world who drinks martinis for the sake of someone else," Nort said, setting his face in an elaborate smile. "How do you want your scotch, Penny, long or short?"

It was the way Nort said her name which was insulting, Ben noted. Obviously he did not like it, and by over-emphasizing it he made it a contemptuous joke.

"On the rocks with a little water," Penny replied evenly.

She turned, and Ben saw that on the back of her dress near the neck there was a piece of paper. He said nothing, but Nancy spied it at the same time.

"You have a tag on your dress, dear," she said.

"Oh?"

"Just a label of some sort. Is it new?"

"Yes," Penny said casually. "Take it off for me, will you Ben?"

"Of course."

He was grateful to her for refusing to be flustered.

"It's a marvelous dress," he said, detaching the price tag.

"Thank you. I rushed out and bought it as soon as you asked me for the weekend."

He had, Ben realized, been given a refreshingly frank compliment.

Nancy looked down quickly and Nort cleared his throat.

"By the way," Nancy asked, "how's your mother doing, Ben? Is she still out in South Bay?"

"She's eighty-two and still pretty active," Ben said, wondering if Nancy knew that any mention of his mother still, after all these years, filled him with painful emotions.

"How's your work going, Ben?" Nort asked, setting down the bottle of scotch and looking at him intently.

"Not too well," Ben said.

Picking up the glass, Nort handed it to Penny. There was an instant of silence during which Nancy sighed, perhaps with regret for Ben's difficulties, perhaps with relief, Ben thought. Nort was keeping his face rigidly expressionless. My God, how all my little successes have galled him, Ben thought. What would he do now if I said I had — in addition to a girl who gives me public compliments — a big musical comedy opening next week?

"I think it's terrible what they've done to television," Nancy said. "Comic strip series, soap opera, and all that. There's nothing like the kind of work you used to do."

"No."

"Is there any hope of getting any real drama back?" Nort asked. "Do they ever talk about reviving *Playhouse 90*, or anything like that?"

"Not very seriously, I'm afraid," Ben said.

"Well, how about Broadway? Are the chances getting any better there?" He handed Ben a glass containing at least three ounces of scotch and two ice cubes.

"Broadway is Broadway," Ben said, shrugging.

"Do you have a new play on the stocks?"

"Not at the moment," Ben said.

"I must admit I'm not sorry," Nort replied with a smile. "I was afraid you might be too busy to be interested in my new project, and ever since I first started it, I've been counting on you."

41

"Please don't get into that now," Nancy said. "We have to eat, or the girls will be furious."

"We have again started to live our lives for the convenience of servants," Nort replied, pouring himself another martini.

"Nonsense," Nancy retorted. "We got some college girls in, Ben, to help out in their spare time. I finally decided it was absurd to try to take care of this mausoleum by myself."

"The truth is, we couldn't get any more colored girls," Nort said. "Even the ones we bring up from Florida quit."

"It's lonely for them here, poor things," Nancy said. "What do you do, Penny dear? Are you an actress?"

"No," Penny said with a smile. "At the present I am unemployed."

"Oh, how nice! I have never really believed that women should have jobs."

Nancy made her voice so light and gay that she sounded as though she were burlesquing herself.

"It's fun to be a lady of leisure sometimes," Penny said mildly, and again Ben admired her poise.

"Don't you get bored?" Nort asked with irony.

"We really do have to go in to eat," Nancy hastily said. "Bring your glasses if you want."

The big dining room with the green silk wallpaper was just as Ben remembered it, but the long formal table had been replaced with a small one in a corner, which was now set with stainless steel instead of silver, and modern ceramic plates. A tall, plain girl in a sloppy gray sweater and denim skirt was putting a casserole on a hot plate on a sideboard.

"This is Virginia Pedrone," Nancy said, and the girl gave a sickly, uninterested smile.

"Pleased to meet you," she said. "You want me to bring in the rest of the stuff now?"

"Yes," Nancy replied. "I'm sorry we're late."

"I don't mind, if you don't care if we leave the dishes until tomorrow. Kathy and I both have tests, and we have a hell of a lot of work to do."

"Of course, dear," Nancy said. "Just bring everything in and forget about us. We'll clear the table ourselves."

Despite the unusual service, the meal was excellent, as Ben had known it would be. Ever since he had known her, Nancy had made a point of serving gourmet food, wearing beautifully tailored clothes, swimming expertly, sailing like a professional and riding well. She was also fairly expert on child care, many aspects of psychiatry, and contemporary books. At least since the age of fourteen, when he had first met her, she had thrown herself into life as though it were nothing but a complicated game that anyone with enough drive and intelligence could win.

All this was easy to make fun of, but Ben felt suddenly grateful for the beef stew which had been simmered in wine without taking the crispness out of the vegetables, the golden spoon bread, the fresh string beans with almonds, and the good red wine, which was dry without being astringent.

"This is marvelous," Penny said, unable to keep surprise completely out of her voice. "I keep forgetting that home cooking can be so good."

"However else I may reproach myself for other things," Nort said, "I must admit that I married a good cook."

Nort's plate, Ben noticed, held almost nothing. Gluttony was one of the vices which had been left out of his character, and Ben, who for years had tortured himself with diets, envied him.

Nort did not eat much, and to Ben's knowledge, which was fairly extensive, Nort had never been unfaithful to his wife, whom he had married when they were both twenty-two. Much against his will, Ben found himself vividly imagining what it must be like to sleep with Nancy now, and the thought appalled him — in fact it produced, for no real reason, a twinge of nausea.

Poor Nort, he thought, no appetite for food, no good sex, no real work — how on earth does the man live?

And that was funny in a way, because he was sure that Nort was pitying him, Benjamin Powers, who at the age of forty-five had lost his money, his wife, the muscular appearance of youth, and even his profession, for wasn't the craft of writing serious little plays about middle-class people for television and even for Broadway or the movies just about as out of date as the manufacture of buggy whips?

He was not only broke, but he was in debt to the government beyond any real hope of recouping, and he was quite sure that Nort knew that, perhaps down to the exact dollar, for Nort had bankers and lawyers who had all kinds of ways of finding out about things like that, and several times before Ben had found that for some reason he kept careful track of his friends' finances. If he was going to talk to him tonight about some business project, Ben could be sure that he had in one of his files a folder with his name on it and all the latest information.

What kind of project could it possibly be? And why, fundamentally, was he, Ben, so apathetic about it? In view of his financial chaos, shouldn't he be trembling with eagerness to hear any proposition made by an old and rich friend? Why was he really so completely uninterested, so almost bored by the prospect of getting into a long conversation about business at all?

Partly because he could not imagine himself succeeding in any kind of business, Ben thought, especially where Nort was involved. Twice before Nort had tried to draw him into some of his enterprises, once in a magazine some friends of his started, and once in a scheme for importing Swedish boats. Both schemes had sounded rather interest-

44

ing at first, but perhaps because Nort was so rich, Ben had been astonished to find that they became a bore simply because their chief purpose was to make as much money as possible in a hurry with a minimum of risk. Although it might have been fun to try to start a good magazine, or to import beautiful sailing yachts, Ben found it impossible to maintain any enthusiasm for publishing a magazine devoted to trash or to selling ugly little motorboats.

The truth was that he wasn't a businessman by any stretch of the imagination, and was lucky to have enjoyed a brief period of prosperity which at least had enabled him to give money enough to his former wife to insure an education for his children. With that primary task done, he hadn't worried much about money.

No, that wasn't true, Ben told himself, as he sipped the mellow red wine. Of course he liked money as much as anyone else did, but the truth was he was scared of it, frightened in the same way he might be by a horse which had thrown him too often. Like his father before him, when money was concerned he always seemed to wind up in a complete shambles, and the easiest way out was to adopt the pose of the artist or the writer who was above it all.

And he was not only afraid of money, he was afraid of Nort, even after all these years, Ben reflected. He was afraid his cynical despair was catching. And why on earth would Nort want to involve so impractical a man as himself in a business enterprise? Did he have some obscure urge to tie Ben to him forever, to keep him captive, a servant, as he had virtually been during so many years of his youth? Had the spectacle of seeing his former flunky, the recipient of so many family favors, become more successful than he in the war and in the first years of peace so twisted Nort's mind that he wanted to devote the rest of his life to putting him again in his place? And did Nort feel some obscure urge to

45

ruin his relationship with this girl, who seemed so full of promise?

Hell, that was absurd. Think how much he owed Nort! Nort's father had paid Ben's way through college, where among other things, he had got his commission in the Naval Reserve. Nort had written him a beautiful letter when Ben got the Navy Cross, in which he had said he felt almost as though he had been decorated himself. The Clay family had helped him immeasurably ever since he had been born, and there was no reason to end up edgy and suspicious at the age of forty-five, when they all, in many ways, were beginning to fall apart.

"Ben?" Penny said. "Please eat some garlic bread. I love it, but I simply can't let myself eat any if you don't."

He had not seen Nancy put the crisp loaf of soft French bread on the table.

"Thanks," he said, breaking off a piece. "There's nothing I love better."

"I can't let it alone," Nancy said, "but I never can get Nort to touch it."

"Please!" Nort said, pushing the plate toward her. "You know I can't stand the smell of the stuff."

"But you wouldn't smell it if you ate some!" Nancy continued. "Really, you ought to — for your own protection. After all, it's three against one."

How little everything had changed! How many times in the past had he heard Nancy and Nort engage in this same ridiculous argument about garlic? What was it about people that made them cling to such small instruments of torture year after weary year? Why did she keep putting the stuff on the table, and why just to surprise her didn't Nort say the hell with it and eat it for once? Or why didn't he pick up the plate and heave it out the window?

Instead, Nort picked up the martini glass he had brought to the table with him and drained it.

"Have you been down to Janus Island this year?" Ben asked.

Putting the glass down with a click, Nort turned to him. "For a short while," he said. "Have you been there lately?"

"No. Laura and I were going to try camping on the site of our old house. I don't know if I'll try it alone."

"I think Janus Island is the only part of Florida that hasn't changed at all," Nancy said. "Do you remember Minnie Lee? She always asks for you."

"Minnie Lee! Is she still there?"

"Very much so," Nancy said.

"Where is Janus Island?" Penny asked.

"Just before you get to Key West, but it's not hooked up to the Causeway," Ben said. "You still have to take a boat."

Ordinarily Nort would have added, "And you always will have to, too, if I have anything to say about it." Any mention of the Causeway was like one of several automatic buttons on Nort which, when pushed, would always cause the same reaction, but now Nort just poured himself a glass of wine and sat gazing moodily at his plate, his lips pressed tight.

Ben wondered whether the "fantastic scheme" Nort had mentioned involved the island. Was it a real estate plan? Did he intend to hook it up to the Causeway and sell lots?

If so, there would undoubtedly be a lot of money to be made, but how would that involve Ben? The lot on which his father's house had once stood was still his, but since the hurricane had carried away the building and much of the nearby beach, that wouldn't be worth much. Did Nort want him to go down and manage a real estate project?

"It sounds lovely," Penny said. "How big is it?"

"Eleven miles long," Ben replied. "In some places it's only a few hundred yards wide. Nort and Nancy own almost all of it."

47

"Wow, you ought to start a resort!"

"I'm afraid I would be very unhappy with that," Nort said, still looking uncomfortable.

Well, if not a resort, what was he planning?

Disappearing into the kitchen, Nancy brought in a platter of French cheeses and a glass bowl of fresh fruit.

"I'm afraid we've grown rather out of the habit of serving dessert," she said. "Nort won't eat it and I'm not supposed to, but there's plenty of ice cream in the freezer if anybody wants."

"Nothing for me," Ben said, wanting the Camembert and the Brie very much. "I'm making myself a monument to self-discipline."

"Indeed," Nancy said dryly, glancing at Penny. "What will you have, my dear?"

"Some of the grapes, please. They look marvelous."

"If you men aren't going to eat, why don't you go out and have your business talk?" Nancy said. "If Penny doesn't mind, we can stay and clean off the table."

"Fine," Ben said, pushing himself away from the table sharply. By his plate the glass of scotch he had brought in with him stood largely untouched. The very suggestion of talking business with Nort had made him long to drain it, and he wanted to get away from the table before he gave in, because he suspected that he would need a clear mind.

"We'll go up to my study," Nort said, and led the way, clenching and unclenching his hands as he walked.

What is it about this great project of his that makes him so edgy, Ben wondered, or is it just this long crazy involvement with me?

Does the hunter always get nervous as he approaches his quarry?

That was a ridiculous thought. Wishing he had taken his glass of scotch with him, Ben followed his old friend and enemy.

CHAPTER 4

THE corridor led to a wide flight of eight stairs at the back of the house, at the top of which were high, white double doors.

"My office," Nort said as he opened a complex brass lock on the righthand door with a key he took from his watch pocket. There was a flicker of fluorescent light as he touched a switch.

Ben found himself standing at the entrance of a large

49

room which seemed to be a panorama of Nort's whole life. At the far end was a huge Italian desk, with legs terminating in lions' feet, which had been in old Corny Clay's study. Behind it was a modern reclining chair of pleated black leather, surrounded on three sides by large gray metal filing cabinets. On the left side of the room was a workbench about twenty-five feet long which held a complete shortwave radio system that looked as though it had been lifted intact from the destroyer escort aboard which Nort had served during World War II as a radioman third class. Plastic bags of elaborate electronic equipment were neatly hung on a long pegboard nearby, together with a complex set of tools.

On the opposite side of the room there was a smaller workbench full of guns, photographic equipment and a section of wall devoted to exercising devices, including a rack of dumbbells and a set of parallel bars. None of these impressed Ben so much as the decorations on the walls, which included large models of the DE 179, Nort's yawl *Hope XIV*, and a succession of yachts which had belonged to Nort's father over the years, some of which were dearly familiar to Ben. There also were enlarged photographs of Nort's five children, all of whom were now in boarding school and college, and a series of photographs of Nancy, taken from the time she was a winsome girl of eighteen. Near the desk, charts of the Florida Keys and of South America covered the wall from carpet to ceiling. The decoration which held Ben's attention most was a large oil painting of Janus Island which had been painted by his own father.

How strange to see one of those paintings after so many years! Toward the end of his life, Paul Powers had done many of these depictions of the island which were nothing more than illustrated maps, but which were almost the only 'kind of thing he did that ever sold. Many of the people who visited Janus Island formed a sentimental attachment to it, and when they went home they liked to take one of these souvenirs which they could say was the work of a local artist. Although he felt it demeaned him to abandon the still lives and the abstractions he loved so much, Paul usually kept on hand a dozen or so of these paintings of the island, and as time went on, they became more and more elaborate, showing fleets of Spanish galleons which had once plied the waters nearby and yachts rendered in enough detail to be recognizable by their owners. This particular painting, which was almost twelve feet long, must have been done especially for old Corny Clay, for it showed his house, even bigger than it really was, and the winter homes of all his friends, as well as their boats. With pictures of palm trees bending in the wind and the intense green of the sea turning to yellow over the reefs, Paul had managed to evoke enough of the feeling of the island to make his son, all these many years later, almost dumb with nostalgia.

"Recognize it?" Nort asked with a smile.

"Yes."

"How would you like to go back there for a while, not just to camp, but to work?"

"That might be fun," Ben said cautiously, but he was surprised at how much the idea of going back to Janus Island to live, a thought which had never before occurred to him, appealed to him now. It wasn't just the fact that his father's poster art evoked so many pleasant memories, it was the pictures of Nort's children, which reminded him of his own two, and made him long for a home. When he was divorced he had given his house in Connecticut, as well as most of his money, to his wife. The thought of living in a small hotel room had not worried him until he had discovered how difficult it was for him to earn his way out of it, and how embarrassing it was to have his children visit him there, where there was no place for them to sleep at all. If he had a house on Janus Island, the children might be glad to visit him on vacations, and he would have a chance to give them some of the advantages and traditions of his own youth. He could teach them how to sail and fish for marlin. It was possible that if a vivid and energetic girl like Penny would join him in such a life, there, after so many years of destruction, he could start building again.

The rush of these thoughts left him wanting Janus Island so much that he could almost smell the soft sea air and hear the bees buzzing in the orange groves. It was not wise to let himself fall prey to such dreams, he thought, for it would be ruinous to bargain with Nort when he wanted what he had to offer so much.

Life on Janus Island wouldn't be any bed of roses, Ben told himself sternly. When all was said and done, he would be Nort's flunky again. He would be saying goodbye to most of his ambitions and would probably end by drinking himself to death in the sun.

Anyway, Ben reminded himself, he was jumping to conclusions. Nort might well be proposing no more than a brief assignment, which he had done many times before.

"I have a little conference room over here," Nort said, leading the way to a door near the parallel bars.

To his surprise, Ben found himself ushered into a small cubicle, not more than ten feet square. It contained nothing but two unupholstered chairs and a glass table, on which there were two telephones. There were no decorations on the windowless walls.

"Sit down," Nort said. "I've got some good brandy. I'll be right back."

Lowering himself into one of the chairs, Ben searched nervously in his pockets for a cigar, but found none.

"Here we are," Nort said, returning with a silver tray on

which there were a decanter of brandy, some snifters and a box of Havana panatelas.

Without asking whether Ben wanted a drink, Nort poured two of the large glasses much fuller than they ought to be and handed him one.

"I guess I better explain this room," he said, sitting down across the table from Ben. "Nance thinks I'm a little nuts, but I do a lot of business trading in the stocks of small companies, and there are quite a few men who could make money from knowing what I say to some of the people who visit me here. Nowadays it's almost impossible to make sure that a large room isn't bugged, unless you go over it almost every day. A little place like this I can keep clean with no trouble at all. Maybe it's a foolish precaution, but I think it's worth it, if only for my peace of mind."

"I suppose so," Ben said, sipping his brandy, and he wondered if anyone actually would plant listening devices in Nort's home, or whether his friend was really heading for another crackup, finally going from eccentricity to madness. What kind of people did he do business with, anyway?

"Electronics is still a hobby of mine, and I know what it can do," Nort said, lighting a cigar and passing one to Ben. "In this world we've got today, it pays to be careful. Even our own government goes in for bugging in a big way. The new devices are fantastic."

"Yes, I suppose you're right."

The cigar was a Partagás, moist as though it had been freshly rolled, and fragrant. Ben lit it gratefully, noticing that Nort was watching him intently.

'Where do you get Partagás cigars these days?" Ben asked.

"A friend gets them for me. I can't really convince myself that I'm helping my country by giving up Havana tobacco."

Ben took another sip of his brandy.

"What is this project you want to talk to me about?" he asked, feeling that directness was the best way to avoid being involved in a game of cat and mouse.

"It's rather hard to explain briefly. I'm afraid that at first blush, you'll think the whole thing is a little crazy."

"Try me."

"First I'll stick to statistics," Nort said in a matter-of-fact voice. "Do you know that just in the last five or six years several hundred thousand dollars' worth of gold has been recovered from wrecks in the Florida Keys? I'm just talking about what has been officially reported to the government for tax purposes."

"I've heard a little about it," Ben said in surprise.

"That's a hard fact. To add an opinion, I believe that much more has been discovered and bootlegged out to the illegal gold market without being reported."

"Perhaps."

Ben felt so tense that he found himself squeezing his brandy snifter almost hard enough to break it. Draining it, he put it on the table.

"Now a familiar fact," Nort said. "The Florida Keys were right on the main route that most of the galleons took from South America to Spain. As you know, I'm sure, historians report that a fantastic amount of gold bullion and silver was lost along the way. I've heard the figure quoted as anything from one to two *billion* dollars. No one knows what it is exactly, because those old Spaniards had tax problems, just the way we do. Their bills of lading didn't always report all of what they carried."

"I've read a little about it," Ben said.

For some reason he was feeling an enormous sense of letdown. A rich man's treasure hunt! Is that all that Nort had on his mind? Although he actually knew quite a lot about the history of the galleons, he could not really imagine anyone finding anything of value unless he set out on a kind of undersea mining operation that would cost more than it could retrieve. Anyway, the whole thing sounded more like fantasy and small-boy adventure than a project which might be counted upon to solve any of his personal problems.

"So far we've just been talking about matters that are public knowledge," Nort said, refilling both brandy glasses. "From now on, everything I tell you is confidential, top secret. Do you promise to honor that?"

"You want me to cross my heart and hope to die?" Ben asked with a smile.

"Damn it, I'm serious! Millions of dollars and the lives of several people may depend on this. At first it all sounds fantastic, I know, but if you stick with me, you'll find that it's just as real as death and taxes, both of which are involved."

"I'll keep your secrets," Ben said.

"That means not talking to *anybody* — not your girl down there or anyone else. Some of this I haven't even told Nance."

"I understand."

"All right. *I* think you can keep secrets or I wouldn't have chosen you for this."

"I'm glad," Ben said, feeling as though they were playing an absurd game.

"Right now I won't go into details, but I have good, scholarly reason to believe that a whole convoy of galleons and naos, some twenty-six ships in all, cracked up in a hurricane on the reef right off Janus Island in October of the year 1681. Later I'll show you the documentation for this. Furthermore, I think that a little of the gold has already been found and bootlegged off the island. Not enough to matter, because many millions of dollars were involved, perhaps thirty or forty in all, but I think enough has already been found to show that something big is there."

"How extraordinary!" Ben said, the exclamation sounding flat. "You have proof?"

"I'm not going to ask you to carry more secrets than you need. Just assume for now that I know that several ingots have been found."

"I don't suppose I should be so surprised," Ben said. "There's always been talk . . ."

"I'm going to organize a major expedition to go after the whole lot, and I want you to help me."

There was an awkward pause.

Nort picked up his glass of brandy, and Ben saw that his hand was shaking. He had never seen that happen to Nort before.

"Why me?" Ben asked. "What are my qualifications?"

"First of all, I know I can trust you. At my age you begin to realize that such people are rare."

"Under the right conditions you can find plenty of people to trust."

"Secondly, you're a damn good sailorman. I haven't forgotten the war."

"When it comes to ships, I'm pretty rusty. Professional captains are easy to find."

"There are other reasons I want you. In organizing this expedition, I have two problems. One is to make as much as possible of it tax-exempt, especially if we fail to find much. It's easy to drop a half million dollars on a thing like this, or even more. If they were after-tax dollars, that would be too much."

"You think I can help you with taxes?"

"Maybe. And maybe with another problem: secrecy. Ever since that big wreck was found summer before last, a kind of gold fever has been sweeping the Keys. Everybody and his brother who can afford an aqualung is combing the reefs. Every time an expedition with the equipment to really recover anything is started, everybody within a hundred miles knows it before the lines are cast off the dock. Every time a wreck is found, they home in like buzzards. If we located a whole convoy, they'd grab most of it unless we had enough people to guard every wreck."

"How could I help with that?"

Nort dropped a dead cigar in his empty brandy glass and lit a fresh one, his hand steady now.

"I've been thinking about this a lot," he said. "What we need to do is learn a lesson from the spy boys, the CIA, and all that. What we need, in short, is a cover story, and you can give me that."

"How?"

"Say we don't start out to run a treasure hunt at all. Say we start out to film an underwater movie — they do that every once in a while down there. We get together all the paraphernalia for the treasure hunt which will be in our script — the salvage boat, the divers, the shore base, a barge we can take in over the reef, the whole fleet. What we do is, we actually produce a low-budget movie — we don't just fake it, we make something we may actually be able to sell. We have a lot of cameras and actresses around. Instead of trying to act secretively, we hire a publicity man to get as much in the newspapers as he can. No one would know if one of the small salvage boats was actually operating in earnest."

"That's clever," Ben said.

"There are many advantages. I own most of a small movie company which would pay the bills, and if there were any loss, it could be deductible. Even if we don't find anything, this whole thing probably won't cost me a third of what it would if I did it straight."

"And there's always the chance the movie itself will make a profit," Ben said with amusement.

"Of course. If we actually find something big, we could release the film as a documentary, or we just might come up with something commercial anyway."

"What part do you see for me in all this?"

"First of all, write me a script — everything about the movie has to be on the up and up, and no one would doubt the legitimacy of a script you did. Secondly, I'd like you to direct the film. It could be awkward if we got a director who didn't understand the whole project."

"I can see that."

"Will you do it? If we can get the details right?"

"I don't know."

"Why not? Frankly, I thought you'd jump at the chance."

"The whole thing sounds a little shady to me, Nort. Tax evasion, cloak-and-dagger stuff. That has never been my bit. You know me — I'm the antithesis of James Bond."

"This isn't cloak-and-dagger stuff, and looking for tax-sheltered investments is not the same thing as tax evasion. I guarantee you that the whole plan will be passed on by some of the best legal brains in New York. What's wrong about making a movie? And what would be wrong if we accidentally stumbled onto something real?"

"I don't know. The whole thing just makes me feel rather uneasy."

"I'll pay you a good salary and a quarter of any profit the film makes. On the treasure we'll make an entirely separate deal, after we've discussed it in more detail, but I guarantee that if the plan works out, you'll be rich beyond anything you imagined even in your best years."

"I'll have to think about it," Ben said. "I suppose I'll need time before the whole thing starts to seem real."

"Don't take too much time. Summer is the season to hunt down there, when the sea is calm. That means we have to get this whole thing organized, both the film and the expedition, in just about two months."

"I'm not even sure I could come up with a good script in two months."

"Then hire help. What I'd like you to do is fly right down to the island now. You can stay at our house. You can work on your script and start noising the word about the movie around, while I'm organizing the whole thing."

"I'll need a day or two at least to make such a decision."

"I don't want to press you too hard — take three days if you want."

Casually, Nort stood up.

"I guess we better join the ladies," he said, and led the way out of the little room.

When they got into the hall outside his office, Nort took his key and turned the elaborate, heavy brass lock. After putting the key back in his watch pocket, he rummaged around in his trouser pocket and held something out to Ben.

"While you're making up your mind, here's a reminder of our conversation," he said, and placed a smooth, irregularly shaped piece of metal slightly smaller than a quarter in his hand.

In the dim light of the hall, Ben opened his fingers, and saw a glint of gold.

"A doubloon!" he said. "I've seen them in museums. Where did you get it?"

Nort gave a low laugh of vast satisfaction. "For the time being, just say I found it," he said. "You can be sure it's an authentic souvenir of Janus Island. Keep it as a lucky piece."

Putting it in his pocket, Ben wondered how long it would be before he lost it. Somehow he never seemed able to keep lucky pieces.

When they got to the living room there was no sign of Penny or Nancy. The dining room and the kitchen, which was as big as a hotel's, were also empty. So was the library.

"Nance!" Nort called with apparent irritation. "Hey, where is everybody?"

"Maybe they went upstairs," Ben said.

"Maybe. You want a highball?"

"I'd better not. I think I need a clear head."

"I think I'll have just a light one."

Going to a bar in the corner of the living room, Nort poured himself a stiff drink. A door slammed, and the voices of Nancy and Penny could be heard in the vestibule. When they came in, their hair had been tousled by the wind, and their faces were wet.

"Where in the hell have you been?" Nort asked, astonishing Ben by the ugliness in his voice.

"I just wanted Penny to show me Ben's car," Nancy said with a great air of gaiety.

"Car?" Nort said, looking as confused as Ben felt.

"It's the newest Ford. Weren't you planning to buy one?"

"I took it out to show it to her, and the damnedest thing happened," Penny said. "I dropped my cigarette case in the crack behind the seat, and I can't get it out. I wouldn't mind, but it's sort of a sentimental gift someone gave me a long while ago, and . . ."

"Would you mind helping her, Ben?" Nancy said. "I think you have to move the seat."

"Do you want me . . . ?" Nort asked.

"I'm *freezing*," Nancy said. "Nort, be an angel, and get me a sweater, will you? I really got quite a chill. And I also need a drink."

Feeling the pressure of Penny's hand on his arm, Ben followed her out the front door. A cold wind was blowing with rain, and she started to run toward the Ford.

60

"Hey, what's this all about?" he asked as she opened the door of the car.

"Get in!"

He did, and slammed the door to escape from the wind.

"This is crazy," she said. "You won't believe it."

"Believe what? Where did you lose your cigarette case?"

"Never mind that. Nancy got me out here to talk to me. You won't believe this, but she says that husband of hers has got the whole house bugged. Anything that anybody says in any room is recorded!"

"What?"

"She says he's been doing it for a long time to check up on business people he brings out here, but now it's gotten to be an obsession, and he listens in on everything. She thought we ought to know, so you won't say anything that might queer whatever he was talking to you about. She's terribly anxious to talk to you. She wants you to meet her at seven in the morning right here. She says he doesn't get up until about ten."

"She's crazy," Ben said.

"Or he is. Could it be both?"

"God knows," Ben replied in bewilderment.

"Let nobody say you don't have fun friends," Penny said with a laugh. "Do you want to get out of this nuthouse now? We could make up some sort of an excuse."

"Like acute appendicitis?" he asked. "I don't think there's any reason to be scared."

"Did he offer you any kind of a legitimate business deal?"

"Maybe. I don't know yet."

"You want to stick around?"

"I think so, unless it bothers you."

"No, I'm fascinated. Come on. Get my cigarette case out of the glove compartment. We'd better go back in."

CHAPTER 5

WHEN they reached the living room, they found Nort and Nancy engaged in a violent argument which stopped abruptly as they came through the door.

"Did you get the cigarette case?" Nort asked, perhaps with a shade of irony.

"Yes," Penny said, holding it up. "If you people don't mind, I think I'll go to bed. For some reason, I feel terribly tired."

"Of course," Nancy murmured.

"I think I'll go up too, after I see Penny to the guesthouse," Ben said. "I enjoyed our talk, Nort. You certainly gave me a lot to think about."

"The world is full of things to think about," Nort said, pouring himself another drink. "Want a nightcap?"

"I'm afraid I've had enough. See you in the morning."

Nancy peered into her glass, and Nort seemed to be glowering at him as he turned and followed Penny to the front door. Until he got out of the room he could almost feel Nort's stare. What was there about Nort which seemed to express such vast sexual hunger and envy, or was that all in his mind, Ben wondered. Yet if he were married to Nancy, who despite her fine features seemed somehow as sexy as a sackful of broken glass, how would he like to watch a contemporary walk to the guesthouse with Penny?

Taking Penny's cape from a closet, Ben draped it over her shoulders. It was bitter cold outside, and still drizzling. In the darkness the lights of the guesthouse looked cheerful and warm, but outside its door she paused.

"I'd like to ask you to come in for a few minutes, but it's a little awkward, knowing that he may be listening."

"Yes. Well, I told you we'd be chaperoned, didn't I?"

She laughed, throwing her chin up sharply, and he kissed her for the first time while she was laughing. She started to respond fully but then she caught her breath and stepped back.

"I don't know . . ." she said ruefully. "It's so quick!"

The phrase "the quick and the dead" came to his mind, but he said nothing, and kissed her again.

"I have to be careful!" she protested. "I'm breakable, Ben. It should be written all over me. 'Fragile! Do not drop!' I've just been through a very hard time."

"I do not intend to drop."

"But we don't know, do we? Right now we're both so

mixed up I don't think we even know ourselves, never mind each other. If we're going anywhere, please take me along slowly!"

"I want you much too much to make a botch of it."

"Let's think and plan and go very carefully. I have an idea that you're in no great need of disappointment either."

"I've taken about all the kicking around I want this year."

"I don't see why anyone would want to kick you around."

"I imagine my former wife would be glad to fill you in."

"Well, I guess there are a few people who would be glad to fill you in about me."

"I'll not ask questions."

"But I'm beginning to want to give you answers. Will you be angry if I turn out to be different from what you hope me to be?"

"What I hope, I guess, is that eventually you will love me."

"Me too!"

Standing on her toes, she gave him a brief but intense kiss.

"Good night!" she said, and disappeared into the guesthouse, shutting the door softly behind her.

Feeling as lighthearted as schoolboys are supposed to feel, Ben walked back to the big house. All but a few dim lights were out now, and there was no sign of Nort or Nancy as he walked through the living room to the stairs. Probably they were in their own suite, arguing or relapsing into a frozen silence, he thought with pity. How were they able to survive without the slightest discernible glimmer of love for each other or anyone else?

Well, he too had wasted plenty of years, and so had poor Rita, the two of them sunk into some terrible paralysis of passion he would never be able to understand. If he were given the opportunity to have just one prayer answered, that prayer would be — please, don't let me ever sink into such a paralysis again!

With a sigh, Ben slept and dreamed of swimming in the tidal basins of Janus Island when he was young and did not know what paralysis meant.

It was a restless night for Ben. Awaking at three, he remembered that Nancy wanted to see him at seven, and his curiosity was piqued. What was the state of Nort's mental health, anyway? Was it wise to take any of his plans seriously, or should he just try to talk him into seeing a psychiatrist?

Seeing an alarm clock on the bedside table, Ben set it for six-thirty, but that really was not necessary, for he found it impossible to get back to sleep. At six he shaved and took a long bath. There was nothing to read in the room, and after getting dressed, he paced restlessly until seven. Going downstairs, he walked cautiously through the apparently empty house to the living room. Nancy, wearing black ski pants and a red turtleneck sweater, was sitting in an armchair holding a cup of coffee on her lap.

"Good morning," she mouthed silently, and for Ben the whole scene became as absurd as a movie when something goes wrong with the sound track. She beckoned and he followed her to the coat closet, where she put on a parka and threw him one. When they went through the dining room she picked up a Thermos bottle she had left on the table. Briskly she led the way to Ben's car.

"Thanks so much for coming, Ben," Nancy said as they got in. "I know how totally ridiculous all this must seem to you."

"Not at all," Ben said, sounding idiotic to himself. The first rays of sun were beginning to hit the frosty windowpanes on the second floor of the house and he had the uneasy sensation that Nort might be up there watching them. A cold wind was still blowing, and somewhere a shutter banged. He shivered and started the engine.

"Let's go get the papers," she said. "If Nort wakes up, that's our excuse. They won't deliver them this far out."

He put the car in gear and glided silently out of the driveway.

"When we get over the crest of the hill, park," she said. "I'll give you a cup of coffee."

"All right," he replied uneasily.

There was a flirtatiousness in her air of conspiracy that bothered him. Nancy was perhaps the only woman in the world who might conceivably make a date with a man through the man's girl. She was carefully made up, he saw, and he smelled a musky perfume that somehow seemed indecent in the crisp morning air.

"Pull off the road here," she said. "Behind that clump of pines. Don't worry about the lawn — it's frozen hard."

She was one of those women who cannot help giving orders. That and the memory that this was a favorite parking place of hers annoyed him, and he couldn't quite keep the irritation out of his voice when he said, "This all right?"

"Fine. Leave the motor running so we can get some heat. Here's your coffee."

She handed him the red plastic top from the Thermos bottle.

"What can I do for you?" he asked before taking a sip.

"Ben, I know you must have thought I was crazy last night when I told Penny to tell you about the bugging, but I was afraid you would say something Nort shouldn't hear. I'm terribly anxious that you go with him down to Janus Island."

"Why?"

"He needs you, Ben! He needs somebody competent

66

that he can trust. You know, in some ways he's still like a little boy, and this is a terribly difficult time in his life. I'm really worried about him!"

"How long has he been doing this bugging thing?"

"When it started it didn't sound quite as crazy as it does now. Do you mind if I tell you the whole story?"

"Go ahead."

"Well, you know, most of Nort's money was left in trust until he was thirty-five. Ten years ago, when he first started making his own investments, he lost a lot. It almost killed him. You see, he'd failed at almost everything he ever did. First the war, in comparison to you, anyway, and then he turned out to be a lousy businessman. It became kind of an obsession to get back everything he had lost."

"I guess that's understandable."

"He got this idea of buying a small movie company to get capital gains. The people out in Hollywood are pretty rough, you know — they had fleeced him once before. So he got this idea of asking them all up here for a long weekend when they were making their big deal, and he bugged their room."

She paused and lit a cigarette.

"It was dishonorable," she continued, "but he assumed they were dishonorable, and it worked. There were three men, and they talked over their plans every night. He found out they thought he was a sucker, and he also found what they thought their stock was really worth. And he discovered that another buyer they kept talking about was entirely fictitious."

"How did it work out?"

"He stuck to his guns and got what he wanted at a pretty good price. But he had got started on the bugging, and of course he couldn't leave it there."

Taking the cup from his hand, she took a sip of coffee.

"You know, he's awfully clever at electronics," she continued. "He used to sit up there night after night with his shortwave set, listening to Tokyo and Moscow and all the rest. The trouble is that radio hams don't say anything very interesting to each other. He found there was a lot more fascination in tuning in to our guest rooms after a party. Even the cook's room."

She handed the coffee back.

"At first," she went on, "I thought it was just sort of a sick phase he was going through, and I didn't object, but it started ruining our lives. You know the way friends talk about each other in private — no one should know what everyone else says. One of his best friends, Stu Nottingham, drank with him all night, and then went up to the Morgan room and told his wife he was quite sure Nort is a latent homosexual. Nort wanted to go punch him in the nose, but of course there was no way he could explain how he had heard. The next morning Nort just glowered at him all the way through breakfast, and Stu never knew why he was never asked back."

"I can see things could get very complicated," Ben said.

"They can get tragic! I had known for a long while he suspected me of being unfaithful to him, but it came as quite a shock when I realized that he had even bugged my car."

"How did you find out?"

"He said he was worried about Judy. You remember Judy, our oldest girl?"

"Yes," Ben said, remembering a pleasant, fresh-faced eighteen-year-old.

"Well, when Judy came back for Christmas vacation, I lent her my car to go on a skiing weekend with a guy from Dartmouth and a whole bunch of kids. When they came back, Nort turned purple. He was furious at her. I asked him for an explanation, and he finally admitted he had bugged the car. He said he had just done it to check up on her, but he hadn't even known I was going to lend it to her.

She took it when her own car broke down at the last minute."

"Oh boy," Ben said, rubbing his face wearily.

"Nobody should know all about the private lives of his own children, and all the servants and everybody!" Nancy said indignantly. "For a whole year now he's been firing people without explanations, dropping friends, and reading these incredible moral lectures to the kids. And he's been in despair. He figures that nobody is moral and no one loves him. It's all so goddam stupid!"

"He won't stop it?"

"The more he finds out about people, the more he wants to know! He says a whole new kind of psychology could be based on bugging. I think he's keeping a dossier on everybody around him, instead of a radio log book!"

"Has he thought of seeing a psychiatrist?"

"He gets furious at the mere mention of that. You know, he had that one long stay in a sanitarium, and I guess it was pretty rough. We've also had psychiatrists here as friends. He bugged their private conversations and lost all faith in them."

"If it weren't so sad I suppose it would be funny," Ben said.

"I'm afraid I'm well past the point where I can laugh at it. You have no idea what it's like to live in a house where nothing is private. And it's not only the house! He's bugged the barn and the garage, the guesthouse, even the bathhouses, everything!"

"You can't talk him out of it?"

"It's like talking an alcoholic out of drink. But I do hope, Ben, that he may forget it if he goes down to Janus Island to look for gold. That whole scheme may sound ridiculous to you, but it could be his salvation. He needs to do something constructive on his own, Ben! He needs a sense of accomplishment and clear goals. If he could find some gold, or some little artifact they could put in a museum with his name on it, that would mean a lot. Just playing the stock market with his father's money isn't enough. He has to do something completely on his own, preferably something which most people think has some danger attached to it. Do you know that ever since the war he has thought of himself as a terrible coward?"

"I don't think he has any particular reason to."

"Well, you know, he asked you to transfer him ashore, and the next month you got into action."

"No one could have foreseen that. Anyway, he was chronically seasick. That wasn't his fault."

"He thinks it is, and Ben, he still feels he has to prove himself. The thing gets worse as he grows older. He thinks it's now or never. I honestly believe he thinks this treasure hunt thing is his last chance."

"I don't like it," Ben said. "The sea is a bad place to go to get cured."

"Haven't a great many men gone to sea to try to prove themselves?"

"Probably. I suspect that they are the ones who cause disasters."

"That's why I want you to go with him. I think that's why he wants you, Ben! In a strange way he's always counted on you, ever since you were both ten years old. Didn't you save his life once when you were kids?"

"Not really. He could have swum ashore alone."

"Well, he's got it in his mind that you've saved his life twice, once when that boat turned over, and again when you transferred him off your ship. Was it true that the radio shack was hit?"

"Yes, but no one could have predicted that."

"Nort is something of a mystic, Ben. He always carries a lucky piece, and I think he feels you're a walking symbol of some kind."

"I'm a pretty damn poor lucky piece," Ben said morosely. "Good God, look at my own life!"

"He admires that too. He sees you as a man of principle, too proud to prostitute your art, too much of a man to put up with a bad wife."

"That's a pleasant fiction."

"You can't let him down, Ben. He'll do anything for you, and there's no real reason he can't find a little gold down there to bolster his ego. Has he told you about his other scheme yet?"

"What other scheme?"

"The movie?"

"He mentioned something about that."

"He talked about tax advantages and secrecy, but you know what I think he really wants?"

"What?"

"I think he wants to be an actor. More than that, he wants to have his exploits recorded. If he does find something big, he'd like to have the whole exploit televised from coast to coast."

"Well, I guess he'll never die of modesty."

"He has the arrogance of the weak, Ben. I can say that because in a motherly sort of way I love him. And you have the modesty of the strong. I guess you know that in other ways I have loved you for a long time."

"Thank you, Nance," he said awkwardly, and kissed her on the forehead.

"I rather embarrass you, don't I?"

"Not at all."

"God, things have turned out to be ironic," she said, lighting a cigarette. "When you were fifteen years old and I was seventeen, remember how you used to follow me around?"

"I remember it well."

"When you're fifteen, a girl two years older is exciting, but not at forty-five, eh?"

"We'd better get back to the house," he said.

"It's not really fair that men like you never really go out

of circulation, while we old girls sit moldering on the shelf. And it's not fair either that Nort always has so much money, while you're always dead broke. He tells me you're badly in debt. Is that true?"

"Yes, but I think we really ought to get back. You know what Nort will think if he knows we're out here."

"He couldn't do anything about it he hasn't done to me a hundred times already."

"I still think we ought to try to get him to a doctor. This hidden microphone thing is really bizarre, Nance!"

"Please don't talk doctors to him! Nothing gets him more upset! Remember, mostly the only person Nort tortures with his microphones is himself. Ben, he's in trouble, and at heart he's a good man. He needs your help now more than he ever did. Will you give it?"

"I've got to think," Ben said doggedly. "Nance, I can't let myself be pushed into this too fast."

"I know, but he's got a lot to offer you, Ben. You two guys are in many ways complementary. There's no reason for you to be poor all the time. Never forget that."

"It's a hard thing to forget."

"We'd better go get the papers now," she said. "He might get up earlier than usual, and I'd just as soon not get him upset."

After picking up the papers at a drugstore, they returned to the parking lot. The big house was totally quiet, outside and in, but Ben again had the eerie sensation of not only being listened to, but being watched. Taking his paper, he went up to his room to await breakfast at ten.

Breakfast turned out to be a puzzling meal. When Ben brought Penny from the guesthouse to the living room, they found Nort sprawled on the couch reading the paper, while Nancy made scrambled eggs in an electric frying pan on a sideboard. Dressed in a freshly starched pair of khaki trousers and a white T-shirt which emphasized his muscular torso, Nort looked at first glance like a college football player. When he saw Penny he jumped to his feet, the picture of gentlemanly attention.

"Good morning, Penny!" he said with new warmth. "Have a good night?"

The sudden shift from the coldest condescension to all this heartiness surprised both Penny and Ben.

"Yes," Penny replied. "Yes I did, thank you."

"Let me get you some coffee. Sit down here!"

His courtesy was not emphasized quite enough to make it a burlesque, and Ben wondered whether it was only his own hostility which made him suspect that Nort was playing out a parody of good manners as a subtle form of insult. After all, maybe Nort felt guilty about the rudeness he had displayed the night before. Or maybe he had decided that he would have to treat Penny well if he wanted Ben's friendship and cooperation.

"Cream and sugar?" Nort asked Penny solicitously.

"Just black, thank you."

"Can I get you the morning paper?"

"Not now thanks," Penny said, and glancing out the windows saw the view of the Sound for the first time in daylight. "How beautiful! I hadn't realized how close to the water we are."

"During the last hurricane, we were a good deal too close," Nort said. "Still, it's marvelous in the summer."

On that gray windy day the Sound seemed menacing, Ben thought. Low scudding clouds obscured the Connecticut shore, giving the impression that they were looking out over the open sea. The waves broke cold and sullen against the muddy shore. Ever since he could remember, Ben had had a secret premonition that he would drown, that his death inevitably would come at sea. Since the war he had almost forgotten the notion, but he thought of it again now as he gazed at the threatening water, funereal as the dirge of the wind that gusted up around the eaves, making the big French windows rattle.

"Coffee?" Nancy asked Ben, cocking an eyebrow.

"Thank you."

"Penny," Nancy said, "I'm going to play tennis this morning. We have an indoor court. Would you like to join me?"

"I'm afraid I don't play tennis."

"I don't know what the rest of you want to do, but in a few minutes, I'm going swimming," Nort said. "Why don't all of you come?"

"Swimming!" Penny said in a horrified voice. "On a day like this?"

"I have a heated indoor pool. It's really the only improvement I've made on this place."

"He designed it himself," Nancy said. "He built a kind of glass house that slides on tracks right over the old pool in winter. Really, it's quite clever."

"I didn't bring a bathing suit," Penny said.

"Well," Nort replied with elaborate nonchalance, "we don't often use them here. We don't mind swimming in the buff if you don't."

"I'm afraid I'm just not in the mood," Nancy said, and there was an instant of silence during which husband and wife glared at each other.

That was a piece of cruelty if I ever saw one, Ben thought. If the four of them had gone swimming nude, it would not have been the carefree sport of uninhibited adults. Nancy, whose figure was painfully contrived from steel springs and foam rubber, would look pathetic beside Penny, and Ben obviously would not show up to advantage next to Nort's triumphs of diet and exercise. In the nude, Penny and Nort would seem to belong together, leaving Ben and Nancy to hide themselves up to the neck in water as best they could. Furthermore, Ben was sure, Nort would be incapable of masking those strangely adolescent, furtive looks he kept darting at Penny even when she was dressed. It was difficult for him to imagine anything much more painful than such a group swim.

"I'm not very modern about swimming in the nude," Penny said. "The truth is, I hate it."

"Why?" Nort asked.

"I don't know. People always think it's going to be so gay and romantic, but I find it uncomfortable and embarrassing. I guess I'm just old-fashioned."

"The truth is," Ben said, "that most of us have been brought up to associate nudity with sex. I find it most frustrating to sport around in the buff with attractive women I'm not supposed to touch."

"You always have been a lecherous bastard," Nort said. "How do you stand him, Penny?"

"I don't mind what you call lechery in the proper circumstances," she said with a smile. "I just don't like to mix it up with swimming."

"A very sensible answer, my dear," Nancy said. "Nort, you go swimming if you want. Personally, I'm going to stay here and mix up some bloody marys before I torture myself on the tennis court. Anyone can join me who wants."

"Ben, I wanted to show you some new aqualungs," Nort said. "Have you seen the ones that actually let you talk?"

"No, I haven't even heard of them."

"I've got a couple I'm trying out, and a few gadgets for working underwater that I've worked up myself. Want to see 'em?"

"Sure."

"Grab a coat. It's the old pool down by the tennis courts."

From the outside the pool looked like a large greenhouse,

which indeed Ben had thought it was. The panes of glass were fogged, and it was a surprise, when he walked in the door, to see the big marble swimming pool he remembered so well, with the little dolphins in the corner spouting water. The glass enclosed most of the surrounding terrace, and in one corner Nort had built a workbench for his underwater gear. The air was warm and moist.

"This is great," Ben said.

"It's a fine way to stay in shape."

Casually Nort took off his clothes and tossed them on a bench by the pool before sitting down on the edge, dangling his feet in the water.

"Did Nance get you aside for a talk this morning?" he asked in a matter-of-fact voice.

The question caught Ben with his pants halfway off, and he didn't say anything until he had freed his legs.

"Yes," he replied after a moment. "Yes, she did."

"Did she tell you all that stuff about my having the whole house bugged?"

"She did mention something about it," Ben said, and sat down on the bench.

"Do you want a cold beer? I have a bar over there."

"That might go pretty well."

Nort bounded like a young athlete to the corner and came back with two opened cans of ale.

"I don't usually talk about my wife to anyone," he said, sitting down on the edge of the bench, "but if you're going into business with me, there are some things you have a right to know. Anyway, you're my oldest friend."

He handed Ben one of the cans.

"Thanks," Ben said.

"I know you've been through enough troubles yourself to realize that marriages sometimes run into periods of crisis. As you know, things have been a bit rocky for us the last few years."

"I'm sorry," Ben said.

"Well, you know, she's going through this change of life thing, and that hits some women pretty hard. She's not the kind of woman who likes to exercise, and she's scared to death she's losing her looks. She keeps saying that I look much younger than she does, that I grow younger every year."

He paused expectantly and Ben took a swallow of ale.

"Anyway, she worries a lot about whether she's attractive to men. That makes a woman vulnerable. You don't have to be much of a psychiatrist to realize that."

"Yes," Ben said.

"I guess we're all old enough to realize there are men who would take advantage of a situation like that if they could. When I came into my trust fund some years back, there was a lot of publicity about it, a lot of exaggeration. A good many people around here think I'm richer than I am."

Ben smiled, he hoped sympathetically.

"There was talk, you know, of hundreds of millions of dollars, and of course I don't have anything like that. I didn't like it. I figured that it marked my family as some kind of target, and I was right."

"How?"

"Well, there was a young fellow who turned up and kind of ingratiated himself with Nance. She hired him to teach tennis and swimming to the kids. I got suspicious — I don't mind saying I got jealous too. He was always fawning over her, and that was a period when I had to take long business trips. And he was always fawning over the girls, both my daughters. I just figured he was out after everything he could get."

"Tough situation," Ben said.

"I was sure he was no good, but I couldn't convince them of it. I had to get some kind of proof before he did any real harm. After all, it's my job to protect this family, and what do you do when you have two wacky teen-age daughters and a wife who's half out of her head? Well, that's putting it too strongly, but Nance is pretty neurotic sometimes."

"I guess we all are."

"Sure, but I had to take steps. So I bugged the guy's room and his telephone. I don't want to go into detail, but I found out quite a lot. Enough to fire him without making my daughters sore and without giving Nance a chance to fight back. But of course, it was humiliating for her, in all sorts of ways I don't want to describe. I guess it was a pretty bad shock for her, and maybe I didn't handle it too gently, because I was so mad."

Nort paused again, apparently expecting sympathy.

"It must have been rough."

"I'll say. She couldn't get over the idea that I had listened in on some of her conversations as well as his. This bugging thing got to be kind of an obsession with her. Before long she started accusing me of having the whole house bugged, of listening in on everything everybody said."

"Did you?"

"What do you think I am, some kind of psychotic? I only use a bug when I have to. Once or twice I've used them in business, when I figured a guy was really trying to do me in. That's not unusual nowadays. Certainly you know that."

"I've heard of it."

"A guy's crazy if he doesn't fight fire with fire. You realize, Ben, if Nance ever decided to divorce me and got some clever lawyer to play her cards right, she might take me for two or three million dollars, at least. Read the papers — it happens all the time."

"I know."

"Well, now she's in such a mixed-up period in her life, as

I say, she's vulnerable. Almost any young punk could come along and offer her the illusion of romance. When women get that age, they start figuring it's now or never. You have to feel sorry for them."

"Yes."

"An ambitious young guy could get her to divorce me with a big settlement, and then he could marry her. That's one of the easiest ways a guy can latch on to a couple of million dollars today."

"It doesn't sound easy."

"For some it would be. Honestly, I worry about Nance more than I do about my daughters, and I worry about them all the time. It's a terrible thing when it's known that a girl has big money. How can you expect teen-agers to keep a level head?"

"I don't know," Ben said, "but to be honest, I think you're probably worrying about this much too much."

"It's easy for you to talk. The daughter of a friend of mine ran away with a chauffeur just last year. She was sixteen!"

"I guess the moral of that is to drive yourself."

"It's no joke, Ben. It's a legitimate worry, something to guard against. The only thing is, I don't want Nance to scare you about it. She has a whole big thing built up about this bugging, and like a lot of neurotic people, she thinks everyone around her is going out of his mind."

"I won't let her scare me."

"She's a fine woman, Ben. God knows I love her very much. She's having a hard time, but I'm going to see her through it, and I hope you'll help."

On the last words, Nort's voice almost broke with emotion. Getting up suddenly, he dove cleanly into the pool and started thrashing back and forth like an Olympic swimmer in pursuit of a record.

After due consideration, Ben dove leisurely in, and

slowly bisected the pool. When Nort climbed out and ominously approached the springboard, Ben turned over on his back and kept cautiously to the shallow end. With a tremendous crack, Nort sent himself flying into the air, where he seemed to hang around for several seconds doing somersaults before he landed with a great splash.

"That's quite a dive," Ben said with honest admiration.

"Well, it helps keep me in shape. Come on up and I'll show you the new equipment."

From a box at the edge of the pool, Nort took two warm Turkish towels and threw one at Ben. After drying his face, Ben followed him to the workbench in the corner.

"Here's the lung that lets you talk," Nort said, taking a complicated contrivance of aluminum and rubber from a hook on the pegboard along the wall. "Want to try it?"

"Not right now," Ben said.

The sight of the scuba tanks stacked under the workbench, the canvas belts with lead weights and all the rest of it gave him a curious twinge of panic. It had been a long time since he had learned how to dive, and he was sure that he had forgotten most of it. Even when he was freshly trained and in far better physical shape than he was in now, he had not liked the sensation of jumping into the water with so many weights strapped to him, and sinking down, down, far away from the light of the sun.

"Don't you want to give it a try?"

"I'm a little rusty. I'll have to check out on the equipment all over again."

"Good old Ben — always so careful," Nort replied. "That's why I need you along on this trip."

"To tell you the truth, I suffer from claustrophobia when I get all that stuff on. I never really liked it."

"There will be plenty of other people to dive. But one thing bothers me. Do you mind if I tell you what it is?"

"What?"

"This is a pretty exciting project I've outlined, isn't it? Wouldn't most people think so?"

"I suppose."

"Why is it you have no enthusiasm?"

"I don't know," Ben replied slowly. "I'm afraid that in a thing like this, I mostly think of the difficulties."

"Isn't it more than that? At heart, don't you think there is really zero possibility of finding anything?"

"Oh, I wouldn't say there was no possibility."

"Ben, you've been around the water for a long time. You know the Keys as well as I do, and their history. You know the gold is there, but you also know it's been scattered over God knows how many miles. And you know that coral has grown over it, sometimes several feet deep."

"Yes, I know that."

"Barrels of coins have been scattered and even gold ingots are pretty small when you have to bust hundreds of cubic feet of coral to find them. Right?"

"Right."

"I don't think I'd go down there if there was nothing but coins or ingots to look for. You might find a few, but the chances of finding enough to pay your expenses are pretty small."

"What else is there?" Ben asked.

"I wasn't going to tell you this until we were farther along, but maybe it will help you make up your mind. As I said, the Spaniards had tax problems, much like ours. About ninety per cent of the gold they gathered was supposed to go to their king. But of course no one knew how much they gathered. It was a perfect situation for smuggling."

"I've read that."

"In Seville they keep some rather remarkable records. I won't give you the full documentation now, but I have reason to believe that it was fairly common practice for some of the Spanish admirals to cast large objects in gold, to put gold in a shape which could be smuggled ashore in Spain without accounting for it."

"I have heard rumors about that . . ."

"You've probably heard of the lost golden table. Well, I think I know of something better. I believe the admiral's ship in the lost convoy which I think cracked up on Janus Reef was equipped with about twenty gold cannon. Do you have any idea what one of those old guns weighed, even in iron?"

"Plenty, some of them."

"Up to about two tons."

"Wow!"

"Now a cannon would be easily cast in gold in South America, because they cast bronze and iron cannon there. And a gold cannon would be quite easy to black up and take ashore, presumably for repairs, and to replace with bronze or iron."

"In theory, I suppose it's possible."

"I have more than theory to go on. There was an inquiry in 1682, and all kinds of letters. Suffice it to say that a good many scholars are convinced that Admiral Valera, who sailed from Panama in 1681, was really sailing into a trap. Some of the people who helped him cast those cannon informed on him. The king paid well for that kind of information."

"But he never got home?"

"Right. The whole convoy simply disappeared in a hurricane, and from reconstructing the weather, on the basis of logs from nearby ships, I figure he must have been right off the eastern edge of Janus Reef."

"It's an interesting theory," Ben said. "I hope you're right."

"I'm fairly sure I am, for reasons we'll go into later. But my point is, those heavy cannon wouldn't have been scattered far, even by three hundred years of surf. And they'd be easily detectable by all kinds of devices. We have the great advantage of looking for something physically big."

"By God, that does sound pretty exciting," Ben said.

"I'd just love to see one of those cannon go into a museum, about twelve feet of it, maybe two tons of shining gold!"

"It's quite a thought."

"Do you think you could use it in your movie?"

"I don't see why not."

"Do you figure you could use a guy obsessed with finding a golden cannon, a character based on me?"

"Perhaps."

"I'm trying not to be self-conscious, and I certainly don't want to tell you how to write your script, but I thought we might keep it as close to a documentary as we can. I mean, you could have a hero who doesn't need money, yet who is obsessed with the search for gold. Is there anything you could do with that?"

"I don't know yet. I'd have to give it a lot of thought."

"It's just an idea," Nort said. "The movie part of this will be strictly up to you."

There was a pause, while Nort toweled himself vigorously.

"Ben," he said suddenly, "there's still something troubling you. What is it? We've known each other too long to play games."

"It's just, well, this bugging business still bothers me, Nort. Will you get angry with me if I tell you what I really think?"

"I'll be angry if you don't. Where can I expect candor if not from my oldest friend?"

"I don't know how much of this bugging you've been doing, but you seem awfully preoccupied with it and with people who may be tapping your wires. Besides that, I hope you don't mind my saying that both you and Nance seem to have been under a growing tension lately. There are, after all, doctors whose business it is to reduce tension. It might do you good to see one of them and talk some of these problems out."

"Do you think I'm crazy, Ben?" Nort asked quietly.

"Certainly you're past the stage where you think a man has to be crazy in order to see a psychiatrist! I just think you're operating under strains which might be relieved."

"Am I the only one operating under strains?"

"Of course not."

"You've been frank, Ben. Do you mind if I'm frank too?"

"Of course not."

"I've been looking for a way to talk *you* into seeing a doctor."

"Me?"

"You're the oldest friend I've got, Ben. Do you think I enjoy seeing you get into such a mess? First your marriage collapses, and then your career goes into a decline. And then you come out here obviously infatuated with a woman half your age . . ."

"She's not half my age," Ben said defensively. "She's twenty-eight."

"All right. Does that make a big difference? Do you really think you can find any stability with her? Or have you given up on stability? Tell me, Ben, are you just out for kicks?"

"No!" Ben retorted. "Listen, Nort . . ."

"Now, don't get angry! There's no reason why old friends can't talk. If you said you were just out for a good time with that young lady, I wouldn't worry so much, because that at least would be within the bounds of reality. But I know you, Ben, God how I know you! You're a

84

master of self-delusion, and always have been. Remember, I tried to talk you out of marrying Rita twenty years ago? Everybody but you knew she was a neurotic bitch! But you wouldn't listen. You had hypnotized yourself into thinking . . ."

"That's water over the dam, Nort, and anyway she wasn't all that bad. Come on. This conversation is too painful."

"But if you won't listen to me, the consequences will be even more painful! You don't know reality, Ben! That's why my listening in on conversations scares you — instinctively you're scared to death of reality, you don't want to know what's going on. Most of all, you don't want to know yourself. You think you're a young lover embarking on a great romance. I think you're a dear old friend succumbing to middle-aged satyriasis."

"That's enough!" Ben said. "You've always been hung up on sex, Nort. If you had your way you'd castrate the whole world."

"Hear me out, will you? Have the guts to hear me out for once! I don't want to see you get hurt, Ben, not all over again! I don't blame you for divorcing Rita — only you could have stayed married to her for twenty years. But why do you have to go over that roller coaster all over again?"

"You think the two women resemble each other?" Ben asked acidly.

"Superficially, no. But this girl isn't anyone who is going to make you a good wife! Obviously she hasn't got the experience, the education or the background to do anything for you outside of bed. If you're just on a sex kick, why don't you line yourself up with some professionals in New York? With them, at least, you know the price. You shouldn't bring them out and introduce them to friends and moon over them the way you moon over that girl! I hate to see you making a fool of yourself, Ben!"

Abruptly Nort stopped. He was breathing heavily. There was an instant of silence during which Ben was surprised to find the anger draining out of him.

"It's funny," Ben said with a curious air of detachment. "I don't feel foolish. I don't feel foolish at all. When I'm with that girl I feel incredibly wise."

"For Christ's sake, Ben! Every man feels wise when he gets a hard-on. For a few minutes at least, he knows what he wants."

"You always make cynicism sound like truth. It isn't, you know."

"What is the truth, the truth about you, your version of it?"

"I'm a pretty confused guy, Nort. I've been through a long hard time, and much of it was my own fault. But I think I've learned a little. I don't think love is just a senti-mental word. I don't think people have to lapse into a lifetime of meaningless work, boredom and petty cruel-ties — I don't think that trip is absolutely necessary. I think you have to be awfully good, unusually healthy, if you like, to give and get love over more than a short period of time, and I think you have to be lucky enough to find someone capable of responding, but I have some small hope Penny and I can qualify. At least I want to give myself a chance to find out."

"Do you have any idea what sentimental garbage that is?"

"To you, of course. Nort, I ask you with compassion and not hate, do you have any idea how tragic your whole loveless way of life is?"

Now Nort flushed. "There are many things that I love!"

"You said it. That's the whole tragedy."

"What the hell do you mean?"

"Never mind, Nort. Let's stop enlightening each other. To you, my world is an illusion, a sentimental or lecherous dream, and to me, yours is a nightmare of suspicion and hate. Now do we fight, let each other alone, or find some small area where we can work together?"

"We find the gold cannon," Nort replied with a shrug. "I love the gold cannon, I suppose, if you want to press me into that, or at least I love the idea of finding them, of bringing them up and presenting them to the world. I love accomplishment and self-discipline. And you love a woman, or some fantasy you think a woman to be, but you'll need money to keep on that drug. If you ever are fool enough to marry her, you'll have two families to support, and right now you can't even support one."

"Yes, I'll need money."

"I can give it to you, and I want to work with you, so we do have common ground if we can maintain any faith in each other, and don't start questioning each other's sanity."

"Yes," Ben said, "and if we don't keep infuriating one another."

"Our friendship has lasted forty years, Ben. To you this may sound corny, but I know that no matter what, I can count on you till the day I die. And you can count on me. Our friendship has long roots."

And sometimes bears strange fruit, Ben was tempted to say, but instead he accepted the hand which Nort held out to him. Feeling that he was involved in some incredibly childish yet touching charade, he squeezed it hard.

"You just think my plan over for three days before you say yes," Nort said with a grin. "Come on! If we don't get back to the house soon, Nance will have drunk a whole pitcher of bloody marys and will be yelling at the top of her lungs that I'm nuts."

CHAPTER 6

T HEY found Penny and Nancy hunched over a card table in the library.

"Nancy has been scaring me to death reading my fortune," Penny said. "It's fantastic. The woman's a witch!"

"Sit down, Ben," Nancy said. "I haven't read your fortune in a long time."

"I'm afraid I've got to go upstairs and start getting my things together," Ben replied. "Nort here has given me a good deal to think about. We'd better get back to town."

"No!" Nort said, sounding stricken. "I thought you were going to spend another night!"

"I've got a lot of thinking to do if I'm going to give you my decision inside of three days," Ben said.

"Don't you already know exactly what you are going to do?" Nancy asked, somewhat sardonically.

The question startled Ben, because he did know what he wanted to do — he wanted to go to Janus Island if Penny would go with him. Despite Nort's warnings, there was all kinds of excitement in that thought, and none whatsoever in the idea of going down there alone, no matter what adventures with gold cannon Nort promised. But he didn't feel he could just ask the girl to go off to the Florida Keys with him for two or three months until they knew each other much better. If we're going anywhere, please take me there slowly, she had said, and he had agreed.

"No, I don't really know what I can work out," he said to Nancy. "Nort gave me three days to make up my mind, and I'm going to need them."

What Ben wanted now more than anything else, he realized, was to get out, to escape all the questions raised by Nort and those wry, quizzical glances from Nancy, to go somewhere where he could be alone with Penny, but the farewells took a long time. It was one o'clock when Ben helped Penny into the car and drove down the long drive-way. In the rear-view mirror he saw Nancy and Nort standing in the parking area waving. Then Nort put his arm around his wife, and like an affectionate old couple they seemed to help each other back toward the house.

For several minutes Penny sat absorbed in thought. It wasn't until he got onto the Long Island Expressway that she spoke.

"Ben," she said suddenly, "did he offer you something that's going to be useful to you?"

He found he had a tremendous urge to talk, to tell her all about the treasure-hunting expedition, the fantastic gold

89

cannon, the movie to be made not for art but for secrecy and tax evasion. If he talked about it enough, it might begin to sound real, but he was quite aware that he had promised not to tell anyone at all about this.

"It's hard to be sure," he said uncomfortably. Stripping himself of secrets with a pretty woman had always been a weakness of his, he reminded himself, but he still hated the awkwardness of evasion while talking with a girl he was beginning to love. In some obscure way it was like going to bed with her but being forbidden to take off his clothes.

She was waiting, obviously expecting him to go on.

"It's no use," he said with a sigh. "I can't do it."

"Do what?"

"Be sensible, keep secrets, go slowly, all that."

She laughed.

"Keep trying," she said.

"No, I enjoy leveling too much. It's the only thing in the world that's any fun, leveling with a pretty woman I'm going to fall in love with."

"You mean you haven't been leveling with me?"

"Not entirely. The situation is really this. Nort offered me a job writing and directing a movie to be made on Janus Island. At the same time he wants to look for gold, and that might not be quite as crazy as it sounds."

"Are you going to do it?"

"If you'll go with me, but the awful thing is, I can't ask you if you will yet. We don't know each other well enough to make such a request even halfway sensible, and you asked me to go slow."

"Ben?"

"Yes."

"I'll go," she said quietly.

"You will?" he asked with astonishment.

"Oh, we could discuss it a lot and wait for days, but in

the end I know damn well I'd go, so I might as well start right off admitting it."

"That's marvelous!"

"Don't be so sure yet. Now can I talk for a minute?"

"The floor is yours."

"I'll go to Florida with you if we agree on the basics. And for me the basics are this: I'm looking for something. I've knocked around the world for twenty-eight years, and I'm sick of it. I don't mean I'm all anxious to get married, because I'm too afraid of making a mistake, but I am anxious to see if maybe, somehow, you and I might eventually be able to work something out, something that might conceivably make sense, some way of life that combines passion with kindness."

"We agree on the basics."

"What we've got to do is to explore each other, and that has to go slowly, but I don't think the surrounding geography will make much difference. On Janus Island or Manhattan, we'll still be the same people. So if you want to go to Florida, I'll go with you on a voyage of mutual exploration."

"That calls for a celebration!" he said. "There's a good restaurant just ahead!"

His voice rang with enthusiasm, but he noticed that she looked sober, depressed.

"What's the matter?" he asked.

"I ought to tell you a little about myself. It's not really fair . . ."

"Do whatever makes you feel best, but first let's order a drink and a good meal."

The restaurant was big, almost empty and dimly lit. They sat in a corner booth and he ordered scotch for both of them.

With a long, carefully manicured pink fingernail Penny

traced a line in some salt which had spilled on the table-cloth.

"You wanted to know what kind of work I do," she said. "Well, it's not very glamorous. I was an airline stewardess."

There was a pause during which she looked at him intently.

"I quit my job in order to get married," she continued. "And then, well, it didn't work out."

"I'm sorry — but, of course, for my sake, glad."

"He married someone else," she said, and he saw that a muscle at the corner of her mouth was pulsing. "Pilots know lots of girls. I quit to get married, but at the last moment he married someone else."

"Oh boy," he said. "That must have been quite a kick in the stomach."

"But of course I deserved it. Fools always deserve what they get."

She was smiling now, and her eyes looked less hurt.

"A real fool never knows he's a fool," he said.

"Thank you."

"As a professional fool of long standing, I know."

"One reason that I like you is that you're so rueful, yet so full of zest."

"The zest is a gift from you. Penny, do you ever want to go back to the airline?"

"I don't know. For about a month now, I've just been sitting around without being able to think. We had rented an apartment to live in, and we had paid a month in advance. It was my money, really. He was always borrowing from me."

"He sounds like a gentleman you may someday be glad to have got rid of."

"Oh, I know," she said with a wry grin. "He has no character at all. He's brutally selfish and he's weak and not very intelligent. My only problem is, why did I stick with

92

him for five years? That's really the question which robs me of all my self-confidence. I didn't know what I was doing for five whole years!"

"I was married for about twenty years before I got divorced."

She looked up at him intently, and her eyes looked hurt again.

"Twenty years!" she said.

"That's the way it worked out, and there is no way to justify it. If she was a good woman, why did we split up, and if not, why did I stay with her for twenty years?"

"I suppose people change."

"They do, and the world changes, and I, at least, find that nothing is quite the way I used to assume it was. My own past is just as mysterious to me as the future. In fact I sometimes think I know more about what will happen than what did happen when I was a child and a young man. I've just met you, and I'm at least under the illusion that I already know more about you than I will ever know about my former wife, whom I've known for twenty-five years. I don't really know my own children. My mother is a mystery to me, and I don't think I ever knew my father at all. The world is all an unknown quantity, except for strangers about whom one can make snap judgments."

"Do you find that terrifying?"

"Of course. I live in terror, and so does everyone I know."

"I don't want always to live in terror."

"It doesn't have to be just that — it can be terror mixed with delight."

"That's your definition of life?"

She took a sip from her glass.

"For some people. For others, I guess it's mostly boredom. Are you often bored?"

"I guess I'm too emotional for that. Either I'm miserable or happy, with very little in between."

"Me too."

"Ben?"

"Yes."

"Will it scare you if I ask some practical questions?"

"Yes."

She laughed.

"I'm going to anyway. A trip to Florida doesn't bother me from my own point of view, because I don't think it matters where we get to know each other, but does it make any sense for you professionally? I want to help you be constructive, not just take you off on a wild fling."

"To be honest, I don't have much of a profession any more," he said. "I was a wonder boy there in television for about ten years, but everything has changed. A lot of people think I'm washed up. The truth is, I think, I'm just not interested in television the way it is, and I'm not too marvelously eager to do anything I don't like for the sake of money. I've made a lot of money in my time — for a while there it seemed to me I always was doing a kind of work I hated in order to live in a way I soon began to hate, with a woman who appeared to hate me. It was all pointless, but profitable. For a long while I've been looking for something else."

"You're not washed up," she said. "But can I ask you a tough question?"

"Temper it if you can."

"Why did you stop trying to write serious plays?"

"There's no market. The mass audience . . ."

Often before he had given that explanation, but under the scrutiny of her dark, serious eyes, he felt phony now, overdefensive.

"I'm sorry if I was impertinent," she said.

"On the contrary, I'd say your question was highly

pertinent. When television went to hell, I could have done legitimate plays and movies the way others did. I did two plays, but they didn't work out too well. Hell, the truth is, as I got older I grew confused. You need standards, a code, if you're going to write drama, or at least I do."

"I'm not sure I understand."

"If you believe in a rigid code of conduct, then it is dramatic when a person breaks it, and dramatic when he returns to it. Sin and repent and be forgiven. That is really the basis of everything I did."

"It doesn't work any more?"

"I don't think I believe in any rigid code. Take all those stories people used to write about young girls falling in love. Would they remain chaste until marriage? If not, would they be forgiven, one way or another?"

"What's wrong with that?"

"Well, nowadays any psychiatrist will tell you that most girls don't stay chaste through high school. A certain amount of sexual experimentation is perfectly normal, and virginity continued too long is judged a disease. This, I don't doubt, is good medicine, but a certain amount of normal sexual experimentation is damn poor material for drama!"

"Do you have to write about adolescents?"

"Isn't it the same for adults? I used to write about adultery all the time, all kinds of modern versions of *The Scarlet Letter*, but how could you write about poor Hester now? She'd just be sitting at the country club bar discussing her latest affair with all her friends."

"Surely you don't think that's typical of modern women?"

"I don't know what, if anything, is typical of modern women. I just know that I've seen so much adultery that it ceases to interest me as drama any more. I can't base a whole play on whether some cheating broad goes back to her husband! I keep hearing the psychiatrists again. A great many people commit adultery at one time or another, and it's generally just a sympton of a fairly complex neurosis. It's a subject for medical study, not dramatization. I'd just as soon try to dramatize athlete's foot!"

She laughed.

"Isn't there anything you can write about except sex?"

"Sure! I used to write about war a lot. That was a great subject, with a fine rigid code to break and return to dramatically. The brave guy turned coward and then brave again. The hero shot Germans while the villain ran. But nowadays, what happens? In my own mind I think the good guy probably is miserable in uniform, and the guy who likes to shoot probably, in my mind at least, is either a simpleton or a sadist. I don't really believe war is dramatic any more. I think it's just a bloody mess, the disease of nations, just as adultery is a disease of individuals."

"I guess it is hard to write war stories about Vietnam."

"That's only part of it. Take business as a subject. When I was young I felt the struggle to get ahead was dramatic. The good guy got the vice presidency, or in reverse, spurned it because he didn't want to sell his soul. Now I honestly don't think his soul has much to do with it. I suppose some vice presidents have souls and some errand boys don't, but I couldn't care less. The truth is that the whole world of business bores hell out of me. I live in a great business nation, but everything about offices and banks and insurance companies bores me to death."

"I'm afraid it does me too. It always has."

"I suppose I'm talking about two things," he said, his voice intense. "Standards have become much less rigid in the last twenty years, and that does make drama more difficult. But not impossible, of course, for some. The other thing I have been talking about is that at forty-five, I've probably become jaded, or at least have temporarily lost my way in the world."

"You don't seem jaded. I don't think jaded people get excited when they talk."

"Confused, then. A writer of any kind has to have a set of beliefs, whether they're right or wrong. The only things I believe in now are abstractions, such as 'love,' 'justice,' words like that, but it's very difficult for me to make people act them out with any kind of reality in my own mind."

"Perhaps you need time," she said.

"Perhaps. But for the present, I'm grateful for the chance to do a movie about a treasure hunt. There, at least, there is clarity of purpose: either they find the damn stuff or they don't."

The waiter came with the menus, but he found he wasn't at all hungry. They ordered hamburgers.

"You know," Ben said, "while we're on the subject of my curious profession, I think I owe it to you to tell you I'm broke and in debt. Everything I had saved went to my wife and kids — and to the government, which keeps re-computing my taxes and demanding more."

"Fortunately, I'm not broke," she said with a smile. "In my savings account I still have sixty-three dollars and twenty-two cents."

Ben laughed. "Nort presumably is going to pay me a salary," he said. "One way or another, we'll get by."

"I've never had enough money to worry about it much," she said.

The waiter brought the hamburgers, and he ate his slowly.

"I wish we could fly right down to Janus Island tonight," he said.

"Is that possible?"

"I've got to work out the details of the deal with Nort

first. And he's become awfully tight-fisted, even with friends."

On the way back to the city, they drove slowly without talking much. As they emerged from the Midtown Tunnel, Penny said, "Would you like me to fix you dinner at my place?"

"Of course, I'd be delighted."

"You will find my apartment very strange," she said, "but I want you to see it."

The lobby of her building on East 63rd Street was ordinary enough. After taking an elevator to the eleventh floor, he followed Penny down a corridor, the walls of which were papered with a design of coconut and banana trees. At the end of the hall she fumbled with a key and opened the door. He followed her into a large living room which was absolutely empty — there were no furniture, rugs or decorations of any kind.

"I said it was strange," she said with a smile.

"I wouldn't say it was too cluttered."

"Come on into the bedroom and sit down."

The only furniture in the bedroom was an austere little cot — that and nothing else. Sitting on this, he leaned against the wall.

"Can I get you a drink?"

"I'd love one."

Going into the kitchen, which was across from the bedroom door, she came back with a glass, ice, and an unopened bottle of scotch.

"I sold the furniture," she said.

"I thought maybe the Friendly Finance Company had paid you a call."

"No. It was all paid for — by me, most of it. We'd been getting this apartment ready for about six months. Do you mind if I talk about it?"

98

"Of course not."

He took a sip of the scotch, which was twelve years old and very good.

"How is it?" she asked.

"The best."

"That was one of the wedding presents. I threw most of the rest out, but it seemed sort of a crime to waste that."

"I'm glad you saved it."

"But I couldn't stand the furniture. We had shopped for most of it together. Every damn lamp reminded me of some weekend."

"Furniture can be very cruel."

"Hank fancied himself a great connoisseur of almost everything. Every table and chair had to be just right. Then when we got the whole place furnished right down to the last teacup, and he told me we were not going to get married, do you know what he said?"

Without waiting for him to answer, she got up from the foot of the cot and stood looking around the apartment, as though she still couldn't believe what she was saying.

"He said not to worry about the furniture. He said he hoped I'd keep on living here, and he'd stop in on this end of his run. That son of a bitch was setting me up as a mistress here at the same time he was planning his wedding in California."

"He sounds like a real idealist."

"I couldn't believe it at first. I'd trusted him for five years. We'd always planned on getting married, just as soon as we got a little money in the bank. I had no idea that he'd been wavering between two women all along."

"What did you say to him?"

"I'm afraid I went sort of hysterical. I think I was about as subtle as a drunken fishwife. All I can remember is pushing him out the door and a lot of screaming. Then as soon as I got the door shut I called the first secondhand furniture store I could find in the phone book, and told

99

them to clear the place out. For the whole lot, all I got was something like two hundred bucks."

"I too have sold furniture at a loss."

"Then I bought this cot and decided to stay here for the month that the rent was paid because I didn't have anywhere else to go."

"It must have been rough," he said, thinking of her wandering through the empty rooms.

"The first two days I just slept, without eating or anything. On the third day the doorbell rang, and I didn't answer it. A few minutes later the door opened. The super let him in. There stood Hank in a new suit, all dapper and freshly pressed. And do you know what he said?"

"What?"

"He said, 'My God, what did you do with the furniture?' And I started to laugh — I think that was my salvation. He looked so surprised, with his face all pink, just fresh from the barber. He just stood there with this look of utter amazement and then he went around opening all the doors to see if I'd piled the furniture in the bathroom or someplace."

Ben laughed.

"And then he was furious," Penny continued. "He wanted to know how much I'd got for it, and whether we could get it back. And I kept laughing harder and harder. He looked so ridiculous, not handsome any more, not really a man at all — just a little old lady worried about the furniture and the money. That was when I realized that I already had him off my back."

"There comes that time," he said.

"When he saw I thought his anger was simply funny, he tried another tack. He began telling me how much he'd missed me, how mixed up he was. Inside of five minutes he was trying to get me to make love. Do you mind if I tell you this?"

Ben shook his head, not trusting his voice.

"Well, I guess it's not very delicate. I asked him how his wedding plans were going, and he said all right, but he would always need me, he couldn't get me out of his system. He tried to pull me down on this cot."

She paused, her eyes suddenly full of laughter.

"I guess I should be ashamed of what I did."

"What?"

"I told him I had to go out and buy a new diaphragm. I told him to take his clothes off and wait for me. Then I went downstairs and told the manager that a man who was not my husband had got the super to let him into my apartment. I asked him to get rid of him, even if he had to call the cops. The manager and the super started up to my apartment, and I went across the street for a drink."

Ben laughed.

"Oh God, I wish I could have seen it," the girl said, laughing. "But I got most of the details. They found him stark naked in the bedroom. He tried to tell them that it was his apartment, but I had signed the lease and put down the rent. After I finished my drink, I went to the lobby and waited. Pretty soon he came down, looking rather rumpled, with the manager on one side of him and the super on the other. He saw me and for a minute I thought he was going to try to kill me. He stopped, but they took his arms and shoved him toward the door. He looked so ridiculous, all ruffled dignity and indignation. He gave me this terrible look. 'Goodbye,' I said. He sort of swallowed then and kept walking, right out the door and up the street. I haven't seen him since."

"It doesn't sound as though you're ever likely to."

"No. That's the way I want it. I went back up to the apartment and cooked myself a meal, the first one in three days. And ever since, really, I've just been sitting here like a prisoner in a cell, trying to figure out how I could have been under an illusion for so long and what I was going to do now."

"You know something, Penny?"

"What?"

"This is no place for you to stay now, and God knows that my hotel room is no place I want to be. Let's just pick up and fly South! I can get my lawyer to make out a contract with Nort. I've got enough money for the airline tickets. Let's just pick up and go!"

"Just like that?"

"Just like that."

"Well, I don't have much to pack. I gave my uniforms away when I quit the airline — I never liked them much. And my trousseau hadn't been paid for, so it was easy to send those things back."

"I don't have much to pack either. But before I start, I'm going to call my lawyer and Nort."

Glancing at his watch, Ben saw it was a little after four, but then he remembered that it was Sunday, and his lawyer, Jerry Grant, wouldn't be in his office. Well, Grant was an old friend, and there was no reason why he couldn't call him at home. Getting the number from Information, Ben sat down on the cot while he dialed it. As always when he called his lawyer, he felt unusually tense.

Somehow, every time he saw Jerry Grant or any other lawyer, he got into big trouble. In the days when he had been making a great deal of money in television, he had hired a whole battery of lawyers to interpret the tax laws, a profession apparently as occult as examining the entrails of chickens for omens of good fortune. He had always followed the advice of lawyers, and in the fullness of time had somehow ended up owing the government so much that he could probably never get out of debt, even if he could find a way to make huge amounts of money again. It had also been in the offices of lawyers that the divorce agreement with Rita had been hammered out, relieving him of whatever tag ends of property remained and attaching a large part of the income from all his work, past, present and future. Ben was quite sure that any adult who found himself hopelessly in debt forever had ultimately no one but himself to blame, but, still, he had always followed the advice of lawyers, and it was difficult to avoid feeling a trifle nervous whenever he entered the building on Madison Avenue where Jerry Grant and his associates always began every conversation with a smile of reassurance. It was a ridiculous thought, but Ben really would not have been a bit surprised if the cigar which Jerry Grant usually offered him exploded in his face, or if the chair in any lawyer's office collapsed when he sat in it. Absurd or not, he had come to imagine every lawyer's office as a huge, rather sadistic fun house, where boxing gloves on coiled springs lurched out to smack anyone who opened a drawer, and where the carpets in the corridors could suddenly start moving, forcing him to run very fast just to stand still. He was glad he was calling Jerry Grant's home, rather than his office.

"Hello?"

It was the nasal voice of Jerry Grant's wife.

"This is Ben Powers, Sally. Is Jerry in?"

"Ben Powers? Oh, just a moment . . ."

There was a long wait.

"It's good to hear from you, Ben! I've been meaning to give you a call. How the hell have you been?" Jerry's voice was hearty as ever.

"Fine. I'm sorry to bother you on a Sunday, but an old friend of mine wants me to write a movie and direct it."

Even in his own words, the statement didn't sound very credible to Ben, and he sensed that Jerry was not so much surprised as tolerant of a has-been grabbing at straws.

"Why, that's great!" His enthusiasm sounded completely artificial.

"If I have him or his lawyer call you, will you hammer out a contract for me?"

"Sure thing. Tell you what. Get him to come around and see me as soon as you're both definite you want to go ahead, and be sure not to agree on any figures."

"O.K."

"Ben?"

"Yes?"

"What I wanted to talk to you about is that I'm afraid the government is starting to question some of those trust funds we set up. Remember, I told you they might."

Jerry's voice was casual, but he might as well have delivered a 225-volt shock from his fun house over the phone.

"You mean, for the kids' education?" Ben asked incredulously.

"Well, it's a question of whether they decide those funds are a tax-evasion gimmick or a legitimate part of the divorce settlement. There will have to be some hearings. We won't know for quite a few months."

"Oh."

"I wouldn't worry about it. There's not a hell of a lot we can do. Meanwhile, if you can work out a movie agreement, we might be able to set some of that money aside."

"I hope so."

"I have some plans for a countermeasure. Can I see you Monday? There are quite a few things we ought to go over."

"I'd been hoping to get off to Florida tonight," Ben replied, but even as the words came, he knew he had been foolishly rushing things. Good as his impulse was to get Penny out of her empty apartment, there were still a lot of details he would have to clean up before he left New York if he were to be fully responsible.

"I guess I can wait," he decided. "What time Monday?"

"Three o'clock?"

"Fine," Ben said. "Thanks a lot, Jerry."

Hanging up, Ben turned to Penny.

"I think you were wise," she said before he had a chance to say anything. "I heard. We don't want to act like a couple of crazy kids."

"No," he said, confused, because he did not want to leave her for the night, and he did not want to spend their first night in these barren rooms which must be full of such bad memories for her, or in his hotel room, which contained a few bad ones for him. Somehow the first night with her was beginning to seem enormously important to him. Could he borrow an apartment anywhere?

"It would be wise to wait a little, anyway," she said. "You know as well as I do that we're both losing track of common sense."

"I suppose so," he said, wondering why one more night alone should loom so horribly.

"I'll fix dinner and then you go back to your place. We'll feel better when we get on that plane."

He agreed, but it was surprising how deeply depressed he felt.

"I have a steak in the freezer," she said. "Do you feel like that?"

"I'm not hungry. I know it's childish, but the idea of leaving you makes me feel terrible."

"Would you like to stay here?"

"I don't think that would be so good."

"Thank you for realizing that. We've had two wonderful days, and I'm looking forward to going to Florida with you more than I can say, but I'm superstitious. If you don't go now, I'm afraid we'll louse it up. The signs are wrong. Call me when you know what time we can board the plane."

"All right," he said, and kissed her.

"I feel like a frustrated teen-ager," he said a moment later. "Adults don't say goodbye with that kind of kiss."

"Get out of here," she said with a laugh.

"I hate it!"

"Go!"

"Will you be ready to get on the plane tomorrow afternoon?"

"Yes."

"All right," he said, kissed her again, and left.

CHAPTER 7

B EN found, somewhat to his surprise, that he was exhausted. Back in his cell, he sank into a profound sleep, and immediately began to dream about Janus Island.

When he woke up he could not remember the details of the dream, but his memories of Janus Island were as fresh as if he had just returned, and there was a moment of confusion when he realized he was no longer there. How quiet his hotel room was! People kept talking about the "noisy city," but this room, which was on an airshaft high up in the stoutly built old hotel, hummed on this Sunday night with the silence of a desert.

In his father's house on Janus Island there had never been complete silence like this. Lying in his bed in his sterile hotel room, Ben catalogued the sounds of his youth. First there had been the surf, which varied from the full-throated roar of a gale to the soft breathing sound of a calm, but which was never still. Then there was the rustle of the palm leaves which grew near the eaves of the house, and occasionally brushed against them. On the seaward side of the house there was the melancholy mewing of gulls, which had always seemed to him to be an echo of the cries of drowning men, and on the garden side there had been the sweeter sounds of mockingbirds, warblers, cardinals with their call of "cheer! cheer!" — an ornithologist's delight. From the kitchen of the house which had been constructed of thin pine boards, came the voices of the Negro servants and their friends, people who in retrospect seemed to have been treated very badly, but who, to a white boy at least, had at the time seemed cheerful and happy. Often there had been the chunk-chunking sound of his mother's chisel as she pursued her ambition to carve statues out of wood. It was strange that out of that whole remembered symphony of sounds, he couldn't remember any associated with his father, a gentle man who spent hours staring at the sea and at the beach, whether he was painting or not.

Ben had no idea what time it was, nor did he know the state of the weather. On Janus Island it had rarely been necessary to consult a watch when he had been young, for it was easy to guess the time from the stage of the tide, the relationship of the sun to the horizon, and the nature of the kitchen sounds, which increased as mealtime grew nearer.

It was necessary to remind himself, he thought, as he lay in the complete darkness of his hotel room, that if he went back to Janus Island now in pursuit of golden cannon, he would only be returning to a piece of real estate, not to the conditions of his youth. The people he had known and loved there were gone, one way or another, and even the house had been blown away, the garden drowned in surf and sand. It was idle to pretend that it could be rebuilt.

Restlessly, Ben sat up and snapped on a light. The walls of the little room seemed to press in upon him like the closing of a trap. The clock on his bureau said it was only a little after three o'clock in the morning.

Unable to sleep any more, Ben got up and poured himself a drink. Looking out the window into the airshaft he saw silver streaks of rain, which would have been rattling like a snare drum against the tin roof of his father's house. How good it was to know that in a few hours he would be heading back to Janus Island with Penny at his side!

At a little after nine Ben was called from his shower by the insistent ringing of his telephone. It was Nort, his deep voice curiously childish in its eagerness.

"Ben?" Nort said. "Gosh, I'm sorry to call you so early, but I'm really going on this thing, and I've had a lot of new ideas and second thoughts I want to talk to you about. I've got to come in town this afternoon anyway. Are you free for lunch?"

"Sure, Nort."

"Are you really going to need two more days to make up your mind?"

"I'm sure I'll want to help you some way, Nort. It's a question of when and how long and how. You know, there are the financial details to be worked out."

"That's why I want to talk to you right away. Can you meet me around noon at the Racquet Club?"

"After the weekend, I think it's time I bought you lunch. How about the Harvard Club?"

"Fine," Nort replied, perhaps with just a trace of annoyance. "See you there."

It was better to stop letting him play host all the time, Ben thought, if he were to avoid falling into an almost menial role. The two clubs would affect their meeting in none too subtle a manner. At the Racquet Club, which Ben felt he had neither the money nor the family background to join, he would be definitely an outsider and an inferior, in his own mind at least, and perhaps in Nort's. At the Harvard Club things would be reversed, and Nort would be reminded that despite his wealth and connections, college and other achievements had always been beyond his reach. Perhaps it was small of him to think about these things, Ben reflected, but if there were to be any bargaining about money and authority over the movie, the atmosphere of the meeting could have an important effect.

Dressing quickly, Ben went to the coffee shop downstairs for breakfast. Staring at a huge globe of "reconstituted" orange juice which was kept in constant motion by a revolving paddle, he remembered that his father had always insisted upon orange juice being absolutely fresh, and would disdainfully refuse it if it had been left in the icebox overnight. How long had it been since he had tasted fresh, natural orange juice, and why should such a small pleasure loom now as an important part of a vast excitement about going South again, as though it were proof that everything on Janus Island would be better?

The boyish enthusiasm in Nort's voice was a warning, Ben reminded himself. How many times had Nort been violently enthusiastic about the prospect of a new sailboat or a new fishing rod, only to forget and abandon it the next day or a week later? It would not be surprising if, after all the plans were made and Ben's expectations were at a peak, Nort decided to drop the whole thing and fly to Spain or Switzerland. Such swings of mood and inconsistencies were a prerogative of the very rich, against which ordinary people had to be on guard.

Ben consulted his watch. A few minutes before eleven. He wanted to call Penny just to say good morning, but she might still be asleep. Feeling restless, he decided to walk across town to the Harvard Club.

It wasn't raining any more, but a strong wind was whipping the awning at the entrance to the hotel, making a noise like a sail luffing in a full gale, a sharp, cracking sound that had always filled Ben's belly with fear, ever since he and Nort had turned that boat over so long ago. Turning up the collar of his overcoat, Ben darted through traffic as the light changed, breaking finally into a full run, as though pursued by ghosts.

This is ridiculous, he thought, slowing down. If I keep this up I'll arrive hot and disheveled, looking as wild as I feel. Play it cool, man, play it cool — that's the expression nowadays. When a man is most in need, he must act most debonair.

Twenty minutes later Ben walked slowly into the cavernous lobby of the Harvard Club. The bar had not opened, and the cocktail crowd of young advertising men and space salesmen had not arrived. In the big room adjoining the bar a few retired old gentlemen sat reading the *Times* and in a corner a well-known banker sat playing chess with a classmate of Ben's who drank too much and was always looking for a job. Leaving his coat at the checkroom, Ben walked to the table where the newspapers were laid out for the members, and, picking up a copy of the *Times*, sat down in a big leather armchair under the imposing head of a huge African elephant Teddy Roosevelt had shot.

The paper was full of news about the war in Vietnam. Forty-three American names had appeared on the latest casualty list, all killed in a valley the name of which Ben couldn't even pronounce. Reading about it, a sudden fear hit him with the intensity of a premonition.

If the government did take the trust funds, perhaps he would not be able to send young Ben to college, and perhaps his son would be drafted. And if he were put in the army, would tall, gentle Benny, who had never even liked to shoot rabbits, be able to survive?

With a pessimism he could not talk himself out of, Ben doubted it. With the clarity of a nightmare he imagined the boy being shot down in the jungle, the final casualty of his father's inability to cope with the world.

Or would it be the final one? Would Laura, who had been reared like a pampered pedigreed kitten, be able to get scholarships and jobs in an alley-cat world? Would Rita herself, whose mind was always full of art exhibitions and charities, be able to survive if the sources of her alimony dried up?

Also on the front page of the paper was a story about the allotment of public funds for education. It was all very confusing, Ben thought. The government was apparently going to take the money he thought he had saved for his children and would use it for building schools, and for sending Benny to Vietnam. This was the state of the world, and whether he thought it was just or insane had nothing to do with it. The only question was, could he and his survive?

I will find a way to keep him in college, Ben resolved, beginning to sweat again. He had a deep feeling of guilt about his son, who had clung to his mother throughout the divorce and rarely wanted to see his father. In time, Ben hoped, those wounds would heal, but there wasn't much he could do now other than pay the boy's bills. How strange that so many paths led back to the need for money — and to Nort.

Would Nort deliberately keep him waiting as a tactic? It

was necessary to learn patience. Leaning his head back, Ben closed his eyes and thought of how Penny would look at the plane.

At twenty minutes to one, Nort came through the revolving door. He was dressed in a black silk suit and he carried a thin black leather briefcase bound in brass or gold. At first Ben almost failed to recognize him. Dressed in his usual T-shirt, or in bathing trunks, Nort looked young, but with only his face showing, he appeared surprisingly old. His handsome features were etched with small lines of pain around the eyes and mouth, and his hair looked thinner than it was before.

"Ben!" Nort said agreeably. "You're looking fine. Nance and I were a little worried about you over the weekend."

"Oh? Why?"

"I don't know, you seemed kind of tired. But I told Nance that all you probably needed was a good night's sleep."

This may have been a mildly bawdy reference to Penny, Ben thought. He said nothing.

"How's Penny?" Nort asked, again emphasizing the name just a little too much.

"Fine, thanks."

Ben led the way to the back of the reading room and they sat down.

There was a moment of silence.

"When would you like me to go to Janus Island?" Ben asked abruptly.

"As soon as possible. I figure we're losing gold every day we delay. Small operators are already picking away at it."

"What are the first steps?"

"The first thing is, you go down to Janus Island to write the script for the movie. We give out a publicity release right away, saying that's why you're there."

"Even before the script is written?"

"You won't need a fancy script for this! While you're working on it, I'll make the arrangements for a camera crew. While they're getting organized, I'll come down and start a search operation. I won't need a lot of equipment for that. Hell, I can put everything I need on one big fishing boat. When the camera crew is ready, I'll charter a boat for them and they can start shooting the initial exploration of the reef."

"What if there just isn't anything very interesting to film?"

"I'll keep looking until I find something! I know the gold is there somewhere, Ben, and for once in my life, I'm going to stick at a thing . . ."

Nort's voice rose with emotion, and with an effort brought it back to a whisper.

"The gold cannon are there!" he said.

"Nort," Ben replied, feeling a need to inject a sense of reality into the situation, "Nort, I agree there may be a possibility of finding gold, but you have to understand that I have to give most of my attention to the movie. There's a probability of doing something good there, if you give me a free hand."

"Sure, I want a movie, and I want it to make money."

"How much of a budget will you give me?"

"How much will you need?"

"You can't do much for less than a million dollars nowadays."

"For a simple documentary-type thing like this?"

"I want to try a dramatic movie. I have some ideas."

"I had in mind about half that. I don't think I could get my board of directors to go for more."

"With a half million we could, I suppose, do something, if we stick to unknown actors."

"I'll leave all the details up to you," Nort said grandly.

"Would you sign a contract?" Ben asked. "Something that would guarantee the money?"

"I'm not sure my board of directors would go along with that at this stage," Nort said blandly. "I had hoped we could begin just playing it by ear."

"My lawyer and agent probably wouldn't let me work on that basis," Ben said.

"No?"

Nort smiled, and it seemed obvious to Ben that he knew exactly what his financial situation was.

"I would have to have some guarantees," Ben said doggedly.

"Oh, I'm sure that as friends we could work something out. The main thing is, Ben, we've got to get started. When can you go to Janus Island?"

"Tonight. *If* we get the financial details straight."

"That's the spirit! Why wait around? I'll fly you down in my new jet! We'll board the yawl in Miami and sail her to the island together!"

This was the last thing Ben wanted, partly because he wanted to be alone with Penny, and partly because he knew Nort to be a highly erratic pilot.

"I already have plane tickets, Nort," he said carefully. "And to tell you the truth, I'm uncomfortable in small planes."

"Suit yourself, but I'll start down this afternoon and meet you aboard the yawl. I'll help you get her down to the island. I've installed so much electronic equipment that you'll need to be checked out on her pretty thoroughly before you try to handle her yourself."

"I don't know anything at all about the new gadgets."

"We've got a fine radar set. If you moor her at the jetty on the island, you can scan the whole reef. Don't you think it would be interesting to see what goes on out there at night?"

"It might. Nort, I have to be able to count on some sort of salary."

"I'll guarantee you five hundred dollars a week for three

months and a quarter of the profits of any movie we complete. You can have that on paper if you like."

There was a moment of silence while Ben wondered if, for the form of it at least, he ought to bargain for more.

"Nort," he said finally, "I haven't worked for as little as five hundred a week in years. I doubt if my agent will be willing to establish a precedent. You know, it's feast or famine in my business, and I have to make it while I can."

"Tell him to call my lawyer, Bert Howell at Jenkins, Morris and Howell. We can make it look as though you're in it mostly for your cut of the profits."

He was going to be adamant about the deal he had offered, partly because he had become so aggressive in business, and partly, Ben guessed, because Nort wanted to humiliate him. Nort had him where he wanted him and he wasn't going to budge an inch, even though five hundred dollars a week was a beginner's salary for a man expected to both write and direct a film.

"One more thing," Nort said suddenly. "Am I to assume you are going to bring that girl with you?"

"Yes," Ben said, his antagonism immediately aroused. "Look, we've been all over that! I refuse to discuss . . ."

"Well, I'm not trying to be moralistic," Nort replied. "I'm not talking about the personal aspects of this, but now I'm talking hard, cold business! If she's going to be down there with us, she's going to be part of my business. For one thing it will be impossible to keep a lot of important information from her. How much do you know about her?"

"She's trustworthy," Ben replied. "I'll vouch for that."

"I hope you won't be hurt if I ask *how* you can vouch for her? How long have you known her?"

"Long enough to trust her."

"Don't be so damn evasive, Ben! I'm going to have

hundreds of thousands of dollars tied up down there, and if we find gold, we should keep a large part of it a secret if we don't want the government grabbing the whole thing. I've got to have people I can trust!"

"I said you can trust her!" Ben said, coloring.

"And I think it's my right to ask how long you have known her!"

"Only a few days, but I can tell."

"Nothing personal, Ben, but you wouldn't be the first man in the world to think a woman is trustworthy because she's got good tits. I hope you won't mind if I have some of my people run a routine check on her. After all, indirectly at least, I'm sort of hiring her."

"No! You're not hiring her, directly or indirectly! Let's not get started on the wrong foot, Nort. My girl is damn well none of your business!"

"Except, as I pointed out, she is bound to learn all the details of my whole operation! Now don't get hot under the collar, Ben! I'm not saying anything against her. I just want to gather a little information about her to make sure she's reliable. After all, you want me to invite her to Janus Island, don't you?"

"Yes."

"O.K.; it's my right to be a little careful about who I invite to my island. Where did this girl last work?"

"She was an airline stewardess, but she's not working now."

"What line was she with?"

"I don't know."

"Well, I can find out. Do you mind if I say something to you as an old friend?"

"What?"

"Right after a man is divorced, he's vulnerable. Give yourself a chance to know a lot of women. Don't grab the first one who comes along."

"Nort, we went all over that! I appreciate your concern, but I'm a little old for fatherly advice."

"That's another thing, Ben. Why do you have to pick a girl with such an age difference? Don't you think that will be a barrier to any lasting relationship?"

"Nort, friendship does not give you the right to say things like that!"

"Because you're afraid to answer them?"

"All over the world men my age from the beginning of time have had relationships with younger women, some good and some bad. It's an American disease to think that only people of the same age can love."

"Or an American sign of health. Of course I know I can't dissuade you, but for the sake of my own conscience, I think I should tell you that Nance and I were very alarmed by this girl — Penny, as she calls herself."

"And just what alarmed you, other than her youth?"

"Well, for one thing, she marches in those goddam peace parades."

"How dreadful. How did you manage to ferret out *that* piece of information?"

"Nance was talking to her when she was telling fortunes and it came out. She walked on that thing to Washington a couple of years ago."

"Well, I probably would have too, if I'd had the guts."

"Come on, Ben! Christ, you were a good naval officer!"

"And I'm still in the reserves, but I don't necessarily have to back every idiot decision of my government."

"You shock me, Ben! I've known you all my life, and suddenly you start sounding like some Commie bastard."

Ben laughed.

"I'm no Commie," he said. "If I lived in China, they'd shoot me. If I lived in Russia, they'd put me in jail. Here all they want of me is my money and my son."

"But for a good purpose, Ben! Would you really like to

see our people in Vietnam tuck tail and run? Do you want to see those yellow bastards win?"

"Don't let's talk politics now, Nort. We aren't going to convince each other."

"Why are there so many questions you're afraid to answer?"

"No, I don't want to tuck tail and run. I just hate seeing an idiotic war drag on year after year, and I don't like to contribute my money and maybe my son for the destruction of men, women and children I can't bring myself either to hate or to fear."

"If the morons in Washington would use the big bomb, the war wouldn't drag on."

"Oh, come off it, Nort! You're making my stomach turn over."

"Why does the thought of victory make you squeamish? Are you one of these people who thinks patriotism is out of date?"

"Listen, Nort," Ben said wearily, "don't question my patriotism. I love this country enough to get angry when I think it's doing wrong. We are the most powerful people on earth, and we should be building, not destroying."

"Why should the destruction of our enemies make you so upset?"

"Nort," Ben said very quietly. "I was at sea four years to fight a war that had to be fought, and my stomach was all right. How was yours?"

"That was a low blow. I couldn't help ——"

"I know you couldn't, but don't come on strong with me about this war business. Of course you're entitled to your opinions, but so am I, and I get angry when people question my motives."

"I guess we'd better make a vow not to talk politics."

"I'm for that."

"Are we still friends?"

"If we don't discuss politics and if you keep your damn investigators away from my girl."

"There should be no *if's* in friendship. But to finish the business, how do we tie this movie thing up?"

"I'll have my agent and lawyer give your man a call," Ben said. "And tonight Penny and I will fly to Miami. I'll meet you some time tomorrow morning aboard your yawl."

"Fine!" Nort exclaimed with satisfaction. "Shake!"

It seemed to Ben that he was constantly being forced into giving Nort great hearty handshakes.

"Now!" Nort said jovially. "Did you invite me for lunch or not?"

Ben led the way to the dining room, where Nort munched the health salad while he ate a steak.

"There's one important thing you haven't yet asked," Nort said as he lifted one of the huge Harvard Club cups of coffee.

"What?"

Nort sipped the coffee and put the cup down.

"What will your cut of the treasure be?"

"I guess I hadn't thought that far ahead."

"You don't really believe in it yet, do you?"

"I believe it's a possibility, but I'm not spending it yet."

"Have you looked at that museum down in the Keys and seen what they've found? Have you seen Teddy Tucker's finds in Bermuda?"

"I know stuff is there. All right, what will my cut be?"

"Of the first hundred thousand dollars, I'll give you half. After that, ten per cent. If we find the cannon, that could be more than you imagine."

"I think that's very generous of you, since I'm risking only my time."

"I hope that's all you'll be risking," Nort said, and on that melodramatic note, stood up. "I've got to run. I'll meet you aboard the yawl as soon as you can get there. She's at Chapman's yard."

With a debonair wave, Nort walked out of the dining room, holding himself as erect as a soldier on parade.

Lost in thought, Ben finished his coffee. Golden cannon, he thought as he ordered a brandy. If I could only find a golden cannon, I could really offer Penny a future, my son would go to college instead of to war, and I would change suddenly from a failure to a success. How strange to think that the solution to all one's personal problems might conceivably lie buried under coral and several fathoms of sea!

Good Lord, now he's got me believing all this malarky! And he started to grin. The depression which had been plaguing him since he had left Penny was beginning to lift. Regardless of what happens, it will be good to get back to the island with Penny, he thought. It would be good to sit at the wheel of a big yawl in the Gulf Stream with the girl beside him basking in the sun. It would be fun to do whatever he could to put together some sort of movie about a modern treasure hunt.

The brandy tasted fine. After a second one he found himself dreaming of walking through the shallows of the reef with Penny, who in his fantasy was already his wife.

But Nort is right about one thing, he thought — I don't really know her. I've got to give myself time to sort truth from illusion.

That seemed a highly sensible thought, but also a terrifying one. Was Nort right when he had called him a master of self-delusion? Where was the line between delusion and love, foolish dreams and credible hope?

CHAPTER 8

AFTER leaving the Harvard Club, Ben went to Jerry Grant's office and told him about his conversation with Nort.

"Doesn't sound like much of a deal," Jerry said lugubriously. "How long are you going to be out of town?"

"Three months at least."

"Well, I've been thinking about your tax situation, Ben. Frankly, these hearings don't look good, but I've had an idea."

"What?"

"You know your mother was in here last year asking me to draw up a will leaving more or less her entire estate to you. After all, she's over eighty, and frankly, if she died in the near future, I think the government would grab your inheritance along with all the rest. It's not much, as you know, but it would be a shame to see it go down the drain."

"Yes," Ben said grimly.

"If I were you, I'd ask your mother to bypass you in the will and leave it all to your kids. Then if she died in the next few years, you wouldn't have to worry about their education, and the whole thing would be entirely free of your tax tangle."

"That's a good idea," Ben said, but he thought: that will be one more thing I can never give a new wife.

"I'll draw up a new will and send it out for your mother's signature, but you'd better explain it to her. When she was in here she seemed — well — a little anxious about this sort of thing."

"I'll explain it to her," Ben said, and he felt a curiously familiar stab of futility.

It was true that his mother was and always had been "a little anxious" about money, just as he himself still was. When, during the depths of the Depression, it looked as though the money had disappeared, his mother had at first refused to believe it.

"Who took it?" she had asked incredulously, for despite her college education, she was apparently incapable of ascribing the loss of money to anyone but a thief.

"Why did you let it happen?" she asked her husband, the artist who had simply followed a broker's advice.

For most of that part of his youth he could remember, Ben's parents had been miserable, not because of actual poverty, from which old Corny Clay removed most of the sting, but from his father's feeling that not only had he been unable to make money, he had even proved incapable of hanging onto it. And this sense of failure and guilt, Ben thought grimly, his mother had done little to ease, just as Rita had shown nothing but contempt for him when he got into trouble with the government.

That was one of the strange things about both women, Ben reflected. They were interested in sculpture and painting and music, and they were forever saying that money wasn't important, but when their husbands managed to lose money, they had been incapable of forgiving them.

Ben had not thought about all this for a long while, but it suddenly seemed relevant to many of his problems. Had he really, for a lifetime, been living in fear that most women in the long run find themselves incapable of forgiving a man for financial incompetence? Is that why he had worked so hard to make big money when he was young, and had his ambition died simply because he had found that not even *that* worked with Rita? That she was fully capable of treating him as badly when he was solvent as when he was broke?

Perhaps. Perhaps he had in his heart a basic distrust of women not too far removed from that suffered by Nort. And that might be one big reason Penny was becoming so important to him: it was impossible for him to imagine her launching into recriminations about money or anything else. Time might disprove him, of course, but he guessed that Penny prized above all simple kindness, without which even passion could mean little over a period of time.

But how long could a woman consider kindness, even combined with passion, enough if a man were such an idiot that he couldn't hang on to an inheritance?

Well, God knew he had always been fairly good in the bill-paying department, Ben told himself, at least until, irony of ironies, his huge salaries had caused the lawyers and the government to complicate everything beyond belief. Still, one way or another, the government would let him live, and it was ridiculous for any consideration of money to throw him into a panic. Certainly he was old enough to realize that money was not love, that some women could love him rich or poor, just as Rita had been unable to love him in either circumstance.

"I never had enough money to worry about it much," Penny had said, and she had not seemed in the least concerned about his talk of debt.

This was a comforting thought, but Ben still found himself dreading the approaching meeting with his mother. One thing he needed, and which Penny, like most women, would expect of him, whether he was rich or poor, was self-confidence, and oddly enough, it was his faith in himself which his mother, after all these years, could still dilute.

His mother would start by being "a little anxious" about the state of the family finances, which would be a good euphemism for panic, and in panic, perhaps hysteria, the old accusing words he had heard so often in his youth could not be kept bottled up: irresponsibility! incapability! And certainly there were plenty more, if he really wanted to review the list.

But he couldn't avoid this visit. His mother would not sign a new will leaving her estate to her grandchildren without knowing why. An explanation would be demanded, and then there would be fireworks. The one unforgivable crime in his mother's code was losing money, and he'd done just that.

Anyway, Ben thought, I don't have to let the loss of money sour my whole life, the way it did my father's. No, I don't have to live with her glum looks and her sighs and her constant questions about what will happen if we get sick. I can see her for an hour, be polite, and get the hell out, for I know something my father apparently never learned: if one woman doesn't love you, it is generally possible to find another who will.

Going to a private conference room in his lawyer's office, Ben telephoned his mother in Connecticut.

"Benny!" she said, her voice sounding curiously young. "Are you coming out to see me?"

"Yes, Mother," he replied. "I'll be there in a couple of hours."

Then he dialed Penny's number. The telephone rang for several seconds without an answer, and he had the panicky thought that she might have changed her mind about going with him. When she finally said "Hello" he felt an incredible relief.

"Penny," he said. "I would have called this morning, but I was afraid I'd wake you up. Anyway, I saw Nort and the deal seems fairly well fixed. I'm at my lawyer's office now, and he says he'll be able to wind up the details, but I have to see my mother on business. I suppose I should see her anyway before I leave town."

"Where does your mother live?"

"Connecticut. Do you want to drive out with me?"

"I don't think you should introduce me to your mother yet. I know mothers. It might get her all upset."

"You could stay in the car, if you want. You've made this disease I have, this inability to be alone, much worse. I'd love to have you along for the drive. When we come back, we can go right to the plane."

"Wonderful! I'm all packed. If I go now, I won't have to finish counting the tiles on the bathroom wall."

"I'll pick you up as soon as I check out of Hotel Horrible. An hour?"

"I'll meet you at the car."

"I love you," he said, the words springing to his lips without thought, and sounding natural.

"Me — me too," she said with a slight stammer, and there was a click as she hung up.

It took Ben only about twenty minutes to throw his clothes into a suitcase and check out of the hotel in which he had spent so many miserable hours. Without a backward glance he hurried to the garage where he rented a car. He was five minutes early when he got to Penny's apartment, but she was waiting beside a small suitcase on the sidewalk, a rather forlorn figure when he first caught a glimpse of her, drawing her coat tighter around her neck, pacing and hugging herself for protection against the wind.

"Get in," he said, pushing the door open. "You look half frozen."

As soon as she slid onto the seat with the suitcase on her lap, she kissed him. Her nose was cold.

"I couldn't wait to leave that apartment," she said. "I've been walking around the block."

He put the suitcase in the back seat.

"I haven't made plane reservations yet," he said. "I thought we'd wait and see what time we get back from Connecticut."

"How far do we have to drive?"

"South Bay — that's about fifty miles."

"Tell me about your mother," she said, settling back in the seat. "I want to learn all I can about you."

The bare facts of his mother's life had of course been familiar to him ever since he could remember, but they sounded strangely incomplete when he related them to Penny. Martha had been born in South Bay, the granddaughter of a man whose father had clawed his way up from a dirt farm to a fortune in a brass foundry. Her grandfather, Benjamin Buchanan, after whom Ben was named, had lived to be seventy-eight, an impressive old man with shaggy white eyebrows and a barrel-like paunch, but her father, Claude, had apparently been something of a wastrel and had died of tuberculosis and whiskey when his daughter was only five years old. Martha had been brought up by her mother and her grandmother in her grandfather's house, where apparently she never heard any good about her father, who did not survive even in paintings or photographs. Who had destroyed such mementoes, or why, Ben had no idea, but the family albums included no trace of Claude, and to this day Ben had no idea what his mother's father had looked like.

Martha had grown up to be a stern-faced young woman passionately devoted to women's rights and prohibition. She had studied to be a concert pianist, but finding she had not the talent for that, she had turned to painting and joined an art school, where she had met Paul, a mild young man who liked to paint pastel landscapes and vases of flowers streaked by sunlight. From the old brass foundry they had inherited enough money to tour Europe and to spend their winters on Janus Island with some pretense of equality with the very rich people who invited them there, until Paul's bad judgment and the Depression made them virtual wards of the Clay family, "objects of charity," as poor Martha used to wring her hands and say.

The truth was, Ben realized for the first time as he talked to Penny, his mother had grown up without ever really knowing a man she could trust. In her experience her grandfather had been only a noisy old invalid and her father a blank space in collections of family photographs. Her husband was a failure as a painter, had no skills for making a living other than the ability to ingratiate himself with rich people, and as things then seemed, managed to lose her money almost as soon as he got his hands on it.

So Martha, in the years that Ben remembered her best, made fun of her husband's clumsiness when he tried to show her how to improve her sculpture, never let him drive the car without a running stream of directions, and constantly berated him for eating too much and getting too fat. Throwing most of her massive energy into her "art," she dressed in khaki trousers and a man's shirt, and spent her days trying to hack statues out of mahogany logs or massive blocks of stone. The greatest embarrassment of Ben's youth was the "one-man shows" she held on Janus Island, when the neighbors were asked to troop through their garden to see the massive Indian chiefs she had made, the wood nymphs and the mothers holding infants to curiously nippleless breasts. The whispered comments of the art lovers had not always been kind and had not always escaped the ears of the boy in the garden. Why should the memory of the ladies in their long dresses and the men in their white suits smiling at the statues still be enough to make him clench his hands and sweat?

No one had bought the statues, not ever, as far as Ben knew, but in 1939, when Ben had been nineteen years old, his father had reported with quiet modesty that a man in California was starting to collect his work.

Almost every month after that his father had crated one of his big pictures and shipped it off. Later he would display a wad of money. Martha had congratulated him effusively, but her main reaction had been to redouble her own already frenzied attacks upon the mahogany logs and the slabs of coquina rock and coral which she used when she could no longer afford marble.

The trouble with a sculptor's work is that there is no good way to get rid of it when it doesn't sell. The house on Janus Island had been surrounded by a growing army of Indian chiefs, wood nymphs, and heavy nudes of both sexes, all of which had been created without reproductive organs. When the hurricane of 1942 finally toppled the whole house, the garden had looked like a battlefield full of maimed corpses. Home on leave to clean up the mess, Ben had spent most of his savings to have his mother's favorite statues trucked to the house she had bought, back in South Bay. The remaining wood carvings he had stacked together in a giant funeral pyre and burned. The leftover pieces of crudely carved stone he had buried for the mystification of some latter-day archeologist. Decent cremation and burial for these figments of his mother's aesthetic imagination had seemed preferable to the ridicule they so often excited from children seeking shells and picnickers who wandered down to that deserted stretch of dune to drink beer and make love in the soft hollows of sand where his father's house had once stood.

The burial of the statues had been a more emotional event in Ben's life than the burial of his father a year before, for Ben had done it alone on a windy day with the gulls moaning overhead. In contrast, his father's funeral had been curiously convivial, with all the friends and neighbors stopping in for a drink. Half stunned with whiskey and exhaustion, after having sat up on the train from Boston all night, Ben had not been able to cry at his father's funeral. The genial mourners had seemed to him to be celebrating a peculiar irony. After years of suffering recriminations about losing money, his father had died leaving his wife's estate well replenished. With the coming of war, stocks had gone up, and so had Paul's reputation in the eyes of his widow.

Ever since, Ben's mother had lived with a series of paid companions in her cottage at South Bay, which was only a mile from the old mansion built by her grandfather, now a nursing home for the aged and helplessly ill. All through her seventies she was a surprisingly cheerful old woman who spent most of her time reading or puttering around her garden, where the undying statues of her youth still stood. She made almost no demands upon Ben, and there was no reason why it should always be so difficult for him to force himself to go out there and sit on the couch in her living room beneath the big oil portrait of his great-grandfather, trying to make conversation.

As Ben told Penny about all this, she listened silently, her eyes large and sad.

"At least you know a great deal about your mother," she said finally. "I know so little about mine."

"Is she still living?"

"No, she died a long while ago. Someday I'll tell you about it, but I always get very emotional, and I don't want to do that now."

When they got to the outskirts of South Bay, he drove slowly past the high school.

"I lived in this town for eighteen years," he told Penny. "I was on the committee that helped to plan that school shortly after the war."

"It must be hard for you to come back."

"I used to think it would be hard — I suppose one reason Rita and I both endured an unhappy marriage so long is that we were afraid to leave everything that was familiar. But looking back, it's funny — I don't think I'm bitter any more, but I see so little in my past that I can honestly regret losing. I'm happier right now than I was all those years. The very thought of the so-called friends we used to have here, the eternal golf and cocktail parties — it all makes me wonder how I stood it so long."

"I'm glad you don't want to go back," she said.

"Never! It's too much fun to look ahead."

He passed a row of expensive stores and turned down a road lined by huge dying elms. Then there was a grove of oaks which still retained a ragged cape of brown leaves, even in the dead of winter. On the far fringe of that were a hill and a church, beyond which was his mother's house.

It was an unpretentious Cape Cod cottage of brown shingles surrounded by a high cedar fence. Driving two hundred yards past it, Ben turned into a field and parked.

"Are you sure you don't want to come in with me?"

131

"She wouldn't like me there if you're going to talk business."

"We could do that in another room."

"You'd better go alone. It would be awkward."

"All right," he said, and kissed her. "Penny," he said suddenly, "can I tell you what my business is here?"

"If you want to."

"I have to ask my mother to leave her money to my kids, not me. If she left it to me, the government would eventually take it."

"I think that's very good of you," she said.

"Not just a sign of financial impotence?"

"It would be irresponsible not to do it, wouldn't it?"

"Yes," he said, and kissed her. "I'm afraid I'll have nothing left to give you but kindness."

"That's enough," she said. "Go and hurry back."

The warmth with which she filled him started to ebb as soon as he opened his mother's gate. With rising apprehension he walked across the garden, through a circle of statues, now weathered and cracked, their faces aged almost as though they had been carved from flesh. Before he raised the brass knocker, his mother opened the door. Despite her years, she was still a bulky woman whose shoulders and hands had not forgotten their strength. The black little-old-lady dress she wore seemed somehow like a masquerade to Ben, who still thought of her clad in her working clothes, hammer and chisel in hand. Her gray hair, which she had always worn straight, was curled and fluffed out in a style that seemed too youthful to him, but he was touched to realize that she had worked hard to make herself look pretty for him.

"Benny!" she said, and placing both her big hands on his shoulders, gave him a quick kiss on the cheek. Immediately, before he had a chance to return the kiss, she stepped back, almost as guiltily as a boy who has stolen a kiss. She did not hug him and he did not hug her, because he knew she would be embarrassed and twist to get away, but her smile was tremulously warm, and taking his hand in both of hers, she squeezed it.

"It's good to see you, Mother," he said.

"Come on in and sit down. I sent Mrs. Craig out because I wanted to be alone with you."

The living room was just as he remembered it, the oil portrait of the big-bellied old man over the couch staring at a large old-fashioned television set at the opposite side of the room.

"Would you like a cup of tea or something?"

She was looking at him intently, and whether it was only his imagination or not, he suspected that she was hoping he would opt for tea, that she was really asking if he was drinking again. Occasionally, and with reason, she had worried about his drinking, and if he were kind, he would be abstemious now, but a thousand mysterious tensions were rising within him and he wanted a drink more than he had in years.

"A little scotch if you have it," he said.

The corners of her mouth tightened.

"I'm afraid we only have sherry or port."

"Sherry will be fine."

He sat down. As she poured the sherry from a decanter on the table in the corner of the room, her eyes were still intently upon him, and seeing himself as he thought he looked to her, he was not pleased. Was it her fault that her criticisms were so clear that they rarely even had to be put into words? During the past year he had put on weight. He was pale, and all the drinking he had done in the last few months had left his face a little splotched. His suit had not been pressed recently, and on the knee of his right trouser leg there was a small spot. Never was he less pleased with himself than when under his mother's gaze.

"You look tired," his mother said. "Have you been working terribly hard?"

"Yes," he lied. "I've been keeping at it pretty hot and heavy."

The falsehood annoyed him. Was it for his or her protection that he did not tell her that for months he had not had any real work to do, and that idleness was the most tiring thing of all?

"I keep looking at the television page every day, but nothing of yours seems to come on any more. Do you have anything scheduled?"

"I've been working on other things," he said. "Do you remember Norton Clay? He wants me to go down to Janus Island and help him do a movie."

"Norty Clay? What on earth does he have to do with the movie business?"

"He's invested in some sort of company. It might be a good opportunity for me."

"I don't know that I'd trust Norty Clay. As I remember, he never had much of a head for business."

"Anyway, I'll have a nice two or three months in the sun. I'm looking forward to getting back to the island again."

"I was never really very happy there."

She handed him his sherry and sat down in a large armchair facing him. He saw that already she had started to move her hands nervously on her lap, as though she were washing them. He sipped his sherry, stifling a temptation to drain the glass and ask for another.

"Janus Island," she said ruminatively. "I never thought you'd go back there."

"I've always loved the place."

"Your father did too, but I hear it's changed. Florida isn't what it used to be."

"No," he said.

"How are the children?"

"Fine. That reminds me, Mother. I was talking to my lawyer today and he suggested that perhaps it might be wise to leave me out of your will, and leave everything to them. It would — well, it would save on inheritance taxes."

This last-minute half-lie he considered an inspiration, for he despaired of ever being able to tell his mother the whole truth.

"I don't want to do that."

"Why?"

"I don't think it's wise for children to inherit money when they are so young."

"We could tie it up in various forms of trust. I don't need the money and it seems silly to make them pay a double inheritance tax."

"Are you really doing so well?"

Her voice was obviously skeptical. That was the way it had always been — first she somehow made him feel it was necessary to lie, then she caught him out.

"Things have been going pretty well."

"Even with your alimony and all that?"

"I get along."

"I don't want to change my will," she said flatly. "Someday you may need it. If it's divided in two for the children, the capital will just be dissipated."

"I'm afraid it may be necessary to change it," he said, trying to keep any urgency out of his voice.

"Why?"

"Well, you know, in my business, taxes are complicated. The truth is that if you leave the money to me, the government might step in and take it."

"You owe the government money?"

Her voice rose sharply.

"At the level I used to be at, these things get complicated."

"You didn't pay your taxes? What did you do with all the money?"

"My lawyers made some miscalculations. They had a deferred payment plan that was disapproved."

"You mean you can't hire lawyers that know how to manage? How much do you owe?"

"I don't know. There will be some hearings to figure that out."

"Hearings? Are they going to send you to jail?"

"Good Lord, no. I didn't do anything criminal."

"If you owe the government, I should think you would need everything you could get."

"The government will settle for whatever I have. If you leave me anything, it will just be lost."

"Are you trying to cheat the government? Surely you aren't asking me to help you do that!"

"No, I'm not trying to cheat anyone. I'm just trying to make sure there will be enough money for the education of my children."

"You have to rely on me for that? What happens if I don't die for another ten years?"

"I'm not talking about that," he said miserably. "I'm just trying to guard against the possibility of the whole thing being wasted."

"You waste money when you pay your bills?"

"Oh, Lord, let's not argue!" he said. "I thought I was suggesting quite a noble thing. You make me feel like a crook when I ask to be cut out of my own mother's will!"

"What are you going to do without money?"

"They will always leave me enough to live on."

"How are you going to save for your old age? What will you do if you get sick?"

He could not tell her that he more or less hoped he would not have an old age, and that if he got sick he supposed he would either get well or die, regardless of his financial position.

"All this isn't under my control, Mother," he said wearily. "You've got to understand, I'm doing the best I can."

"What do you mean, it isn't under your control? You've got brains, haven't you? You made hundreds of thousands of dollars. How did it all disappear?"

"It's not unusual for taxes and divorce to leave a successful man broke."

"Successful!" she said, breathing hard. "Successful! And you come here at your age and tell me you don't even know how much you owe!"

Getting up, Ben poured himself another glass of sherry.

"And how much are you drinking now?"

"I think I've got it under control," he said evenly.

"You ought to quit, if only because it makes you gain weight. It's not good for your heart."

"Yes, Mother," he said.

"How often do you see your children these days?"

"I saw Laura Saturday. I'm not supposed to visit Benny at his school."

"How can they come home for weekends when you just live in a little hotel room?"

While his mother's inquisition continued, Ben tried to remind himself that he was there simply to get her to change her will. Anything he said should be directed toward that. Leaving her chair, she now began to pace up and down the room, wringing her hands, a woman so obviously tormented that it was almost possible to forgive whatever pain she inflicted.

"Irresponsible!" she moaned. "Incapable of undertaking a man's most primary job, that of feeding his own!"

How familiar the words were, how remembered from a

hundred muffled conversations overheard in the middle of the night!

"Nothing set aside for an emergency!" she went on, like a tape recorder crazily out of control. "Appealing for help for your son's education!"

The sweat was trickling down Ben's neck.

"Mother, you know you really are exaggerating all this," he said, making his voice light. "I can always make a living. I still have my brain and my hands."

Throwing her own hands out in a gesture of helplessness, Martha abruptly sat down. Gripping her fists tight against her belly, she began to rock back and forth.

"Oh God," she moaned, "why did I have to live to see this? What can I do?"

"You can change your will and cheer up," he said. "Mother, what in the hell ever made you think money is so important?"

"Important!" she said tragically. "How are you going to live?"

"Well," he said. "I'm going to live *well*. I always have been pretty good at that."

"At least your father always paid his bills. We were never in debt."

She started to rock and moan again. He wanted more than anything in the world to get out, but he didn't think he should leave her alone like that. He poured himself another glass of sherry.

"Stop drinking!" she gasped.

"A glass of sherry isn't going to hurt."

"You've had three."

"When is Mrs. Craig coming back?"

"You're planning on leaving already? You just got here!"

"I have to get back to New York," he said. "I'm leaving for Florida tonight."

"I'm glad your father didn't have to know about this," Martha said. "At least he was spared."

"Yes, he was spared," Ben agreed.

"Your father was never in debt. He had his weaknesses, but he never was in debt."

"I'm glad," Ben said, and he thought, only the damned can be as cruel as this woman is. How did my father ever survive so long? His own presence was probably exciting her far more than his departure would, he thought. Was he really helping her by remaining?

"You had such a good start in life!" his mother said. "I had such high hopes!"

"I still have high hopes," he said, his voice sounding oddly debonair. "I have to run, Mother. Now don't get yourself all upset."

"It's been quite a shock," she said. "Help me up before you go. I think I'll take a nap."

Her hand was strong on his as he guided her to the bedroom at the back of the house. She lay down on her bed and he covered her with a comforter.

"I thought you were doing so *well*," she said.

"Well, I was flying pretty high there for a while."

"Call me in the morning. I'll think about the will. It's all so confusing . . ."

"Of course it is. Would you like me to get you a cup of tea before I go?"

"No, I know you're in a hurry."

It struck him that she was as anxious for him to leave as he was. Histrionics like hers were obviously as exhausting to give as to receive.

"Goodbye, Mother," he said, bending over to give her a peck on the forehead.

"Goodbye, son," she replied, and then added the incredible two sentences she always used in ending such scenes: *"Don't worry! I love you!"*

"Thank you, Mother," he said, gave her hand a reassuring squeeze, and fled the room.

"Penny!" he said when he got to the car. "Come on, girl, let's go to the airport!" Giving her a hug which almost crushed her, he started the car and roared away.

By the time they got on the airplane, they were both so exhausted that they fell promptly asleep. It had been necessary to wait two hours as standbys for tickets, and they had paced, Ben thought, something like a hundred miles.

In the chair next to him, Penny now slept with her hand affectionately placed on his knee. Leaning his head back, Ben too dozed, but awoke with a start half an hour later. Penny had shifted her position and was now leaning forward, almost as though she were praying. Outside the window of the plane there was a bank of clouds glowing in moonlight.

"Penny?" he whispered.

There was no reply, and he realized that she was still asleep in that curious position.

Sitting up in his chair, Ben picked a menu from the pocket at the back of the seat in front of him. Appropriately enough, it was decorated with drawings of Spanish galleons, anchors and crossed cannon which actually looked as though they might be gold, and he noted that the airline was calling this flight the "Golden Galleon Service."

This got him to thinking about the basic job he was being paid to do, the writing of a movie script. No matter what else happened on Janus Island in the next few months, he owed it to himself, even more than to Nort, to come up with a good script that might eventually be filmed by someone, even if Nort proved incapable of producing a movie.

Why not call the movie *Golden Cannon* and concentrate on telling the story of their creation, their loss and their recovery? The whole concept of those big guns was beginning to fascinate him, even if they had never existed. During his youth he had read a good deal about the history of the Keys and the Caribbean, and there were plenty of tales to be told which were both true and fantastic.

The script could begin, Ben thought, with the screams of a native Carib Indian being tortured by the conquistadores for information about gold. That of course had happened often enough. The Spaniards had occasionally roasted an Indian alive over a barbecue pit, and in retaliation the Indians had occasionally poured molten gold into the mouth or anus of a Spanish captive. This would be one movie which no one could complain lacked action.

From the shot of the tortured Indian, Ben thought, he could cut to a scene in which the Spaniards were looting a South American village temple. It would not be hard to re-create that on Janus Island, and perhaps he could find a local man to play the old admiral who had tried to avoid paying ninety per cent of his find to his king by casting some cannon in gold. Perhaps the cameras could show the natives being made to drop their pretty bracelets, necklaces and idols into a great iron pot with a charcoal fire being fanned by bellows. How did they cast those ancient cannon, anyway? Did they dig a hole the shape they wanted in the sand?

Research could find the answer to that. It would not be hard to construct a mockup of part of the hold of an old galleon where the heavy cannon were laboriously placed in the gun carriages, and someone out in Hollywood could shoot the whole hurricane scene with models. Or would it be more dramatic to have the ship sunk by pirates which the golden cannon failed to repel? In any case this part of the film could end with the cannon sinking to the bottom and a long shot of the empty sea with gulls circling the spot. The scene could then shift to the present with a man like Nort studying a pilot chart, reconstructing the voyage of that lost Spanish convoy, studying the currents and probable winds for that part of the world at that time of the year, and finally drawing a circle near Janus Island.

Then the interesting part of the movie and of his own life would start, Ben reflected as the airplane soared above a sea of golden clouds. What would be the mechanics of a realistic modern treasure hunt? What kind of men would elect to risk their time, money and perhaps their lives on such a long-shot chance? How would these men compare to those ancient mariners who for mysterious reasons had left the fertile plains of Spain and sailed their dangerous, clumsy ships thousands of miles into unknown waters to seek and fight for gold?

Well, he could stick pretty close to life, Ben thought. He could base one character on Nort, a rich man who had inherited more gold than he could ever spend, but who was still driven to prove something to or about himself. And perhaps there could be another character, an aging script writer left over from that short golden age when television had been concerned with more than comic-strip characters and soap opera, a man hopelessly and forever in debt, but who still, improbably enough, was a good deal more interested in finding a woman than gold.

Outside, the sea of clouds was changing to silver. When a stewardess offered him a martini, Ben sipped it slowly, and settling back on his pillow, closed his eyes.

Just because a thing is fantastic, it doesn't mean it's not true, Nort had said when discussing the golden cannon. Ben was forty-five years old, yet still somehow felt exactly as he had when he was seventeen, lonely and eager and confused. He was thirty thousand feet up in the air flying at six hundred miles an hour back to Janus Island to look for golden cannon, and by his side was a girl who now seemed to him all good.

"Ben?" Penny said suddenly.

He turned to her with a smile.

"Gosh, I really conked out. I get a big kick out of just relaxing on an airplane, instead of running up and down the aisles with a tray."

"Do you feel rested now?"

"Yes, but also a little guilty. I don't think I'll ever be able to ride in one of these things without thinking that I really should be working my way. Every time anyone rings for a stewardess, I'll jump."

"How long has it been since you had a long vacation?"

"Lord, I don't know. I never could get the money together for more than a couple of weeks, and then there was usually work to do, like fixing up the apartment, or organizing some part-time job. Hank is one of those pilots who always has to have some business on the side. He tried raising cattle, and when he lost his shirt at that, he bought a part interest in a store that sells uniforms. He always had me typing out tax or order forms."

Glancing at Ben, she added, "I'm sorry I talk about him."

"That's all right."

"No, I'd hate to hear about your former wife, and I shouldn't inflict my past upon you. Anyway, I'm much more interested in the future. Do you mind if I ask some questions about Nort? I'm going to have to learn to get on with him, and it might help if I understood more about him."

"What can I tell you?"

"Has he always been the way he is now? I mean, I know you've been friends for years, but frankly, it's hard for me to see why. He seems so tensed up, so arrogant and so suspicious of the whole world."

"No, he wasn't always like that," Ben said sadly, and he had a vision of Nort, a boy laughing as he ran along the beach on Janus Island, trying to fly a big red kite that he and Ben had made, long, long ago. "He used to be proud, not arrogant, and he had a lot to be proud of."

"You mean family and money and all that?"

"All that and a lot more. When we were kids, he was better at everything than anyone we knew. He could swim better, shoot better, ride better, dance better — there was a kind of natural superiority about him that set him apart."

"I should think that would have made you hate him."

"It did sometimes, but he was very generous then. When he got his week's allowance, every kid in the neighborhood flocked around. When I admired a big model airplane he had, he gave it to me, and I was furious when my mother made me give it back. He was a good giver — he was never condescending about it. There was just an air about him of having everything that was good, and wanting everyone he liked to share it. He made a gift a sort of compliment."

"What happened to him? Why did he change so?"

"I didn't realize it at the time, but he was under a lot of strain. His parents insisted upon impossible standards of excellence. They were always building up this big mystique about the Clays as a family of supermen. Come to think of it, I suppose they were always trying to rival what some people call the real Clays, the ones descended from Henry Clay, and Cassius Clay, the Clays of Kentucky, all that. Cornelius Clay always made a point of saying they were not related to that family, but you could tell, he always wanted to be. His grandfather was nothing but a bricklayer, yet they are the kind of people who feel a great need to pretend they are related to emperors and kings. The unusual thing about Nort's family is that most of them worked terribly hard to live up to their own pretenses."

"Do you think Nort works terribly hard now to achieve any real kind of quality?"

"He might still be capable of it, but a lot's happened to him. The first thing was when he discovered he wasn't really better at school than everybody. His father kept him at home with tutors until he was twelve years old, and then shipped him off to one of those New England prep schools that pride themselves on being tough. I think Nort just assumed he was going to be president of his class and captain of the football team, the way his parents wanted him to be."

"Did he come anywhere close to making it?"

"Not really. He's bright enough at some things, but he never could learn languages, and he'd had so much discipline from others all his life that he couldn't discipline his own mind. He hated studying, and the school threw him out when he was fifteen years old. That really did something awful to him."

"Poor little superman," Penny said.

"He tried other schools, but he began to rebel against the whole system. Three schools threw him out. Then the war came along, and that made everything worse. All his friends became officers, but without even a high-school diploma, it was impossible for him to get a commission."

"But other people get through such disappointments without turning permanently sour on life. He still had more to go on than ninety-nine per cent . . ."

"Not really," Ben replied. "I've been thinking a lot about that. Sure, he had money and social position of a kind, but he had lost all his self-respect as a competitor in any important kind of game, and worse than that, his marriage started to go sour almost before the minister finished the ceremony."

"Why?"

"Who knows all the reasons for that sort of thing? Maybe Nort simply isn't capable of loving a woman. Maybe love is like money — you can't give it if you never have had any. Nort's parents never really loved him, in the sense of being with him a lot and forgiving his failures. He was brought up by a long series of hard-nosed nannies and tutors whose business it was just to teach him how to be better than everybody else, not to enjoy life. His father was always out somewhere making more money, and his mother was far too busy social climbing at Newport or Palm Beach to give any time to a child. In those days rich people just handed their children over to servants. Nancy's parents did the same to her. What experience did those two have of love?"

"Did your family do that to you?"

"In a way, but I was lucky. My father was always around the house, and though he had troubles, he was a very affectionate man. He hardly ever passed me without touching my face with his hand. And though Mother has some pretty painful disabilities, she may have realized that, or maybe Dad did. Anyway, I had a wet nurse when I was a baby, and she stayed with me until I was five or six years old. Her name was Lillian Lee, and I still used to visit her a lot until I was fifteen years old. She was a nice warm Negro woman, not one of those crisply uniformed English nannies who can talk about nothing but discipline and the great need to avoid spoiling a child." He paused. "Lillian Lee. Gosh, I haven't thought about her for a long time!"

It was strange how the very sound of the name could still arouse in him all kinds of conflicting emotions.

"Don't keep running over to Lillian's house!" he could remember his mother shouting. "It's not proper for a boy your age."

"Is she still alive?" Penny asked.

"No, but a lot of her children are. Nort and I used to play with them back before the color thing built up in our lives. Those were good days, back then on Janus Island. It's good to be going home again."

Sighing, Ben closed his eyes and slept. When Penny shook his shoulder an hour later, the plane was circling high over Miami, which looked like a handful of jewels in the night.

CHAPTER 9

WHEN Ben and Penny got out of the airplane he did not recognize the airport at all. It had been ten years since he had been to Janus Island, and twenty since he had come by airplane. Miami had changed so much that it looked like a foreign city to him, some new place in a new land he had never visited. It made him feel peculiar to reflect that this was the recorded city of his birth, for his mother had come from Janus Island to the hospital here a week before he had been born. In his youth he had often come to Miami for shopping, for dentists, and later, for his secondary schooling, but that Miami of the Thirties had been a relatively small and quiet city compared to this fantasia of glass, chromium and concrete.

A fat man with a camera swinging from his neck jostled past Ben on the way from the plane to the gate, and in the terminal there seemed to Ben to be an unusual number of people with cameras, all snapping one another. The practice of recording each moment suddenly seemed sensible to Ben. Go ahead, he thought, get it all down! Tomorrow it will be different, and I hope you have a fast shutter.

The airline terminal was crowded with people arriving for a convention. Some pretty girls representing a hotel were putting brightly colored imitation Hawaiian leis around the necks of a group of arriving businessmen, some of whom already sported straw beachcomber hats. The atmosphere of frantic gaiety made Ben feel more anxious than ever to be alone with Penny.

"This way for the baggage," Penny said. "I know this terminal pretty well."

Ten minutes later they got in a taxi and headed toward the boatyard where Nort kept his yawl. The evening was cool for Miami, and Penny put her tweed coat back on.

The sleek yawl with the providential name *Hope XIV* lay in a slip near a bridge in the Miami River with lesser craft nestled all around her. As Ben jumped from the pier to her immaculate teak deck and turned to help Penny aboard, a burly bald man dressed in dungarees stuck his head from the forecastle hatch and switched on floodlights.

"You Mr. Powers?" he asked in the soft accent of the Keys.

"Yes."

"Mr. Clay told me you were coming. He just got in a few minutes ago. He said to tell you he was tired and turned in. He'll see you in the morning."

Climbing from the hatch the man revealed a muscular torso with tattoos covering his arms and chest. It was difficult to tell whether he was a white man deeply tanned or a mulatto. His dungaree trousers were held up by an elaborately spliced and knotted rope around his waist. Among the many tattoos on his left arm was a dagger dripping blood and the words "Death Before Dishonor." On his right arm was the picture of a tombstone inscribed "Mother," and an American flag encircled by the motto "My Country, Right or Wrong." An American eagle spanned the full width of his enormous chest.

It was like Nort, Ben thought, to hire a nautical apparition like this to take care of his boat for him and to provide local color for his guests.

"I'm Flint," the big man said. Keeping his eyes on Ben, he seemed to be avoiding Penny, as though the sight of a pretty girl was somehow disturbing.

"Captain Flint?" Ben replied in astonishment.

"Fred Flint," the man said, scratching his ear miserably. "I know, people keep kidding about the name."

"It must be difficult," Ben replied, wondering whether this was a professional yacht captain smart enough to realize that many people who buy boats like to play romantic games which require character actors rather than any particular knowledge of the sea.

"It's my real name," Flint said earnestly. "My grandfather came from Maine. There are a lot of Flints up in that country."

"I know," Ben said. "Fred, I'd like you to meet Miss Penny Savodi. She's going along with us."

"Pleased," Flint said grudgingly. "Mr. Clay said to put you in the guest stateroom."

"Thank you."

"I was a boatswain's mate in the navy — that's where I met Mr. Clay. He said you was his skipper once, on a D.E."

"For a very short while."

"Anyway, glad to have you aboard," Flint said, and reaching up, swung Penny's and Ben's suitcases from the wharf.

Going aft to the polished chromium wheel on a pedestal in the cockpit, Ben let his eyes travel over the deck and rigging. God, how good it was to get back aboard a boat again! Here everything was manageable and understandable, dearly familiar, even though he had never before been aboard this particular yawl. The sheets, the halyards and the backstays all were clearly identifiable, of simple purpose, totally reliable if renewed often enough and handled right. In its chromium binnacle by the wheel, the compass gleamed, silently offering directions to anywhere he might want to go.

"She's a beauty," he said.

"Yes," Penny said, making the one word an exclamation of admiration.

"Looks good now. We just got her off the ways. Mr. Clay punched in her bow."

"How?"

"Ran her right up on the jetty at Janus Island. When the current gets her there, she's pretty hard to handle sometimes. With a vessel this heavy, that little engine doesn't do much good in reverse."

"No," Ben said.

"But we got a whole new stem now, and she's better than new. Want to come below?"

Following Penny down the companionway, Ben saw a main saloon in gleaming white and mahogany. Against the forward bulkhead was a small tile fireplace with a handful of charcoal briquets glowing in a grate to ward off the dampness. Amidships was the guest stateroom, with two narrow bunks and a writing desk. Aft was the owner's stateroom, behind the closed door of which Nort presumably slept.

"Here you are," Flint said, dropping the suitcases in the guest stateroom. "Good night."

Perhaps Ben imagined a stern note of disapproval in Flint's voice, and he cursed his New England ancestors for making the situation so awkward. Penny looked at the narrow bunks dubiously and began to unpack her bag, putting her clothes into drawers.

"I'm sorry this isn't more comfortable," Ben said.

Standing on her toes, she gave him a quick kiss on the cheek, which confused him. She was so short and slight that she suddenly reminded him of his daughter, a thought that was both welcome and not welcome.

"Let's go on deck," he said, a little gruffly.

Sensitive to his tone, she stepped back, looking puzzled.

"You reminded me of my daughter," he said, feeling an explanation was needed. "That's sort of complicated. I guess I don't want you to think I have to be fatherly with you, yet sometimes I feel terribly protective."

"You do look a little like my father did when he was younger. I loved him very much."

"Really?"

"Why are you so astonished?"

"I don't know. I guess I've begun to seek adults who really like their parents the way some people seek rare coins. You're practically the first in my collection, but to have *any* makes me feel good."

"Are you really such a cynic? What kind of people have you known?"

"Come on," he said. "Let's go on deck."

They sat on canvas-covered cushions damp with dew.

"How long will it take us to get to Janus Island?" she asked.

"It depends a lot on the weather. A day and a night usually, if we go outside, and a little longer if we take the inland route. It's fairly rough out there now. Do you think you'll be seasick?"

"No," she said with a laugh.

"What's funny?"

"We still have so much to find out about each other. I used to be a nurse aboard the Cunard Line, before I was a stewardess. I spent two years at sea."

"A seagoing nurse!" he said. "I know now what I've always wanted."

"I don't know anything about sailing yachts, though."

"You'll learn."

A slender Negro in a white uniform approached them.

"My name is Lawson," he said. "I'm the steward. Would you like anything?"

"I'll have a scotch," Ben replied. "How about you, Penny?"

"The same," she said, and brushed her hair back with her hand. "But first I think I'll go below and change."

"Fine," Ben said.

The yawl was beautiful, but it was not a good place to take Penny for their first night together. With Nort sleeping directly below them and with Flint and Lawson padding about on rope-soled shoes, there was no sense of privacy. The staterooms were made for ocean racing and nothing else — the bunks were narrow, high-sided, and uncomfortable-looking.

"Lawson," he heard Penny say, "I don't think there are any towels in here. Could you please get me some?"

She was in the cabin just forward of the cockpit, beneath the doghouse, but her words came up through ventilators as clearly as through speaking trumpets. Aboard this craft Nort would not need any bugging equipment.

"Your scotch, sir," Lawson said a moment later. "Shall I leave the lady's here?"

"Please," Ben said.

She kept him waiting for what seemed a long while, but when she came up she was wearing a flowered green print he had never seen, and her rich brown hair was freshly brushed. Standing up, he kissed her, breaking off the embrace quickly when he saw that Flint was sitting on the anchor windlass, stolidly watching them.

"Damn!" he said, sitting down.

"What's the matter?"

"There's no privacy here and that damn little stateroom is going to be uncomfortable."

She laughed.

"We are star-crossed lovers," she said.

"Let's go ashore and find a hotel."

"If you want, but I must admit I enjoy the waiting. Is that horrible of me?"

"Yes."

"We're having something I had never really hoped for again: a courtship. Nobody I know in New York really courts anybody any more. Everybody is so sophisticated, nobody waits for anything. All the fun of anticipation is lost."

"I've had all the fun of anticipation I want," he laughed.

"I consider your eagerness a compliment, Ben. Please don't mind my playing coy! It's just that I'd forgotten how well people treat each other during a courtship. No cross words, no temper tantrums, no arguments over who makes the coffee or gets the laundry. It's so good I want to make it last. All those melting looks you give me, the feeling I get just when your hand brushes my arm — it's so good, Ben! What are we rushing for?"

"Who's rushing? Those bunks down there will be worse than bundling beds!"

Throwing up her chin, she laughed again.

"I don't want you to think we're going to be good for each other only when we're courting," he said seriously. "I've had enough arguments, deadly glances, wounding jokes and all the rest to last two lifetimes. I hereby promise

153

that I shall cut my tongue out with a carving knife if it ever says one cross word to you."

"Do you think we could really live long without arguments?"

"I don't know, but I think I'll treat arguments the way alcoholics treat drinks. The important thing is to avoid the first one."

"Yes. I too will cut out my tongue if it wounds you."

"Anyway, we'll be a remarkably silent couple!" he said.

She laughed again.

"To avoid the first argument, I'll get my suitcase and we'll find a hotel," she said, getting to her feet.

"No!" he replied. "To avoid the first argument I shall wait until I have been driven mad by anticipation! We will live like sister and brother aboard this bloody boat until we get to Janus Island."

"Hotels do seem sort of sordid to me," she said. "When I was a stewardess, I always had to live in hotels. I want everything with you to be different. Can you understand that?"

"Yes," he said. "Penny, I love you very much. Let's go to our torture chamber and go to sleep. We'll need the rest if we're going to get an early start."

"Thank you, Ben," she said, and picking up his left hand in both of hers, kissed each of his knuckles separately, while he stroked her hair with his other hand.

"Let's go below," he said.

As soon as they got into the little cabin, his arms went around her automatically and she answered his kiss so hard that he was afraid of bruising her lips. In the dim light with four small portholes, her eyes gleamed as she stepped back, leaned against the lavatory door and shook her head, tossing her hair back from her face.

"All right, Ben, I'll be right out," she whispered, turned and disappeared into the lavatory.

His whole body rigid with tension, he took off his clothes and laboriously climbed into one of the narrow bunks, finding that his shoulders barely fitted, and that when he lay on his back, the deck was barely three feet above his face. What he should try to do was just to go to sleep, reserving the act of love for a nice big flower-filled room on Janus Island, with a long private beach glimmering in the moonlight outside the windows, but he knew he would find it impossible to lie there rigid, knowing that Penny was also lying sleepless in a bunk three feet away. Then the lavatory door opened, and she came out, wrapped in a large white Turkish towel, which she had wound around herself like a sarong, leaving the tops of her breasts exposed.

"Are you asleep?" she whispered.

"Are you kidding?"

She gave a low laugh.

Stepping toward him, she undid two pins at her side, and casually tossed the towel on her bunk. In the dim light her breasts seemed to glow white against the darker skin of her suntanned shoulders and midriff. Unafraid of his own violence, he pulled her to him. Suddenly the smallness of the bunks didn't offer any problem — they fitted into one surprisingly well. The high sides he began to welcome, for her supple body strained against him so hard that in one moment of panic he feared she was trying to get away. Then he felt her fingers caressing his groin, guiding him. At first he found her so hard to enter that he had the hallucinatory suspicion that she was a virgin.

"Go!" she said. "Hard!"

She arched her body under him, ripping her mouth from his to get air. Afraid of premature ejaculation, he began holding his breath to stave it off. Suddenly her body opened for him, and she seemed to pour out warmth, manipulating him in subtle ways.

"Don't wait for me," she said. "I don't need that! Let yourself go!"

He did, and suddenly it was all over. Beneath him he felt the tension go out of her body. Her eyes were closed and she was breathing deeply.

"Thank you, Ben," she said softly.

"I was afraid I was too fast."

"Just right. I came twice."

She gave another low laugh.

"That anticipation, I tell you," she said. "It's a great invention."

"Yes."

She sighed.

"We're good together, Ben. Thank God. I was worried about that."

"So was I. Want a cold drink?"

"Water, yes."

Getting up, Ben dressed and went to the galley. A light was on in Nort's stateroom, he saw, and suddenly music started there, a stereophonic phonograph playing Bach. Why should that worry him? Finding Lawson had gone to the forecastle to sleep, Ben took ice cubes from the refrigerator and filled two glasses with water. When he got back to the guest stateroom, he heard the shower in the lavatory running. Almost immediately Penny came out, and stood toweling herself in the doorway.

"Thanks," she said, when he handed her a glass, and hanging up the towel, took it.

"I'm never going to get enough of looking at you," he said.

"Good. I love to be looked at. I'm very vain about my figure. I work hard to keep it."

"If you were made of marble, millions of art lovers would cross oceans to see you. You are most improbably beautiful."

"And you are most improbably appreciative."

Gracefully she climbed into her bunk, pulled a sheet up to her chin, and closed her eyes. Leaning over her carefully to avoid cracking his head, he brushed his lips across hers.

"I always knew there was some good reason for staying alive," he said. "Good night."

He climbed into his own bunk, and lay staring at small lights dancing on the overhead, the reflections of dock-lights on the water outside the portholes. There was a moment of silence.

"Ben?" she said suddenly.

"Yes?"

"Are you disappointed because, well, because we didn't last long together tonight?"

"Disappointed is exactly the wrong word to describe the way I feel."

"I'm glad. Sometimes, like tonight, I love it sudden, but that doesn't mean there won't be other times when we can make a game of seeing how long we can make it last. Will you be looking forward to that?"

"A little."

She laughed, and then there was only her deep breathing. With one open hand extended almost supplicatingly over the edge of the bunk, she slept.

CHAPTER 10

T HE next morning when Ben awoke, the first thing he saw was a dazzling splash of sunshine on the white bulkhead. There was no sound but the phonograph in Nort's stateroom which was still playing Bach very softly. "Penny," he said.

There was no answer, and opening his eyes, he saw that her bunk was empty. Filled with panic, he wrenched on his trousers and went into the main saloon. That too was empty.

"Penny?" he called.

"She's on deck, sir," Lawson said, opening the door from the galley.

Looking crisp and neat in a white tennis dress, she was sitting in the cockpit drinking coffee. Standing when she saw him, she kissed him lightly.

"Good morning." she said. "It's a wonderful day and Flint says there's a good weather report."

"Good," he said, shielding his eyes from the sun and looking up at the sky, where puffy cumulus clouds were scudding across their own pale blue sea. "Yes, it looks like a great day for a run to the island. Where's Nort?"

"He's not up yet."

"What time is it?"

"About nine."

"Well, he must be awake. At least he's got that music going."

"Maybe he went to sleep with it on," Penny said. "It seems to be playing the same piece over and over again."

This seemed somehow sinister, and Ben nervously paced the decks while Lawson prepared breakfast.

"I think I'll knock at his door and say breakfast is ready," Ben said as they sat down to scrambled eggs and sausages in the main saloon.

"I'd be careful," Lawson said. "He don't take kindly to being woke."

"Hell, we've got a fair wind and a fair tide," Ben retorted. "We shouldn't be sitting here!"

"Maybe we should take it easy, Ben," Penny said. "After all, it's his boat."

"I know, but he was in a hurry to get to the island, and he's got that music going. Maybe he's just lying there, waiting for us. I'll go give him a try."

Walking swiftly aft, Ben tapped lightly on the door of Nort's stateroom. There was no answer but the unbroken rhythm of Bach's *Toccata and Fugue in D Minor*. He knocked louder, but still there was no reply. After slapping the door with the palm of his hand and calling "Nort!" several times, Ben tried the door and found it locked.

"There's no answer and the door's locked," he reported when he returned to the main saloon.

"That's funny . . ." Penny said.

"No, ma'am, there's no reason to worry," Lawson said.

"Why?" Ben asked. "What's going on?"

"Well, Mr. Clay, when he gets on board this boat, lots of times he likes to drink. He was right tired after flying that plane all the way from New York, and he was on that telephone of his half the night. He had me bring him a bottle of scotch. I expect he'll get up around noon and everything will be all right."

"Well, I think that when he does wake up, he'll want to get out of here fast," Ben said impatiently. "Let's anchor out in the harbor and take the sail covers off."

"You sure he'd want us to do that?" Flint asked.

"Mr. Clay and I have been friends for forty years. I know that when he wakes up he'll be grateful to us if we have made all the preparations instead of wasting time."

"All right, Mr. Powers, but I'm no captain here, I'm just a ship keeper," Flint said. "If you want to anchor her out in the stream, you'll have to be in charge."

"I'll take her out. Warm up the engine and single up the lines."

"Aye," Flint growled.

A few moments later there came the deep cough of the diesel. While it warmed up, Ben and Penny drank coffee and ate their eggs.

"Mr. Powers?" Flint said coming to the main saloon, cap in hand.

"Yes, Fred?"

"We're ready to go, but I think I ought to tell you something."

"What?"

"I'm not much on sail handling, and neither is Lawson. With Mr. Clay not feeling well, you won't have much help. This boat is a bitch when you get the genny on her. I'm not really a sailboat man. Truth is, I hardly ever got offshore when I was in the navy. I was on repair ships anchored in harbors."

"Don't worry, Fred. I won't push her."

"I guess I ought to tell you that I get seasick when we go offshore. I've got some dramamine, but . . ."

"It won't be bad out there today," Ben said, thinking how little appearances meant. "Let's get started."

"Couldn't we just run down inside under power? The lady . . ."

"The lady worked two years with the Cunard Line, Fred. I'll go out and anchor inside the breakwater so we can make sail slowly."

Going to the cockpit, he sat down at the wheel and fingered its polished spokes. Beside him Penny sat sipping a cup of coffee quietly.

"Cast off all lines but number three," Ben said to Flint.

"Cast off all but number three," Flint repeated dourly, and there was a splash as Lawson, jumping to the wharf, released the bow line.

"All lines but number three are in, sir," Flint growled a moment later.

Touching the reverse gear, Ben pulled the bow away from the wharf.

"Take in three," he said.

"Three's away!" Lawson replied.

Shoving the gearshift ahead, Ben steered the yawl smoothly away from the wharf.

"It's good to see a thing done well," Penny said.

"There's great fun in mastering small problems."

Behind the breakwater Ben anchored and helped the two

men take off the sail covers. He had hoped that moving the boat would wake up Nort, but when the big diesel was turned off, there was still no sound from Nort's cabin but the same record played over and over again. When all preparations for making sail had been made, Ben glanced at his watch and saw that it was a little after ten-thirty.

"Usually he's up by now, even after a night of drinking," he said.

"Does he take sleeping pills?" Penny asked.

"Sometimes. That's what I've been worried about."

The thought of sailing with a corpse lying in the owner's stateroom sent a chill through Ben, and picking up a piece of new mooring line, he began to put an eye splice into it for something to do.

By the time it was noon, and there was still no sign of movement in Nort's cabin, Ben was genuinely worried. The same record, repeated endlessly, was getting on his nerves more and more.

"Damn it, I think it's my responsibility to take a look in there!" he said. "Flint, do you have a master key?"

"That door is bolted on the inside."

"If this goes on, we'll have to force our way in."

"Wait," Penny said. "Maybe we're getting too worked up about this. After all, the poor guy probably just has a hangover."

"I'm going to break that record as soon as I get my hands on it," Ben said.

By one o'clock Ben was in no mood to wait longer.

"After all, he may need help," he said. "Flint, do you have a big drill and a keyhole saw? It would do less damage to try to get at that bolt than to smash the door in."

"I got the tools, sir, but will you give me written authorization?"

"You really are a navy man! Sure, but let's get started."

"Couldn't we look through the portholes first?" Penny said.

"He usually keeps the curtains drawn, but we can try," Lawson said.

To look in the portholes of Nort's cabin it was necessary to lie down on the deck. As Ben did this he reflected that he had accused Nort of spying on others. What would Nort do if he should look up and see Ben staring in? That was an entirely academic question, Ben found, because thick curtains were drawn across all Nort's portholes.

"Let's get on with the door," Ben said, climbing stiffly to his feet.

After Ben had written a note authorizing the action, Flint methodically cut a hole in the door big enough for him to insert a hand and draw the bolt. Ben thought that the sound of the saw might arouse Nort, perhaps to great anger, but still there was no sign of life.

"There you are," Flint said, stepping back and leaving the door still discreetly closed.

"I'll go in," Ben said.

Somehow it took a lot of courage to swing the door open. The first thing Ben saw was that Nort had converted the luxurious owner's stateroom into a radio room and electronic workshop. Surrounded by transmitters, workbenches, boxes of spare equipment and a big generator was one narrow bunk. In it Nort lay on his back fully dressed without any covering. There was no discernible movement of the chest, and at first glance Ben thought he was dead.

"I'd better look at him," Penny said. "Do you mind, Ben?"

"No," Ben said, and stood away from the door. Seeing the phonograph on a shelf over Nort's head, Ben reached up and shut it off. The silence was both welcome and eerie.

Brushing past Ben, Penny leaned over Nort's bunk, taking his wrist.

"He's alive," she said. "The pulse is slow but steady."

"I smell booze," Ben said. "He probably just knocked himself out."

"It's more likely these," Penny said, picking up a bottle of yellow capsules from the bunk. "Nembutal — bought without prescription, from the size of the bottle. It must have held five hundred. God knows how many he took."

"Should we call a doctor?"

Expertly Penny peeled up one of Nort's eyelids, and put her ear on his chest to listen to his heart. Then she took his pulse again.

"I think he's just in a deep drug-induced sleep," she said. "He'll probably wake up in a couple of hours."

Trusting Penny's judgment, Ben felt his concern for his friend subside into irritation.

"God, I hate to waste this day swinging at anchor," he said. "I've got a good mind just to set sail."

"Will he be angry when he wakes up?"

"I suppose it would be presumptuous of me to run off with him in his own boat. Maybe we'd better wait. Penny, do you want to see if we can catch some fish?"

Flint brought them tackle and almost immediately Penny caught a baby hammerhead shark about two feet long.

"Keep your hands away from his mouth!" Ben said. "Here, let me take him off the hook."

"How vicious he is!" Penny exclaimed.

"You know what Nort used to do when he caught these?"

"What?"

"He'd break their necks in such a way that they couldn't use their head planes to get under the water. Then he'd throw them back, and they'd scoot around on the surface like speedboats. It takes a shark a long time to die."

"How cruel!" she said with distaste.

"Most people down here hate sharks so much that no cruelty is too great," Ben said, but then remembered another boyhood trick of Nort's — nailing a small fish onto a thick plank painted the same color as the sea. When the pelicans dived on it, they broke their necks. By what process of self-protection had he chosen to forget Nort's youthful cruelty to animals, and why had he chosen to remember it now?

"There!" he said, rapping the shark over the head with a winch handle. "Now he won't suffer or cause pain."

Taking the shark by the tail, he threw it back into the sea.

"Thank you," Penny said. "Oh, look!"

There was a swirl of water by the floating fish, and it disappeared.

"The fresh blood draws them," Flint said. "They eat their own."

"And people skin dive in these waters?" Penny asked.

"Sharks hardly ever bother divers except in the movies," Ben said.

At three in the afternoon, Ben decided to try to wake Nort up and get permission to set sail. Taking a cup of hot black coffee from the galley, he went to the stateroom and knocked at the door. When there was no answer he went in and shook Nort gently. To his surprise, Nort opened his eyes almost immediately and tried to sit up.

"Ben?" he asked in confusion. "Ben? What time is it?"

"Three o'clock, Nort."

"Oh, afternoon," Nort said, blinking. "I did a lot of work last night."

"Here's some coffee," Ben said.

"Don't feel like it now. There's some aspirin there in that drawer."

Ben got him a glass of water, and Nort swallowed three pills.

"There's no reason for you to get up," Ben said, "but do you mind if we sail? We've got a fair wind for the island."

"Sure, set sail. I showed Fred how to use the radar if you need it. Just go ahead as though I weren't aboard."

"All right," Ben said.

"I was talking to Hollywood last night on the phone," Nort said. "Big things in the wind. Changes of plan, all for the good. Possibilities of all kinds. Talk to you about it later. Right now I want to go back to sleep."

"Fine," Ben said. "Nort, I got a little scared this morning when we couldn't rouse you. I had Flint saw a hole in the door so we could reach the bolt."

"That was a silly damn thing, Ben! What did you do that for?"

"Your machine was playing one record over and over again. I thought you might be ill."

Nort gave a crooked smile.

"At heart, you still think I'm nuts, don't you, Ben?"

"I think alcohol and Nembutal make a damn poor combination. I knew two people who died of it."

"Hell, I know how much to take, Ben! Sometimes I just get all worked up and I need something to knock me out. How's your little girl doing? Before I conked out last night, I heard her dulcet tones purring away there for quite a while."

"She's fine," Ben said coolly, wondering just what Nort had heard. "You go to sleep and get a good rest."

"Thanks, Ben. Will you have Lawson bring me some ice?"

"Right away," Ben said, and wondered uneasily if Nort was going to start drinking again. After a prolonged binge, Nort really got hard to handle.

This was not a good way to start either a movie or a treasure hunt, Ben thought as he saw Lawson disappear into Nort's cabin with a tray of bottles, as well as an ice bucket. Still, there wasn't much he could do about his host's drinking habits, and there was one big compensation: with Nort self-confined to his cabin, Ben would have some measure of privacy with Penny, and he could have the pleasure of sailing the big yawl.

"Let's stand by to get under way," he said to Flint with sudden exuberance. "Ask Lawson to come on deck and help."

Penny too wanted to help, but she was also afraid of getting in the way. The result was that she kept making little excursions from the cockpit to help the men roll up a sail cover or coil a line, and then would retreat to the edge of the coaming, where she perched and watched all the preparations intently, seeking some activity she understood well enough to lend a hand. Both her reticence and her eagerness seemed charming to Ben. She was very nervous, he saw as she repeatedly brushed her dark hair back from her forehead.

"It's not going to take you long to be a great sailor," he said. "Most women either hide when we're making sail, or keep getting in the way. You're doing it exactly right."

Her quick smile of gratitude told him how much she loved compliments, and he wondered why such a pretty girl had apparently received so few.

"With this wind the way it is," he said, watching a pennant flutter from the masthead, "I don't see why we can't just sail her away from her anchor. I don't think we'll need the engine at all."

"The tide by the breakwater can be pretty tricky," Flint said. "If the wind drops us, she'll be hard to steer."

"There's plenty of wind to give us steerage way, and the tide is slack," Ben replied.

"Aye," Flint grunted.

"Stand by the mizzen halyard," Ben said.

"Aye."

Ben went and sat by the wheel, his fingers caressing the

smooth metal spokes. Ambling aft, Lawson took his place beside Flint.

"Hoist the mizzen," Ben said.

"Hoist the mizzen!" Flint echoed in his deep voice, and there was the sound of the winch turning and the clatter of blocks. Up the mast climbed a growing triangle of gleaming Dacron, cream-colored against the azure sky. Briefly the sail filled and then slatted as the boat rounded into the wind.

"The mizzen halyard is secured, sir," Flint said.

"Very well," Ben replied, finding that his tongue savored all the old marine phrases like candies remembered from his youth. "Stand by to hoist the mainsail!"

"Stand by to hoist the mainsail!" Flint echoed glumly.

A big winch made the mainsail go up easily but slowly. The girl stood watching the white triangle grow, her hand shielding her eyes from the sun, her lips slightly parted in awe at the size of the great expanse of shining sail. A slight puff of wind made the big boom slat back and forth impatiently, rattling the polished blocks.

"The main halyard is secured, sir," Flint said, "and I've taken down on the downhaul."

"Very well. Let's get in the anchor before we set the staysail."

"Get in the anchor," Flint growled, and walked forward. A moment later the big electric windlass started to grind.

"Tell me when she's ready to break out," Ben said.

"Aye!"

Standing by the wheel as the vessel inched forward on her cable, Ben glanced over his shoulder, noting that he had plenty of room to fall back, turn and sail under the stern of a Coast Guard cutter anchored nearby. As the boat fell off a little, the big mainsail started to fill. The wheel kicked like a living thing in his hands as he rounded her up. Sitting in the bottom of the cockpit where she was entirely out of the way, the girl watched him, smiling, with her chin in her right hand.

"She's over the anchor now," Flint called.

"Very well. Break out the anchor and stow it. Lawson, stand by the mainsheet."

Looking rather sullen, his white shirt stained with sweat, Lawson came and sat by the coil of white nylon line.

"The anchor's aweigh," Flint called.

"Very well."

Released, the big yawl hovered in the wind as though she were not yet aware she was free. Slowly she started to drift astern. Spinning the wheel fast, Ben let her come back until the graceful bow edged past the stern of the Coast Guard cutter. Gradually the sails filled.

"Let the mainsheet run," Ben called, and himself released the mizzen sheet, which was near his hand.

"Let her run," Lawson said, and the nylon line purred through the blocks.

Her sails quivering, the big yawl continued to drift astern. When they were well clear of the Coast Guard cutter, Ben said, "Sheet that mainsail in now!"

"Taking her in!" Lawson said, throwing his back into it.

Reaching for the mizzen sheet, Ben saw that the girl had come to stand near it.

"Do you want me to take this in?" she asked.

"Fine," he said with a grin.

"The anchor is aboard," Flint called. "Do you want me to set the staysail now?"

"Set her and sheet her in!" Ben said as he spun the wheel fast.

Gathering headway, the stately yawl turned toward the mouth of the harbor, her big sails taut in the wind. There was the rattle of the staysail going up, and then that too went quietly to work. There was no sound anywhere except the water beginning to chuckle under the bow. The vessel began to glide through the still water of the bay with surprising speed. On the fantail of the Coast Guard cutter a group of men stood watching them go. Cupping his hands to his lips, a young officer shouted, and Ben leaned forward to hear.

"She's a beauty!" the officer yelled, and the men waved.

Stepping from behind the mizzenmast, the girl waved back, looking pretty with her white dress and brown hair fluttering against the cream-colored sail. She was rewarded by another wave and a chorus of wolf whistles.

"A beauty!" the young officer called again, and Ben had the curious feeling that when he finally was lying sick and dying, this was one moment he would go over and over again in his mind, this instant of splendor which was his now. How sad to think of Nort, who really owned this boat, lying in a stupor, unable to enjoy this day or the beauty of a pretty girl!

The tide grew stronger than Ben had expected as the mouth of the harbor narrowed, and the big yawl flew along effortlessly, needing hardly a finger on the wheel. Two children in a fast outboard motorboat came out and circled them in wonder, and an old man stood up in his flat-bottomed rowboat, forgetting his fishing to watch the tall-winged yawl sweep by. For a moment the wind slackened, and Ben kept his hand near the starting button of the engine as the tide pushed them down toward a concrete jetty. If the wind did leave them now and if the engine didn't start, could they get the anchor over in time, or would this magnificent afternoon end by piling the great yawl ashore at the mercy of a four-knot current? In his mind Ben felt the jolt, heard the splintering mahogany, and heard Nort's indignant curses, but then a puff of wind appeared gray on the water, and the graceful boat heeled to her work, leaving the ugly jetty safely astern. Ahead now there was only the ocean, the green shallows shading to deep blue as they met the Gulf Stream.

"Want a cold beer?" Lawson asked.

"Let's everybody have one."

"That would be good," the girl said, and sat in the cockpit, her eyes still traveling over the sails and the boat in wonder.

"I've never been on a big sailing boat before," she said, and it gave Ben a strange feeling, both melancholy and pleasurable, to think that this, which might well be his last great sail if he couldn't get on with Nort, was also her first.

"There's nothing quite like it, is there?"

"No."

Lawson handed them cans of beer still frosted from the freezer where he had put them to cool quickly, and the first sip was sharp, incredibly good.

"It's these simple pleasures that make life worthwhile," Ben said. "A can of beer, a beautiful girl, a hundred-thousand-dollar yacht . . ."

She laughed explosively, spilling a little beer as she took the can from her lips, the white foam running down her neck and breast, and she looked so good laughing there in the sun that he realized the yacht was not really as important as he had thought. Without the girl, he would be rather bored now as the thrill of getting under way wore off, but without the boat the day would still be exciting on any beach, in any room where she cared to stand laughing with a can of cold beer, dabbing with a Kleenex to mop up the little rivulets of foam that sparkled on her skin in the sun.

When they got well clear of the shoals, Ben changed course to parallel the shore. The wind seemed to be dying, and, close-hauled, the yawl lay drowsily bucking the current of the Gulf Stream, the chuckling of water under her bow sinking to a whisper.

"We ain't getting nowhere like this," Flint said, squinting at a beacon about three miles off their beam. "We're just about holding our own."

"Just about," Ben said.

"Do you want me to put the engine on?"

"Nope. I'm quite content to sit here waiting for a breeze."

"Might be here for days," Flint said disgustedly, and went below.

"I've just realized there's no point in hurrying," Ben said. "I feel too good now."

"That suits me," Penny replied. "I think I'll put on a bathing suit and get some sun."

"Good idea."

She went below. Over the starboard bow a school of porpoises broached, their arched backs gleaming in the sun. A large gray gull floated solemnly on the water, effortlessly drifting alongside the yawl. Coming up astern a big fishing cruiser pounded along at thirty knots, her heavy engines thundering, her bow sending up showers of spray, almost blinding white in the sun. Offended by the noise, perhaps, the big gull took off disdainfully, soaring away on silent wings.

"Do you mind if I lie down here?"

Turning, he saw that the girl had come back and had put a pillow by the deck alongside the cockpit. She was wearing a white bikini of the kind that only a young and slender woman can wear, and in the harsh sunlight he was surprised again at the perfection of her body. It had been a long time since he had known a woman with breasts that held up her brassiere instead of the other way around, and her thighs were so trim that they made him think of a teenager. Perfectly proportioned and delicate, she made him remember so many things so many years ago that he felt a little confused.

"Will I be in the way here?" she asked.

"Not at all," he said. "That's a pretty bathing suit. I think the only appropriate comment is *wow!*"

"No, I'm getting out of shape," she said, patting her tiny stomach, which seemed to him to be perfectly flat, with concern. "I'll be glad to be where I can swim again."

On her back she lay with one arm covering her eyes. How slim her legs and ankles were! The sight of her carried him back to places he did not want to go. Suddenly recognizing the familiar image of the young girl lying on a teak deck, he knew it was not his daughter she reminded him of, but Rita before he married her, back when they first met at the age of sixteen.

"Don't look at me," Rita had said. "I don't like to be looked at like that!"

And he had looked away, ashamed of what she had seen in his young eyes. Now, how sad it seemed that a pretty young girl had been thrown into such confusion by the avid eyes of a young man who loved her! Poor Rita, during all those years of their youth, she had been afraid or ashamed of nudity, even after they were married.

"Don't look at me!" she would say when she was dressing, and even on their honeymoon, she would always lock the bathroom door while she was taking a shower.

"But you're beautiful!" he had said.

"I have to have privacy," she had replied.

She had been willing to make love only in the dark, and how desperate those first nights had been when he had realized that the transports of young love were entirely his, that she was not sharing them at all, that her sighs and groans expressed almost every emotion except pleasure.

If he had been older and more experienced, would he have been able to handle a reluctant bride better? Would he know now how to treat a woman who did not want to make love, even after months of trying?

Yes. Now he would just walk out the door after having

expressed his sympathy as best he could. But then he had not imagined that the fault might conceivably be in part hers. Then it had seemed clear to him that somehow he had stumbled upon a game he simply couldn't learn to play well enough to please his partner, and just as he would do when trying to master any other skill, he had gone out and bought a lot of books.

In retrospect it all seemed as funny as it was pathetic. Much embarrassed, he had bought out practically the entire sex department of the one bookstore in Key West, and had sat up all night studying as hard as though he were preparing for final examinations at college.

"Oh, please don't!" Rita had said when he had tried the first of his newly acquired techniques. "Ben! You stop!"

"Please read the books," he had said miserably.

She had tried to read two, but said they were ridiculous and disgusting. In despair he sent away for a book called *Sex for the Sensitive Woman*. When it arrived he found that it was written in such flowery prose that it was hard to discover whether the authoress, who was pictured on the back cover as a thin lady at a piano, was talking about poetry, flower arrangement or copulation. There was a chapter on the female orgasm, however, which likened the phenomenon to the climax of a symphony orchestra, complete with trumpets and kettledrums. The language was less than clear, but at least Rita had consented to read it, and had not put it down until she was through.

"It sounds marvelous," she had said. "I want to have one."

"All right," he had replied, and that was the first of a long desperate attempt to get Rita to hear trumpets and kettledrums in bed. Somehow, despite all their frantic grapplings, she had never been able to get the orchestra tuned, and when he gave up, content with a few squeaks from his own flute, she was always furious at him.

"You just don't know how to do it," she said.

"I'm sorry. Next time I'll try harder."

"Maybe if you were physically bigger . . ." she said.

Unable to figure out how he could get physically bigger, he had shrugged hopelessly. The time had come when he dreaded going to bed with her, because in her desperate search for trumpets and kettledrums, she began telling him what to do from the first kiss on, directing him as though he were an inexperienced actor on camera. Without spontaneity, with frustration growing to hatred, the act of love soon became a nightmare. Perhaps he would have walked out then if things had worked out differently, but what actually happened was that in pursuit of trumpets and kettledrums, Rita got herself a baby, and what decent man of twenty-one could walk out then?

No, it had been easier to hope that they were just going through a normal period of adjustment, as all the books called it. How full of confidence, how careless of warnings his youth had been! He had gone to war sure that he had a beautiful, warm and responsive bride waiting for him at home, and such were his aspirations that he had actually been faithful to her, or the illusion of what she was going to be, for four years, the entire time he had been overseas!

When he came home, he found that she had changed. She had been going to see a psychiatrist, she had said, and she had looked thin and drawn, beginning to grow old at twenty-five. He had felt pity then for the first time, but it had also been mixed with despair. She had wanted to make love right away, as soon as he got home, and there was the old desperation he could not help her with, the impossible striving, the gymnastics, the exhaustion, the tears.

So sex isn't important, they had both decided without admitting it. Laura was already four years old, a remarkably pretty young girl, and very soon Rita got pregnant again, without the echo of a single trumpet or drum.

Sex isn't important, he had told himself, and had worked day and night, first as an assistant to a television producer, and then as a writer of scripts. And he had almost convinced himself that sex wasn't important, or at least was something he would never be any good at, when at the age of thirty-five, he met a jolly actress who insisted that they go over scripts in her hotel room.

"You're marvelous!" she had said on that first occasion, and it was as though he had found that he wasn't crippled after all, that he wasn't ugly, not contemptible, not weak, not incompetent, but all right, a perfectly healthy young man.

He had loved the jolly actress, even when she insisted upon going home to her husband in California.

"You'll be all right," she had said with amusement. "I'm glad I was able to open a few doors for you."

With a light kiss on the cheek she had gone, the first of several women, as even at the time he was beginning to suspect, but none of them had ever inspired in him the dumb longing he had felt for Rita when they were very young, the first lyrical hopeful desires of youth which had been denied so long that they were different, blunted, before they were satisfied. Always at the back of his mind there had been that picture of the young girl he had loved for so many years, but who had always begged him not to look and not to touch, a girl who even when he was at the peak of young manhood, had never found him handsome, strong or kind enough.

The tragedy was not his alone, Ben told himself, thinking of Rita now, trying to get a job as a receptionist, hoping an old lawyer who had been taking her out would propose marriage. After her own youth and beauty had gone, as they had with such incredible speed, she had gone through a stage of trying to make herself hugely attractive to him, buying fancy negligees of black lace, but by then he had not much wanted to look. For years the only way he had brought himself to make love to her at all was by conjuring up in his mind the image of the young girl in the bathing suit he had wanted so much, but whom he had never really been able to have until she had changed beyond recognition.

"What are you thinking about?" the girl at his feet now asked.

"The betrayal of youth," he said in sepulchral tones.

"I thought it must be something like that. You looked so sad."

"You give me an illusion, and I suppose any illusion is in some sense sad."

"What is the illusion?"

"By offering me your youth you give me the illusion of offering me my own back again, so that I can live it better."

"I'm not really all that young."

"But your youth is magic. It lasts."

"Can you say that, looking at my face?"

"Yes."

"Thank you," she said.

There were perhaps five minutes of contented silence before she said, "Any chance we can take a swim?"

"I guess we could, but I'm always leery of sharks out here. Sharks don't bother divers much, but swimmers on the surface look like dying fish. If I have a hose hooked up, how would you like a squirt bath?"

"That would feel great," she said.

Going to the hatch, he asked Lawson to take the wheel. Flint hooked up a hose to a saltwater pump while Ben changed into bathing trunks.

Five minutes later Ben stood on the fantail with Penny, laughing while they squirted the hose back and forth between them.

Hearing a slight squeak behind him, Ben wheeled and saw that Nort had opened the hatch of his cabin. Half hidden in shadows, Nort was standing there staring at him and Penny playing with the hose, his deep-sunken dark eyes gleaming above a stubble of dark beard. As soon as Ben turned, Nort slid the hatch closed with a thud. Reaching for a towel, Penny wrapped it around her as though she had been discovered naked by strangers. Feeling angry at Nort and frustrated by the thought that he had no right to object to the man looking out over the stern of his own boat, Ben turned off the hose.

"I think I'll get dressed," Penny said, and demurely walked below, keeping herself covered with the towel.

"We hardly got steerage way, Skipper," Lawson said.

"The stream is pushing us north," Flint added. "We're losing ground."

"You got a ballooner aboard this bucket?" Ben asked, trying to forget Nort's face.

"Oh sure, Skipper, but that's a hell of a lot of trouble!" Flint said. "The genny is bad enough."

Standing up, he took a bottle of pink pills from his pocket and popped one in his mouth.

"Are you feeling all right?" Ben asked.

"I don't like this ground swell much."

"I hadn't even noticed there was one. Get the Genoa jib on deck. Lawson and I will put it on."

Snapping the big sail to the headstay and rigging the sheets was a good deal of work. By the time it was up and drawing Ben found that his shoulder was beginning to ache, but the water began to plash under the bow contentedly, and the big yawl was beginning to leave a wake.

"What are you steering?" Ben asked Flint.

"A hundred and fifty degrees."

"You got a pelorus?"

"In the rack over the chart table."

Getting the instrument out, Ben fitted it to the binnacle. Coming from below with her hair newly combed and in her green dress, Penny sat watching him while he took bearings. Going to the chart table, he plotted them and said, "Do you want to see where we are?"

"Sure," she replied, and came to lean on the chart table beside him, her skin smelling of pine-scented soap.

"We're right there," he said, tapping the place where his lines crossed on the chart. "So far today we have progressed backward precisely three miles."

She laughed.

"But it's been a lovely voyage," she said.

"Now we've got the genny up we'll do better," he replied, and, picking up the parallel rules, he laid a course that would take them well offshore for the night.

"Can you show me where we're going? Is Janus Island on this chart?"

"On the next one."

Taking the chart from a rack overhead, he unrolled it, and there was Janus Island, looking incredibly small and insignificant, but the center of a network of reefs and shoals that stretched for sixty miles into the South Atlantic. Looking at this large-scale chart for the first time in a long while, Ben saw why Nort might be right when he said the lost convoy of Spanish galleons had ended up in a hurricane there. The chain of reefs extended from the southern tip of the island like a giant scimitar cutting into the sea. The Spaniards would have been hugging the shore there after having made a landfall on Key West, it was logical to assume. They would have kept close to the keys to get the full strength of the Gulf Stream sweeping them on their way north. Twenty miles south of Janus Island they would have hauled out to the eastward to clear the reef, but if a hurricane had hit them there they would have been caught, their clumsy ships inexorably driven into a semicircle of coral islets that were barely awash at high tide. The danger of this trap even for modern ships was clearly apparent on the chart, where three wrecks were marked within ten miles of Janus Island.

"There's the place," Ben said. "We come in through the reefs here."

"It looks difficult."

"Not with all the gadgets we've got aboard here."

"I can't wait to get there," she said, examining the chart closely. Her hair was soft as it brushed against his face.

"If the wind doesn't come up, I guess we'll have to put on the power," Ben said restlessly.

The heat aboard the boat and the lack of privacy were making him more and more nervous. He had a dread that something might happen to force him and Nort into some kind of blowup if they stayed cooped up together too long.

Well, if it did, what then?

Even without Nort he could write a movie script which might sell to someone else and if that didn't work he might get a job somewhere down in the Keys selling real estate or taking care of yachts. No matter how much he owed the government, there was always some way to keep body and soul together, and it would not be absolutely necessary to go back to that dismal hotel room in New York.

Would Penny continue to be interested in him if he ended up the seedy manager of some motel, stripped of the glamour of the movie business and the yacht? Or would she eventually, like so many others, turn out to be the kind of luxury one had, one way or another, to find gold to keep?

From her quiet face bent over the chart it was impossible to tell, no matter what convictions his heart held. The girl was a story that only the future could reveal, and the future could not do much talking until they got to Janus

Island, that small beanlike shape on the chart on which so much of his life always seemed to depend.

"Skipper!" Flint called. "Could you come here a moment?"

"What's up?" Ben asked, going to the wheel.

"I think we got a rainsquall making up over there." Flint pointed toward a gray cloud billowing up over the land.

"Might be," Ben said.

"Do you think we ought to get that genny in?" Flint asked nervously.

"I don't think so yet," Ben replied, and he was thinking how good it would be to get the big yawl really bowling along at eight or nine knots. If they got a good breeze they could reach the island before dark the next day.

"She's a bitch to get down in a blow," Flint said. "I hate that damn sail."

"Don't worry about it," Ben replied. "The course is one four three."

"One four three," Flint replied, and scowled at the rain cloud. "You might know it would rain and blow. What else can you expect when you get a good weather report?"

"You want to eat on deck or below?" Lawson asked. "It's ready any time you want."

"Below," Ben said, simply because he did not want to share his meal with Flint, who sat grumbling at the wheel.

The meal consisted of a good avocado salad, cold ham and more beer. Penny ate daintily, in the European fashion, Ben noticed — she kept her fork in her left hand, and used her right hand only for her knife.

"You're quite a riddle to me," he said with a smile.

"Why?"

"You eat like a European. Your accent is American, but as I told you, I can't guess what part of the country you're from."

"I told you, the Cunard Line," she said.

"The Cunard Line! Are you English?"

"Of course not. Do I look English?"

"No, but you're the first girl I ever met who gives a line of steamships as her nationality."

She laughed.

"Those ships are really where I feel most at home. The *Queen Mary*, the *Mauritania* . . . I was practically brought up aboard them as a child. Do you want the whole story? It's been such fun hanging onto a little mystery."

"You'll still be mystery enough for me when I know where you come from."

"All my life I've never known what to say when people asked me where I came from. My mother was Irish, and my father Italian. They met aboard a boat when both were coming to America for the first time. They married, and tried to live in New Jersey, but they hated it. So every time they got a little money together they went to Dublin, which my father hated, or to Rome, which my mother loathed."

"That sounds very complicated."

"It was. The only time my parents were really happy was on the Cunard Line, when they were going or coming from some place they didn't like. All during my childhood the Cunard Line was my idea of heaven. That's why I studied to be a nurse. But after two years it dawned on me that it wasn't really home," she said. "And being a nurse was rather different from being a passenger. No room service."

"But your voice still puzzles me," he said. "There's no hint of Italy or Ireland in it, and I never would have guessed New Jersey."

"I suppose all the different accents I was brought up with canceled each other out. What you're hearing is probably high-school voice lessons. One of my many ambitions was to sing."

"Are you good at it?"

"No. I can't sing and I can't act, but I am very good at giving back rubs. Aboard the *Queen Mary* that was my forte."

"I could use one. My shoulder has been giving me a bad time lately."

"Where?" she asked, and began kneading the muscles of his right shoulder.

"There! That's marvelous."

"It's better with your shirt off."

Her hands confused him. They felt so richly loving, but how much of that was just professional skill? He had never learned how to take love without giving, and it bothered him to sit there passively under her hands.

"If you get some rubbing alcohol and some mineral oil, I can do really a good job for you."

"I'm sure. But I've got to go up on deck and take a look at that rainsquall."

The clouds were building up rapidly now, and Flint had already put on a yellow slicker and rubber boots.

"Looks like it's going to be bad," he said morosely, and swallowed another pink pill.

"It won't last long."

"Maybe. Don't you think we better get that genny in now?"

It would be prudent to do so, Ben thought as he stared at the clouds, but a feeling of recklessness was building in him, and the idea of plunging along through the rain with the big jib drawing like a hundred horses pleased him. The sail was of fairly heavy Dacron and looked brand-new.

"I doubt if that squall is going to be more than we can handle," Ben said. "Let's let the genny take us for a ride."

In anticipation of the squall, the wind was beginning to die, he saw. The sails hung limp, slatting back and forth, reflected crookedly on the still surface of the sea.

"You better put on a slicker," Flint said.

"I think I prefer my bathing suit. You better warn Mr. Clay."

Lawson went below. When he returned a moment later, he said, "Mr. Clay's gone back to sleep."

"It's going to rain," Ben said to the girl. "You'd better put your bathing suit on again or get a slicker."

"The bathing suit will be fine," she said.

The prospect of taking the big yawl through a squall with the rain beating on his face excited him, bringing back memories of sailing in the bay behind Janus Island when he was a boy. There had been a time when he and Nort had gone sailing every time a big cloud appeared on the horizon, and he could still remember how good the rain felt splattering on the hot deck.

"You're crazy!" Rita had said. "You're absolutely soft in the head!"

"Not if we stay in the lee of the island. Come on, it's a marvelous thrill!"

Rita had never liked to go sailing even when the weather was good. Like Flint now, she had gulped seasick pills and had sat darting apprehensive glances from the sea to the sky, making Ben feel genuinely sorry for her, but also irritated because her fears robbed him of his joy.

"I'll take the wheel," he said to Flint now. "You and Lawson stand by the genny's sheet. When this thing hits, I imagine we'll have to pay her out a bit."

"Liable to take the whole bloody mast out of her," Flint said. "That's what Mr. Clay did."

"I'm not going to take the mast out of her."

The wheel kicked idly back and forth in his hand as the yawl lost steerage way. In a few moments the girl came and sat in the cockpit with a towel knotted around her waist.

"It does look like quite a storm," she said, peering up at the clouds.

"Are you scared?"

"I love storms. On the *Queen Mary* sometimes they let me climb up to the crow's nest. You can't imagine what it was like up there in a gale."

"You're wrong," he said.

"You've been there?"

"Aboard a destroyer. The mast of a destroyer in a gale can give you quite a ride."

"I'll bet."

Her lips parted in admiration of the scene she was imagining.

"You see that big tanker off the port bow?" Flint asked, pointing toward a ship approaching.

"Yes," Ben said.

"I wouldn't want to get close to him in a rainsquall. Those guys can run you over without even knowing it."

"If the visibility gets bad, turn on the radar. It's working, isn't it?"

"Supposed to be, but who can trust the damn things?"

"Turn it on," Ben said. "I'd like to take a look at it."

The radar was mounted beside the chart table. As Flint turned the dials a dim light appeared on the screen in roughly the outline of the coast.

"I guess it's working," Ben said. "There's the tanker, about six miles away."

"And it looks like a collision course," Flint said lugubriously.

"I'll bring her to starboard," Ben replied, and taking the wheel from Lawson, looked at the compass. "We're not going anywhere right now."

"Here she comes," Lawson said. "Man, look at that!"

A curtain of rain had just obscured the shore from view. It advanced slowly across the water, preceded by cat's-paws of wind which darted over the sea like the cavalry of an advancing army. With her sails slack the big yawl waited passively, like a young girl for her lover, half frightened, half eager, it seemed to Ben. There were a few scattered drops of rain, and then the first warning puff hit, tightening the sheets with a jerk. Heeling, the yawl gathered way and began to answer her helm. Whitecaps danced under the current of rain, which now was almost upon them.

"Here we go!" he shouted. "Slack off those sheets!"

There was the creak of blocks as he put the yawl on a broad reach before this new wind. Suddenly the squall was upon them, and the air was so full of rain that he could barely see the bow. With the rain was wind, enough to send the big yawl leaping ahead as though she were attempting to leap free of the water. Astern, the wake stretched like that of a speedboat, and all the rigging vibrated in the wind, twanging like the strings of a demented guitar.

Ben kept his eyes glued to the clew of the big jib, which was straining against its heavy nylon sheet like a frantic horse.

"By God, you'll take the sticks out of her!" Flint shouted.

"No!" Ben shouted back, his exhilaration growing as he found he had judged this squall right. "Come on, baby! You're made for this!"

The stately yawl dug her caprail into the smooth sea and began to tremble all over as he eased her a little into the wind. The big Genoa luffed with a crack like thunder, but when he paid her off again, she stood up all right, and it was obvious now that she could take the strain. Glancing from the sails to the cockpit, Ben saw that Penny was jumping up and down, partly to keep warm in the cold rain, but mostly from excitement. With her right hand she was holding on to a backstay, and she was dancing like a marionette on a string, her face radiant. The wind was so loud in the rigging that he could not make out what she was shouting, or perhaps singing, but her lips were moving, and her chin was tilted as though she were an opera star.

"That tanker's about two miles off the starboard bow now," Flint called from the radar set.

"Very well. Keep track of her."

With the passing of the edge of the rain curtain, visibility was improving, but Flint continued to be pessimistic.

"Skipper, we're still closing with her!" he shouted.

"I can see her now," Ben said. Mountainous in the mist ahead, the tanker loomed, close but far enough away for safety. She was steaming at a good sixteen knots, and her whole enormous black hull was glistening with the rain that spouted from her many scuppers, rain turned red from her rusty decks, like blood gushing from some great wounded beast.

"My God," Penny said as the tanker pounded by, "what a monster!"

Swallowed by the mist and the rain, the tanker disappeared as suddenly as she had come, and there was no sign of her but the distant beat of her engines and her huge propellers churning the sea.

"She like to kill us," Flint said, and he swallowed a white pill this time — probably a tranquilizer, Ben thought.

"But she was beautiful," Penny said. "Ben, that's a sight I'll never forget. So queerly beautiful!"

"Yes," he said. "Were you afraid?"

"I was scared to death, but what was your phrase — 'terror mixed with delight'?"

"Yes, I guess that's part of it. For a minute there I was afraid I had guessed wrong about the squall."

The wind was already beginning to ease now, and the yawl bounded along effortlessly, as though proud of having survived. The rain too was letting up.

"You damned near took the masts out of her," Flint said accusingly.

"No. We might have blown out a sail, but that's all. Nort must have gotten her into a hurricane to take the masts out of her."

"Damn near," Flint said. "Or so I hear."

"You weren't aboard?"

"I wouldn't go in one of them races for nothing! He leaves me ashore."

Ben laughed.

"Well, if this wind holds, we ought to have you back ashore by tomorrow. And I think I can handle her now if you want to hit the sack."

"I think I will," Flint said. "Do you want me to call Mr. Clay later?"

"No, let him sleep," Ben said. "Get Lawson to bring me some coffee, and one of those slicker jackets. Better bring two — it's getting cold."

Penny's hair was dripping and bedraggled, and the yellow oilskin much too big for her.

"You look about twelve years old," he said, smiling.

"I don't want that!"

"Why not?"

"That was an unhappy time for me. I'm sorry — I always feel gloomy when I hear about anyone being twelve years old."

"Do you mind if I ask what happened?"

"I don't mean to be morbid."

"Sharing sorrows isn't morbid."

"My mother died when I was twelve. She was hurt in an automobile accident and was in the hospital a long time."

"I'm sorry," he said, imagining the girl at the age of twelve walking down a long hospital corridor.

"She knew she was dying, and she kept saying to me, 'Anyway, you're twelve years old, and that's old enough to get along pretty well.' "

"I'm sorry," he said again.

The girl shrugged.

"All she worried about was me while she was dying. I hope I'll have a daughter. It must be wonderful to love someone that much."

"Yes."

"Of course, you know. I forgot. I guess it's not fair to ask whether you love your kids so much."

"I don't get to see them often," he said, feeling a small knot of pain in his stomach. "Maybe they'll come to the island for part of their summer vacation."

"I would like to meet your children," she said.

He tried to imagine what it would be like to introduce this girl as his wife to his children. Laura would be very polite, and would tell him she was happy for him, but he guessed that her eyes would be clouded. Benny would be silent, drawn into himself to the point of rudeness.

"I think my children would be astonished by you," he said.

"Why?"

"I'm afraid that all the women they know are strident and loud. No woman in my family stops talking for as much as an hour at a time, or denies herself the pleasure of telling the nearest man exactly what to do. My former wife never learned how to sail a boat, but if she had been aboard, she would have told me exactly how to weather that squall."

Penny laughed.

"She should have met my father," she said.

"Did he have a cure?"

"He wasn't an Italian-American, he was an Italian-Italian until the day he died, and yes, he had a cure."

"What was it?"

"One look. It was indescribable, but with it he could close any woman's mouth, even my mother's."

"Did it make your mother angry?"

"She adored him. Of course he made her angry, but she adored him."

"Silently?"

The girl laughed.

"Often silently. My mother came from a big Irish family in which the women talked all the time, and the men never said anything. She didn't like that. She told me once that my father was the only real man she had ever met in her life."

"It's good to hear about people who loved each other. Sometimes I catch myself forgetting that sort of thing ever exists."

"Me too," the girl said, and she fingered the clasps on the front of her coat absently. "It did exist for them," she said.

With the passing of the rain, the sun was trying to come out again, but the wind remained fair and strong.

"If this keeps up, we might be off the reef before noon," Ben said. The needle of the Kenyon log trembled steadily at eight knots.

"I'd like that," the girl said. "It's funny, you've talked so much about the island, I've half begun to think of it as home. Maybe it's because you call it that all the time. You're always saying, 'Home to the island . . .'"

"It was my home for a long time."

"When I was a kid I often dreamed about living on an island. In Ireland and in Italy I never felt at home, and in New Jersey I was kind of different too, because I went away almost every other year. I used to dream about an island. Somewhere I was sure a special one existed."

"I hope Janus Island won't be a disappointment. Perhaps I've built it up in your mind too much."

"I don't know what I'm hoping for, but it's good to hope for a change. For a long time there I forgot all about that dream of the special island that I would know was home."

"Dreams are good if they don't make reality disappointing. This island has mosquitoes, sand flies and a few rattle-snakes."

"Sounds like home, all right!" she said.

He laughed. The clouds cleared, and there was a splendid sunset, dying slowly over the distant coast. Curled up on the deck, Penny half slept, but sometimes he caught her studying his face as though she wanted to ask him many questions. All evening the big yawl charged along like a young mare homeward bound, while gulls circled and swooped around them.

When dusk came, Ben got the sextant from its box under the chart table and took star sights. They were not really necessary, but it was fun to use again the skills he had acquired so painfully in his youth. During all the years he had not been to sea, he had kept up with his navigation, occasionally taking sights in his back yard with a bubble sextant, as though unsure where his house was. This practice had helped, and now he found the calculations easy. A line from Arcturus, a line from Venus and a line from the moon crossed in a tiny triangle two miles from the spot he had estimated from his dead reckoning.

"We've begun to make some progress," he called from the chart table.

"Let me see!"

It was Nort's deep voice. He had shaved now, and wore immaculate white ducks and a blue shirt.

"You been taking star sights?" he asked, bending over the chart. "My God, you don't need a sextant any more. I got buttons I can push."

"I know," Ben said. "I still like the old way. You feeling better, Nort?"

"Feeling fine! But I've got to call the Coast. I'm getting a cast together, Ben. There's a lot of interest."

He went to his cabin, and from time to time Ben could

hear him talking, the voice urgent, but too low to be understood.

The night that followed was a strange one which Ben knew, while he was experiencing it, that he would never forget. Shortly after dusk the sky clouded up again, and instead of dying, as Ben had half expected, the wind gradually increased, and a short humpy sea made up. In the head below decks, Ben could hear Flint retching and cursing. Lawson rather sullenly asked whether he was expected to stand watches at night as well as cook the meals, and Ben told him no, he'd stay at the wheel as long as necessary. After a supper of hot soup and sandwiches, Penny took some pillows and blankets to the cockpit and curled up near Ben. The port running light turned the clew of the big Genoa jib and the arch of spray at the lee bow ruby red, and the dim light of the binnacle made the white blanket, in which the girl had wrapped herself like a shroud, give off a ghostly glow in the dark. At about nine o'clock the moon broke through the clouds and cast a pale golden path across the sea to a string of low sand keys which looked silvery in the distance. It was an eerie night, with wispy black clouds obscuring the stars overhead, the very kind of night, Ben thought, when the helmsmen of the Spanish galleons long ago must have been edgy, searching the dark shadows of the sea for the flash of breakers on an unknown reef, or for a glimpse of a sail which might mean that pirates had put out from the nest of islands abeam.

"These are strange waters," he said to Penny. "A movie about treasure here doesn't have to be entirely fiction."

He told her then a little about the old galleons and the naos which for centuries had groped down this coast on their way from South America to Spain, their holds laden with gold ingots consigned to the king. He told her too about the many modern wrecks in this region, about the hulk of a Hog Islander which had gone ashore in a gale during World War I which he had seen once through a glass-bottom bucket when he had been fishing as a small boy. The vessel had broken apart in the middle and had been festooned with seaweed streaming in the current. It had looked so ghostly that he had kept on rowing, despite the fact that a big grouper had slowly been circling the crazily tilted smokestack.

"It's a strange part of the country, made for violence," he continued, and told her about the rumrunners who had fought pitched battles with the Coast Guard cutters here during his own youth, giving him his first experience with the sound of distant gunfire, and the rumble of explosions while men were dying far off in the night. Later, during World War II, German submarines had sunk two tankers in this region, scattering the sandy beaches with corpses covered by black oil, and even now, he said, no one knew what illicit trade existed between the Keys and Cuba, less than ninety miles away.

She shivered, wrapping the blanket tighter around her.

"You seem to like it," she said.

"I guess I'm a romantic still. When I was a boy I studied the history of all the pirates. Old Blackbeard himself used to hide out here when the British got too close to Nassau. He was a great big man with a long black beard in which he used to burn little torches while he was fighting, so his victims would think they were up against the devil himself. I suppose nowadays we would think he was just a psychotic, but he seemed almost a hero when I was a boy."

"I'm glad I didn't live in those days," she said.

"In those days evil at least had the look of evil. In some ways Blackbeard seems quite innocent to me now. He didn't kill as many people as can be wiped out by proud patriots with one small bomb."

Close by the stern there was a loud slapping sound.

"What's that?" she asked in alarm.

"Probably a manta ray, a big devilfish. They jump and land with a sound like that, but they don't do anybody any harm."

"You're at home here," she said. "I can't imagine you going back to New York."

"Now, there is a place full of terrors!" he replied with a laugh.

"New Jersey too," she said. "When I have nightmares, it is always about New Jersey."

"What was it so terrible there?"

"Oh, my parents used to leave me there alone with an old aunt sometimes when they had to go away on business. My father was an importer, he had to travel all the time, and they got worried about taking me out of school."

"It's no fun to be alone."

"I hated my poor old aunt. She looked like a witch to me, but she was very nice when my mother died."

A big comber came hissing up astern, and he had to concentrate on his steering. When he turned again to Penny, she was asleep with the blanket drawn tight under her chin. For perhaps an hour he sat steering, content with the graceful motion of the yawl and the feeling of companionship the girl gave him. Then, just as the moon went under a cloud, she gave a sharp cry, followed by three low moans.

"You all right?" he asked sharply.

"Yes."

Sleepily she sat up, shaking her head.

"Have a bad dream?"

"I haven't had that one in a long time."

"Want to talk about it?"

"There was the screech of tires," she said. "That's all, and the feeling I had when my aunt told me my mother had been in an accident."

"I suppose talking about the past brought it back."

"I never saw the accident," she said. "They were driving back from New York and some drunken kid swerved right across the highway and hit them. Ever since, the screech of tires has done something to me, and I keep dreaming about it."

"Would you like a cup of coffee?"

"Can I get you one?"

"I think Lawson left a pot on the stove."

She disappeared and in a moment returned with two heavy mugs.

"I told my father about my dream once," she said, "and he said there was no screeching of tires. He'd had no warning at all."

"I used to dream about the screeching of tires too," he said.

"Did you ever lose anyone in an accident?"

"No, but almost. Whenever my wife got mad, she used to run out of the house and drive fast. We were terribly angry at each other at the time, but the thought of her killing herself terrified me. She used to threaten it sometimes. She said someday she would drive her car right into a bridge on the Merritt Parkway. She even had the place all picked out."

"Poor Ben."

"Poor Rita. She was in quite a few small accidents. Every time the State Police called, my heart flipped over."

"Is she all right now?"

"Apparently. She always said that the only thing wrong with her was me."

"It's hard for me to imagine that."

"I don't think I'm the same person with you that I was with her. Maybe men differ when they're with different women, and no two women know the same man."

"And no two men know the same woman," she said.

She went back to sleep. Almost immediately Nort came on deck.

"Do you want me to take her for a while, Ben?" he asked.

"I'm content," Ben replied. "I don't get a chance to sail much."

"Then I guess I'll turn in," Nort said with a yawn.

Toward dawn the wind started to moderate. In the last hour of darkness, there was a quick stab of light on the horizon, one point on the starboard bow.

"Janus Light," Ben said aloud.

Penny sat up quickly.

"We're here already?"

"The light makes the island look deceptively close. We have to keep well out to sea for another thirty miles, following the reef before we can double back and come in."

"I don't want to miss anything. Can I get you another cup of coffee?"

"That would be great."

It was a sullen sunrise with long low clouds on the horizon which made it look as though they were surrounded by islands of banked fires. The first rays of the sun glinted on the breakers foaming over the first barrier of Janus Reef about five miles away. Sending up geysers of spray, the reef stretched as far as the eye could see, and even at that distance could be heard the ominous booming of the distant surf.

"Imagine what it must have been like for those poor old Spaniards if they were driven onto that one dark night!" he said.

"Have they ever found any of the old wrecks here?"

"An occasional coin or two. Some old anchors and ballast stones . . ."

"Do you suppose any of them escaped alive?"

"Not much chance, but who knows?"

His mind was suddenly full of visions of what it must have been like to be shipwrecked here. First the sickening glimpse of the reef, with the old square-rigged ships helpless before a gale. The men probably jumped into the rigging when they hit, cursing, praying and sobbing as the masts went over the side. Most probably died right then, crushed by the breakers on the coral, but maybe a few grabbed pieces of wreckage and were driven ashore to Janus Island, there to be tortured by the very Indians they had tortured in their search for gold. Or had they wandered alone for years through the barren keys, dreaming of Spain and the women they had left behind?

Sitting on the lee side of the cockpit, Ben's gaze drifted from the compass to Penny's face to the luff of the big Genoa jib and back again, making sure that they were on course, that Penny was happy, that the sails were full. With a spoke of the wheel in one hand and a hot mug of coffee in the other, with good memories of one night with her and the anticipation of many more to come, he felt that no matter how painfully death might eventually come to him, he could honestly look back on this moment and say there had been more pleasure in his life than pain.

At about six in the morning the sun emerged from the clouds, and the wind shifted a little to the south. The sails began to luff, making that sinister cracking sound which Ben associated with so many storms of his youth. Giving Penny the wheel for a few seconds, Ben grabbed the mainsheet and looked up to trim the sail. To his astonishment, he saw Nort, whom he had supposed to be in his bunk, sitting high up on the crosstrees, his left hand nonchalantly hooked around a shroud, drinking from a silver flask held in his right hand. As he tipped the flask to his lips, the sun flashed so brilliantly on the burnished metal that Ben had to look away, but in that first glimpse he had seen the most curious look on Nort's face. The big man had been sitting there staring down into the water with a rapt expression, as though he could see not only the clear blue depths of the Gulf Stream with the occasional shadows of sharks, but the treasure of centuries: gold cannon, chests of coins — and a somber aquatic parade of all the men who had sailed these waters and had left their bones here. Perhaps that was his own imagination, Ben thought, but when he looked again, Nort still had that curiously intense stare, like the face of a child at the theater for the first time.

"Nort!" Ben called. "Good morning!"

Nort did not move, nor did he speak. He just sat there, sixty feet above the deck, gazing out over the sea, resting the flask on his left knee. As the yawl rolled in the ground swell, he swayed but did not tighten his arm around the shroud. There was something about him which made Penny think of a corpse propped in the rigging, and involuntarily she reached out a hand and gripped Ben's arm.

"Do you suppose he's drunk?" she whispered.

"Perhaps," Ben said, and he called, "Nort! *Nort!* Are you all right?"

Casually, as though Ben had not called before, Nort looked down and smiled.

"Of course, Ben," he said. "Are you?"

"Yes. How long have you been up there?"

"Oh, an hour or so. It's a great place to watch a sunrise."

Putting his flask in his hip pocket, Nort casually stood up and stepped into midair, lowering himself effortlessly hand over hand down the shroud. Landing lightly on deck, he gave a rather stiff nod to Penny and disappeared below decks.

"What is it about that man . . ." Penny began, and tightly compressed her lips.

"I don't know," Ben sighed.

The sight of Nort silhouetted against the sky had left them both strangely shaken, he realized, but why? What was wrong about going up the mast to watch a sunrise?

All morning Ben felt on edge. It was not until they got close enough to Janus Island to see the familiar outline of the beaches of his youth that his spirits were fully restored. The yellow sand of the point where his father's house had stood looked as though it had just emerged from the sea. All along the seaward side of the island a line of royal palms grew with their leaves rippling in the morning wind, yellowish-green in motion against the still deep green of the pines behind them. Penny looked at the shore without saying anything, but her whole face reflected her delight.

"The houses are hidden in the foliage," Ben said. "As soon as we get ashore, I'll drive you around."

"The houses have red tiles," she said.

"Can you see them yet?"

"Just behind those pines, but I think I always knew it."

"Do you want me to call Mr. Clay?" Flint asked Ben.

"No. He knows we're here."

Passing the end of the island, they coasted into the quiet bay which separated it from the keys inshore. On a long concrete jetty at the other end of the island from the ferry landing a blue station wagon appeared.

"That's probably George, the caretaker," Flint said. "He must've been watching for us."

"Better get the fenders over," Ben said to Flint. "I'll bring her in port side to."

"Aye, aye, sir," Flint said, sounding much more cheerful now that land was near. "Hey Lawson! Give me a hand."

"Tell me when your mooring lines are ready," Ben said, pushing the engine into neutral.

"The lines are ready now, sir!" Flint boomed. "Had them ready for half an hour."

Ben steered the big yawl nearer the wharf. Closer and closer he edged, until Flint could step ashore with the bow line.

"Put out all lines and double up," Ben said.

"All lines and double up!" Flint sang out joyfully.

Ashore, George Grey was studying the girl, Ben saw, his

big dark face impassive. Sitting on the piling by the car, Grey made no move to help Lawson and Flint put out the remaining lines.

"Everything's secure now, sir," Flint called.

Standing on the doghouse, Penny was looking around eagerly, her lips parted. Ben switched off the big engine, and there was a moment of profound silence.

Immediately Nort came on deck. He was, to Ben's surprise, dressed for the city: polished black shoes, dark blue suit, light gray felt hat.

"Ben, I've been in touch with some of my boys in New York and on the Coast," he said. "These new developments are snowballing, and I've got to get back for a day or two. Let me check you out on some of this equipment before I go."

"All right," Ben said. He was curious about the mysterious "new developments" and delighted to be left alone with Penny for a few days. As so often happened, Nort seemed to fill him with so many emotions that they all canceled each other out, leaving him with a restless feeling of confusion.

"Of course you'd better not monkey with the radio gear," Nort said, leading the way to his cabin, "but you'll have to know the generator and the switchboard if you get away from dock current. Flint is a mechanical moron— you can't count on him for anything much but deck work."

For half an hour Nort briefed Ben on the complex electrical system he had installed in the yawl. Before Ben was sure he had mastered it, there was the whine of a light plane overhead.

"Oh, that's the float plane I called to Miami for," Nort said, squinting up through an open hatch. "He's going to take me to my jet."

While the little yellow airplane landed in the bay, Nort

conferred with George Grey about opening up various buildings on the island. Then he ripped a piece of paper from his wallet, wrote something on it, and gave it to Ben.

"At three P.M. tomorrow go to a pay phone in Key West and call me at this number in Los Angeles," he said. "Pay phones we can trust."

Then, without a word to Penny, Nort jumped into a dinghy and Flint rowed him out to the plane, which was drifting just off the end of the wharf. As soon as he climbed into the little cabin, the pilot started the engine, turned into the wind and raced across the bay, taking off just before he reached the beach. Within a minute there was nothing left of Nort but a small yellow dot high up against the sun.

Both Ben and Penny stood watching, shielding their eyes from the glare with their hands. As the buzz of the little plane faded into silence, Ben heard the call of a swamp thrush loud and clear, answered by many more. With a sudden rush of exuberance, he turned and gave Penny a hug.

"We're finally here, with nobody to watch over us!" he said, and holding out his arm toward the expanse of tropical vegetation and shining beaches, announced with relish, "I give you Janus Island!"

"Complete with mosquitoes and rattlesnakes?" she asked with a laugh.

"Complete with mosquitoes, rattlesnakes and acres and acres of the best oranges you ever ate!"

"Are those oranges growing over there?"

"A whole grove of them."

"I want an orange," she said. "Suddenly I want an orange more than I ever wanted anything in my life!"

Jumping ashore, she ran rapidly toward the orange trees which lined the beach by the other end of the jetty. He wanted to follow her, but the long night crouched at the wheel had left him tired. His shoulder still ached and his legs felt stiff as he climbed to the wharf. With the other men, he stood watching her as she swooped down upon a heavily laden orange tree. She returned with her arms full of fruit.

"I never knew a place in California where I could pick them," she said, smiling. "I always used to dream about picking oranges."

"That's one thing you can do here all you want."

George Grey stepped forward as though noticing them for the first time. "Hello, Mr. Powers," he said.

Physically George had changed surprisingly little in the past twenty years, Ben noticed, but his manner was far different from the cheerful man Ben remembered.

"It's good to see you, George," Ben said. "This is Miss Savodi. Penny, George Grey here takes care of the island."

"Pleased, miss," Grey said, and perhaps Ben imagined that a slight emphasis on the "miss" showed disapproval, the moral judgment of an old man who had long been a deacon in the Baptist church.

"Hello," the girl said, and held out her hand, but the big man looked away and busied himself with starting the car.

Quickly Penny returned her hand to her lap, where Ben covered it with his own. Raising the back of his hand to her lips, she kissed it, then picked up an orange from the seat.

"Some things are perfect," she said. "Look at the colors! Can you think of any way this could be improved upon?"

CHAPTER *11*

T<small>HE</small> back of George Grey's head somehow discouraged talk, and they rode silently toward the big house. The road from that end of the island led through sand dunes and groves of grapefruit and banana trees to the first of the row of houses on the beach. Obviously entranced, the girl sat erect, looking all around her like a child surrounded by Christmas presents. Just inside of the dunes, shortly before they reached the houses, Ben saw half-buried in the sand the skeleton of an old Bahaman sloop which had been tossed there by a hurricane long ago. It was, he realized with a kind of shock, a boat his father had once owned, or one very like it. In the old days his father had spent a lot of time aboard a sloop without sails in which he had installed a one-lunger. Loading his easel aboard, Paul had taken long solitary voyages over the reef, anchoring where the colors appealed to him most. Now the bleached bones of the sloop seemed to Ben almost to be a desecrated grave, and he averted his gaze. What would his father say to him now if he could see his son arriving on the island, a man close to his own age when he had died, with a young woman he had known only a few days?

He would have been deeply shocked, Ben was sure. His father would probably be able to understand him no more than he was able to understand the way his father had lived, apparently without passion, patient under the constant abuse of his wife, dedicated to painting pictures of the sea and the clouds. My God, how much I loved him, Ben thought.

"How much my father would have loved all this!" Penny said, her thoughts curiously parallel to his own. "He loved gardens and hot weather. He always planned to retire to Florida someday."

At the edge of the property surrounding Nort's house, the road cut inland to avoid disturbing the Clays' beach, and circled around by a chapel.

"What a pretty little church!" the girl said. "Can we go in?"

"I think so. George, will you stop the car for a few minutes?"

Wordlessly, George drew to the side of the road.

"A retired Episcopal minister used to be in charge," Ben said as they got out. "I don't know if anybody is here now."

He wondered if she was a practicing Roman Catholic who might stop at the door of a Protestant church, but without hesitation she walked up the three steps and took hold of the big brass doorknob, which had not been polished recently. Silently the door opened. The one room with a high-peaked roof was dimly lit by the sun streaming through blue and green stained-glass windows which old Cornelius Clay had had imported from Italy. There was the smell of the cedar rafters, dampness and old incense. Stepping into the shadows, Ben was almost suffocated by a thousand memories, as though all the ghosts of the past had been waiting to trap him here.

This was the church in which he had been married and where his father's funeral services had been held. In a corner behind the altar a wooden statue of Christ which his mother had carved stood staring down at him. In his own mind he had depreciated his mother's work, but this figure was surprisingly powerful, a muscular, brooding Christ that looked something like a defeated heavyweight prize-fighter.

That statue had made him nervous when at the age of twenty-four he had stood by this altar to get married, and Rita's hand had trembled as he slipped on the ring — how reasonable in retrospect their fears appeared! His mother had cried softly in the first pew and his father for the first time in years had sat stony-eyed and drunk. It had not been a happy wedding, and there was no reason to mourn it now.

"It's a beautiful chapel," Penny said.

Crossing herself, she knelt and made a brief prayer. Watching her lips move, Ben felt that no matter what her experience had been, the innocence of her face demanded some ceremony of love, an exchange of vows, songs to be sung and promises to be kept.

"Did you come here Sundays when you were a child?" she asked.

"Yes."

"My parents had a thing about religion. They were both Catholic, but Dad turned against the Church. It made me feel strange when I went to Mass. It seemed so beautiful and I couldn't understand why he hated it so much."

"Did he ever tell you why?"

"He said it made Mother hell to live with. She wouldn't practice birth control, and he was scared to death of having a lot of children. During the Depression, he was barely able to make a living, and had to travel all the time."

"That must have been very difficult."

"She finally gave in to him, as she always did, but she died thinking she was a sinner. I think she was sure she was going to hell."

The girl paused, and Ben saw that she was close to tears.

"When she talked about it, my father would start cursing," she continued. "He said, 'Any God that would put you in hell would be a damn idiot!'"

Saying this, she unconsciously fell into an Italian accent, and when she went to quote her mother, this was replaced by a strong Irish brogue.

"Mother always got furious at this. 'And don't be making it worse with blasphemy!' she'd say. 'Isn't one mortal sin at a time enough?'

"'Now is it blasphemy to say that a God that would set a fine woman like you on the coals is a demon? Never did a more noble, virtuous woman live!'

"My mother," Penny continued, "never knew whether to get more and more furious at the blasphemy or more and more pleased by the compliments."

"I wish I could remember things like that about my parents," Ben said.

"What do you remember?"

"Arguments about money and discussions of art."

In the corner the great figure of Christ his mother had

fashioned seemed to scowl at him. The atmosphere of the chapel was suddenly oppressive.

"The grounds outside are pretty," he said. "I'll show you around."

She preceded him. When they emerged into the sunlight, they saw that George Grey had gone.

"It's only a short walk to the house," Ben said. "I suppose he had work to do."

"He doesn't seem a very friendly type."

"I suppose he has plenty to be angry about. To be a colored man on a feudal estate, with an overlord like Nort isn't easy."

Ben looked up at the steeple.

"That's an old ship's bell somebody found out on the reef."

"Does it have a good sound?"

"I'd ring it for you, except everyone would think there was a fire or some sort of disaster. For years it's been used as an alarm. Once in a hurricane it was queer: the rope got loose and it rang like hell all by itself."

Going around the church, Ben pointed to a steep hill that looked like a high dune behind the cemetery.

"That's an Indian mound," he said. "When the first settlers came here, they found human bones buried there, so they decided to put their own cemetery next to it and make the whole thing hallowed ground. In my day, the Negroes wouldn't go near this place at night — see, there's a path beaten all the way around it."

"It's a pretty cemetery," she said.

"All neatly segregated for hundreds of years — and from the look of those new graves, it still is. I suppose that's one of the things George is bitter about."

On the white side of the cemetery there were several freshly made graves, probably from the retirement community Nort had developed at the northern end of the island, Ben thought, and in the far corner of the Negro side there was a new wooden cross before which a Negro woman knelt, planting pansies.

"My father is buried over here," Ben said, and led the way to a weathered marble slab with elaborate scrolls his mother had made, how could he say without love? In large letters she had carved the words: HERE LIES PAUL POWERS, A PAINTER, GONE TO THE SEA AND SKY HE LOVED SO MUCH.

"I like the inscription," the girl said.

"When I was younger it somehow embarrassed me, but now I like it, too."

Looking across the cemetery, Ben saw the Negro woman stand up. Silhouetted against the sky her heavy figure looked familiar. Slowly the woman walked toward them, and as she got closer, Ben recognized Minnie Lee, the daughter of the woman who had been his nurse.

"Minnie!" he said.

"Hello, Ben," she replied as though he had been away only a few days. "I see you got yourself a new girl."

"Penny, this is Minnie Lee, whose mother nursed me to life when I was a baby. Minnie, Penny Savodi."

"Hello," Penny said with a smile, and held out her hand.

"I'm glad you're pretty," Minnie said seriously. "Ben deserves a good woman."

Here at least there was no hint of disapproval.

"I'm sure he does," Penny said.

"Which is your mother's grave?" Ben asked.

"We just put up a new cross," Minnie said, pointing. "The old one crumbled clear away."

Slowly Ben walked through the gate of the low picket fence that separated the two parts of the cemetery. It was strange to see the new cedar cross with the freshly carved letters LILLIAN LEE, as though she had just died. Looking down at the bed of freshly planted pansies, he seemed almost to smell the warmth of the woman's house he had visited as a child. All his life, it seemed he had been oscillating between puritanical, intellectual women like his mother, and giving, sensual women like this half-remembered wet nurse.

"My mother sure was crazy about you," Minnie Lee said, staring down at the grave. "She talked about you more than any of her own."

"I guess she knew she gave me life, too," Ben said. "Even my own mother said I never would have lived without her."

"Did she look like you?" Penny asked Minnie.

"Lord no, not much. She was a lot prettier than I ever was. The men came running to Mama, and she left eight good kids behind her. Only one of 'em's dead and not one of 'em's sick or in jail!"

"I envy her," Penny said.

"You still got time!" Minnie retorted with a laugh.

"How many children do you have now?" Ben asked.

"Only four. Ben, stop by and see me before long, will you? There's a lot I'd like to talk to you about."

"I'll make a point of it."

With a friendly nod Minnie Lee walked down the path that led around the Indian mound toward the center of the island.

"She's nice," the girl said.

They started down the road which led to Nort's house. Penny seemed almost to dance beside him, exclaiming over the bougainvillaea vine which covered one garage and the hibiscus and the poinsettias which lined the road. When they came to the row of big houses, she paused.

"This must have been quite a place once. Doesn't anyone live here now?"

"Very few. They go to the Bahamas or Europe."

"If I had a place like this, I'd never leave!"

The road curved toward the beach just before they got to Nort's big house, and the boom of the surf was loud.

"Is this it?" she asked when she saw the high old imitation Spanish villa. One wall was covered by a trumpet vine in full bloom.

"This is it."

"Be it ever so humble . . ." she said with a laugh. "I think it's beautiful."

"Let's go in. I could use a drink."

Before he rang the bell, George opened the door.

"I was sorry to leave you," he said. "I have so much to do . . ."

"I understand."

"I put your things in your rooms, the ones old Mrs. Clay used to have."

"Thanks," Ben said. "I know the way."

"Is there anything else you need?" George asked.

"Does Mr. Clay have a bottle of scotch around?"

"Yes. I'll have the maid bring one."

"What time is lunch?"

"In about an hour."

"I wonder," Ben said, hesitating, thinking he should do something special for Penny to celebrate their arrival. "I wonder, does Nort still keep a wine cellar?"

"A few bottles are left."

"Do you have any champagne? I'll straighten it out with Mr. Clay later."

"I don't think it's champagne, but there's wine. I'll have the cook put a bottle on ice."

"Thank you," Ben said, and to the girl added, "Having you here is a festive occasion for me. I was alone on this island for such a long time."

"A yacht, a mansion, wine, a thoughtful man!" she replied. "This is pretty festive for me, too!"

They walked through a big living room with some of the furniture still shrouded in sheets.

"Here's our place," Ben said, opening the door to a downstairs suite.

"How grand!" Penny said, looking through the French doors to the terrace and the beach beyond. "How long do you think we'll have all this to ourselves?"

"Maybe we'll find out when I call Nort tomorrow. We have twenty-four hours of privacy at least!"

There was a knock on the door, and a Negro maid appeared with a tray, on which was a bottle of scotch and two glasses beside a bowl of ice and a pitcher of water.

"Want a drink?" he asked Penny.

"I think I'll wait for the wine."

Looking through the open door to the bedroom, he saw that Grey had placed her suitcase on the big double bed.

Sitting down in front of a bureau, Penny began to comb her hair, her face serious, or just tired, perhaps.

"Is there time for me to take a shower before lunch?" she asked.

"Plenty."

His shoulder was aching and he poured himself a drink. She disappeared into the bathroom and shut the door. In a few moments he heard the water running.

Finding that his sleepless night was catching up with him, Ben took off his clothes, removed the suitcase from the big bed, and lay down. He was almost asleep when Penny came out with a towel loosely draped around her waist.

"Damn!" he said.

"What's the matter?"

"Here we're finally alone in a marvelous room, and I'm so tired I can't move a muscle!"

She laughed.

"How's your shoulder?"

"There's a twinge now and then. Bursitis, I guess."

"Are you too tired for a massage? Tell me if you just want me to go away and let you sleep."

"I don't want you to go away," he said. "I'm in terrible shape. You're so pretty I can't take my eyes off you and I'm so tired I can't keep them open."

"Just lie on your stomach and see if I can make you comfortable."

Kneeling over him, she pulled back the sheet and he felt her fingers expertly kneading the muscles of his shoulders and back.

"Thank you," he said. "God, that's marvelous!"

"Do you like it harder or more gentle?"

"Every way. You've got good hands!"

"And you've got a good strong back. Relax! Your muscles are all tense."

"I can't relax. I feel I should be doing something for you."

"You can do me later if you want, but I enjoy this."

"What are you doing now?"

"Does it hurt?"

"No, it feels lovely."

"Then relax. Go to sleep if you like. I'll be right here."

"I can't go to sleep. You're making me feel more and more sexy."

"Would it help if we did something about that?"

"I'm too exhausted for any gymnastics."

"Just relax, but turn over," she said. "Let's see what I can do for you without making you move a muscle."

The last sensation he remembered before slipping into a deep sleep was Penny sponging off his sweating body with a hot towel followed by cool ones.

"Penny, do women ever remain this wonderful for long?" he wanted to ask, but there was the luxury of weariness so strong it was taking possession of him like a drug, making it impossible to form the words, and all he could manage was a contented sigh.

CHAPTER *12*

BEN not only missed lunch, but slept clear through dinner, for Penny would not let anyone disturb him. When he finally did awake, it was dark, and there was no sound but the rhythmic breaking of the surf on the reef. For a moment he lay confused, half thinking that time had reversed itself and he was in his father's house near the tip of the island before the hurricane. Either memory or imagination carried him far back, back to the time when he had lain waiting to hear the Negro servants laughing and banging dishes in the kitchen as they prepared breakfast; even further back, in fact or fantasy, when he had perhaps lain waiting for Lillian Lee to come in and playfully spank his bottom before pressing his face to her breast. Turning restlessly in the bed, he felt his arm touch Penny's hand.

"Ben?" she asked sleepily.

"Yes."

"You all right?"

"I'm fine. You?"

"Happy. Sleepy."

"Go to sleep," he said, and groping in the dark, kissed her fragrant shoulder. "I'll be in the next room."

Feeling his way in the dark, Ben found the curtains at the French doors of the sitting room and drew them, flooding the floor with moonlight. Glancing at his watch, he saw that it was a little after three in the morning. On the coffee table was a tray covered with a white napkin, and he realized he was hungry. Shutting the bedroom door, he put on a light and removed the napkin.

There was a cold boiled Florida lobster with mayonnaise on a paper plate and two cans of beer in a pitcher of ice water. There were also some big navel oranges and some tiny red sugar bananas. A note beside the plate said, "Darling, I thought you should sleep. I got this from the kitchen. If you want anything else, don't hesitate to wake me up. For years on ships, in planes and in hospitals, I have gotten up in the middle of the night to serve strangers. Why shouldn't I do it for a man I love?"

The note was signed with a very small "P," and he sat looking at it for a long while before he began eating. Somehow he was growing apprehensive. It was almost too good. After all, he had had other affairs which started well, if not with quite the intensity of this one, and within a few months or a few days, each girl had turned into a sad creature whose attractions he had been unable to understand at all.

It would be good to do everything he could to make this happiness last for him and this girl, he thought. It would be good to see how long he could actually go without letting one unkind word escape his lips, not one question which might cause pain, not one hint of accusation. And when the inevitable process of boredom and mutual irritation set in, it was time he was able to avoid feeling monumentally hurt each time a woman did something to nick his self-esteem, it was time and past time he found out how to keep silent in the face of insult, to be reassuring in the face of fear, to meet boredom with cheerfulness. All these things he had rarely been able to do, and he doubted if anyone had a perfect record, but certainly he ought to be able to improve on his own past performances. This day, after all, had been a sweet day, and so had each of the days he had spent with Penny. The days of the future, he felt, were like a big collection of multicolored candies in a fancy jar his father had brought him from Miami years ago. It was fun to turn the jar over in one's hands and guess how many candies it contained. That could never be estimated correctly, but he had tried to eat the candy slowly, making each one last as long as possible, until he had dropped the jar and his mother had thrown the whole thing out, because she said the sweets were mixed with splinters of broken glass. That, in a way, was the story of his life, but this time he would be careful, trying to savor each day, taking care never to drop anything.

The lobster and the cold beer tasted fine, and so did the sweet little native bananas. Consulting his watch again, Ben realized that in about nine hours he would be calling Nort. Now that things were going so well in his own life, he found he was much more interested than he had been in making a movie and even in finding gold or anything else that would help him out of his financial straits.

For months he had felt too defeated and depressed to make any concrete plans. For instance, would it be possible to ask Rita or the court for a reduction in alimony? A rather fantastic schedule of payments had been set on the basis of his past earnings, which had proved to be a poor prediction of his present and future capacity. His savings and the various incomes from reruns, residuals and all the rest were pretty well used up now, even if the government didn't clamp down further. Would Rita fight a reduction of alimony, or would she ask the court to send him to jail?

The thought of that raised the hair on the back of his neck, but many men had gone to jail in such circumstances. If it were within Rita's power to have him locked up, would she?

He did not know. Toward the last they had both been so vindictive that anything could happen, but in the old days she had never willfully hurt anyone. Yet what if she were still jealous of him and learned that he wanted to remarry?

Anything could happen. After calling Nort he probably should call Jerry Grant and ask him what could be done. What if Jerry said there was no hope? Would he go for the rest of his life dragging the chains of his past? Would Rita ever remarry, thus setting him free, or might she die soon, perhaps carrying out her threat of suicide? How terrible to find himself hoping for the death of a woman he had lived with for so many years, the mother of his children, the center of all his youthful dreams! No, I would not want her to do that, he told himself. There is still some part of me that would have to die along with her.

Was there any realistic chance of her remarrying? What were the odds for a woman in her mid-forties with two children? And what were the odds of a woman giving up an income guaranteed for life when she might much more prudently just live with another man, adding her income to his? What kind of man was the elderly lawyer she was reputed to be seeing a lot of? Was he the kind of idealist who would want to marry her, making the break with her past a clean one?

The odds didn't seem too good.

If all the tax hearings went against him, he might owe the government a couple of hundred thousand dollars, Jerry Grant had said. Compounded at whatever interest they charged, five or six per cent, he would owe much more every day of his life. It was all rather like trying to sail a boat against the Gulf Stream in a light wind. One had the illusion of progress, but one was always going backward, and the only salvation was that sometimes that backward voyage could be pleasant.

The future was simply too complicated to think about, Ben concluded. Whatever happened, there was this beautiful *now*, this day which in a few hours would dawn. Finding he was getting sleepy again, Ben went back to bed.

"Ben?" Penny murmured as he climbed under the covers. "You all right?"

"Never better."

She sighed.

"Love you."

"And I love you."

Grateful that those old words rang true, he went back to sleep.

When he woke up the sun was in his eyes, and he was alone in bed. Blinking, he looked around the empty room, and he was filled with an old forgotten sense of loss which was no less powerful for being irrational.

"Penny?" he called, trying to keep the alarm out of his voice.

"I'm in here."

The door from the sitting room opened, and she came in, wearing only the bottom of her white bikini. Sunshine streaming through the window dappled her tanned skin, dancing on the white of her breasts, where her bathing suit had been.

"By God, that's a sight to wake up to!" he said.

"Sorry to be such a nudist, but I've washed all my dresses. They're drip-dry, but when you only have five you can't let them lie around."

"We'll get more in Key West today. I'm broke, but Nort's paying me five hundred dollars a week, and I have credit cards."

"Broke like this I want to be!" she laughed. "Come on in and have breakfast. I thought it would be nice to have it in here."

Putting on a bathrobe, he went to the sitting room, where he found an electric coffeepot going and an electric frying pan with bacon sizzling in it.

"They had all this stuff in the kitchen, and they didn't seem to mind if I took it here. They even lent me this."

She pointed to an old-fashioned glass orange squeezer.

"Did you tell me that you like absolutely fresh juice?"

"I did."

"Maybe it's silly when we can order it from the kitchen, but I find I like playing housewife. It's supposed to give us both ideas."

"You don't need the orange squeezer for that. Penny, I'll marry you any time that seems sensible to both of us. Don't you think that will take time?"

"Yes, but I love your good intentions!"

She gave him an enthusiastic kiss, and returned to the orange squeezer.

218

"What kind of oranges do you want?" she asked, eyeing a big wooden bowl of fruit she had picked that morning. "I never knew there were so many varieties."

"The navel oranges are good this time of year."

Picking a big plump one, she sliced it open.

"It's pink inside!"

"Those are called blood oranges. I used to love them when I was a kid."

"Do they taste different?"

"When your eyes are open."

"I almost played a joke on you this morning!" she said, squeezing the orange.

"How?"

"I felt very good when I got up, and I got this idea that it would be fun to dress up like a real island girl and surprise you. I put a kerchief around my waist and I put some of those flowers in my hair. Then I started to squeeze oranges and that ruined it."

She started to laugh.

"How?" he asked.

"Two squeezed half-oranges make a perfect bra for me, but instead of making me look sexy, they just made me look funny. I was going to come prancing in with these oranges stuck on me, doing the Queen of the Island bit to the hilt, but it got too ridiculous and I just broke up! I was afraid you'd think I was out of my mind."

Ben touched her face with his hand.

Giving him a quick smile, she took an egg from a bowl and cracked it into the frying pan.

It was exhilarating to sit there in the morning sun, drinking fresh orange juice and hot black coffee and looking forward to every hour of the day.

"Aren't you going to eat your eggs?" she asked.

"After that nice meal you left me last night, I'm not terribly hungry, and anyway I'm too excited to eat. I'm dying to show you the island. We don't have to be in Key West until noon."

"I'll slip into a dress," she said.

Borrowing a jeep from George, they started driving west across the island, away from the single row of big homes.

So far, nothing has changed, nothing at all, Ben thought, looking around him. On both sides of the road scrub palmetto, century plants and mangrove roots made this part of the island almost impenetrable, even for small boys. There was the peculiar smell of pitch dripping from pine trees in the sun, a thousand wild blossoms hidden in the undergrowth, drying seaweed and mud flats. Ahead the road seemed to lead directly into the azure sky, but then they reached the crest of a low hill, and turning, they got a breathtaking glimpse of the seaward side of the island, a long irregular beach of yellow sand laced by white breakers stretching on either side into the mist as far as the eye could see. In his childhood Ben had often boasted that the island was eleven miles long, curiously proud of a private estate that size even if it was not his, but of course the habitable part was only about three miles long, and the rest was a maze of sand strips that were awash in any storm, islets and reefs of coral. Now the beach looked as though it went on forever, without human habitation of any kind. On the seaward side of it, after the lacy ribbon of surf, there was a wide band of green water humped up by the ground swell that rode over the distant coral reef, lavender in the sun. Beyond the reef whitecaps flashed on the crest of rollers pounding in from the broad Atlantic. At the top of this, the only hill on the island, Ben's father had liked to sit and paint, or stare endlessly out over that distant expanse of blue water, his eyes enchanted, as though he could see all the way to Africa or perhaps beyond.

"Let's get out of the car," Penny said. "I want to look around."

Standing at the highest point, Penny looked first to the north and then to the south, following the beach into the haze with her eyes as far as she could. Then she looked landward, where the beach was fringed with royal palms old Corny Clay had planted, some still stately, some tortured and stunted by hurricanes. Within the row of palms was a bright green belt of carefully watered lawns, gardens and orange groves, above the leaves of which appeared the red-tiled roofs of the old houses.

"I never could have imagined such beauty," she said happily. "Drive slowly. I want to see the rest!"

Everything seemed created to increase their pleasure. As they rounded a turn to parallel the beach, they passed a grove in which Ben had often pilfered oranges as a boy, the joy of stealing increased by the knowledge that nothing would happen if he were caught, since Nort's father owned everything. This was a special grove in which many varieties of fruit were grown, big richly fleshed navel oranges, little sugar-water oranges, tart wild oranges with pitted skins, king oranges one could peel with no trouble, and dwarf tangerines. The branches of the trees were heavily laden now, the fruit shining brightly in the sun.

Paralleling the beach, the road passed the first of the houses friends of old Corny Clay had built. In Ben's youth these mansions had seemed more grand than the castles of England, and they still looked impressive with their sharp-peaked roofs rising in gables, and the wings spreading out in old-fashioned hospitality to embrace courtyards and patios, swimming pools and hidden gardens. In front of them the lawns glistened with water jetting from twirling sprinklers and there was a high row of bushes with bright red flowers, the name of which Ben forgot, while remembering how he used to pick them and suck honey beneath the stamen from a tiny cup. In passing he could almost feel the crisp flower-flesh in his teeth. He was so beguiled by this and by the other gardens they passed, containing lime trees and loquats he could remember climbing, that he did not notice until he came to the fifth house that the shades of almost all the windows were drawn, and that several doors were boarded up.

"Where is everyone?" Penny asked. "Hasn't the season started yet?"

"I guess maybe it's over," Ben said sadly.

"What do you mean?"

"As I said, rich people go mostly to the Bahamas now, and ordinary people don't like to come where there's no highway."

"You mean, *nobody* is here?" she asked. "What a waste!"

"Oh, I wouldn't say no one. Of course, Nort comes down every once in a while, and a few old people still use their houses. Nort sold a little land down at the north end, and some retired people have built some little places. A few of the natives stick around, but most of the colored people have gone where work is."

Stopping the jeep by the beach, Ben said, "Let's take a walk."

Slipping off their shoes and socks, they followed the shore for half an hour without seeing anyone. This seemed all the more eerie because the air, the sea and the land all seemed to be bursting with everything but human life. A dozen different kinds of gulls wheeled overhead, and pelicans skimmed over the sea just beyond the breakers, collapsing into an improbable bundle of feathers as they dived for fish. A school of porpoises rocked in the waves inside the reef, their backs glistening in the sun, and at their feet small fiddler crabs scurried back and forth in borrowed shells. When they sat down on a log to rest, a small striped lizard darted away, pursued by another. Troops of sandpipers followed the waves in and out. A white land crab retreated behind a clump of dried seaweed and raised its claws, preparing to fight.

But there were no people in sight. Getting restlessly to their feet, they continued to walk toward a bend in the beach where a forest of pines marched down to meet the sea.

When they rounded this curve, they saw two figures, two old men standing on the beach with big poles as they fished in the surf. Quickening their pace, they felt almost like running toward them. On the dunes beyond them they saw some small cinderblock houses, the retirement colony. The men were standing in rolled-up khaki trousers beside buckets in which they kept their bait. Heavily tanned, they were stripped to the waist.

By the time he came up to them, Ben was rather winded.

"Hello!" he said cheerily. "Catching anything?"

"Not yet," the bigger of the two said. He had three yellow teeth, and his chest was so emaciated that his ribs were clearly outlined. His friend was fat, with gray hair matted in the sweat of his belly, which fell in a series of folds from sagging breasts almost as developed as those of a woman. Penny glanced down at the sand. The man gave Ben a toothless grin.

"We never catch much," he said.

These certainly were not the trim-bodied people, elderly only by reason of the gray in their hair, which the advertisements for retirement homes depicted. Shocked as much by his own capacity for disgust as by them, Ben tried to smile pleasantly.

"Anyplace I can buy a Coke around here?"

"Up by the pool," the fat man said, waving his pole in the direction of the small houses.

"Thanks!" Penny said, and turning from the fishermen

with relief, they walked toward the settlement. As they left the sea, the sand was hot and dry on their feet. Ahead a stand of bamboo waved, cool and green in the sun. Pressing forward, they clambered over a low dune, and stopped in bewilderment.

Ahead of him was a small swimming pool surrounded by an expanse of concrete on which were concentric circles of deck chairs. Lying in the deck chairs in various stages of undress were a great many very old people. To Ben's eyes they looked almost like a collection of corpses, the pathetic remains of a Nazi death camp. The sun gave no illusion of health to these wasted bodies, shriveled legs, and arms as thin at the shoulder as at the wrist. Beyond this gathering was a red Coca-Cola machine by a table with a pitcher of water, but although Ben's throat was dry and his tongue parched, he could not force himself to go on, and he saw that Penny too was hanging back. In the center of the group an emaciated woman with a red kerchief covering her head stood up and rubbed suntan oil on her thin chest and sticklike thighs. Seeing Ben, she waved.

"You Mr. Clay?" she cried shrilly.

"No. No, I'm not."

With a skeletal arm, the woman beckoned.

"Can't hear you!" she said in a piercing voice.

They had to go nearer, and they did so, with Ben telling himself it was childish to be so strongly affected by the sight of what age does to flesh.

"I'm not Clay!" he shouted, and the whole fallen army looked up, staring at him out of sunken eyes.

"You work for him?" the standing apparition asked accusingly.

"No," Ben shouted back, reflecting that of course he now did.

"You tell him to come here! The air-conditioning doesn't work. He said he was going to have it fixed, but he never did."

"He said he was going to plant trees," a small man with a stubble of gray beard said, sitting up in his deck chair.

"I'll tell him when I see him," Ben replied, and hurried around the group to the pitcher of water. Taking a paper cup from a box, he drank greedily before putting a dime in the slot for a soft drink.

"Won't you join us?" the standing woman asked, holding the front of her bathing suit over shrunken breasts with a clawlike hand.

"No!" Ben said. "No, thank you! We have to be getting back!"

With waves they hoped were cheery, Ben and Penny strode rapidly toward the shelter of the dunes. As soon as they found themselves hidden from the rest of the world in a deep hollow of sand, they turned to each other without a word and fell into an embrace so strong it was as though each were trying to carry the other away from the portals of death. With the desperation of a boy who had never before made love, he found himself pulling off her dress, finding in her firm breasts and strong thighs a tangible youth he could cling to.

"I don't have a diaphragm with me, but I don't care. I want every drop of life you've got. I want to feel you in me, Ben!"

"But that's crazy," he said almost with a shudder.

"Is it? How long will it be till we're like them?"

"A long time. For you, at least."

"But not long enough to waste!"

"I've got to be responsible!" he said miserably. "I'm not even sure I can educate the children I've already got."

"I'm sorry," she said, seeing the look of torment in his eyes. "I don't want to make you feel bad. Let's go back and I'll get that damn piece of rubber."

But the mood had passed when they got back to the house, and they had to hurry to get to Key West on time to call Nort. After a sandwich and beer, Ben drove with

Penny to the old landing craft that acted as a private ferry between Janus Island and Pine Key, which in turn was connected with the Causeway. When the ferry left the landing with them aboard, a mulatto sailor came up to Ben.

"Hello, Ben Powers," he said.

"Hello. You're —— ?"

"They call me Navy. I'm one of Lillian Lee's sons."

"Of course. Glad to see you."

"I know you're a friend of Mr. Clay. Do you think you could talk him into putting this ferry on a scheduled run? The people here would sure appreciate it. Now half the time they have no way to get ashore."

"I can try."

"I know he don't like to have people telling him what to do. They keep writing him petitions, and it makes him angry. He still figures it's his island, and nobody is going to push him around."

"Would it cost more to make hourly runs?"

"Sometimes it would cost less! When the Clays are here, we're going all the time. They got a hundred friends they let call me any time they want to. And those retirement people! He promised them ferry service on demand, but they don't like me to bring over anybody else. The man before me on this job used to make a nice buck sneaking over tourists when no one was here."

"I'll talk to Mr. Clay," Ben said, thinking back to the days when knowing how to get around Nort's whims was a special talent of his. "I'm going to speak to him on the phone in a little while."

"If you can get hourly runs, a whole lot of people will be grateful to you," Navy said. "They'll say you're just like your old man used to be."

"My father? You knew him?"

"A little, like. I guess you know he helped a lot of people around here."

"How?" Ben asked in astonishment. Somehow this image of the good Samaritan did not fit the memory of the absentminded artist he had always considered his father.

"People could talk to your father. Colored people could, and in those days that wasn't too common. He was always willing to do what he could to help."

"I'm glad," Ben said, and he felt an unaccustomed surge of pride, along with surprise.

The ferry was approaching the opposite shore.

"That man knew my father," Ben said to Penny. "He liked him."

"I bet a lot of people did. You don't seem like the son of a completely ineffectual man."

"I need to feel that," Ben said. "I wish he had lived longer. I wish I had really known him."

The drive to Key West was a short one. It was only half-past two when they arrived.

"Let's have a beer before I put through the call," Ben said, feeling more and more nervous about talking to Nort.

Sitting down in a booth by a pay telephone in a bar, Ben nursed a scotch while Penny sipped a beer. All around them sailors sat, moodily staring into their glasses, and Ben remembered a hundred afternoons in navy towns where there was nothing to do but sit and drink beer. Several of the sailors kept glancing hungrily at Penny.

At a quarter to three a big boatswain's mate went into the telephone booth with a glass of beer in his hand, and showed no sign of completing his call.

"Let's get out of here," Ben said. "I'm supposed to call promptly at three."

In a glass telephone booth on the sidewalk down the street, Ben pulled Nort's letter out of his pocket and gave the operator the Hollywood number. In a surprisingly short time there was a click, and Nort's voice said, "Hello."

"This is Ben, Nort. How are you?"

"Good! Say, Ben, what was the name of that boat, that old sloop your father put the engine in?"

"The *Sea Swallow*," Ben said in astonishment. "Why?"

"Some people can imitate voices, and anybody can read a piece of paper. Call me nuts if you want, but I was afraid someone might have gone through your wallet and gotten the number I gave you. I wanted to be sure it was you."

"It's me," Ben replied, his heart sinking. Was he really dealing with a madman?

"I know you think I'm crazy, but the tax men are after me, just as they're after you, and they're not the only ones. Now listen, Ben, things are going great!"

"How?"

"I've got Dick Drake!"

"Who?"

"Dick Drake! Don't tell me you don't recognize the name!"

"The old movie actor?"

"He's not so old, and he has a pretty young wife. I've signed them both for our picture. We're going to be there in a couple of days!"

"We don't even have a script yet! I've hardly started!"

"Don't worry. It's all working out marvelously, Ben! Dick has always been fascinated by skin diving, and he loves this treasure idea. The only month he has free is right now. He and his wife and I and a few divers are just going to start looking. I've got a powerboat coming down, loaded with diving gear!"

"Good," Ben said, "but what about the movie?"

"I have another boat chartered for the camera crew. The whole technical gang will be there in a couple of days. Tell George to get all the guest cottages ready. He can use the men on the yawl and hire anyone he needs."

"A camera crew! Are you going to start shooting without a script?"

"They're going to film the search! A lot of underwater stuff with a pretty girl in it. And a major star. How can we go wrong? You can write a script about the historical part, and we'll have that shot in Hollywood."

"Just that and a long search aren't going to make a movie!"

"They will if we find the cannon! And if we don't, we'll fake an ending for the screen. We'll bring up cannon, even if we have to plant some!"

"O.K.," Ben said. "But I think it's going to be a wasteful way of shooting."

"All tax money," Nort said with satisfaction. "I can charge even the historical research up to our company, and Drake has bought in. It's a great chance for him to give his new wife a part. She can't act, but she's a beautiful kid."

"Does Drake think we can make a movie this way?"

"We're thinking of it as a documentary. I know we'll find something, Ben! I've got a lot of new documentation from my man in Spain. I have a graduate student digging up stuff there all the time."

"I sure hope *we* do!" Ben said.

"Even if it was just a historic relic of some kind, it would be good for a documentary. Drake says it will be marvelous publicity for him and his bride, even if nothing else. A lot of people are saying he's washed up. It will be great for all of us if we really find something."

"I'll say! It could save my life!"

"Don't forget, you're still cut in. I'm going to need you, Ben."

"I'll do what I can to help."

"How are things going for you, Ben? Is your little girl still keeping you in a fool's paradise?"

"Come on, Nort! We agreed —— "

"Don't blame me for being a little concerned, Ben! I depend on you to help me in my business, and I know that when she gets through with you, Nance and I are going to have to pick up the pieces."

"They will be happy pieces. Listen, Nort, I have something to talk to you about."

"What?"

"The people on the island are all upset about the ferry."

"Christ, they always are. They think it's their yacht. Tell them to go screw themselves."

"The thing is, I got to thinking that when we have a camera crew down here, and all those people, it might be more efficient to put the ferry on an hourly schedule. I've just been trying to get things ready for you. Anyway, I talked to some of those old people you sold houses to, and one of them raised hell."

"How do you mean?" Nort asked belligerently.

"He said too many tourists would come over if you had a regular schedule. He said you had no right to do it. He started talking a lot about law, and said he wouldn't let you do it."

"Screw him!" Nort said. "Put the ferry on a regular schedule tomorrow! When we get this whole gang down there, it will save money."

"Thanks, Nort. I knew you wouldn't let anybody push you around," Ben said with satisfaction.

"Not me, boy! Nobody pushes old Nort around. Now listen, Ben, I got one more job for you. Set up a press conference on the movie for me a week from today. Drake will be there. Get George to hire someone to clear off the airstrip. Put the bulldozer on it. That float plane is too small to bring in the press boys, and I want to keep my jet there anyway. Remember, the news conference is important if we're going to throw people off the scent of the real hunt. I bet people are trying like hell to figure out what you're doing there now."

"There haven't been any questions."

"Those people don't ask, they listen."

"All right. I'll set up the press conference."

"If George can't get the airstrip cleared in time, hold it in Miami. I want that press conference to stop rumors."

"O.K.," Ben said. "It will be held a week from today. I'll have to check the paper's deadlines to find the right time."

"That's the spirit!" Nort replied enthusiastically. "We're on the glory road, Ben! Can't you see those golden cannon coming up out of the sea right now?"

"Almost."

"I've already chartered a ten-ton crane on a barge. They'll be towing it down in a few days. It will be just right for working over the reef."

"That's great!" Ben said, bewildered and stimulated by the speed of developments.

"Hang on, Ben boy! We're going on quite a ride! The real glory trail after all these years!"

"I'll be with you!"

"See you in a couple of days. I'm taking delivery of the new powerboat in Miami and running it down with Drake."

"Great!"

"Keep your fingers crossed and your mouth shut, boy! Hope you haven't talked too much to that girl."

Ben said nothing.

"Can't tell about people, not till you've known them for years," Nort continued. "It's not beyond the realm of possibility that she was sent to you for a purpose."

"Come on, Nort, remember? We don't discuss my girl!"

"You can't trust people, Ben, unless they're you or me. Remember that!"

With an abrupt click, Nort hung up, leaving Ben exasperated. To him Nort was such a mixture of madness, shrewdness and high imagination that it was impossible to judge him. One thing was fairly clear: no matter how

231

insane he might be, Nort had come up with a way of recording himself on film in the company of an actor well enough known to insure distribution, and all at very little after-tax cost with some possibility of great gain. He might be crazy, but never stupid.

And Ben could still handle him a little, as the ferry incident proved, he reflected with satisfaction. Maybe, after all, his forebodings and premonitions of doom had been absurd. Maybe he was standing on the threshold of a profitable and exciting new adventure.

"Is everything all right?" Penny asked when he came out of the telephone booth.

"Keep your fingers crossed, darling," he said.

CHAPTER 13

W HEN Ben and Penny got back to the big house on Janus Island, they found George Grey sitting in an armchair in the back of the garage moodily drinking a can of beer. Still excited by his telephone call with Nort, Ben said, "George, we've got a big job ahead of us," and went on to relay the messages about opening up the guesthouses and putting the airstrip in shape.

"It can't be done," Grey said. "Not so fast."

"But he wants you to hire all the extra help you need!"

"Where?" Grey asked with passion. "Don't he know everybody's moved away? People won't put up with his kind of stuff nowadays. No ferry they can count on, no . . ."

"He told me to have the ferry put on a regular schedule."

"Does he think that's enough?"

"We can call the State Employment people," Ben continued.

"And get every drunk between here and Miami?"

The old man sounded not only angry but confused, perhaps baffled by so much activity after so many years of near solitude.

"I can help," Penny said. "Putting the house in shape doesn't seem to me to require too much work."

"It's not just putting the house in shape!" George said. "One cook can't take care of all these people he's talking about! Why are all these people coming here anyway?"

"Mr. Clay is planning to make a movie," Ben said.

"A movie?"

"That's right. There will be a lot going on here for quite a few weeks. I'm sure we can get together an adequate staff."

"It's not like the old days, Mr. Powers! If your father wanted anything, he could get it for a few bottles of whiskey. People want a lot more than that now."

"Whiskey?" Ben asked, puzzled.

With a grimace, George turned and walked toward the kitchen.

"I'll help him," Penny whispered to Ben. "I think he's just floored by all this."

Going to her room, she put on her bikini, tied a kerchief around her hair, and went to the kitchen to ask where the vacuum cleaner was kept. With that machine firmly in hand, her whole personality seemed to change. Gone was the somewhat languorous, sensual approximation of the dreams of his youth, and in her place was a grim-faced female fighting dirt with the fierce energy of a tennis star engaged in a championship match. Armed with broom, mop and dustcloth, she charged from room to room, seeking new worlds to conquer.

"Don't exhaust yourself," Ben said. "I'm going out and hire some people."

"Meanwhile, I'll do what I can. Don't worry about me. Working like this always makes me feel terribly virtuous, like going to church."

The first person he decided to try to hire was Minnie Lee. Driving toward her house he thought about her mother. According to all the tales he had been told, he had had colic badly, and had lost weight until it was feared he would die before he was six months old. A doctor had recommended a wet nurse, and Lillian Lee, who at the time had been only sixteen years old, had been found. She had just had a baby, but had no husband. Her lack of morality, the old physician had felt called upon to explain to Martha gravely, would not affect her milk.

Lillian had been given a room over the garage, and for five years that had been Ben's real home. Of course, he did not remember that part of his life, but he did remember being told he must not go there all the time, when he was perhaps six or seven. About that time Lillian had been fired and sent to the cottage in the center of the island from which she had come. Till the time he was fourteen or fifteen, Ben had often visited her there in secret, because he had learned that the very mention of her name made his mother angry.

"Who do you love best, Lillian Lee or me?" Martha had asked him often when he was six or seven, trying to make the question a joke, but it had never been funny to either of them.

"You!" Ben had replied dutifully, always knowing it was a lie. How curious to recollect that from the very beginning, he had so often been involved in some sort of triangle.

He had known it was wicked not to love his mother, not to be interested in sculpture, music, art and all the books she talked about. He had not really disbelieved his mother when, as he grew older, she explained that Lillian Lee was an evil woman who kept having babies without benefit of marriage, and who couldn't even read or write. But Lillian's cottage had had a peculiar aroma of geraniums, of cakes baking in the wood stove and of unwashed bodies, perhaps, but the very smell of the place had always made him feel joyous and relaxed. When he went there at the age of ten or eleven, Lillian had always hugged him silently, pulling his face down on her copious breast, and then sometimes she let him sit drinking sweet tea at the kitchen table while she rocked in an upholstered chair from Sears, Roebuck, and nursed her latest child.

Lillian had had no husband, and little money, but she had never gone to the law for child support. The many men she knew brought her chickens, hogs and vegetables when they could, and in huge iron kettles behind her house, she boiled most of the island's laundry and hung it out to dry in the sun. Perhaps it was sentimental to think of her as a happy woman, but Ben had seen her cry only once, when one of her children died of diphtheria. What he remembered about her most was the way her hands had touched him, hands like Penny's, always seeming to give a benediction, and the way she threw her head back when she laughed. Those were the things he remembered, those and the sight of her leaning over one of the big pots, stirring the laundry with a heavy paddle while steam rose in clouds around her head and the lines of sheets and dresses danced in the morning sun.

But no, those were not the only things he remembered about Lillian, Ben found as he prepared to visit one of her daughters. There was one more thing he remembered — a misty recollection of a day almost like a story told about somebody else, a morning when he was about fifteen years old and had sneaked away from his mother's house during Christmas vacation to see Lillian. He had approached her through veils of laundry, for in those days the island had been crowded at that time of year. A dozen lines of tablecloths and bedspreads had screened the spot where she usually worked. He had approached silently in the sand without meaning to surprise her. Then between two sheets parted in the wind, he had caught a glimpse of her sitting on a stump where she cut kindling wood. She had taken off her blouse and with her big chocolate breasts was nursing a boy two or three years old, who was standing at her waist. She was laughing, and she was not only nursing, she was teasing and playing with the child, moving her shoulders to take the nipple from his mouth, and brushing it over his eyes and face. The child too was laughing as he tried to grab first one breast and then the other.

To Ben at fifteen, all this had been more stimulating than just a pretty mother-and-child tableau. Behind the sheets he had stood watching her until she finally satisfied the child, holding his face firmly against her breast with her left hand while she massaged his plump little buttocks with her right. Only when she had finished and was buttoning her blouse did Ben walk through the lines of laundry as though he had just arrived.

"Hello, Lillian!" he had said.

"Benny!"

Pushing the child from her knee, she had come toward him, giving him her usual wholehearted embrace. There had been the familiar smell of sweat and laundry soap. He had not been able to help the fact that his breath seemed to be coming hard. Instead of stepping back after the hug, he pressed closer, and with his right hand fumbled at her breast.

It was softer than anything he remembered, and there was one delicious instant before he felt her body stiffen. Suddenly one strong arm pushed him back, and her hand came down, slapping him sharply across the face.

"You get outa here! Benny, what make you act like that?"

The indignation on her face sharpened the sting of his guilt.

"I'm sorry!"

"Don't you know better than fool around me like that? What you think your mother say?"

Choking, Ben whirled and ran through the lines of laundry, the wet sheets and dresses slapping him in the face just as Lillian had.

"You watch out!" he heard her shout behind him. "You get me and you both into a peck of trouble!"

With his heartbeat thundering in his ears, he kept on running until he collapsed in the soft sand of the dunes.

She knew him now, he thought. She knew his wickedness, the sinful thoughts that lay at his inner core. They had always been his own dread secret, but now one other person knew. Would she tell?

When he got home that night Ben sat through dinner stiff with fear, but his parents talked of sculpture and paintings, nothing else. A woman who came to the door wanted only to sell fish, and a tall Negro man who approached from the direction of Lillian's cottage kept on walking by, picking up empty bottles on the beach.

For a week Ben had lived in terror, but Lillian had kept his secret well. When, two weeks later, he met her bringing a wicker basket of laundry to his house, she smiled as though nothing had happened.

"Good morning, Benny!" she had said.

But that, he had known, was just an act for the benefit of his mother. Turning his face away, he had blushed.

Within a few days he had gone away to school, where he had been plagued by fantasies of Lillian. The other boys at the school in Miami had talked a lot about shagging colored girls, and he had begun almost to imagine that he had made love to Lillian there in the hot sand by the swaying lines of drying laundry.

"You got to watch out," a tall freckled boy had said. "That's a good way to get the syph and the clap."

The intensity of Ben's fantasy had been such that he had begun examining himself to see if had the dread symptoms the boy described. When he went back to Janus Island for Easter, he had been afraid to visit Lillian at all. That summer they had gone to Huntington, and it wasn't long after that that he had heard of her death, an exhausted old woman with eight children at the age of thirty-three.

"They don't live long on the island," his mother had said. "They don't eat right, and they have no idea of how to take care of themselves."

"And they don't get medical care," his father had added. "The Clays should start some sort of a clinic."

Ben had not gone to Lillian's funeral, because he had been away at school. He had never seen the place she was buried until, visiting his father's grave five years later, he had chanced to wander through the Negro part of the cemetery and had seen her name clumsily carved on a wooden cross. Without warning a storm of emotion had hit him, and choking with tears, he had gone to stand by his father's slab of marble, where it had seemed less embarrassing to let the grief out.

Since then he had rarely thought of Lillian, but the rutted sand road to the part of the island where the Negroes lived was as familiar as though he had traveled it yesterday.

"Isn't it crazy?" his mother had said. "With all this coastline to choose from when they first came here, they built in the very center of the island, where they get neither a breeze nor a view."

It was crazy, all right, all the winter visitors had agreed, for none of them had seen the island in a hurricane, when even their solidly built houses were menaced by the surf.

In a few minutes Ben came to a driveway leading to a tin-roofed shack with a wide porch on which geraniums and nasturtiums still grew in rusty coffee cans. Slowly Ben climbed the steps to the front door.

"Come in, Ben!" Minnie's soft voice called before he knocked.

The sweet, pungent smell was the same. In the dim light from shuttered windows he saw Minnie sitting in the same old rocking chair, the upholstery of which was now tattered. She was wearing a spotless yellow housedress. In her arms she held an infant, which she was feeding with a bottle. Perhaps she looked a little like her mother, perhaps not — it was strange that there was no picture of Lillian in his mind, only a feeling.

"Will you sit down?"

He sat at the same old table where he had drunk tea with three teaspoonfuls of sugar and great dollops of Carnation milk.

"Will you have a Coca-Cola?"

"No thanks," Ben said. "I just had breakfast."

"I wanted to see you," Minnie said. "Mother always set such store by you. I thought you might help."

"In what way?"

"Things are bad here, Mr. Powers, and we can't get nowhere with Mr. Clay. I was sure surprised when I heard you got him to run the ferry right."

"What else is wrong?"

"He fixed it so they ran the highway right by us without hooking us up. We got hardly any work here now, no schools, no doctor, nothing! People are leaving their homes here. Mr. Clay isn't the only one has land here, though he thinks he owns the island. We can't sell our land and we can't live on it. Nobody wants to come here any more, 'cepting them old people, and they don't have no money."

"What do you want me to ask him to do?"

"Stop raising hell every time the government wants to put in a bridge! Let us try to bring in some business."

"I'll talk to him," Ben said. "To be honest, I doubt if it will do any good."

"He won't listen to us. I think that man going plumb crazy! They already call this place Crazyman's Island around here!"

"What's he done to earn that?"

"You ask anybody! Running motorcycles on the beach and motorboats right up on the reef. Drinking and raising hell. His daddy never carried on like that."

"No."

"Can you tell me how you got him to run the ferry right?"

"I just exercised a little black magic."

"You sound just like your daddy when you say that! I can remember when he got the state to give my uncle a pension after the tree spraying made him blind. 'Just black magic,' he said when those checks started to arrive."

"Minnie, did you know my father very well?"

"You might say."

"It's funny, but I don't think I ever knew much about him. George told me my father could get anything he wanted, for just a few bottles of whiskey. I never saw whiskey in our house, and I can't imagine what he means by that."

Throwing her hands up, Minnie Lee laughed.

"You sure *don't* know much about your daddy!"

"What did George mean?"

"You really don't know?"

"No."

"Maybe that's what he wanted."

"I hate mysteries. Please . . ."

"Your daddy — well, for a time there, he was in the liquor business, you might say. Back in the Twenties . . ."

"My father was a bootlegger?" Ben asked in astonishment.

"He wasn't just no ordinary bootlegger. He was the best and he was honest."

"An honest bootlegger?"

His image of the ineffectual little painter was hard to dislodge. A bootlegger! Was that what he had been doing while he was puttering around the reef on his boat?

"He wasn't just a man who ran the stuff in," Minnie continued. "He worked with all of them. Liquor was a big business down here in them days. Fishermens, truck drivers, all kinds of people was in on it. Your daddy, he could work with all of them. He was the one man they all could trust."

"I can't imagine it," Ben said, trying to reconstruct his whole past. When his father had lost his mother's money in the Depression, was that the way he had got it back? Had his mother known about it? If so, how had she reconciled her need for money with her fanatic puritanism?

"He was a generous man," Minnie said. "My mother said she could always count on him. He paid for most of this house."

"He did?"

"You don't know about him and my mother?"

"Not very much."

Minnie Lee laughed.

"Well, they really thought a lot of each other. Your daddy, you know — my, he really liked the girls!"

242

"He did?"

"I wouldn't be surprised if you had more half brothers and sisters around here than you expect."

"I'll be damned!"

"Maybe I'm one, for all I know. My mother never thought things like that counted for much. She just said God was the father of us all."

"I never knew him at all," Ben said, thinking of how things must have been for his father when the money first ran out and his wife embarked on a career of vituperation. The bootlegging — had it been a desperate solution, or a joyful revenge against a world which had rejected his other work? And the girls, how well Ben was able to understand the need for them! He could see his father bringing him as an infant to Lillian Lee's house, when Lillian had been only sixteen years old, but already with a baby and sweet-flowing breasts. Seeing her with the baby, Paul Powers must have felt much as Ben did fifteen years later when he stood behind a curtain of laundry watching a kind of love play that made everything else seem unimportant. Was that why Lillian had been so shocked? Because she had even then been committed to his father?

"I guess he was afraid to talk out to you, because of your mother," Minnie said. "He never wanted to upset her."

"No," Ben said, and he realized with astonishment how different his mother was beginning to appear to him in this new light, his mother who had been so full of dire warnings about the results of illicit love. Had she simply been the wife of a philanderer at a time when venereal disease in Florida was unchecked? Had she turned to her wooden statues because she was afraid of her husband's touch?

"Ain't nothing to be ashamed of," Minnie said now. "There wasn't nobody on this island didn't like your old man."

Except my mother, Ben thought, and with bewilderment

he remembered the inscription on his father's tombstone: "Here lies . . . a painter, gone to the sea and sky he loved so much." He admired his mother's capacity to stick so stubbornly to memory or illusion, whichever it was. Perhaps his father had lived as a philandering bootlegger, but he had been buried as an artist, and his widow had worked night and day for a week to carve his tombstone.

"It's all very strange," Ben said. Pulling himself out of the past with enormous effort, he added, "A lot's going to be going on here. Mr. Clay is going to produce a movie."

"Is that what it is?"

"Had you heard something else?"

"Always been a rumor that Mr. Clay's going after gold."

"The movie's going to be about that."

"I don't know nothing about movies, but bits and pieces of gold been found for a long while. Your old man saw to selling some of it. The fishermens brought it to him. He knew all kinds of stories."

"Do you remember any of them?"

"A few. You remember the story about Big Sam?"

"No."

"I don't know if it's true, but the people tell it like it was. Big Sam was getting old, and his girl left him for another man. So Big Sam goes off in his boat, most people thought forever. Two, three days, though, Big Sam comes back, and he's got this big bar of gold."

"Does the story say where he found it?"

"That's what everybody wanted to know, but Big Sam don't say. He move back to his shack with that big bar of gold, and pretty soon his girl come back. Big Sam takes out his knife and he carves a piece off that gold bar. He cuts it like butter. He gives a piece to the girl to take to Miami to sell.

"Well, everybody start watching Big Sam. They figure when that gold is gone, he'll go back to look for more, and they want to see where. Big Sam can't even go to the woods to relieve himself without being watched.

"His girl come back from Miami, she got lots of new clothes. Everybody know Big Sam found gold. Two, three days later a boat full of mean men come from another island, and they break into Big Sam's shack. The girl scream and they kill her. Big Sam fight and they kill him. They take what's left of the gold and they go, but nobody ever did find where it all come from."

"That's quite a story," Ben said.

"Some say Big Sam told his brother, but his brother was afraid to get the gold, afraid people would start following him."

"Maybe he was sensible. Minnie, if you hear any more stories like that, will you let me know?"

"I'll let you know."

"What I came for," Ben said, feeling that his errand was quite an anticlimax, "was to ask if you'd like to help George put the house in shape. With so many coming, he has quite a job on his hands."

"No, not me," Minnie said. "George and me, we don't get along. Do you get along with him?"

"Not too well."

"Not even your daddy got along well with George. No, I wouldn't work with him. He's a man finds it too easy to stay mad."

"All right," Ben said, getting back in his car. "Don't forget to tell me if you hear any more stories about finding gold. This whole movie is about that."

Ben drove next to the big yawl to recruit Flint and Lawson for work on the airstrip and the house.

"You got to leave one of us here," Flint said. "They'll break in and steal everything."

"Who? Hardly anyone's here."

"They come from the other islands in all kinds of boats. Soon as they see someone's aboard, they go away. Last year Mr. Clay made me do some work ashore, and when I got back aboard, I found all the diving gear was missing, along with the sextant and a lot else."

"Did you ever find who did it?"

"Hell, no! How you even going to start looking? In these keys there must be ten thousand small boats. Some steal from the yachts, some trap crayfish out of season, and some trade with Cuba, but you can be sure of one thing: nobody rats on anybody else."

"I guess you'd better stay here," Ben said, "but Lawson can help out at the house."

"Lawson's gone," Flint said.

"Gone?"

"He just took his pay and said he needed a week off. Didn't say why."

Feeling frustrated, Ben went back to the big house, where Penny was still industriously cleaning.

Why had Lawson gone?

Had he, to use Nort's phrase, been "sent" by people who wanted to keep track of activities aboard the yawl? Was he making some kind of report, or receiving additional instructions? Or was this simply more evidence that Nort's paranoid vision of the world was catching? Probably the poor man had simply gone off to see his girl.

Why was he growing more and more suspicious of everyone? Old George Grey with his deep, unquenchable anger seemed more sinister all the time. Was he really just upset about getting the house ready, or did he want to do everything possible to discourage visitors and delay them? There was no real reason to suspect that, except that on this particular day Ben felt he had no reason to be sure of his estimates of anybody. Anyone could turn out to be entirely different from what he seemed. Fred Flint, for instance, looked like a sailor to outsail all other sailors, but he could neither navigate nor stomach the sea. Minnie Lee looked like no one he knew well, but might be his half sister. The light-colored ferryman might be his half brother, Ben found himself thinking, and he suddenly realized that this could become a mania, this business of staring into the eyes of every mulatto on the island, seeking some sign.

We are all brothers, he thought wryly.

If he hadn't known his own father well enough to write a character sketch of him that anyone else could recognize, how could he be sure of anyone? Penny, a pretty girl in a bathing suit, was apparently turning out to be a latent cleaning woman, lusting for the destruction of all dirt, and she also took better to the sea than Flint did.

"Penny!" he said as she flew by, brandishing a broom. "Stop!"

"Only six more rooms to go!"

"Let's take a swim. You don't have to do this."

"I told you. I like it. It makes me feel clean."

Leaving her to her work, he drove up to the old airstrip. Soft sand had drifted across it, and the last hurricane had erased the seaward end. Perhaps it would be possible for him to start working with the bulldozer himself, he thought, and drove to the garage where it was kept. Climbing onto the seat of the heavy machine, he fingered the huge levers and decided against any experimentation. If Nort wanted the airstrip cleared, he could hire an expert or try the job himself.

A few more days and he'll be here, Ben thought with a mixture of excitement and dismay. Of all the people he knew or thought he knew, Nort Clay was certainly the biggest enigma, the greatest mystery. Was Nort really mad or was he sane? And even if he were in part mad, wasn't it possible that he could stumble onto some great find? Who could doubt that there really was gold in the keys, or that Nort, sane or not, was capable of shrewd organization?

That night Ben was far too restless to sleep. Exhausted by her housecleaning and perhaps rendered too full of a feeling of virtue by it, Penny was disinclined to make love. In the dim light from the window, she lay sleeping contentedly beside him, a slight smile on her lips. How good a mask, he thought, the human face is! How bland his father had looked as he sat on top of the island's highest hill, staring out to sea, perhaps watching for signals! The *Sea Swallow!* Had his father had a sense of humor?

I didn't know him at all, Ben thought for the hundredth time that day. Not at all!

Did Benny and Laura understand *him?* And what did he really know about *them?*

What did he really know about Rita, whom he had loved so desperately for so many years, and then hated with such intensity? Had she changed, or had it been him?

And when he came right down to it, of course, what did he know about himself? Was he, after all, an idealistic man hopefully embarking on a new love affair that could lead to a happy marriage, or just another middle-aged lecher kidding himself? Was he a fairly clever man embarked on a movie and a treasure hunt which could prove immensely profitable, or was he a fool who had involved himself with a madman who really was pursuing death?

A deep sense of mystery and uncertainty engulfed him. Hour after hour he lay sleepless, and somehow he was not surprised when, at three in the morning, there was a quiet tap on his door. Jumping quietly from his bed, he opened the door and saw a small Negro boy.

"Mr. Flint, he says please come to the boat right away," the boy said. "He says to tell you it's mighty important."

Leaving Penny asleep, Ben hurried to the jetty where the yawl was moored. At the gangway, Flint met him, his clay pipe glowing.

248

"Sorry to wake you up, but Mr. Clay said to call you if . . ."

"What's happened?"

"You know, he wanted me to keep a radar watch on the reef. That's why he wanted the boat here."

"Oh?"

"He said he's tired of people poaching crayfish out of season, looking for wrecks and all the rest. Anyway, I been keeping a spot check, and tonight two boats are working off the reef."

"Let's have a look," Ben said and went to the doghouse. For several minutes he stared at the radar tube, which showed two small dots moving near the outer edge of the reef.

"They could be working lobster traps," he said.

"Yes."

Or, Ben thought, they could be working a wreck, perhaps taking their last big crack at it before the arrival of Nort. In the dark it would be impossible to tell what they were doing without close inspection. At that time of night it would be hard to take the big yawl out through the channel, and she drew too much water to go to that part of the reef anyway. For this trip, there was only the dinghy, which would have to be rowed if they were to avoid giving a warning.

Rowing a dinghy over the reef at night did not appeal to Ben greatly, because it would be easy to be drawn by the current into the surf and disaster. Furthermore, illegal fishermen or divers could be armed. Was it cowardice or good sense to avoid such an encounter?

"I don't know what's out there," Ben said, watching the dots, which were now standing still. "I think if I went out there to find out, I'd want more than two men in a dinghy."

"Don't have no dinghy," Flint said. "That's another

thing I wanted to tell you. I had it tied up astern. About midnight, I woke up and it was gone."

"Stolen?"

"Painter cut clean. Of course, they steal lots of dinghies around here, but it's never happened to us before."

"Then there's not much we can do for now," Ben said.

Getting out a chart he carefully marked the bearing and range of the activity on the reef. When Nort brought his powerboat down, that spot could be inspected, and perhaps it would turn out that they had been shown the way. At any rate, Nort would be pleased that his instructions had been followed.

Bidding Flint good night, Ben went back to his room, but still could not sleep. Outside, the surf pounded, sometimes seeming like a whisper, sometimes like an orchestra with many drums. Beside him the girl breathed rhythmically, her face seeming more a mask than ever. The shadows of the room, the curtains waving softly in the breeze, all seemed as if they could conceal mysteries. Somewhere in this room, as in Huntington, did Nort have his miserable little microphones hidden? If so, was that because he really had reason to fear people, or only because he was suffering from some perversion of wanting to know the truth about his friends and relatives, just as Ben always yearned to know, to break through the mysteries surrounding the people he loved?

Only time could tell, Ben thought; only time could unravel answers to the thousand questions in his mind. Gently kissing the girl's enigmatic face, he finally slept.

CHAPTER *14*

Wʜᴇɴ Ben woke up the next morning it was almost eleven and Penny had gone, perhaps to take a swim, perhaps to return to her cleaning. The sight of the empty place in the bed once again filled him with a vague sense of alarm, a legacy from all the angry women he had ever known, beginning with his mother, who had often exorcised her demons or eased her torment by rushing out of her bedroom and working all night. Dressing quickly, Ben

251

strode rapidly through the house. "Penny!" he called. "Penny!"

"She's not here."

The words were uttered in Nancy Clay's amused, sardonic voice. Whirling around in surprise, he saw her sitting in a black Italian campaign chair. She was wearing elaborately tailored white slacks and a white shirt, and she was, as usual, sporting her long cigarette holder. Once again Ben had the impression that there was something curiously witchlike about her. The chair was exactly like one she had in Huntington, and he had a vision of her being magically transported through the air in it, her cigarette held at a jaunty angle.

"Nance!" he said. "How did you get here?"

"I flew."

"You mean a plane was able to get down on that airstrip?"

"Nort hired a seaplane for me and a few of the others. He and Dick Drake are bringing some boats down tomorrow."

"Oh. Well. It's good to see you, Nance."

He had a feeling that he should get away from her as soon as possible, to tell Penny that she was there. The thought of the two women together made Penny seem vulnerable.

"Sit down," Nancy said. "I've got a lot I want to talk to you about, Ben."

"I'll be right back," Ben replied, making for the door.

"If you're looking for your girl, she's out in the guesthouse, cleaning. She's a darling to help."

"Thank you."

"Please sit down, won't you? We may not get many chances to talk alone."

Her invitation was uttered in the tone of an order.

Feeling the resentment that Nancy's orders always aroused in him, Ben sat down.

"You're looking well," Nancy said. "A suntan always did become you."

"Thank you."

"Have you been having fun down here, shacked up with that pretty little girl?"

"I'm not sure that's the way I would have phrased it, but yes, I've been having fun."

"It's really too bad, isn't it, that Nort has to come busting in with all his divers to interrupt your idyl?"

"He's got an interesting project going."

"Good. He's what I want to talk to you about, Ben. A lot depends on you — one hell of a lot."

"Why do you believe I'm so important to Nort?"

"Because you are the single human being in the entire world that he trusts. I've told you that. I'm not trying to be melodramatic, Ben, but I honestly think you are his last link to sanity, as well as to humanity. If you trust *no one*, you are insane. If there's one person left whom you *can* trust, you are still in communication with mankind."

"I shall try to deserve his trust," Ben said, sounding a little false to himself.

"It will take more than that. It's going to take understanding, Ben, and total care. You must never say anything critical of him anywhere, because he is always listening. This bugging craze of his is getting worse."

Nervously, Ben glanced around the room.

"No, not here yet," Nancy said. "At least, not so far as I know. But he's got the equipment on the yawl — he has it fitted out as a regular floating laboratory. Once he's been here a few days, you must assume he knows everything you say, even when you're on the beach. That sounds ridiculous, I realize, but he can put one of those little microphones in the seam of your bathing suit, in your girl's sunglasses, anywhere. Or he can aim one of those damn listening devices at you. And if he hears you say anything the least bit critical of him, his whole faith in you will snap. You have no idea how sensitive he is."

"I'll be careful," Ben said.

In this new world of suspicion he was suddenly unsure of whether Nancy was trying to build Nort's confidence in him or destroy it. What would Nort think if he already had this room bugged and could hear him now? Uneasily, Ben added, "I have nothing to hide. Anyway, I like Nort."

Nancy smiled.

"I want you to try to understand him," she continued. "In the last year this electronic craze of his has destroyed his faith in me, in the children, and every employee he has. There's not one of us who hasn't said something to hurt his feelings or done something he regards as immoral before we were aware of what was going on. You've got to understand that his mania has gone past simple eavesdropping. In some rooms he's got videotape, so that he can watch. Nort thinks of himself as a sort of censor of all human activity. I hope he never realizes what he really is: a voyeur."

"All this is hard for me to believe."

"I'm not asking you to believe, I'm begging you to be careful. He is also hiring detectives now to check up on everybody's past. The present is not enough for him. He lusts for our pasts."

"There is nothing in my past I can do much about."

"I'm not worried about you, I'm worried about that girl of yours. He has a whole team of detectives digging up everything they can about her."

"About Penny? I told him not to do that!"

"You can't stop him. He has detectives working full time for him, checking up on the divers, on Dick Drake's new wife, on everybody. He has a big filing system worked out, with a folder for everyone."

"I'm sure Penny has nothing to hide," Ben said.

"I hope not, but warn her, Ben. Nort can be such a bastard when he thinks he has something on anybody. He's such a puritan, you know — no one is quite so puritanical as an impotent man. You knew about that, didn't you?"

"No."

"I've always thought it was the whole key to his character, really. There's nothing physically wrong with him, he's just not interested. Once he had enough children to prove he was a man, he gave it up."

"I don't really think this is any of my business," Ben said.

"It is your business because you have to understand him, if only to protect yourself and your girl. I'm telling you, if he digs up something on her, he'll use it to torture her. That's his favorite cat-and-mouse game. There will be just a few allusions at first, and then the hints will get stronger until she is sure he knows."

"Knows *what?*"

"Does any of us have a completely clean past? Would you like to read her dossier when Nort gets it? I'm sure I can sneak you a copy."

"No," Ben said, "I don't want to see it."

Much to his dismay, he found that he was lying.

"You'll read it," Nancy said with a tinge of malicious amusement, "and she will never seem quite the same to you again."

"You're assuming that ignorance is the only basis of love."

"Isn't it?"

"Only for fools," he said.

"I must admit I'm curious to see whether you will turn out to be a fool. That's the trouble with Nort's mania, Ben — it's so terribly contagious. I find I'm looking forward to his detectives' reports, and when guests go to their rooms, I find myself drawn to the loudspeakers and ear-phones, despite myself. That's another source of his enjoyment: the corruption of those who disapprove of him."

"I don't think Nort is essentially an evil man," Ben said.

"That's right, be careful — you can't be dead sure he's not listening."

"Whether he is listening or not, I have confidence in his basic intentions."

"Marvelous! But let me tell you one more thing, Ben — never forget how self-destructive he is. His hiring you is the one self-protective thing he's done for a long time, and he really counts on you to keep him out of trouble."

"How?"

"Don't let let him fly a plane when he's drunk. Don't let him dive drunk, or drive drunk."

"How am I supposed to stop him?"

"He'll listen to you."

"He doesn't always listen to me. I don't want you to think I'm assuming a responsibility I can't handle."

"You'll handle it because he intends to keep you with him, and if he destroys himself, you won't have much of a chance. If you don't believe me, wait and see."

"Are you trying to scare me?"

"By no means. I'd do anything to prevent you from quitting if I thought gold fever wasn't enough. But it is."

"I wouldn't be too sure."

"I know you, Ben — you're the only person I really knew well, even before I saw your file. You're broke and in debt and often you are stupid, but you are incorruptible — almost."

"I never pretended to be incorruptible."

"That's wise. But like me you are corrupted only by small luxuries, or you wouldn't be here. You like a good boat, an island in the sun, good food, a girl — all small luxuries compared with liking power over people, too much knowledge about friends, cruelty, torture and death."

"Those things don't tempt me."

"No. Ben, treat me well. We'll need each other."

"How?"

"I have a feeling Nort isn't going to live very long, a feeling that can hardly be called superstition if you've seen him fly a plane lately. For some insane reason I still love him, and when he goes, I'm going to need you."

Ben said nothing.

"You have at least the memory of love for me," she continued. "I'm going to need someone I can kid myself into thinking loves me for more than Nort's money."

"If the need ever arises, I'm sure you'll find many men."

"Don't dismiss me too easily, Ben. That little girl of yours who is so industriously cleaning my guesthouse — do you think she will really stay with you for long?"

"I hope so."

"It's a forlorn hope. You need either youth or money to keep a woman like that."

"Perhaps."

"Why do you always try to link morality to the yearnings of your flesh? You want a poor young woman, not a rich old one, right?"

"I want a woman who loves me."

"If she has good breasts. Right?"

"Do you really think I'm all that simple?"

"Yes. But I love you for not pushing your simplicity further."

"How?"

"It has not yet occurred to you that life is not a matter of choice for intelligent people. If you married me, I would understand the lust for young flesh. I have a good deal of it in me, and before I realized that Nort was bugging me everywhere I went, I saw nothing wrong in indulging it from time to time. What do you think beach boys are for?"

"I'm one of those simpletons who had the idea that they were supposed to act as lifeguards and bring people suntan oil," Ben said evenly.

"Of course. Has it ever occurred to you that if you married me and the eighty-four million dollars I expect to receive, you could set yourself up in the motion-picture business and have a different starlet every night?"

"I can be perfectly honest when I say that that never has occurred to me," Ben said with a laugh. "What are you trying to play, beat-the-devil?"

"Perhaps," she said with a smile. "You know, I find your brand of honesty magnificent, but more than a little sad."

"Why?"

"Because you're going to end up so lonely and so broke. This girl will go eventually, and the next won't be quite as pretty. If Nort dies and you don't play ball with me, where will you work? You know perfectly well you're washed up as a television writer. I suppose you'll end up as the manager of a small motel somewhere in the Keys."

"Perhaps."

"I can see you now, prowling the bars for someone to pick up and being awakened in the middle of the night to plunge out some drunk's toilet."

"You make it sound so attractive."

"The future isn't really so hard to predict. You don't need a crystal ball or a deck of cards."

"Nancy, if you'll pardon me now, I think I'll find my girl and take a walk on the beach. My crystal ball tells me that we may have a great afternoon."

"I'm glad. But remember: treat me well, Ben. We will always be on the same side. Have fun looking for gold with Nort, but when you really want to find some, here I am."

"Nance, I think you like to play at being cynical."

"Is honesty cynical?"

"Sometimes. If, right now, I played ball with you, as you put it, you wouldn't want me any more, because the one thing you really like in me would have been destroyed: my poor battered virtue. You're playing a game with me, and a damned dangerous game at that. If Nort actually is bugging and checking up on everybody, he's of course sick, but that sickness seems less to me than this business of manipulating people's futures. Let me go, Nance. I like you, maybe only because we've known each other so long, but let me go — I can't be a friend if you put a chain around my neck."

Nancy took a long drag on her cigarette.

"How much do you owe the government?" she asked.

"What the hell has that got to do with it?"

"How much? One hundred thousand? Two hundred thousand? I forget what the report said."

"I don't think the hearings have established the exact sum yet."

"You never will be able to own anything, will you? No house, no boat, no money to leave your children or a young wife."

"Unless I get lucky, I'll be always without property," he said.

"And the debt will get bigger every year, won't it? And if you ever make enough to pay it back, the tax on your earnings will be so big there won't be much left to count against your debt."

"That's about the way it stands. Does the thought give you pleasure?"

"Then there's the alimony you owe. I left that out, didn't I?"

"I didn't know you were such a sadist."

Nancy smiled. "You were talking about chains around your neck. How much will it cost to send your children through college? Are they bright and tough enough to get scholarships?"

"I don't know."

"I'm not being sadistic," Nancy said quietly. "Sadists torture for pleasure, and I torture to get what I want."

"And what is that?"

"I want you to see something. See these hands of mine?"

She held out her hands.

"I see them," he said.

"They are old, aren't they? Age shows first in a woman's hands, and they're one part of the body one can't do much about. I know my hands are a little clawlike now, the skin wrinkled, the veins showing on the back."

"None of us is getting any younger," he said mildly.

"I know, but just look at my hands. And remember that with one stroke of a pen they could wipe out your debts and put your children through college. With another stroke they could give you everything you want in the future, including young girls with soft hands and creamy, saucy breasts."

"You really are a witch," he said.

"Of course! They would have burned me in Salem, but this is Janus Island, and they don't burn witches here. Remember my hands, Ben, the hands of a witch with artificial fingernails. But these gnarled fingers have strange powers which are recognized by the First National Bank."

"I'll remember," Ben said, and he had the rather sickening sensation that he would in fact never be able to forget them.

"Good," she said, and touched his forehead, almost in benediction. "Now go have fun on the beach with your pretty little girl, while this old woman sits with a drink and waits for her impotent husband to kill himself."

"Is it really that bad?" he asked with sudden compassion.

"It's really that bad. But don't feel sorry for me. My

hands have power. And when Nort dies, they will have more, if I just play my cards right. My hands won't really grow old, Ben. Nothing that grows more powerful can really be said to be growing old."

"I suppose that's true."

"Go on now. If you make love, take a blanket and do it well in the cool shadows of the dunes. Make it last a long time. I hope you can make that young woman tremble with enough joy to forget that, unlike me, you have no power in your hands, no power to do anything at all."

"Thank you for your blessing."

"Would you like to take some cold wine? A present from me and Nort?"

"That would be most welcome."

"The loaf of bread is a little out of date these days, but my freezer is loaded with steaks."

"If you insist."

"Would you like black satin sheets? Nort bought some once because he thought they would be marvelously sexy, but they didn't work for us. Want to give them a try?"

"That won't be necessary."

"Get out of here, you lucky bastard, and collect your lucky little girl. You'd better start making a habit of the beach, and use a different place each time, because next week you'll never know whether you're being bugged or not, or even whether you're being filmed. Do you have any idea what a telescopic lens can do?"

"No."

"Nort gets the most remarkable close-ups. Please be careful, Ben. You're one man I don't think I want to watch, and I don't want you to make Nort too envious. That could be dangerous."

"I'll be careful," Ben said.

"Shall we shake hands? I'm glad we had this little talk."

He shook her small dry hand and fled.

CHAPTER 15

When Ben got outside, the bright sunshine blinded him a little. Overhead, a small seaplane circled for a landing near the jetty. On the terrace two muscular young men in swimming trunks were unloading diving equipment from a jeep and putting the yellow scuba tanks in the shade under an awning. Two other young men were carrying big pasteboard cartons from a truck to the back door of the house. The clutter of equipment and the roar of a seaplane gave Ben the impression of a small invasion, and it was of course true, he reflected, that the island would soon be occupied by a fairly large army of motion-picture photographers, divers, and all the other people Nort had assembled. Already the plane was apparently establishing a shuttle service to Miami, and Nort himself would soon be there with two big boats for the cameramen and divers.

Even without any elaborate listening devices, the island would soon offer little privacy, and there would be much frantic work, Ben reflected. Checking over their equipment, the divers moved with the urgency and impatience of young men who feel themselves on the brink of great discoveries. They looked as though they could hardly wait to put on their elaborate rubber suits, festoon themselves with tanks, and go charging into the surf, there to break gold from the coral with their bare hands. As Ben watched, a young woman who had come with them walked from the truck with a box of regulators. About eighteen years old, she wore a bathing suit which exposed most of her tanned buxom body, but the young divers were so preoccupied with untangling rubber hoses that they didn't so much as glance at her. Across the courtyard, Penny came out of the guesthouse, her bikini stained with dirt and her face smudged.

"Hi!" she said. "I'm through."

"Thank God! How about a picnic on the beach?"

"Wonderful. I'm sick of cleaning. My urge to clean up the world has spent itself."

"We'll get some wine and steaks from George, and I'll see if I can borrow a car."

"This is a good place to get away from today," Penny said, rubbing the smudge on her cheek. "All hell is breaking loose. A whole line of cars and trucks is backed up waiting for the ferry, George said."

"I'll take you to see the place where my father built his house. It's the only part of the island I really own myself."

"I've been wanting to see it," she said with a smile. "And I do want to get out of here."

Whether he was living in a fool's paradise or not, he was beginning to love this girl very much, Ben realized as they climbed into the Ford station wagon and headed for the south end of the island. Filled with the enthusiasm of a child for a picnic, she had not waited to wash her face or comb her hair, because they were going to swim as soon as they got to the site of the old house. Laughing and chattering beside him in the car, she seemed the picture of innocence.

Why would anyone want to set detectives raking through the past of such a girl? What could they possibly find?

A good many lovers, Ben supposed, but why should that set his teeth on edge? How could he, a man who hated to spend a week alone, expect any twenty-eight-year-old woman to come to him without a fairly complicated sexual history?

If Nancy gives me some horrible dossier on her, I shall simply burn it without reading it, Ben told himself.

Does a man have to be ignorant in order to love?

Perhaps I do, Ben thought—perhaps I am sick enough for that.

Despite himself, the mental picture of a manila folder with Penny's name on it was beginning to obsess him. This is absurd, he thought. How would she feel if Nort handed her a complete dossier on me? What if she had to sit and hear tape recordings of every argument Rita and I ever had, every shabby proposition mumbled to a woman in a bar?

Ben was beginning to sweat. Could anyone love anybody on the basis of complete knowledge? Hadn't the good

Lord shown infinite wisdom in limiting the range of the ears and eyes, and making memories short?

No, Ben told himself — a man *could* love on the basis of complete knowledge. Nort's horrible electronics and his detectives do not expose other people as much as they expose him, his own incapacity for forgiveness, his own sickness. If I let Nort or Nancy give me their unholy knowledge of other people, I shall run only the danger of exposing myself.

I will burn her folder if it's offered to me, he concluded firmly.

"You'll read it," Nancy had said with amusement.

Why was she so bent on testing him in every conceivable way?

There was no answer to this, at least none that he could see.

"Look at those pelicans!" Penny said. "Wouldn't it be fun to glide like that?"

"Yes," he said, and he remembered that Nancy had told him he should warn Penny about Nort. What could any warning do but upset her? If Nort actually started to play some cat-and-mouse game with her, hinting he knew things she would not want him to know, then would be the time to take action. At any rate, this one beautiful day, when the whole island seemed to be theirs alone, should not be marred by dire forebodings about either the past or the future.

When they got near the southern tip of the island, the road turned to nothing but two ruts in soft sand. Afraid of getting the car stuck, they parked and walked. After only a few hundred yards the ruts faded out and a narrow foot-path led to that part of the island which had been almost torn in half by the hurricane that had destroyed his father's house. Plucking a piece of dune grass, Ben put it in his mouth, and the taste of the salt brought back so many memories of his youth that he half expected to see the house standing intact when they breasted the ridge of the last dune. The surf boomed louder on the end of the island as they approached, and there was something about the place which made the land seem hallowed, causing them both to walk in silence.

"There it is," Ben said as he reached the crest of the tallest dune.

Ahead of them, on a knoll which had once seemed safe near the very end of the island, was the ruin of his old home. Nothing stood now except a fireplace on a big hearthstone, a low wall of coquina rock outlining the basement, and some bricks tumbled about in the sand. On three sides of the knoll were wide flats of yellow sand containing shallow pools left by the retreating tide. There was little wind, and the pools reflected the blue sky and white clouds overhead.

"It's very beautiful," the girl said, sounding as though she were in church.

"Yes," he said. "Laura and I were going to come here for a couple of weeks. I don't think it would have worked. Soon she would have been looking for kids her own age."

"Or some man other than her father," Penny said with a smile.

"I'm not quite sure why I wanted to bring her here," Ben said. "For me this house has somehow never been really destroyed. You know, I can still see it the way it was, the veranda here, the garden over there. The living room had nice cypress paneling."

The enduring fireplace, Ben noted, had been left full of charred driftwood by other picnickers. On the heavy hearthstone there was still the figure of the god Janus which his mother had carved, one bearded face looking out to sea, the other inland.

"The god of beginnings," he said to Penny. "Old Janus

266

himself — his temple was closed only in time of peace, and that wasn't often."

"An old Italian god," the girl said. "I know him well."

Sitting down, she brushed sand from the hearthstone.

"It's a nice carving," she said. "One face is turned toward the future, the other toward the past."

"My mother did it. When I was younger I was embarrassed by her work, but now I'm beginning to think it's pretty good."

"When it gets dark, let's light a fire and cook our steaks here," she said.

"My father used to do that. He had a big iron grill. I can still remember how the pine logs blazed up to the fat. I always used to think that the steaks would be burned to ashes, but they never were."

"Tell me what the house was like."

He described it in detail, showing her on the sand where the piano had stood, where the kitchen had been, where his own bed had been built against a fragrant pine wall.

"My father was a bootlegger," he said, the phrase still sounding strange in his ears. "I used to think he was just an ineffectual artist who never made it, but he was a good bootlegger, much loved around here. I'm not sure what the morality of the situation is, but I think I'm glad."

"My father was an importer," she replied. "He used to say that an importer is just a smuggler who doesn't get caught. God, how he hated customs men! Free trade was almost a religion with him."

It was hot on the knoll with the sun high overhead.

"Let's go swimming," he said. "Those pools are marvelous. The shallow one next to the dunes is the warmest, because the tide has left it longest in the sun. As you go closer to the sea, the pools get cooler, and the one the breakers are spilling into is as cold as the ocean itself. I used to love to run from one to another when I was a boy."

"Can anyone see us here? I'm tired of this grimy bathing suit."

"Off with it!" he said, and taking off his own, ran down the side of the knoll to the warmest pool, where the water proved to be as hot as a bath. Splashing through it, he made a circuit of the pools, running through the shallow ones and diving into those that were deep enough. Beside him the girl ran like a slim tan shadow, whooping with joy as they plunged into the coolest pool, which was still churned to foam by the breakers.

When they tired, they walked back to the ruin of the house and spread out the blanket they had brought.

"We'll be roasted here," he said. "Maybe I can pile up some driftwood for a spot of shade."

Driftwood abounded all around the point. While he gathered it, she piled up a hill of sand on which to set it. Within half an hour he had erected a crude wall which effectively shadowed the hollow she had dug.

"This is nice," she said, lying on the cool, newly exposed sand. "Why don't you rebuild this place?"

"Because the hurricanes hit here almost every fall, and because the government would take it if they thought it was valuable enough to bother with."

"Couldn't we build just a temporary shack around the fireplace?"

"That would be fun," he said.

It was pleasant to lie on the cool sand, napping, with her hand casually stroking the muscles of his back. When they felt rested they swam again, plunging from the pools into the surf, and he showed her how to lie stiffly on the surface, riding the big ones in. After that they slept, and when they awoke the sun was just beginning to set in a bank of golden clouds.

"I'm famished," he said. "Let's build a fire and cook the steak."

"How do you do that without a grill?"

"We cut it in strips and hold it over the flames on sticks."

The wood left by former picnickers in the fireplace was dry and there were enough old paper cups and plates crammed between the logs by later visitors to make a search for tinder unnecessary. It was strange, Ben thought, to come back to the ruin of his father's house after so many years and be able to light a fire simply by striking a match. To get the sticks for the steak he had to walk along the high-tide line, looking for thin boards he could split with his knife. When he came back he found Penny shaking the blanket to free it from sand. Seen against the flames from the fireplace, she looked like a young Indian girl sending smoke signals, the blanket flying against the indigo sky, her lithe body looking black in silhouette.

"You are an ornament to the evening," he said, coming up beside her.

"Keep talking," she said with a laugh. "Flattery will get you everywhere."

Spreading the blanket on the sand, she lay down, gazing up at his head, which seemed to be balanced exactly between two stars.

"I wish we could live like this always," she said.

"I think you'd get tired of the sand flies."

"I don't mean just here. No fights, no arguments. You know, I'm scared to death of lousing it up?"

"Maybe we're more durable than we think."

"Are you going to be able to stand me when I get bitchy? I do, you know — sometimes I just can't help it. I have spells, sometimes three or four days at a time. I don't know why, but I lash out at everybody."

"I'll be all right if I don't think it's my fault."

"It wouldn't be. Sometimes I think my past just catches up with me. I get to thinking about the convent, and all that."

"You were in a convent?"

"When my mother died, my father didn't really know what to do with me. My aunt couldn't take care of me forever, and he had to travel all the time."

"It must have been very difficult."

"He took me back to Ireland to my mother's people, and they arranged for the convent. The nuns tried to be nice, I suppose, but it was such a dark place, so full of shadows and sad music. My father and mother had always been cheerful people. On the boats, when we traveled, they were always dancing."

"How long were you in the convent?"

"Until I went to nursing school, about four years. The only reason I wanted to be a nurse, I think, was so I could go back to the Cunard Line. I had to be either a nurse or a stewardess. I wanted to get back to all that dancing. Even in Third Class they always had some kind of orchestra."

"Was it fun when you finally made it back?"

"I loved the boat whistle, when we were leaving the first time. That brought everything back. But of course I was only twenty then, and I was very lonely. The whistle didn't bring my parents back."

Cutting up the steak, he held the strips over the fire, and the flames blazed up.

"I met a good many men," the girl said. "I was always in love." She looked at him quickly. "Do you mind my saying that?"

"I guess most people are always in love when they're twenty."

"It took me a long while to learn that most men don't take a little nurse they meet on the Cunard Line very seriously. I've never been smart that way."

"Neither have I."

"I guess I've always been so damn lonely I fell for anyone who'd give me a smile. After a few trips I stopped thinking of the Cunard Line as home. That was when I started to dream about an island."

"Is this place anything like that dream?"

"You'd be surprised how much! That's why I don't want to do anything to mess it up. All these people flying in scare me — I have a feeling that everything is going to change."

"We can keep this spot here just as it is."

"Will you still like me when there are a lot of people around? I mean, I know you were terribly lonely when we met."

"I will still like you."

Taking the wine bottle from the place he had buried it to keep it cool, he wiped it off and opened it.

"No glasses," he said, passing the bottle to her.

Holding the bottle in two hands, like a child, she tilted it up.

"That's good!" she said. "What is it?"

"I don't even know — there are a lot of old bottles down there in the cellar with all the labels mildewed off. I suppose there's some slight chance that my father 'imported' it."

She handed the bottle to him, and he found it a good red wine, slightly effervescent.

"Your steak, madam," he said, handing her a stick. "It's rare and it's hot."

"Marvelous."

"If you wave it around a little, it will cool."

"How efficient!"

After tracing several circles in the air with the stick, she took the strip of steak off and began chewing it with relish.

"Best steak I ever ate," she said. "Better than the Cunard Line can do, even in First Class."

"It takes years of training," he said modestly, putting another strip over the fire.

"Ben? Will you be angry if I ask you something?"

"I suppose that depends."

"Were you serious when you said we might get married if everything works out all right?"

"Do you want a man who can never own anything, who will always be in debt?"

"That doesn't seem real to me. You said they'd let you live."

"But not accumulate property."

"I don't want property, but I do want a husband, Ben, and someday I want children. I know it isn't fair to ask you that. I mean, you have two already, and . . ."

". . . and I am a little old to be taking on new responsibilities, when I can't even discharge the old ones very well. I don't know. I'm hardly the ideal man to choose as a father."

"I wouldn't want you to father children just for me. Do you like children?"

"If one has a happy marriage, yes. If I can just make sure I can provide the necessities . . ."

"I can help. I can always make six or seven thousand a year, anywhere there's a hospital."

"I wouldn't want you to have to work."

"Do you have any idea how much I ache to have someone to work for?"

"Yes. I think I do."

"I've got lots of energy, Ben. I can take care of a child and work too, if you'll help. Or does that all sound terribly grubby to you?"

"No. It doesn't sound at all grubby."

"How long do you think we should wait before taking a chance that we're not making some terrible mistake?"

"I don't know that we can ever be completely sure."

"I feel reckless, Ben! I know it's wrong, but I feel wild tonight. I think what I really want to do is to make love

272

and have a child and make the future instead of waiting for it. I still want to make love without any goddam piece of rubber or pills to prevent life. I want to squeeze all the life there is in you into me, where it can grow and be born into the world. I don't want to be afraid any more."

"But I'm too old and too cautious for that," he said, his voice melancholy.

"I'll bet I can make you feel young and reckless!"

"But — be-before I have a child, be-before . . ."

To his astonishment, he was stuttering.

"Before you have a child? Oh, Ben! I'm good with children. I've taken care of whole wards of kids. I always applied for the children's ward, every hospital I went to. There was a time when I thought seriously of having a child even if no one I liked would marry me."

"That would not have been wise."

"Are you sure? Is complete loneliness wisdom? If I wasn't supposed to have a child, God wouldn't have made me ache for one the way I did. I've kept monkeys, Ben, and kittens in a one-room apartment, even when I was traveling and had to pay the janitor to take care of them. Really, I've been half crazy on the subject. Once I bought a puppy and took it home and put it to my breast, just to see what it was like."

"There are hundreds of lonely men who would marry you."

"I know quite a lot about lonely men. Loneliness is easy to find, but not kindness. Damn you, the more you tell me what a lousy father you'd make, the more I think you'd make a marvelous one. I never met anyone so responsible in my life! You're always thinking of everybody except yourself."

"That isn't true."

"I can make a good wife to you, Ben, believe me I can.

What if the gods are against us, and it only does last a few years? That's better than nothing, isn't it?"

"Yes."

"Isn't everything temporary? The main thing is to use what time we've got as best we can. Come here, damn it! Let's stop talking!"

He made love to her then, feeling he was being drawn into a hurricane totally beyond his control. The wine bottle got turned over, and he found himself picking it up and pouring it over her body, anointing her, perhaps, or following out some half-forgotten libidinous fantasy, but forgetting that in a surge of release which made him feel as though he had dropped a thousand chains. Her breasts were salty before they flowed with wine, and her laugh was a shout of exultation.

"I want to be washed in wine," she whispered. "It's an old dream of mine. Let's have a real orgy, Ben. Pour it all over me."

It was the only orgy he had ever had which, miraculously, left him feeling clean.

"The bottle's empty," she said afterward, "but at least we won't have a hangover."

"Abstinence, at last I have found you!" he said with a laugh. "Let's take another swim."

The tide had come up, but had not yet reached the pool nearest the dunes, which lay like a mirror, with the moon in its center. The water there was still warm from the sun and just deep enough to allow them to float on their backs.

"Thanks for tonight, Ben," she said. "Probably I won't have a baby, but it would be a lovely night for the miracle to begin, wouldn't it?"

"Yes, it's a very good night for that."

"I don't want you to worry about me. No matter what happens, I can always take care of myself."

"I'm not going to worry, but I'm going to work. When

all is said and done, I've got to get some money together. And I used to wonder why those old Spaniards roamed so far and fought so hard for gold."

"I don't need gold!"

"But babies do. And regardless of what happens as a result of tonight, I can see that if we stick together long enough, there are going to be some sparks from this fire."

"Have you ever heard of a baby crying for gold?"

"Call it tuition, call it life insurance, call it money for medical bills. It's still gold, and I aim to get some."

"Do you really think it can be found, like in a movie?"

"There are many ways to find it, but one way or another, I'm going to get us our share."

It was still warm, and after drying off before the fire, they decided to spend the night there instead of going back to the big and now busy house. Stretched out on the warm sand with the blanket over her, Penny went to sleep almost immediately, but for a long time Ben lay awake. Somehow he felt he was preparing for an enormous battle which he did not understand, knowing only that he had to win. Beside him Penny slept, perhaps already pregnant. How many savages had slept on this very beach, while the man cradled a spear to protect his woman and his child?

It is an old battle and perhaps I am too old for it, Ben thought. There was no really rational way of justifying the hope he found growing within him, a feeling amounting almost to a conviction that finally, despite all, he might possibly emerge victorious.

CHAPTER *16*

In the morning they drove back to the house. More trucks were arriving from the mainland, the seaplane was again buzzing overhead, and the beach looked more like a staging area than ever. As they got out of the car, looking rather bedraggled with a rumpled blanket, towels and an empty picnic basket, Nancy stepped from the front door. She was dressed in an immaculate white tennis dress and carried a long silver cigarette holder which flashed in the sun.

"Good morning, kiddies," she said, arching an eyebrow. "Did you have a good time?"

"Yes, thank you," Ben said. "Good morning, Nance."

Flustered, Penny said, "Hello, Nancy. If you'll excuse me, I'll run along. I'm a mess."

She headed for their rooms, and Ben started to follow her.

"Just a minute, Ben," Nancy said. "I have various messages for you."

"Oh?"

"Nort is coming in this morning with Dick Drake. He'd like you to meet him down by the jetty about noon."

"All right," Ben replied, again aware that he was being given an order, and that Nancy enjoyed giving it.

"Also, there's mail for you. Letters from your children, I believe. Very touching. Mine never write me. I had them put in your room."

"Thank you."

"There are some letters for your young lady, too. You'll find them all on the coffee table."

"You are very kind."

"Kindness is my middle name."

Tapping the ash from her cigarette, Nancy smiled ambiguously and went back into the house.

Hurrying to his room, Ben found Penny curled up in an armchair reading a long letter. On the coffee table near her were two envelopes addressed to her in a large masculine scrawl.

"Hi," Penny said to Ben as he approached, and casually she put the envelopes in her handbag. "There's mail for you over there."

Who, Ben wondered, had written to her? How had they got her address? But what right did he have to monitor her mail?

Impatient with himself, Ben picked up his own letters and saw there was one from each of his children, written in answer to brief notes he had sent them to say he had gone to Janus Island and suggesting that they spend part of the approaching summer there.

"Dear Dad," young Ben wrote. "I'm glad you're back on the island, because I know you like it. I wish I could join you, but Muth is talking about going abroad next summer . . ."

I can't blame him, Ben thought, but there still was a sinking sense of loss, a feeling that he was more alone than he had ever admitted. Quickly he opened the letter from Laura.

DEAREST DADS,

I'm glad you went on down to Janus Island without me — I hated to think of you in that awful hotel. The idea of visiting you next summer is great, and maybe I can make it for a few days, but the truth is that I want to go to summer school at Boston University. You have always told me that we should be able to level with each other, so I'd better admit that I don't want to get too far away from Bill. This Bermuda thing is working out marvelously for us. He really is a great guy, Dads — when you get to know him, I'm sure you'll see that. He's been through a hard time since his father died, and he needs someone, just as, I guess, I do, and you do — everyone?

One reason I don't want to leave him is that he graduates in June, and will probably be drafted. His mother can't really afford graduate school — this house in Bermuda was lent to her by a friend. Bill wants to go to work, so the army will probably grab him. How I hate that! He's an English major interested in poetry and music, so the government figures there's nothing "essential" about him at all which would be worth keeping in civilian life. But oh how "essential" he is to me!

We don't have any heavy plans for the immediate future or anything, but I do want you to know that I'm terribly happy and not lonely any more.

Much love,

LAURA

Ben found himself both delighted and alarmed by her letter. Picking up his pen, he wrote:

DEAREST LAURA,

Believe me, I'm glad you are in love. I expect that maybe you're a little like me, and find life intolerable alone. That could be called a sickness, but personally I believe it's the people who can live emotionless lives who are ill.

Still, your letter filled me with a lot of conflicting thoughts. You have to understand that I myself got married when I was very young, and as you know all too well, that marriage didn't turn out to be made in heaven. Yours is a risky age at which to attempt marriage — there are statistics to prove that.

What can I tell you? You are nineteen and I know a little about the world and you are in love. In my own odd way I am a moralist, and I could never give my daughter all the arguments for "free love," because love never turns out to be free in the long run, not if it's really love. If you just took to living with this guy, you might find yourself hurt terribly, for such arrangements often turn out to be more temporary for the man than for the woman. I could not honestly advise you to do that.

So what do I advise? Love but be chaste during the months before your young man goes away to war? I too went away to war. I know what it's like.

So what does a father advise in a case like this? I guess there is no real advice which can be honestly given, because the factors of your emotional makeup and his are too complex, even if I knew him as well as I know you, for anyone to predict the result of any course of action. You might be wildly happy if you chose any of the possibilities, and you might get a terrible kick in the face. You just have to make your choice and take your chance. The only good thing about such a crisis in a person's life is that he or she is bound to be better off than the poor souls who never feel strongly enough to confront such problems.

I would just like to give you one warning. Of all the terrible things that conceivably could happen to my darling daughter, I think the worst would be getting married, having several children, and then getting divorced while still very young. As you know so bitterly, divorce tears people apart even when there is a good deal of money involved. When the very poor get divorced, there is even more hell. Few men can afford to support two households. The poor have a chance really for only one marriage. If that cracks up, it's hard for them to make a stable relationship ever again.

Of course, I know that no one marries with the expectation of divorce, although everyone knows there is some risk which has to be run. All I am saying is, be as sure as you possibly can. Don't let sexual guilt shove you into marriage. An affair is not always pretty, but it hurts far fewer people than a bad marriage, and the hurt doesn't last as long.

In saying all this, I feel a little ironic, not only because my advice is related to my past, but because it is part of the present. I too, dear baby, think I am in love, and even though I must seem very old to you, I'm scared to death of making a mistake. Yet I just don't have it in me to live alone, and there is something in me which wants to regularize everything, to put love on the up and up.

So I too am going to have to make my choice and take my chance — my last one, in all probability, just as this is your first. Pray for both of us.

Of course I want you to come here when you can, and bring your young man. I shall introduce you both to Penny Savodi. Is it all very romantic, or the makings of a terrible mess?

Maybe it's better to cross our hearts when we say we love, rather than crossing our fingers.

Come as soon as you can. I love you very much.

DAD

Sealing his letter, Ben glanced at Penny, and saw that she too was answering her mail. Looking up, she said, "You look worried. No bad news, I hope?"

"No," he said. "How about you?"

"Just letters from a couple of old friends. Nothing important."

She put her letters in her handbag, snapped it shut, and,

picking up a comb, walked toward the bedroom, leaving her bag on the coffee table. When she shut the door he had the ridiculous impulse to steal a look at her mail. I'm getting as bad as Nort, he thought with indignation. Anyway, if there were anything I shouldn't see, would she just leave her bag there?

Impatiently dismissing these thoughts from his mind, Ben went into the bedroom, where he found Penny sitting before her bureau mirror, combing her hair.

"I've got to shave and get dressed," he said. "I'm supposed to meet Nort at noon."

"I find I'm a little afraid to see him again. And Nancy terrifies me."

"They can't hurt us, Penny," he said, touching her shoulder. "Not if we're careful not to hurt each other."

Rising impulsively, she threw both arms around him and buried her face in his neck.

"If you hurt me," she said, "you're damaging your own property."

"You too."

"Let's be very careful. I don't know why, but this time I feel I'm made of glass. Don't drop me!"

"You're a glass full of wine for a thirsty man. I won't drop you."

"Good," she said, and kissed him. "Now go meet your boss, if that's what he is, and I'm going to try to make myself beautiful. Right now I look as though I'd spent the night sleeping with some man on the beach."

George Grey drove Ben to the jetty in a jeep. The old man said not a word as he steered past a truck of movie lights and cameras which was being unloaded.

"Things at the house pretty well under control?" Ben asked.

"Mrs. Clay told me not to worry," George said, "and I'm just going to follow orders."

The bay around the jetty was so still that the big yawl was mirrored in it as clearly as though a sister ship had sunk on her side in the clear water beside her.

"Good morning," Flint said, looking up from the mahogany caprail he was varnishing.

"Good morning. I understand Mr. Clay is due pretty soon."

"Yes, sir, and I'm afraid he's going to be damn sore. Lawson gone, the dinghy gone, and I've been so busy I haven't had a chance to get anything really in shape."

"Did you check the reef with the radar last night?"

"Four or five times. Not a thing moving."

"I think someone was just setting lobster traps. They're out of season now, aren't they?"

"Yes, sir. There's a five-hundred-dollar fine if you're caught."

"No sign of Lawson or the dinghy?"

Before Flint could answer, they heard far down the bay the distant hum of powerful marine engines.

"That's probably Mr. Clay now," Flint said. "He told me to have the air-conditioning on."

Picking up his can of varnish, he went below. Walking slowly aft, Ben sat down at the wheel of the big yawl and stared out over the reflection of the tall masts toward the end of the island, where the sea and a shimmering heat haze met. Louder and louder the distant vibrations came, growing to a deep mechanical growl that seemed peculiarly ominous to Ben, who had first experienced that noise when, as a small boy, he had heard the big Packard engines of rumrunners whining in the night, a sound which had made such a deep impression on him that years later he had shivered when he first heard a squadron of torpedo boats roaring across a bay in New Guinea, magnifying the whole pattern of violence which in childhood had frightened him so, even though he had no idea then that his father was connected with it. Shielding his eyes against the sunlight dancing on the water, Ben saw two high plumes of silver spray emerge from the haze off the end of the island. The pounding of the engines became louder as the arching wings of spray materialized into two high-powered cruisers racing along beside each other, so close that the broad wakes they cut across the polished bay met and became one road of foam.

As the boats approached the wharf, they slowed, and the bigger of the two circled in for a landing while the other waited a few hundred yards off. High on the flying bridge of this craft, Ben saw Nort, spinning a chromium-plated wheel that stabbed light rays back to the sun. Wearing only brief black swimming trunks and a long-visored swordfisherman's cap, Nort looked tanned and young. The white hull of the new cruiser was spotless, but on the bow a davit had been left with a large patent anchor dangling from it, and a heavy boom which projected over the cockpit from a stubby mast was dripping with a tangle of mooring lines and other cordage. Several people stood in the cockpit and stared toward shore.

"Somebody get up on the bow," Nort called, and a chubby young man in purple bathing trunks gingerly made his way around the cabin.

Coming from the cabin of the yawl, Flint took one look at the approaching cruiser and hurriedly began to put fenders over the side. The engines of the cruiser growled in reverse and the bow swung out uncertainly. On the flying bridge Ben could see Nort frantically manipulating the controls as the tide began to sweep the big boat past the end of the wharf. Suddenly the engines threatened to explode as Nort raced them in neutral at too high a speed. That noise died abruptly when he shoved the gearshift forward, but the heavy boat lunged toward the yawl at much too great a speed. Realizing his mistake, Nort jerked his engines into reverse but it was too late. Broadside to the tide, the big cruiser slammed into the bow of the yawl, crushing the mahogany caprail which Flint had just been varnishing and staving in the bulwark. With the engines still churning in reverse, the cruiser started to back off, but the anchor hanging from the davit caught in the stays, ripping the rigging and pivoting the cruiser in such a way that she slammed back against the side of the yawl, splintering more mahogany.

"Cut your engines!" Ben yelled. "Cut your engines!"

There was so much noise that his voice was not audible, but he motioned with his hands as though trying to tell a car to slow down. Almost directly above him on the flying bridge, he saw Nort staring at him, startled and helpless. With the anchor still caught in the rigging and its engines churning in reverse, the big cruiser continued to bang against the yawl and trying to pull her away from the wharf. Then Nort suddenly seemed to come to, flicked some switches, and there was silence.

"The goddam gearshift isn't working right!" Nort yelled.

"Anyone hurt?" Ben called.

In the cockpit several men and a girl stood in a clump, looking shocked. No one said anything.

"Throw me a line," Flint said. "Give me a line from the stern there!"

"You'd think that for sixty thousand dollars they could give you a gearshift that'd work!" Nort complained.

Looking up and down the splintered rail of the yawl, Ben felt sick, as if he were looking at the body of a beautiful woman crushed in a needless accident. It was perfectly obvious to him that there was nothing wrong with the gearshift except the man operating it.

"I don't think there's any heavy damage," Flint said, making a line fast. "Not much more than the caprail."

"I'll make the bastard who installed those engines pay for it," Nort said.

"No real harm is done, Nort," Ben said. "Come on ashore."

"You saw the gearshift wasn't working, didn't you, Ben?"

"Not being aboard, I couldn't tell."

"She jammed on me!"

"Flint and I will have a look at it."

"Did I hurt the hull? Christ, I don't care about the yawl, but we're going to need this baby right away."

"Your hull's all right," Ben said, examining the cruiser, and he thought how strange it was that a glass hull like that should prove tougher than mahogany and teak. What would he have thought in his childhood if someone had told him they were going to build a glass boat?

"Well, we're here, anyway," Nort said, and with some embarrassment the people in the cockpit started to climb across the yawl to the wharf. The one girl among them was wearing enormous dark glasses, a wide-brimmed hat and a voluminous beach coat with black and white polka dots. She was so encased it was impossible to tell what she looked like, but from the attentive way a tall man beside her helped her ashore, Ben guessed that she must be very pretty. When the tall man turned toward him, Ben recognized the handsome, if somewhat faded, features of the old movie actor Richard Drake.

"The jeep will take you folks up to the house," Nort said. "Nancy's waiting for you. I'll be up just as soon as I take care of things here."

The tall man helped the girl into the jeep and sat down beside her. Two young men got in behind them and George drove off.

"Come on below, Ben," Nort said, walking to the companionway of the yawl. "Christ, it's good to see you!"

"It's good to see you, too."

"Man, it's nice and cool down here," Nort said, sitting down at the table in the main saloon. "Where's the damn steward? Want a drink?"

"Lawson took off, for some reason."

"He's got a girl in Key West and he drinks too much, but he's harmless. I had him checked out."

Sticking his head up the hatch, Nort called, "Hey, Fred, get me a bottle of scotch from the cruiser. Never mind the damn camera boat. They can take care of themselves."

Returning from the other side of the wharf, where he had been helping the other cruiser to tie up, Flint jumped aboard the cruiser and came back with a half-empty bottle of scotch.

"Drink?" Nort asked Ben.

"No, thanks. Not now."

"You look tired. Been working hard?"

The voice was sardonic, the implication clearly bawdy.

"I feel great," Ben said noncommittally.

"So do I. We had a fine trip down. We made it from Miami in four hours, better than thirty knots all the way."

"That's fast."

"She's some boat, except for the damn gearshift. I'll show her to you later. Right now I've got a thousand things to tell you about. Some of it I want you to know before you meet Drake."

"Maybe I will have a drink," Ben said, and poured himself a short one.

"When I told you I wanted you to write and direct the movie, I didn't know I could get Drake," Nort continued. "Now it turns out that what he really wants is a documentary that would be good publicity for him and his girl. If we find anything, great, but he wants to plant something the papers will like even if we don't."

286

"What do you think of that?"

"A documentary could make money if it were really good. There are so damn many phony so-called underwater dramas."

"Won't it still have to be written and directed?"

"Yeah, but Drake is a bug on that stuff himself. He's always wanted to be his own director, and he's always wanted to write his own scripts. Now he's put part of the money up, he wants to do the whole thing himself."

"Which leaves me out of a job," Ben said, his heart sinking.

"Not at all! We'll still need your help, not only with the movie, but everything else. I just didn't want you to get into a tangle with Drake. When it comes to the movie, he insists on being in charge."

"I understand," Ben said coldly.

"As for finding the gold cannon, that of course is my job — and that's where I really need your help. I've got a lot of divers hired, Ben. We're putting quite an organization together."

"Are they all still supposed to think that you're just interested in making a movie?"

"A highly realistic documentary of underwater treasure hunting that probably is just a publicity stunt for Drake's new wife — that's what most of them think."

"You still want a press conference?"

"Of course. And I've decided I definitely want it here on the island. There are all kinds of benefits involved here, Ben! Eventually I'm going to sell Janus Island. Lot of money to be made in real estate here. The publicity won't hurt a bit."

It was remarkable, Ben thought, how all Nort's madnesses seemed to blend into the single art of making money. All his life Ben had tended to make fun of that, but now he found himself almost admiring it. How could a man so in debt do anything else?

"I suppose we can have a bus bring the reporters down from Miami," he said. "The airstrip isn't ready yet."

"I've got some new plans for that. But first I want to talk about you, Ben. Your lawyer wanted me to sign a lot of papers, a contract and all that."

"I thought you were willing to guarantee me three months' pay at least."

"I was, but then I got to thinking. If I pay you five hundred dollars a week, it will all go to the government, won't it?"

"Most of it."

"Well, let's make a deal that will be good for both of us. I'll pay you nothing. You stay here as my guest, or just work for the percentages we mapped out. Then I'll take the money I would have paid you and put it in my foundation. Did you know I had a philanthropic setup?"

"No, but I don't think I want to contribute to it."

"Hold on! We give scholarships, and you've got some bright kids, haven't you? I could send them all the way through college, and it wouldn't cost me an after-tax cent."

"I'd have to think about that," Ben said.

"Why? Do you think 'tax evasion' is immoral?"

"Frankly, I haven't got that figured out in my own mind yet."

"Well, we promised not to talk politics, but you know I love this country. The thing is, though, these boys in Washington know no limits. The United States government is obviously the finest government in the world, but when you come right down to it, it's like you said: they always end up taking your money and your sons — every government does. Personally, I regard the Mafia as a fairly benign institution compared to all big modern governments. They don't take all of a rich man's money, and if your sons mind their own business, they don't take them."

"I suppose they would if we didn't have a government," Ben said. "Don't set me down as anti-government yet."

"I can also get your ex-wife taken care of by my foundation," Nort said. "She's always been interested in art, hasn't she? Maybe we can get her a grant. I bet she'd rather have that than alimony anyway. It would be something she could brag about."

"That's a nice thought," Ben said.

"You're thinking that maybe the government wouldn't let us get away with it?" Nort asked.

"I don't know if they would. The whole tax world is a mystery to me."

More and more, Ben found himself repelled by the whole scheme. Not only did it make him feel blatantly dishonest, but obviously it meant that he was having to place himself more than ever in Nort's hands, who could change his mind at any time. Of course, he was at the mercy of the government as things stood, but at least there was the possibility of appeals. How would he feel if his children were in jeopardy and there were no one to appeal to but Nort in one of his less attractive moods?

"The tax world is no bloody mystery to me," Nort said. "And neither are the draft laws. They both represent a government controlled by the majority of unproductive people compulsively grabbing whatever they can get. Have you considered the fact that your son will be drafted if you can't afford to keep him in college and graduate school?"

"I've considered that."

"Have you wondered whether you can ever get remarried while you're head over heels in debt?"

"Yes."

"I'm just trying to show you a way out. I don't pretend there's no advantage in it for me, and not only the financial ones. You don't have to be afraid of taking a favor."

"What is the big advantage for you?"

"I need people I can count on — in my position, I need that more than anything else. I know that your children would be in some sense hostages to me, under this plan, but I claim that time should have shown you that you can trust me a hell of a lot more than you can trust the government."

The more Nort talked against the government, the more Ben found he wanted to defend it, for despite his own predicament, life without any government at all seemed preposterous, but this was no time, he realized, to start a political argument with his employer. It was difficult to keep his promise not to talk politics, but the situation really had little to do with politics anyway, he realized. For some reason he could never fully understand, both Nancy and Nort wanted in their various ways to buy him, to own him, and he had to fight to stay free of them both.

"I appreciate your concern for my tax problems," he said carefully. "Let me think about it, and in the meantime, let's leave our financial arrangements where they were."

"Have it your way," Nort said, sounding somewhat peevish. "Now listen: we've got to operate at top speed, because Dick Drake has only got a month."

"You expect to make a movie in a month?"

"His part of it. He's got all kinds of commitments, and we're lucky to get him at all. The whole diving team ought to be here today, and his camera crew is already here."

"I hope we get good weather."

"I know, summer would be better, but this is the only month Dick had. If we want, the rest of us can stay for the balance of the year."

"What do you want me to do? I already made some calls about the news conference. All we have to do is set the exact time and place."

"The first thing we've got to do is get that airstrip ready. We've got to have a regular shuttle service to keep people and supplies coming in and going out. That damn little pontoon plane can't carry nearly enough."

"I haven't been able to find anybody yet who can run the bulldozer. I had a look at the strip and it's pretty rough."

"I can run it, and those boys I brought with me are tough. They can help."

Ben had assumed that after taking the power cruiser all the way from Miami, Nort would want to have lunch and rest. But after finishing his scotch, Nort suddenly stood up and said, "Let's go! I want that plane in just as soon as possible, even if we have to put up lights and work all night!"

Although Ben had known Nort all his life, he had never seen him worked up to such a pitch of feverish energy. As soon as they got to the house, Nort rushed to the bulldozer and started the big noisy diesel engine. Manipulating the levers much more skillfully than he had handled his boat, he steered the huge machine for the airstrip, lowering its big blade occasionally to smooth out the ruts in the road. Behind him came the jeep with four of the young men he had brought from Miami, all armed with picks and shovels.

Borrowing the blue station wagon, Ben followed. When he got to the strip, Nort was charging the big bulldozer at top speed, sending up cascades of sand. He had a cold can of beer in his left hand and there was an expression on his face which, improbably enough, Ben thought, made him look like the happiest man in the world.

CHAPTER 17

Tʜᴀᴛ night Nancy served a buffet dinner to the multitude Nort had assembled. Contrary to her appearance of languor, she was entirely capable of messing an army engaged in a major campaign. Despite George Grey's lack of enthusiasm and the inefficiency of the pickup help, the living room of the big house was suddenly transformed into a good restaurant for thirty-four people.

When Ben and Penny entered the room shortly before

seven o'clock, they found Nort setting up a bar in the corner. Tanned and dressed entirely in white, he looked as fresh as though he had been lying idly on the beach all day. Sitting on a sofa was Dick Drake, wearing Bermuda shorts and a monogrammed sport shirt, and beside the aging actor was his wife, whose first name he had changed from Elizabeth to Donna. Wearing a wisp of a low-cut green cocktail dress, Donna Drake seemed to Ben to be the epitome of all the young starlets he had ever seen lounging around swimming pools in California, their bodies implausibly beautiful, their heads full of movie and television contracts.

Standing in the center of the room, glasses in hand, were about fifteen athletic-looking men varying in age from twenty to fifty, some dressed in natty sports attire, others in dungarees and faded khakis. These, Ben learned as Nancy made introductions, were the divers whom Nort had assembled, some of them professionals, but most of them highly skilled amateurs, the kind of people who belonged to clubs which organized elaborate expeditions all over the world. Gathered in a circle which excluded the softer-looking cameramen and other movie people, the divers were talking animatedly about the underwater conditions they might find on the reef in the morning. Obviously excited by the prospect of searching a new location, the divers talked and moved with the animation of football players just before a kickoff.

They were so absorbed in discussing the history of the reef and the location of known wrecks that they hardly seemed to notice the food piled on the table beside them, and when, at Nancy's insistence, they did help themselves, they gulped down their cold roast beef and shrimp salad as though impatient at the interruption. Hardly a man in the room so much as glanced at any of the four women present, despite the fact that Penny, Donna Drake and the young beauty who had come with one of the divers all seemed to Ben to be unusually attractive. The high-pitched hum of conversation and the whole atmosphere of breathless anticipation in the room seemed to Ben to be as curiously sexless as the gaming casinos of Nevada, where semi-nude chorus girls wander around without causing men to look up from their dice.

Wearing a white linen dress Ben had bought her in Key West, Penny looked demure and thoughtful. She had said a woman is different when seen among a lot of other people, often far different from the way she appears when one is alone with her, and in this she was right, Ben realized, for at this party Penny was unusually quiet; not shy, but far more interested in listening and observing than in talking.

"Sit down," she said to Ben. "I'll get you a plate."

Already he had learned to accept her services, and he did not recognize how unusual they were until he saw Dick Drake waiting on his wife hand and foot, offering her delicacies, drinks and cigarettes. There was a kind of reverse pattern in progress on the two sides of the room. On her side Donna Drake kept up a steady stream of demands of every man within earshot, and her husband kept running back and forth, bringing her peanuts, more ice for her drink, another drink, plates of food, an ashtray. Every few minutes the young actress put a cigarette between her lips, which she had colored a pale orange, and said, in a flat tone of voice, "Light me."

Before smoking half the cigarette she would grind it out, put another in her mouth, glance at the nearest male, and again the flat command: "Light me."

In contrast, Penny kept handing things to Ben, and when he took a cigar from his pocket, she was there with a match. Never before in his life, Ben reflected, had he had a woman wait on him, and he found he enjoyed it.

"Penny," he said, "thanks very much for doing all this for me. It's a novel sensation."

"What is?"

"Finding a woman who wants to please, rather than be pleased."

She laughed.

"You never knew the daughter of an Italian before."

"Do all Italian women wait on their men like this?"

"Not any more, I guess. But my father thought the purpose of women was to wait on him."

"Didn't they rebel?"

"No — that was his art."

"I wish he could have taught me."

"You seem to be learning pretty fast."

"Yes, but it's beginning to make me feel guilty."

"That's not the way it should work. It should make you love me very much, and then you should show it by being especially kind, and then that should make me want to wait on you all the more."

"Sounds like a very good system."

"A benign circle," she replied. "You'd be surprised how well, sometimes, it works."

The "system" was, Ben realized, a game which, almost without being aware of it, he and the girl had been playing with each other ever since they had met. She was continually serving him — at the table, in bed, everywhere. His dirty laundry miraculously disappeared, to be replaced by piles of fresh linen in the top bureau drawer of their room. The bottom drawers, which were awkward to open, she had taken for herself. The side of the bed near the reading lamp she had given to him. When they were eating together, she would put the choicest morsels on his plate. All this might seem subservient or masochistic, he thought, if it weren't for the fact that it made him feel so deeply grateful to her that he was constantly devising ways to pay her back. She was the only woman he'd ever known who made him really want to jump to open doors, to stand when she

entered a room, to play out the whole pleasant little charade of chivalry which his mother had always sternly
insisted upon. Beyond that, she already had him aching to
give her marriage and a child, despite all the practical
difficulties, because these obviously were the only gifts she
really wanted, and which could be appropriate to the spirit
in which she gave of herself.

Did this mutual desire to give inevitably degenerate into
a strident insistence on taking, he wondered? Or might a
woman like this actually be capable of making it a permanent way of life? How long, if he himself made every
effort, could this miraculous atmosphere of mutual care be
preserved?

He didn't know, but he suspected that it might be a great
deal of fun to find out, playing the game as carefully as
possible, doing everything he could imagine to please. The
more he thought about the game, the more he found himself
stimulated by it, all the more so because it was the only
contest he had ever heard of which both players could
win.

But of course his part in the game, his basic contribution
as time went on, would have to be the money that would
be necessary to make her desire for a child practical. All his
life he had given money away so freely to people who had
given him little in return that it was maddening to think
that now, when he had found someone so intent upon
being deserving, he had little to offer but debts.

"Do you people ever really find gold at the bottom of
the sea?"

The question was asked by Donna Drake, who had
grown tired of being ignored by the divers and had aggressively invaded their circle. It was followed by the short
ghastly silence that usually follows a *gaffe*. All heads in the
room turned toward her, as though she had entered a
convent and asked the nuns if they really found comfort in
religion.

"I mean, do you really *find* anything?" she asked brightly. "Or is it all just a *thing?*"

"Oh, quite a lot has been found," a rather tough-looking bald man said, sounding bored.

"It's like this, Mrs. Drake," a young, dark-haired man added. "When you begin, you always think you're going to find gold. I mean, you do some reading and you know it's there, and every time you go down you think you are going to stumble over tons of it, just under the next ledge."

"But do you ever?"

"A few do, but it happens so seldom that most people would get discouraged."

"Diving is hard work," the bald man said. "It's harder than mining coal, and I know, because I've done both. Often it's boring, and often it's dangerous, and I've known men who have dived for a lifetime and never found anything worth more than ten dollars."

"Then why do they do it?" Donna asked.

"The adventure, the excitement," the young diver said.

"And the stuff we do find is interesting, even if it's not worth much," a tall young man said. "I've found ballast stones, an old anchor, some cannonballs, a pewter spoon. Altogether, it's not worth much, but when you reach out and touch it, it's almost like touching the hand of the man who touched it last."

"That's spooky," Donna said, and sensing that she wasn't really wanted, she retreated to her husband on the couch. "Light me."

It's curious, Ben thought; these divers are interested not in winning a game but in playing it — not really much different from redcoated hunters who risked their necks riding over hill and dale to kill a fox. He felt himself far removed from them. Shortly after the war he had done enough diving to know the fun of going down about thirty feet in clear, current-free waters to see the coral and fish, but it was rather terrifying to dive in the murky currents on the edge of reefs pounded by breakers where wrecks are usually found. Sucking sand out of wrecks with heavy equipment, splitting coral with crowbars and hoisting heavy weights aboard small vessels in heavy seas — all this was an exercise he hated and would never go near if there was not some hope of solid gain.

The very fact that the divers did not play up the possibility of actually finding gold somehow gave Ben more confidence in the expedition than he had ever had before. Not even the amateur divers thought gold could be scooped from the bottom of the sea like sand. In their discussions of equipment and of previous searches they had made, they all sounded thoroughly professional, and Ben found his respect for Nort's organizational abilities growing. Maybe, after all, they would find the gold cannon, and the shining solution to all his problems would rise, dripping with mud, from the bottom of the sea!

"Are you actually going to start diving tomorrow?" he asked Nort eagerly.

"I want to check out the whole reef with some new gadgets I've got for detecting metal," Nort said. "I guess we can begin that."

"How's the airstrip coming?"

"Fine! I've got a couple of boys up there now, working under floodlights. They ought to be done by morning. I want you to bring the press in as soon as you can. There's no point in waiting."

"My publicity department in New York can give you a hand," Dick Drake said. "They've got the releases all ready to hand out."

"With pictures," Donna added. "They got some really good shots of me."

"I don't want the publicity originating entirely in your office, Dick," Nort said aggressively. "We'll get a better play if the whole thing doesn't stink of Hollywood."

Under his tan, Nort's face was flushed. The tumbler in his hand, judging from its color, was full of straight scotch. Only Nort and Drake were drinking heavily, he realized — abstemiousness on the eve of an important dive was obviously part of the divers' religion.

"Any publicity concerning my wife and me," Drake said slowly, making a great effort to be dignified, "must be approved by the specialists I hire for that purpose."

"I can use their help, Nort," Ben said quickly. "I'm sure they'll cooperate with us."

Seeing the belligerent expression on her husband's face, Nancy came up and said, "Nort, can't we have some music? I can't make the stereo work at all."

Answering the tug of his wife's hand, Nort walked to an elaborate phonograph built into the wall and started to adjust it with expert hands. A moment later the booming brasses and the soaring strings of a symphony filled the room.

"Light me," Donna said to her husband.

"We won't get far with magnetic equipment," the bald diver said, raising his voice to be heard above the music. "There's too much iron out there. When that big tanker broke up, she spread steel plate all over the reef."

"Do you want a scotch?" Penny asked Ben.

"No thanks. Can I get you one?"

"Not now."

On the other side of the room Ben saw the small Negro boy who acted as Fred Flint's messenger come in. Startled by the music and the crowd, the child hesitated for a moment before going up to Nort. The symphony was abruptly cut off.

"Ben," Nort said loudly in the ensuing silence. "Come outside. I want to talk to you."

Striding through the divers, Nort made his way to the

front door, followed by Ben. Outside it had grown dark, and the beat of the surf was loud.

"They're out there," Nort said. "Somebody's working the reef. Flint picked them up on the radar."

"I think they may just be poaching crayfish," Ben said.

"Let's go see!"

"Wait!" Ben said, because he wanted to know exactly what Nort planned to do. If someone was diving over the reef at night, there was presumably nothing illegal about that, but if Nort were drunk enough, he might start some sort of fight. And if someone was working illegal lobster traps, Ben didn't particularly want to get into a row with him now, for he sensed that it might be useful to remain friendly with the local fishermen. In any case, he doubted whether the big cruiser roaring through the night would surprise anyone. A man engaged in any kind of activity he wanted to hide would probably have a light boat that could disappear into a maze of reefs and islands the moment the sound of engines announced the approach of a larger craft. The intelligent thing to do, Ben thought, was simply to send divers down on the site of the activity in the morning.

"I said let's go!" Nort said, his voice tense. He ran toward the car. Dick Drake, who had been watching from the front door, followed him.

"What the hell's going on?" Drake asked.

"Some bastard is working the reef right now. Let's go take a look at him!"

"Great!" Drake said. "Come on, Donna!"

Donna came, followed by Penny.

"Everybody in the car!" Nort called. "Hurry up! I don't want too big a gang."

"Do you really need me on this?" Ben said.

"Go ahead," Nancy whispered, coming from the shadows at his side. "He's drunk, and so is Drake. You'd better go."

"All right," Ben said unenthusiastically. "Penny, you stay here."

"I want to go."

"Come on, damn it!" Nort said, blowing the horn of the car. "What's the matter with you, Ben? Didn't I say I wanted you?"

"Coming," Ben said.

"You stay here," he said again to Penny. He got in the car and shut the door. Before she could answer, Nort started with a jerk and roared off.

Bracing himself in the back seat as they swerved over the narrow roads, Ben was glad that Penny had been left safely behind. From the way Nort was handling the car, he guessed that this was going to be one night when he would earn his five hundred a week. In the front seat Donna Drake was laughing mindlessly while her husband tried to drink from a highball glass, despite the violent motion. At least it would be impossible to work the car up to really dangerous speeds on those curving sandy roads, Ben thought. The real danger would start when they got to the boat.

The big white cruiser lay glistening in the moonlight alongside the splintered rail of the yawl. Her decks were slippery with dew, and Drake fell as he climbed aboard.

"Are you all right?" Ben asked, giving him a hand.

"Yes, damn it!" the actor said, and he looked pleadingly at his young wife, hoping she would not look at him with contempt or amusement. Throwing back her head, Donna laughed, perhaps because she actually thought a fall was funny.

Getting to his feet, Drake straightened up and adjusted his ascot, his mobile face trying to find an expression of hurt dignity combined with gallant tolerance. Suddenly the sound of Donna's laughter was drowned out by the roar of the big engines being gunned in neutral.

"Cast off!" Nort shouted. "Let's get out of here!"

For an instant Ben hesitated, but from the tone of Nort's voice it was obvious that any attempt to dissuade him would only infuriate him and make him more dangerous. There was, of course, still time for Ben to jump ashore. Would that be cowardice or common sense? Did he feel a real responsibility to protect these people from themselves, or was he simply aware that Nort had become a meal ticket too valuable to lose?

Ben cast off the lines.

"All clear," he called, jumping aboard.

"I hope this damn gearshift doesn't stick again," Nort said. The engines growled in reverse.

"You got any scotch aboard?" Drake asked.

"In the galley," Nort said. "Ben, will you come up here and take over?"

"Sure," Ben replied with relief, thinking that if they would only content themselves with drinking while he handled the boat, the evening could turn out to be relatively safe after all.

As soon as Ben got to the flying bridge, Nort hurried below decks. Checking the unfamiliar controls, Ben let the boat crawl slowly toward the channel, where the moonlight danced on the swirling eddies of the outgoing tide.

"Here," Nort said, suddenly appearing at Ben's side.

Turning toward him, Ben expected to be offered a drink. Instead, Nort handed him a 12-gauge automatic shotgun.

"Just in case there's trouble," Nort said. "I have eight of these babies aboard."

The possibility of Nort's impulsively opening fire on some hapless fisherman appalled Ben.

"Is this thing loaded?" he asked.

"You bet. I'll take over now."

Going to the controls, Nort shoved the throttles to full ahead, and the heavy cruiser leapt into the night. Sitting on a stool beside the helmsman's seat with the shotgun on his lap, Ben felt that all sanity, all reality was being left behind in the foaming wake. A scattering of gray clouds overhead occasionally obscured the moon, leaving them in complete darkness.

"You'd better cut that speed," Ben shouted at Nort.

"We're all right. This thing doesn't draw much water."

"But it's not made for beaching on coral!"

"Don't worry!" Nort shouted. "I know the channel. See if you can get Flint on the ship-to-shore."

Flint was standing by the radar aboard the yawl.

"Those boats on the reef are heading in," he said on the radio. "They're moving pretty fast toward the mangrove swamp."

"It's no use," Ben said to Nort. "They've already heard us, and they're going in over the reef."

"I'll head 'em off," Nort said.

"There's hardly any water there! They've probably got nothing but an outboard skiff."

"It's almost high tide," Nort shouted back. "We can make it!"

"You'll take the bottom out of her!"

"Want to bet?"

Turning sharply, Nort left the channel and headed toward a mass of small sand islands which surrounded the mangrove swamp.

Well, Ben thought with a curious air of detachment, we probably won't be killed, not here. Before staving in her hull, the big cruiser would probably rip her screws off, and they could anchor until the Coast Guard came to tow them in.

But what if Nort tore the bottom out on a reef?

It would be no fun trying to make it ashore without a dinghy, crawling over jagged coral, attempting to swim against the tide in the deep spots. With a life preserver, he thought he himself might make it, but Nort and Drake had drunk too much, and Donna would probably panic.

"Why don't you cut the engines?" he shouted to Nort. "Maybe you can hear something."

"All right," Nort said, and abruptly cut the ignition on both engines.

There was the surging sound of the wake catching up with them and the crash of breakers. Cupping his ear against the wind, Ben also heard the distant whine of outboard motors.

"They've gone," he said to Nort. "They'll go up one of those mangrove creeks and you couldn't find them in a hundred years."

"We'll take a look around anyway," Nort said. "I remember the channel near the beach."

The starters growled, and the engines coughed to life. With a deep roar they were off again at thirty knots.

Perhaps I could knock him out, Ben thought. Perhaps I could hit him from behind and put him in his bunk until I can get him safely ashore. On the stern was a staff with a flag rolled up on it, an ideal weapon for a blow designed to knock someone unconscious without killing him. Even while these thoughts were going through his mind, Ben knew he could never do it. There must be some way to get around Nort without resorting to violence.

From the deck below, Donna and Richard Drake climbed to the flying bridge. Invigorated by the rush of wind and the speed, Donna stood hanging onto a rail with her lips slightly parted and her eyes wide with excitement. Obviously she had no idea that any real danger was involved, Ben thought — quite naturally she assumed that Nort knew what he was doing. Beside her, Drake looked badly frightened and even more scared of showing it. In his right hand he clutched a glass from which he kept sipping nervously. If the boat did hit a reef at this speed, Ben thought, they would all be pitched onto the deck below, and would probably be in no shape to try to swim.

They were getting close to the maze of reefs which surrounded the sand islands, and if he were going to do anything, he had better do it fast. Carrying the gun with him, he climbed awkwardly down the ladder to the cockpit. The engines of the boat were under the deck at the stern. Somewhere there must be valves to turn the gas off.

While Ben hunted for them, he wondered what Nort would do when the engines suddenly stopped. One thing Nort understood fairly well was engines, and it wouldn't take him long to find out what the trouble was if he were sober. Could he be persuaded to have another drink while Ben checked things out? Would it be possible to stall him long enough to allow his crazy excitement to die, or would he simply be furious when he discovered Ben had sabotaged the mission?

There was only one way to find out. Ben traced the gas lines out and found the valves. After twisting them closed as tightly as he could, he hurried back to the bridge before the gas in the lines was consumed.

For about thirty seconds the boat roared on. Then with a sputter, the port engine quit and a second later the other engine died.

"What the hell?" Nort demanded indignantly.

"You sure you had plenty of fuel?" Drake asked.

"Damn near a full tank!"

"The lines are probably clogged then," Ben said. "Why don't you people go below for a drink? I'll drop the hook and check the lines out."

"Good idea!" Drake said with relief.

"What the hell would get in the fuel?" Nort demanded. "They're brand-new tanks!"

"Sometimes workmen leave shavings or rags in them."

"And sometimes there is sabotage," Nort said darkly. "I'm going to take a look at those engines."

Leaping to the cockpit, Nort tore open the hatches over the engines. It would only be seconds, Ben thought, before he found that the gas had been turned off. Ben glanced from the engines, where Nort was poking about with a flashlight, to the low-lying islands toward which the boat was drifting, spinning slowly as it lost way and hung between wind and tide. The moon was out now, and just ahead there was a dark patch on the water. Was it a reef or the shadow of a cloud?

Jumping to the deck, Ben picked up a sounding pole and plunged it over the side, finding bottom at five feet.

"Son of a bitch!" Nort howled suddenly. "Some bastard shut off the gas!"

"What's that mean?" Donna asked.

"Ben, you bastard, you did it!"

"I'm very sorry," Ben said.

Picking up the pole, he plunged it over the side again. The water was down to four feet.

"What are you doing?" Nort demanded. "Listen to me!"

It came then, the first tremble, the first light jar as the boat drifted against the edge of the reef. Rising on the slight ground swell, the boat came down hard enough to make them all grab for the nearest support.

"If I hadn't cut the engines," Ben said, "you would have hit this reef at thirty knots."

"Christ, Jesus Christ!" Drake said. "What's the matter with you, Nort?"

"I knew what I was doing!"

"We'd better start the engines and get out of here," Ben said. "It's bad enough as it is."

"I tell you, I knew what I was doing! We drifted out of the channel!"

Nort's voice had become high and querulous. Obviously bewildered, he sank down in a fishing chair. Going to the flying bridge, Ben started the engines. Choosing a moment when they were at the crest of a ground swell, he gave the boat a quick jab of reverse power and started working her off the reef. In five minutes he had jockeyed her into water deep enough to allow him to turn her and head back for the channel at slow speed. At first he was afraid that Nort would soon appear to demand control of the boat again, but Nort remained slumped in his chair, explaining to the Drakes that Ben had almost run them ashore.

Donna believed him, Ben saw, but that wasn't impor-tant — the important thing was that the more he talked, the more Nort started to believe himself.

"That was a damn foolish thing you did, Ben," Nort said, coming up on the flying bridge just before they moored alongside the yawl. "I mean, a joke's a joke, but you can't monkey around with high-speed boats like that. I was following a very narrow channel, and we drifted right out of it when you cut the gas."

"Anyway, the boat's not hurt," Ben replied. "I don't think we even nicked a wheel."

"Damn it, aren't you even going to say you're sorry?"

Ben looked at him and suddenly Nort glanced down. There was a moment of silence.

"We didn't hit until you took over!" Nort said.

"That's right. Let's both be more careful now. If this boat gets piled up on the reef at high speed, nobody will get ashore."

"Hell, Ben, we could walk ashore."

"Like all the Spaniards who piled up here?"

"Hell, it wasn't rough tonight. We could have walked ashore."

"Maybe."

"You're overcautious, Ben, you were always overcautious, and you can't be that in this business. I would have caught those bastards and maybe we could have learned something."

"You'd better leave your treasure hunt to the professionals," Ben said. "This isn't a game of cops and robbers."

"Well, maybe, maybe not. Next time don't foul me up, Ben. Next time . . ."

He let his voice trail off in a way that frightened Ben. Next time? How many times would Nort create some dangerous kind of situation, and how many times would Ben have to find ways to control him? Could he really continue at this job of being keeper to a madman?

Nancy and Penny were sitting in the cockpit of the yawl when they got back.

"We didn't find anything," Nort announced. "Ben here went chicken, and they got away."

"Thanks, Ben," Nancy murmured.

"Are you all right?" Penny whispered.

"I'm all right."

Wanting to be alone with her, he declined a ride back to the house and started to walk. There was a temptation to tell her everything that had happened, but he suddenly realized that she would insist upon leaving the island if she shared his belief that Nort was suffering from some kind of destructive mania. Of course, that would be the sensible course of action if he believed that disaster lay ahead. Had he really contracted enough gold fever to make him forgo common sense?

"What really happened out there?" Penny asked.

"Nort got a little reckless. That was why I didn't want you to come along."

"I appreciate that," she said. "Ben, I wish we could get out of here."

"Why?"

"The whole thing is beginning to scare me. Nancy was

so nice to me tonight, and that scared me even more. She offered me a job setting up a dispensary here."

"They could sure use one."

"But she offered me ten thousand dollars a year. She could get somebody for not much more than half that. I'd feel dishonest."

"Opportunity knocks but once."

"I think I'd rather go on being a kept woman. Do you mind?"

"Not as long as I can do the keeping."

"You're good at that," she said, catching his hand. "Ben, is Nort crazy, or is his wife crazy, or are they both nuts?"

"I'm no psychiatrist."

"I'd rather get a job in Key West than work for them at any price. At least I wouldn't be scared to death all the time."

"Scared of what?"

"I don't know. That's the worst of it."

When they got back to the house they found that everyone had gone to bed. Not a light could be seen. As soon as they got into their rooms, she almost threw herself into his arms, and they made love as though they would never be able to do so again.

CHAPTER 18

IN THE morning Ben awoke not so much in the middle of a dream as in a rush of remembered emotion, the fear he had felt screaming through the darkness over reefs in a high-powered boat with Nort at the wheel. The recollection of this was somehow worse than the experience itself, during which he had controlled his emotions, measured his chances, and had never really been conscious of fright.

Safe in bed, however, he began to sweat and mumble "no, no, no," over and over again. When he sat up he found his mouth was as dry as if he had spent the night drinking.

"That must have been quite a nightmare," Penny said.

"It was."

Dressing quickly, they went to the dining room, where breakfast was being served to the entire diving and camera crews. Dressed in bathing trunks and a T-shirt, Nort looked healthy, cheerful and efficient.

"Good morning, Ben!" he said, as though nothing had happened. "I want you to make the final arrangements for the press conference first thing. While you're doing that, we'll be putting the equipment aboard the boats. About noon, we'll be ready to go down and see what those boats were doing out there last night."

"Fine," Ben said. He took a cup of coffee to the small room where the telephone was.

It took only a few minutes to complete the arrangements for flying in reporters the next morning. When he was finished, Ben sat staring at the telephone, thinking that he should call Jerry Grant to find out the latest developments in his tax situation and to ask whether some reduction of alimony would ever be possible if he simply could not meet the present schedule. For several days he had been meaning to do this, but at the last moment had postponed the shocks he almost always got when he called his lawyer. That of course was absurd, he told himself — one thing he owed Penny was some clear statement of his financial woes, an accounting rather than a hopeless admission of chaos. If Nort had this telephone bugged, as Nancy was sure he had, it might be better to go to Key West for the call, but it seemed likely that Nort already knew more about his financial affairs than he himself did anyway.

Reluctantly Ben put the call through to Jerry Grant.

"Ben?" Jerry said. "How the hell are you?"

"All right. I'm just calling to see if there are any developments in my progress from riches to rags."

"Nothing to worry about, Ben, nothing at all. I don't want you to worry about a thing."

"That's kind of you. But what the hell is happening?"

"Things don't look so good on the trust funds you set up for the kids — some similar cases are getting pretty rough treatment."

"What else?"

"Well, your mother signed the new will I sent her. It took a bit of explaining, but she came through. You're out of the will entirely."

"Well, that's a triumph. Jerry, is there any hope of getting Rita to reduce the alimony payments? Can't they ever be a percentage of my earnings rather than a stated amount?"

"I'm not sure we'd want that. Anyway, I have some more news for you, Ben. In cases like this, I'm never sure how a guy is going to take it."

"What?" Ben asked, steeling himself.

"I talked to Rita the other day, and there seems some possibility that she might get married."

"To that old lawyer?" Ben asked incredulously.

"No, somebody else she's met. A fairly young fellow. I think he's in the advertising business."

"She said she was going to marry him?"

"She said they were trying to work it out. With the children and all, there are problems, but she said their intention definitely was to get married. They're going to Europe together."

This information was the last thing Ben had expected. If Rita did get married, he would be relieved of an enormous financial burden, but the prospect of that impressed him less than this added proof that he knew almost nothing about the people he knew best. During some of those bitter final arguments, his former wife had promised that she would never let him go, that she would hold him in bondage for the rest of her life. For a middle-aged woman with a comfortable income guaranteed for life, marriage was an especially idealistic act, and idealism was the last thing he had come to expect of his former wife.

Yet she had said her intention was to get married, to let him go in exchange for "a fairly young fellow" who in this context seemed also to be somewhat idealistic, that last of all creatures Ben had ever expected to hear about, an idealistic advertising man!

"Ben?" Jerry Grant said. "Are you all right?"

"I'm fine," Ben said. "I hope she's happy."

"She sounded fine over the phone. She said she was very much in love."

Ben tried to picture Rita very much in love, Rita who had been so vindictive toward him for so long, who had told him once that she thought the act of love much over-rated. How much had he himself been responsible for making her that way? Would the young advertising man find in the same woman a completely different person?

Perhaps, Ben thought. Perhaps we create in our imaginations all the people around us, and then have to live with those fabrications. There was Nort, wrestling with his world of suspicious monsters, and there was Penny, wanting to give as much of herself as she could. Or was Penny too a creature of his imagination who might change suddenly, or seem to, when some odd fact destroyed the texture of his vision of her?

"Ben?" Jerry said.

"Yes."

"As a lawyer who has handled a good many divorce cases, I have a piece of advice for you."

"What?"

"Don't pretend that it isn't a shock when your former wife remarries. It always is."

"Yes."

"There's always some little tag end of jealousy."

"No, it isn't that," Ben said with conviction, for he hadn't felt a pang of jealousy in connection with Rita for many years. "It's just, well, it's astonishment. I just realized that maybe I never knew her, I never knew her at all."

Jerry Grant laughed.

"People who get married never know each other, and people who get divorced never know each other," he said. "If you had my job, you'd realize that."

"I suppose so," Ben said, and he thought, of course, people marry angels and they divorce devils, and they never understand how one can turn so quickly into the other.

"From the financial point of view, this can of course be marvelous," Jerry said, "but don't get too excited about it."

"Because it might not happen?"

"Nothing is sure, but my point is that even if it does happen, we've still got the government to deal with. Just about everything that would have gone to her, they'll take."

"My Country 'Tis of Thee," Ben said.

"Come on, now. Where else in the world could you have made it in the first place?"

"I don't know, but Jerry, could you try to write some understandable statement of my assets and liabilities for me? The truth is, I too am thinking of getting married again."

"Congratulations, boy! I've been a little worried about you, rattling around alone."

"Will I ever be able to support a wife?"

"If you work, they'll always let you live. What more can you ask?"

314

"Will I ever be able to own a house?"

"You can rent one. They can't stop you from doing that."

"Good. Well, thanks a lot, Jerry."

"It's a pleasure. And don't worry, Ben boy, don't worry! It's my job to do that for you."

"Thanks," Ben said. "I'll look forward to getting the financial statement."

When he came out of the telephone room, he found Nort deeply engaged in a conversation with Dick and Donna Drake. The elderly actor had recovered sufficiently from his ordeal of the night before to have started drinking again, and his voice was argumentative.

"You must realize we've only got a month!" he was saying. "If I'm not back on the Coast a month from now, I'll be penalized five thousand dollars a day."

"Dick wants to start shooting right away," Nort said to Ben. "I wanted to check out the reef first to get some idea of what's there."

"If it's a documentary, that's part of it, isn't it?" Drake asked.

"I'm just afraid the cameras will slow us down," Nort said.

"Let's get one thing straight," Drake retorted. "For me the treasure is what we take back in cans. It's the film I want. When we get that, you can play around down here for the rest of your life."

"I don't think there has to be a conflict," Ben said, noting that Nort's face was beginning to flush. "Let's go ahead with a straight documentary. Let the professional divers dive and let the professional cameramen film."

"All right," Nort said. "I'm in charge here, and that's the decision I'm going to make. We're going to check the spot where those boats were. Come on along and take all the film you want."

"I'll notify my boys," Drake said, and stalked off, languidly followed by his pretty young wife.

It was a bright and cheerful scene, Ben thought, as the young divers loaded their underwater equipment aboard the big cruiser, and the movie people put theirs aboard the other boat Nort had brought in from Miami. The yellow and aluminum scuba tanks flashed in the sun, and the air was full of laughter, the sound of men about to embark on a new adventure. The divers did not appear to be in the least tense about the melodrama Nort had spun about boats working the reef in the night. There were often boats out on the reef at any time, the bald diver said — perhaps they had been lovers out for a moonlight spin, or one of those fanatic fishermen down from New York to make the most of a one-week vacation. But regardless of that, here was a chance to dive in one of the most historically interesting spots in the world; here was the cruiser and all the equipment provided, along with meals and a place to stay ashore. The day was fine with little wind; the sky was clear, and the divers laughed and bantered as they checked over their equipment.

The movie men too seemed to be enjoying the outing. The camera crew had been carefully assembled in New York and Hollywood by Drake, who had worked with most of them over the years. They knew precisely what he wanted of them, and they set out to provide it with the cheerful competence of experienced professionals. As Drake and his wife boarded Nort's boat, a camera already was on them.

"Do you want to come, Penny?" Ben asked.

"Is there room?"

"We can always use another girl in the background," Drake said.

Penny jumped aboard, and Nort started the big engines. "Cast off!" he said eagerly.

Folded in Nort's hand was the chart on which Ben had marked his radar fix of the midnight activity on the reef.

"Give me a course, Ben," Nort said, handing the chart to him. "Then stand by to take bearings. I want to make dead sure we're right over it."

When they got past the tip of the island, the sea was so calm that it shone like a great mirror, making the small mangrove islets appear to dance in the air. There was a slight ground swell rolling in over the reef, and when Nort cut the engines to give Ben a chance to take bearings, the boat rolled enough to make one of the scuba tanks slide across the cockpit deck.

"Is it always this rough?" Donna Drake asked innocently.

In a fetching red bikini she sat in a fishing chair, combing her long blonde hair.

"Steer two six eight," Ben said to Nort. "Go one point six miles and we should be on it."

In his impatience Nort gunned the engines and had to circle back to get the bearings right. Looking over the bow, Ben saw a whiskey bottle floating neck-down. Studying it, he saw that it was not drifting with the tide.

"There's a buoy," he said. "Probably it marks an illegal crayfish trap."

"Why are you so sure it's only that?" Nort asked with irritation.

"Do you think a man would mark the spot where he was diving for gold?"

"He might put fish traps out for a blind."

"He might," Ben said, marveling at Nort's ability to sustain his vision of the world, to twist every fact into supporting evidence.

"Let's anchor here," Nort said. "We'll get the divers down as soon as we can."

While they anchored, the camera boat circled slowly while two men operated a big camera they had set up on tripods in her cockpit. Aboard Nort's boat a man with a hand camera filmed Richard Drake helping his wife to inspect her regulator.

"I think we'd better wait for the pros to go down first and see what's there," Drake said nervously.

"Will the cameras have to show that?" Donna asked.

"No," he said.

While six young divers helped each other to strap on their tanks, Nort lowered a black box which was attached to a long wire over the side. Studying a gauge he held in his hand, he said exultantly, "There's one hell of a lot of metal down here!"

"Part of that old tanker, probably," one of the divers said. "We'll let you know in a minute."

Strapping on his face mask, he sat on the edge of the cockpit, waved, and did a backward somersault into the sea. One after the other, the remaining divers followed. There was an instant of complete silence, broken only by the sound of cups clinking in the galley below as the boat rolled in the ground swell. Spreading around them were bubbles from the divers as they circled out.

"Aren't they afraid of sharks?" Donna asked.

"They hardly ever hurt you," Drake said. "Anyway, that's what all the books say."

Ben was surprised that Nort did not immediately dive. Instead he stood studying the shore with binoculars.

"You can be damn sure somebody's watching us," he said.

"Do you want to learn to dive, Penny?" Ben asked.

"Will you think I'm terrible if I say I'm scared?"

"No, but you'd probably get over it. In clear shallow water it's fun."

"It looks scary here," she replied. "How deep is it?"

"Only about thirty feet, but the water's pretty roiled up. I doubt if they can see more than ten feet."

"Lousy camera conditions," Drake said. "Can't we go where the water is clearer?"

"Later," Nort said. "What the hell do you suppose is keeping those guys? They must have seen something by now."

Still there was no sound but the clinking of cups below decks, and the water boiled around them in a widening circle.

"I'm going to rig an underwater telephone tomorrow," Nort said. "This waiting around is ridiculous."

Picking up his binoculars, he started studying the island again.

Glancing over the bow, Ben saw a diver climbing up the anchor line. Surfacing, the diver pushed back his face mask and casually said, "There are two lobster traps down there, and the body of an old Ford."

"Nort, the fishermen dump old cars out here to attract the crayfish and groupers," Ben said. "The fish like to hang out in them."

"I know," Nort said, "but what if you did locate something? One way to protect it from people with metal detectors would be to sink an old car over it."

"I suppose so," Ben said.

"I'm going down to look," Nort replied. "Help me with my tank, will you, Ben?"

As Ben tightened the straps around his shoulders, Nort kept flexing his hands compulsively. He had done enough diving not to be afraid of a routine plunge like this, Ben thought. Did he live in terror of having his whole series of dark plots about the gold disproved?

"Keep an eye out for boats approaching," Nort said, just before he put on his face mask. "Keep a gun handy if one does. Anything can happen out here."

Clapping the mask on his face, he took a fancy speargun from a deck box and leapt over the side.

"Do you want to go down, Mr. Drake?" a man with a hand camera asked.

"I don't think the visibility is right."

"A few murky underwater shots might help to give an idea of actual conditions."

"Come on, Dick," Donna said. "I'm dying to go."

"All right," he said reluctantly.

Two divers who had stayed behind helped him and the girl put on their tanks while the cameras started to grind again. Donna's face was avid, her lips slightly parted as they had been the night before when she was enjoying the speed of the boat and the wind. She did not seem the least afraid as she did her backward somersault off the deck, but her husband hesitated, his face tight with fear, before he followed. Picking up underwater cameras, the two divers casually stepped into the sea.

"Donna makes me envious," Penny said. "She's not only pretty, she's got courage."

"Yes, but her lovers are with her."

"Lovers, plural?"

"The cameras — not the cameramen, but the cameras. She sees fame down there."

"And poor old Mr. Drake?"

"He sees his beautiful young wife down there. She always has to be pursued. Everybody sees something different. Nort sees gold, and the professional divers — all they see is some fish traps and an old Ford."

Penny laughed.

"What do you see?" she asked.

"For me down there? I see only discomfort and fear. I like it much better up here with you."

"I'm glad," she said with a smile. "Would you like a cold beer? I saw some below."

"That would set very well."

For about twenty minutes they sat drinking cold beer and watching the bubbles surface around the boat. From time to time Ben glanced toward shore, but there was no evidence of boats putting out to do battle with them. The sun was pleasant on their backs, and a line of diving pelicans provided diversion. When they passed, Penny sat staring into the sea, absorbed in her own thoughts.

Suddenly Nort's head popped up by the stern. He had a big grouper on the end of a spear, which he held up to Ben. Leaning over the side, Ben grabbed the fish, and wordlessly Nort returned to the depths. The boat had no fish well and the grouper was far too big for the icebox, so Ben put it in the shade under a gunwale, where it twitched and bled.

"At least he found something," Penny said.

Ten minutes later the divers started coming aboard, clambering to a platform at the waterline on the transom where they took off their tanks before continuing up the ladder to the cockpit. Taking cigarettes from the shirts they had left in the cockpit, they all seemed happy and relaxed, despite the fact they had made no great find. After the underwater cameramen returned, Donna Drake bobbed up by the stern, and four men helped her aboard. She was followed by her husband, who immediately asked for a drink, and sat cursing the poor visibility below. Last to return was Nort. As he climbed over the side, he let his fish spear fall to the deck with a clatter, and sank exhaustedly into a fishing chair.

"There might be something down there," he said. "To really tell, we'll have to suck up a lot of that sand. I'll get the equipment ready tomorrow."

"Don't you think we should check out the whole reef first?" one of the divers asked.

"Yes, I think we should," Nort replied, brightening. "There's no reason to concentrate on this spot right away."

His energy returning, Nort began to prepare a towing apparatus for his metal detector. When it was ready, Ben got the anchor up, and they began to follow the outer edge of the reef, working a systematic search pattern. The ground swell was more pronounced here, and the boat rolled monotonously. The big grouper Nort had speared slid across the cockpit deck, leaving a trail of slime and blood which smelled. It was hot, and they had to tow the metal detector at such a slow speed that there was no wind on their faces.

"When are we going in?" Donna Drake asked plaintively, and Nort sternly replied, "You have to learn, Donna — looking for treasure is often nothing but hard, boring work."

He sounded as though he were repeating something he had read, not something he believed, but the truth of those words was all too apparent to Ben. If the whole reef were to be checked out at this speed, it would require days of patrolling and many more days of diving to investigate the many deposits of metal which were recorded. If an old wreck were finally located, it might take weeks to suck up the sand with air hoses and break away the coral. Despite his longstanding efforts at skepticism, he found he was disappointed. With so many people and situations turning out to be something other than he thought them to be, had he half hoped, after all, to find gold easily?

Perhaps, but whatever the reason, he had not adequately prepared his mind for what might be months of nothing but grueling work much like that of a commercial fisherman. Dark plots he had been prepared for, even insanity, but the hard labor that was involved came as a disappointment.

Although he had not gone diving himself, Ben's muscles were sore that night from bracing himself against the constant motion of the boat and from helping the divers with their heavy tanks.

"I guess I'd better get in shape," he said to Penny as she rubbed his back, first with oil and then with alcohol. "Nort is going to want to be out there every day, and I have a terrible feeling that where Nort goes, I go."

But in his expectation of having to spend months on the reef, Ben, as so often happened, was proved wrong. The next morning the professional divers went out promptly at eight-thirty, like commuters going to work, but Ben, Nort and the Drakes had to stay behind for the press conference, which proved to be a routine, if fairly successful, affair. And the day after that, Drake asked him to help make revisions on the rough script of the "documentary" he had prepared. Nort, too, remained ashore. Apparently the methodical combing of the reef had disenchanted him during just one long day, and he concluded that the job was best done by the professionals, who were instructed to call him in when they found anything worth seeing.

"I've got lots of research to do," Nort said to Ben. "I'm convinced that the key to this whole thing lies in research."

He did not specify what kind of research, and something in his tone kept Ben from asking.

Nort might be poring over old documents which he said he got from Spain, but which Ben never saw. Or was he, as his wife had said, mainly interested in rigging his listening devices and keeping track of everything everyone was saying and doing?

Ben gradually came to believe this. During most of the days Nort did not leave the big room at the top of the house which he had made into his study, but at night Ben often saw him wandering through the house like a fussy housewife, moving a lamp here, adjusting a picture there. Seen from Nort's distorted point of view, this activity made sense, for if he believed that there was an "enemy" who knew where the gold was and opposed his search, his private intelligence service, if that was what it was, might turn up more information than a minute examination of every fissure in the reef.

During the next two weeks, a kind of pattern developed in the life on the island. About an hour after the professional divers went out to comb the outer reef, the Drakes and the camera crew went to the inner bay to make their film. The water was much clearer there than where the bottom was stirred up by surf, and gradually all pretense of an honest documentary film was forgotten. The real treasure hunt was too boring, as well as almost invisible in the murky waters off the edge of the reef where the divers felt wrecks were most likely to be found. What Drake wanted were pictures of himself and his pretty wife swimming through showers of colorful fish and having adventures from which they could save each other. When Ben showed them where the old Hog Islander lay, Drake had his wife pretend to enmesh herself in a coil of ancient steel cable, from which he rescued her, with four professional divers hovering just out of camera range to rescue them both if they got into any real trouble.

At this sort of amiable nonsense the movie crew was as skillful as the real treasure hunters were at their difficult trade offshore, and every night Drake grew more confident that within the month he had allotted himself he could indeed come up with a marketable film that would be good publicity for his wife, and would earn him her gratitude if nothing else. Drake's enthusiasm knew no bounds when, on only the sixth day of the "expedition," the men offshore actually found a four-pound cannonball, some grapeshot and some bits of broken china.

"This whole deal is turning out to be legit after all," he

said, and had the objects moved to the clearer water, where Donna could find them for the cameras.

All this highly professional activity had a curiously depressing effect on Ben. In the beginning, he had actually hoped he could produce a good movie here, but now it was silly to imagine that Drake was making anything but a quickie suitable only for Saturday afternoon television. In the beginning the dream of the gold cannon had sometimes grown so intense he had almost felt he could reach out and touch them, but the growing pile of almost valueless, if interesting, relics which the divers brought in from the reef gave mute testimony to the fact that gold cannon were about as rare aboard ancient Spanish ships as aboard modern American ones. Instead of gold cannon, the divers found broken bottles, a belt buckle, the handle of a sword, a horseshoe, the bones of a cat clearly outlined in a chunk of coral, a glass inkwell, and a blunderbuss which disintegrated almost as soon as it was broken from the coral.

In all likelihood that was all there would ever be, Ben thought. It was time to force himself to stop building his life on dreams. Every day Nort appeared to be growing more restless. At any moment he might simply abandon the whole project in disgust, leaving Ben without a job.

"You'll wind up plunging out toilets in a motel," Nancy had said.

He did not talk much with Nancy now. Convinced that her husband was always listening, Nancy contented herself with smiles and bland remarks about the weather, but often when he was in the dining room or living room, Ben found that her eyes were upon him, burning into him. When their eyes met she smiled, and holding up one of her prematurely desiccated little hands, she gave him a casual wave.

The only good thing in his life, he realized, was Penny, but even she appeared to be changing subtly, or perhaps his own subjective vision of her was undergoing some revision.

325

Almost every day she received more letters, which she read in private and never discussed. After the arrival of one large envelope, which was addressed in the same bold hand, she said she had to go into Miami on business, and when he offered to drive her, she looked annoyed.

"I have all kinds of things to do, and I want to see an old friend," she said. "I'm only going to be gone for a day!"

It was only a day, but it seemed long to him, full of gathering suspicions and questions. Was the man who had left her trying to get her back, and was she tempted? In any case, was her interest in him, Ben, dying, and was this whole interlude on the island going to turn out to be just another temporary arrangement, a pleasant memory with a painful end? He could see himself in a few weeks returning to his hotel room in New York, alone, middle-aged, and not only disillusioned but hurt enough to make it much harder to sustain an illusion ever again. How long could a man live who had lost the ability to believe that any human emotion is really lasting?

When Penny came back from Miami she said nothing of what she had done there, but she seemed tired and depressed. In moments of tension, she had a habit of snapping her fingers soundlessly and chewing her lower lip, and now these mannerisms were intensified.

"Is something troubling you?" Ben asked after a long evening of silence.

"I told you I got bitchy sometimes, didn't I?" she demanded accusingly.

"Yes."

"Well, this is just one of those times. If you can't stand it . . ."

She let the sentence trail off.

It was difficult to stand, Ben thought — the loss of affection was always difficult for him to stand, even if he knew it was temporary, and he wasn't sure this was. Still, it could be fatal to start an argument now, to respond with sharpness to sharpness.

Doubling up his fists in his pockets, Ben took a long solitary walk along the shore. When he got back Penny said, "I'm sorry — I just feel lousy. I didn't mean to bark at you."

"Is there anything I can do to help?"

She shrugged.

"It's just a mood, I guess. Give me three or four days. It will wear off."

And she was right. On the fourth day she awoke as warmly cheerful as ever, and teased him into making love for so long before breakfast that they got nothing but lukewarm coffee served to them alone in the dining room.

"Thanks for riding out the storm," she said. "I'll make it up to you."

"It was a very short storm," he replied, but he realized that it had left a kind of scar on both of them, a renewed realization that whatever the mysterious force was that made them so good together, it could mysteriously disappear, leaving them like any other querulous, disenchanted couple.

But the good days obviously could come back, Ben told himself, and if nourished carefully like a small flame, they might continue. That afternoon, he borrowed Nort's jeep, and they spent the night in the ruin of his father's house, building two walls of driftwood which, when covered by a tarpaulin, kept out a fairly heavy rain.

There followed a week which could have been perfect, Ben thought, if it hadn't been for the increasing tension generated throughout the island by Nort. Although Nort was rarely visible, his growing frustration at the divers' failure to find anything of value was felt everywhere. When the barge with a big crane for raising heavy objects off the bottom was late in arriving, Nort flew into a rage, despite the fact that the divers had not yet located anything heavy they wanted to raise. Ben was ordered to fly to Miami immediately and get a crane without delay, regardless of cost. When he returned, he found that Nort had chartered another large powerboat and had made arrangements with a skin-diving club in New York which sent down twenty expert amateurs to join the hunt.

CHAPTER 19

B<small>EN</small>! Nort called, and knocked hard at the door of Ben's room.

"Yes?" Ben said.

"Drake wants to have some kind of conference about the movie. Let's go down to the yawl."

"All right," Ben said. "I'll be right there."

It was about three in the afternoon, and he had been trying to prepare some dialogue Drake had requested. Ben hurried to the mooring.

"Good to see you, gentlemen," Drake said with an air of formality. "We've got to do something about this movie."

He was sitting on a bunk beside Donna, who was licking an orange popsicle.

"What's wrong with it?" Nort asked.

"Not enough action. We've got some great sequences of Donna, but for contrast we need some blood and guts. What we need, in short, is sharks. Lots of them."

"Oh, can't we do something better than that?" Ben groaned. "That shark bit has been done again and again."

"I'm going to have a new angle. First of all, the film is going to show me killing a lot of big sharks with a speargun. It's easy to fake that. But if I'm going to be killing sharks, there has to be a reason. We have to get the audience to hate sharks. So I thought we'd show the sharks killing something."

"What?" Nort asked with interest.

"I thought a dog," Drake said. "We can build it into the story line, Ben. Donna here has a favorite dog, something like a Newfoundland retriever. Anyway, this dog goes in the water a lot and the sharks get it. That will make my anger at the sharks understandable."

"Will you show it?" Nort asked.

"Show what?"

"Will you actually show the sharks killing a dog?"

"Oh, hell, we can fake it. There's no problem there. What do you think of the idea, Ben?"

"I guess it's all right," Ben said. "But if you want to keep this within shouting distance of a legitimate documentary, I don't think you should present sharks as a great menace to divers."

"Just what are the circumstances in which sharks actually attack?" Drake asked.

"Anything flopping on the surface is in danger, and blood brings them. Blood drives them into a kind of orgy."

"A killing orgy!" Nort said. "Fantastic. Have you ever seen one?"

"Not since the war," Ben said.

"I mean the real thing," Nort continued. "I saw a movie of a genuine killing orgy once. Sharks attacked a whale that had just been harpooned. More and more sharks came homing in. The water was full of blood and the sharks got so excited they began eating each other. There was one shot of a shark eating the whale while another shark ate him."

"Boy!" Donna said.

"It would be great if we could show something like that in our film," Drake said, "but where in hell would we get a whale?"

"It wouldn't have to be a whale," Nort said. "It could be anything big — maybe a cow or a horse. A dog would be gone in no time."

"You've got an idea there!" Drake replied. "Say we forget the dog and give Donna a favorite horse. We could get some great shots of her riding on the beach. On hot days she likes to ride the horse right into the water, the way they do in rivers out West, and the sharks get him. We show a killing orgy right near the beginning of the film."

"Will we do it with real sharks?" Donna asked.

She put her popsicle in an ashtray.

"What do you think, Ben?" Drake said. "Could we stage a thing like that for real?"

"You're damn right you could!" Nort retorted before Ben had time to speak. "You can draw all the sharks you want out there. All you've got to have is enough blood."

"You could undoubtedly draw a lot of sharks if you want to throw enough pork or beef into the water," Ben said. "Whether they'd go into a killing orgy or not, I don't know."

331

"You're going to have to have something big and bleeding, preferably something alive," Nort said. "Hell, we could send up to Kissimmee for a big old Brahman cow or a horse headed for the glue factory. They have all kinds of livestock up there."

"That's a good idea," Drake said. "Of course, we'd get into trouble with the animal lovers if we showed too much of it on film, but we could tell them we faked a lot of what was real."

"I think we ought to keep the whole film as *real* as we can," Donna said.

"I don't like to be a spoilsport, but I really think this is a terrible idea," Ben said.

"Why?" Nort asked.

"It's revolting — using some old cow or horse as shark bait. And I also doubt if you'd get much that would look particularly good on film."

"We could get some great underwater shots," Drake said. "We can put our cameramen in underwater steel cages, so they won't be hurt."

"I guarantee you all the sharks you want," Nort said. "Hell, we'll throw a barrel of waste from some slaughterhouse off the end of the jetty every day. Sharks soon learn where there's a steady supply of food. And I can bring more in when you want them by towing the carcass of a hog clear around the island. Hell, I'll have dozens of them following the boat. Then you take an old horse or cow and slit a few arteries, but not enough to kill it. We want the thing to kick around. We can put the animal on the ferry, and when the time comes, just push it off."

"Won't it be terribly dangerous?" Donna asked.

"No, honey," Drake said. "We show you riding your horse into the water. Then, say, he gets caught in a current. I come out in the boat and save you, but I can't save the horse. I try, but he panics. We can film all that any time, and then we cut to this terrific shot of sharks actually killing the horse."

"What's the matter with you, Ben?" Nort asked. "You always look so sour."

"I don't know," Ben said, shrugging.

"It's commercial as hell," Drake said.

"I suppose so," Ben replied, feeling curiously weary. "It's just not my sort of thing, I guess. To tell you the truth, I hate the whole idea."

"Come off it, Ben!" Nort retorted indignantly. "Listen, you've got to get with this. At least you can give us some practical help. Tomorrow take the truck and drive up to Kissimmee and get an old horse. You might as well get a couple, in case something goes wrong the first time."

"No," Ben said, "that's not my job, Nort. For that you'll have to find somebody else."

Quietly Ben got up and started ashore.

"Ben, where are you going?" Nort asked.

"To get some fresh air," Ben said, and jumped to the dock.

Behind him he could hear Nort cursing and calling, "Ben! Ben! You come back!" but he walked away from the boat without a backward glance. When he got to the beach he gave in to an impulse to run, and he pounded along on the hard sand until his breath was gone.

"What's the matter?" Penny asked when he reached their room fifteen minutes later.

"I got into a kind of argument," Ben replied. "To tell the truth, I'm not sure why I got so upset."

Unwilling to worry Penny unnecessarily, he talked her into going for a swim and said nothing further about the incident.

The quarrel with Nort was an essentially harmful one, Ben recognized. The tension between him and his employer

333

had become acute. All the next day Nort kept glaring at him. When he saw Ben the following evening, he gave him a sardonic grin and said, "I hate to do anything to upset your squeamish stomach, but the horses arrived this afternoon. I've had a place fixed for them out in the orange grove. Why don't you go out and have a look at them?"

"I thought you were going to look for gold, Nort," Ben said. "Won't all this nonsense louse up your treasure hunt?"

"Oh, there's time for everything," Nort replied easily. "Don't tell me that you've been in the television business for twenty years without learning that there's gold in blood?"

And the horrible thing is, he's right, Ben reflected; Nort would probably make a lot of money by throwing an old horse into the sea for sharks. And I'll take my share, Ben thought grimly — I'll take my share, like all the rest.

Feeling rotten, Ben went to ask Penny if she wanted to go for a walk. As they passed the orange grove on the way to the beach, he saw two decrepit brown horses standing in a hastily improvised corral. Penny insisted on stopping to pat them.

"The poor things are very old," she said. "What is Nort going to do with them?"

"I don't know," Ben said, thinking the lie was justified because she would find the truth so hard to live with, but still feeling very uncomfortable.

"Why would he buy two oldtimers like these?" Penny insisted.

"Do you really want to know?" he asked, wondering whether he hadn't also been protecting himself in some fashion with his lie.

"Yes," Penny said. "What's going on?"

"Nort and Drake are going to throw those horses to the sharks and try to film a killing orgy. Now, can you tell me why that makes me so upset that I just want to get the hell out of here?"

"I'm glad it makes you upset," Penny said quietly.

"But it's silly. Thousands of animals are killed in stockyards every week. Men, women and children are being killed in Vietnam every day. Why do I worry about two old horses?"

"The exploitation of cruelty is worse than cruelty itself."

"It's done on television in a thousand stereotyped forms every day!"

"Which is one reason why you don't want to go back to television — right?"

"Penny, sometimes I get scared. I'm too old for the sensitive bit, but sometimes I feel I'm becoming less fitted for this world all the time."

"Yes," she said with a smile. "I've felt that way often. But where shall we go?"

The next day Nort approached Ben at breakfast.

"Ben boy, I've made a decision I think will please you," he said jovially.

"What's that?"

"Drake has been talking to some of his technicians, and they're going to film that shark bit painlessly. They stand one of those old horses up on the edge of the deck of the ferry and shoot it. It will be dead when it hits the water, and it was going to be shot anyway, so I can't see how anyone can have a gripe."

"Not on cruelty-to-animals grounds, anyway," Ben said.

"On what grounds, then?"

"Do you really want to talk about it?"

"I certainly do!"

"This kind of contrived violence bothers me. If Drake wants to show how sharks actually live, all right, but to show them killing a horse, whether he fakes it or not, is providing a Roman circus. What he really wants is oceans of blood, and he may be right in guessing that this is what the public likes. That's exactly what revolts me."

"You actually are quite a prude, aren't you, Ben?" Nort asked with a contradictorily pleasant smile.

"I don't like violence, I don't like killing, and I don't like catering to the blood lusts of other people. If that makes me a prude . . ."

"But you don't mind sex in any form, right? That's all you ever think or write about. Every so-called drama you've ever done hinges on who gets whom into bed. Don't you think that's catering to the lusts of the public? What effect do you think all that stuff has on the young?"

"I would rather have my children see people making love on the screen than see them killing each other or torturing animals," Ben said.

Nort laughed.

"Ben Powers, the self-righteous pornographer!"

"I didn't say anything about pornography, I said making love. Oh hell, Nort, let's break this up. You don't know what I'm talking about!"

"Perhaps I don't have enough formal education," Nort said nastily. "Well, there's no use busting up an old friendship over that. I have an assignment for you — that's what I really came to say."

"What kind of an assignment?"

"I've guaranteed Drake plenty of sharks. Will you go into Key West or Miami or wherever the hell you have to go to find an abattoir, and arrange to have a barrel of some kind of blood and guts delivered here every day? I'm going to chum for sharks just the way we used to chum for perch."

"Is this really to be one of my duties?"

"I can't do all the organizational work myself, Ben! I

have to have some help on details. After all, you are on salary. Is it really so wrong of me to ask you to do this?"

"No," Ben said. "I'll see to it." He wondered whether Nort had imposed this small demeaning task purposely to humiliate him.

He strode angrily to his room.

"Penny, do you want to go into Miami?" he asked.

"Sure, what's up?"

"Nort has won a small victory over me. Come with me, my love, as I go out into the splendor of the morning in pursuit of blood and guts."

CHAPTER 20

Every day more people arrived on the island. Nort made arrangements to rent two of the big mansions which had been closed for years, but even so it was necessary to bring in a half-dozen house trailers. More and more Janus Island seemed to Ben to resemble a beachhead during an invasion, and there was the same kind of rising excitement he had experienced as D-day approached.

At first the tension was entirely Nort's, for the divers

and the movie people seemed perfectly content to go from day to day enjoying their work. The trouble with Nort, Ben felt, was that the longer the reef was explored without success, the more fanciful became his plan for discovering great riches. Nort was afraid of looking foolish. Many of the divers were on salary, and what with all the boats and equipment he had rented, Nort was spending many thousands of dollars a day. He could afford the money, but not the sense of failure, of feeling he had blundered. As a result, he was like a gambler in over his head, spending yet more money on additional divers and equipment, and on the rare occasions he left his rooms, he seemed thinner and more charged with violent nervous energy than ever.

Days went by when Ben never saw Nort, and there were times when he got the eerie sensation that he had imagined the man, or that Nort's peculiarities were simply the product of Nancy's mind. On the other hand, the indications were that he was busy with his electronic eavesdropping: a lot of people kept getting fired without explanation. George Grey was the first to go, but the old man was so surly that his departure was hardly a surprise. The next day the bald diver, who was the best of the professionals, found a note on his dinner plate saying simply that his services were no longer required, and that the ferry would take him ashore in an hour. A check was enclosed. When the bewildered man asked to see his employer, Nort sent word through Nancy that he was extremely busy and did not wish to be disturbed.

Almost every other day after that some member of the boat crews or one of the divers was summarily discharged, to be replaced by a new recruit flown in from Miami. The men made a joke of these sudden departures, but they enjoyed their work, and the apprehension they felt was reflected in their faces each time they came into the dining room and inspected their plates. Was Nort simply an

339

erratic employer subject to sudden dislikes, Ben wondered, or was he listening all the time to what the men said in their rooms? The bald diver had been an outspoken critic of Nort's reckless boat-handling, and it was possible that Nort had overheard enough to wound his sensitive feelings.

With Nort invisible almost all the time, there was no way Ben could verify his speculations, but the conviction that everything he said was being heard grew into something of a mania with him, and he found himself whispering to Penny even on the beach.

The first concrete proof that at least some of his suspicions were well founded came about a week later in circumstances which made it seem almost unimportant. At about ten o'clock in the evening a servant came to Ben's room and said there was a telephone call for him. He hurried to the telephone in the little alcove off the living room. It was a wire from Massachusetts, where Laura had returned to Wellesley College. The moment he heard the phrase "Western Union" he steeled himself for bad news, and the message he received was more emotional because it was read by a young girl whose voice, far from being impersonal, quivered.

"Dads, please don't be worried, but we've done it. Bill and I were married today. Know eloping is cruel, but almost everybody disapproved except us. This is the choice we both made. He is going to be drafted in June, and we need a little time together. Thank you for making me know you will understand. We both have part-time jobs now, so won't be able to travel this summer, but come see us soon. Best compliment I can give you is that my beautiful husband reminds me a little of you. Love, Laura."

There was a pause when the Western Union operator finished reading.

"Do you wish to make any reply, sir?" she asked.

"Yes," he said, and hesitated, finding it difficult to word his thoughts.

The line hummed.

"Please take this down," Ben said. "Congratulations! Blessings! Good luck! See you as soon as I can get away. Wedding gift of five hundred dollars is in mail. If your husband is anything like me, he loves you very much. As ever, Dad."

"Thank you," the Western Union girl said. "We will mail you the telegram."

"Good."

Feeling oddly light-headed, Ben went back to his rooms.

"Is everything all right?" Penny asked.

"I hope so."

"What happened?"

"Laura got married."

"Oh, Ben! Maybe it's for the best."

"Maybe. I know it isn't true that my personal history must inevitably repeat itself."

"Of course it isn't."

"I know how rough things can be when you're nineteen."

"Only then?"

"Kids have so few defenses! I keep thinking that if I'd been able to give her a good home, she wouldn't have had to do this so soon."

"Was that within your power?"

"It might have been."

"Nineteen isn't really so horribly young, you know. How old is the boy?"

"I don't know. He graduates from B.U. in June."

"That doesn't sound so abysmal."

"Then he's going to be drafted. It's all exactly the way it was with me."

"So far."

"So far," he said.

There was a moment of silence.

"Tonight I'm very glad I have you," he said. "At least I

can worry about them without any deep sense of personal loss. Before I met you, I really depended on Laura more than was fair."

"I'm glad you have me, too."

"Would you like to go to Boston with me to see them? Tomorrow I'm going to tell Nort I'll be gone for three days."

"Do you want me to go?"

"Yes. I'd like them to meet you, and more than that, I'll be happy if you're there and miserable without you."

"Then I'll be there."

Feeling suddenly exhausted, Ben went to bed. Almost immediately he fell asleep, but two hours later he awoke, edgy and restless. Beside him, Penny was sleeping peacefully. Afraid he would disturb her with his tossing, Ben got up and went outside to take a walk along the beach. Just outside the front door of the house, he saw the glow of a cigarette in the darkness.

"Is that you, Ben?"

It was Nancy's voice.

"Yes," he said.

Slowly she walked toward him.

"Should I say I'm sorry to hear about Laura, or should I offer congratulations?"

"How did you hear about it?"

"Nort told me. Were you still under the illusion that you could keep any secrets from him?"

Ben shrugged.

"Do you have to go to Boston soon?"

"Tomorrow."

"Please don't! Nort is reaching some sort of a crisis, Ben. Call it nothing but a premonition if you want, but I have an idea we're going to need you terribly in the next few days."

"I have my own crisis!"

"I know, but have you thought that your daughter might not want you to break into her honeymoon?"

Oddly, he had not thought of that, and he was chagrined.

"O.K., I'll wait a couple of weeks," he said.

"Thank God. I think you ought to know, Ben, that this news about Laura has upset Nort in a strange way."

"How?"

"You were so calm about it. Our oldest girl wanted to get married, and Nort became almost hysterical. He raised so much hell that the poor kids finally got disgusted and broke up. Do you know how he managed that?"

"No."

"He asked the young man up to his study and explained very seriously that his daughter had deep emotional problems — that she was, in fact, promiscuous. When the young man refused to believe him, he played him some tapes he had made of her and another boy. The poor young fellow turned white and ran."

"That's incredible."

"But it worked. Our girl now knows she can never marry without her father's approval unless she finds quite a man."

"Nort ought to be locked up," Ben said.

"Of course. But do you have any idea what I would have to go through to do it? He has a dozen lawyers in his employ, and miles of tape of me he wouldn't hesitate to play in court."

"If he got me in that position, I think I'd kill him."

"No."

"I could not allow another person to control me."

"If you could help it . . ."

"Yes, if I could help it."

"You've got to remember that Nort doesn't think he's controlling people. He thinks he's upholding high moral standards. He gets terribly upset at the tapes he takes of people in bed. He thinks God should strike them down, and since God doesn't . . ."

"Good old Nort steps in to help."

"Exactly. He thinks of himself as God's right-hand man."

"Then he is mad."

"Of course. But he's worth saving, Ben, and I think we can do it if we can get him over this particular crisis. We've got to get him through his frustration when this whole wild scheme of his fails."

"I'll try," Ben said wearily. "I'll try."

Finding that his restlessness had turned to extreme fatigue, Ben went back to bed.

In the morning he explained to Penny that it would be best to postpone the trip to Boston, both for the young couple's sake and for Nort's.

"Nancy is afraid he's on the edge of a real crackup," he said. "What will he do if he finds there simply are no gold cannon? What does a man like that do when all his certainties turn out to be illusory?"

"What do any of us do?" Penny asked, and he guessed from the look in her eye that she was thinking of her onetime fiancé, now married to someone else.

What would he himself do, Ben wondered suddenly, if once more all his own certainties turned out to be illusions? What if this girl turned out to have another man she might return to; what if the strange depression she had suffered became chronic, and the two of them found themselves quarreling like any bored married couple, convinced that love was only a mirage or a dream?

He had survived one marriage that had ended that way, but he had a dreadful feeling that he was too old now to go through it again. In all likelihood he would start drinking heavily, and that ache in his shoulder which had been letting him alone lately would come back and grow, with bouts of dizziness such as his father had suffered until there had been the final, merciful stab to the heart.

In a strange way Ben felt a certain kinship to Nort: they both lived in dread of discovering that the goals they pursued existed only in their imaginations. Just as Nort drove himself to a frenzy, calling in more men and more equipment to widen his search and firing those who "betrayed" him, Ben was trying harder than ever to make his relationship with Penny not just his last big affair, one more bittersweet memory at best, but the start of a life, as he phrased it to himself, "that might begin to make some sense."

To escape the feeling that Nort was always listening, Ben and Penny went often to the ruin at the end of the island. It was entirely possible, Ben knew, that Nort could have placed listening devices even there, buried in the sand or hidden behind the last remaining bricks, but somehow he felt more private on his own land. For hours they lay under the tarpaulin talking to each other as though there would never again be a chance to communicate. Often in the afternoon there were thundersqualls, and the beat of rain on the tarpaulin overhead somehow increased their sense of privacy and warmth.

"I love to talk to you," Penny said on one such afternoon. "It's like breaking out of a cage. Even when I was in love before, I felt I was in one wire cage and the man was in another. The two cages might be so close together that it was possible to touch, but it was never really possible to feel united."

"I too have been cut by wire," he said.

She stretched out on her back and reached out her hand to touch a stream of water which was falling from a wrinkle in the tarpaulin to a gutter he had dug in the sand.

"You know, when I get depressed," she said, "I think I

kind of go back into the past. I got quite a shock when I was twelve years old, after my mother died. Do you mind if I tell you about it?"

"I want you to," he said.

"When Mother died, Dad decided to take her back to Ireland to be buried. He said she had always wanted to go back there. So we went over with her casket on the boat."

"That must have been difficult for a young girl."

"Well, it was pretty emotional, getting the casket loaded and unloaded and all. I'll never forget that big oblong crate outlined against the sky as it was hauled up by the crane, and the sound it made when they set it down. I had this terrible fantasy that it was going to break open . . ."

Ben took her hand. He had found that when she wanted to unburden herself in this way, it was better to say nothing.

"Of course my father was under a terrible strain," she continued. "On the boat he drank a great deal. The voyage lasted nine days."

Her hand tightened on his, but her voice was calm, almost detached.

"People didn't know the nature of our trip," Penny continued. "There were a lot of lonely women on board. My father was a very handsome man, and they saw he was unattached. They pursued him, and he drank."

Her fingernails started to bite into his hand now.

"One night I woke up scared, and I went to his state-room, which was right next to mine," Penny said. "I found him with a woman. They were so drunk they hadn't even thought to lock the door."

Her voice suddenly grew tense.

"He saw me. He said, 'Goddammit, get out of here!' I went back to my cabin. The next morning, he didn't even remember."

"He was lucky," Ben said.

"If I had been older I would have understood, but at twelve, I could only think of my mother down there in the hold, and my father with that awful woman, cursing at me. It had a terrible effect on me."

Again her voice became detached.

"I guess I thought that obviously there was only one way to hold a man, or maybe I just wanted to get even with him. Anyway, I started, right then, at twelve, flirting with the sailors and the busboys. I pinned balls of Kleenex under my sweater, and I bought lipstick in the ship's store. My father was drinking so much he didn't realize what was going on at first."

Once more her voice grew tense.

"But I stuck at it," she said. "One night when he came to my stateroom, he found me there with a busboy, and he got the shock of his life. That was the night he decided to put me in a convent."

Ben remained silent, a sick, hollow feeling in the pit of his stomach.

"I was in agony," she continued. "I hated my father and despised myself and envied my mother. When we got to Ireland, there were all those relatives keening at the wake, and my father kept crying and saying how much he had loved my mother, what a saint she was. Well, I knew I wasn't a saint, and I knew he wasn't. I thought we were both going to fry in hell forever. Then there was the convent and all those nuns and the eternal praying . . ."

"For how many years?"

"Four. And when I got out I figured I was going to hell anyway, so it didn't make a damn bit of difference what I did."

"That's understandable."

"I was never able to confess," she said. "Not about the busboy, when I was only twelve years old. You're the first person I ever told that to. It's strange, how I make you into my priest."

"Do you want me to absolve you?"

"I know you do, or I wouldn't have told you, but I think I want to hear you say it."

"I forgive you," he said. "You are forgiven."

"I know it's silly, but, God, those words sound good!"

"Do you forgive me?" he asked.

"For what?"

"Ten thousand sins."

"Describe one."

"I have lived forty-five years without knowing anyone around me, not my father, not my wife, not any of my mistresses, and I think not my son."

"Do you repent?"

"God knows I do."

"Then I forgive you, but I won't ever forgive you if you don't get to know me. I won't let that happen."

"Good," he said, and there was a pleasant silence broken only by the beat of the rain on the canvas and the distant crash of breakers.

CHAPTER 21

Two days later Nort strolled up to Ben in the living room of the big house shortly before dinner.

"Ben, we're going to do the shark bit tomorrow if the weather holds," he said. "Do you want to come?"

"Not if I can help it," Ben replied.

"Nance is going to be there, and she particularly asked me to request your presence," Nort continued. "Come on, Ben! This could be tricky. We'll need your help."

Indeed it could be tricky, Ben guessed. If things went

wrong with the intricate preparations for feeding a horse to the sharks, Nort might drink and grow exceedingly hard to handle. Seeing he was apparently being paid to be his brother's keeper, Ben felt he might as well try to do a good job of it.

"All right, Nort," he said. "When does this marvelous operation start?"

"At nine sharp they're loading the horse aboard the ferry. I'm going to have two boats dragging fresh-killed hogs all around that area for an hour beforehand, and that kid of Minnie Lee's has been dumping that stuff you had them deliver from Miami on every outgoing tide for a week. I'll bet we'll have a hundred sharks out there. Some of the cameramen have already tried out those cages they put down, and they say the area is swarming with them now."

"Your horse is going to be dead when he hits the water?" Ben asked.

"That's the plan. The kid is going to hold him by the bow ramp, and I'll put a .303 bullet right in the side of his head."

"O.K.," Ben said resignedly. "I'll see you at nine."

"You can bring your girl if you like," Nort replied. "A hell of a lot of people want to go, so I kind of have to hand out reserved tickets."

"Penny won't want to go," Ben replied. "You can give her ticket to somebody else."

"Are you sure she won't?" Nort said, cocking an eyebrow. "Have you ever seen women at bullfights or wrestling matches? There's nothing most women like better than the sight of a little blood."

"Not Penny," Ben said. "Maybe, like me, she's seen enough."

On the way back to his room, however, Ben found himself wondering whether he had been right to turn down the invitation for Penny. Although the spectacle of feeding an old horse to a hundred sharks did not seem to smack of high sport, a killing orgy was a phenomenon of nature she might want to see.

He found her sitting in an armchair knitting a sweater.

"Penny," he said. "They're going to try to film the killing orgy tomorrow. Want to go?"

"You mean they're going to throw that old horse to the sharks?"

"They're going to shoot it first."

"Ugh," Penny said shivering. "I think I'll pass this one up. Are you going to go?"

"Nort wants me there, and I guess it's part of my job. If he gets excited and starts drinking, the thing could turn out to be an even worse mess than has been planned."

The next morning Ben got up at eight o'clock. The sky was a bright azure with only two small fluffy white clouds, and the sea was so smooth that the roar of the breakers on the reef had sunk to only an affectionate-sounding whisper. It was, Nort said jovially at breakfast, a great day for a killing orgy.

Ben drank two cups of black coffee. His stomach felt so tense that he didn't want to eat anything at all. During the war he had lost any trace of squeamishness about the sight of blood, but the preparations for the death of the old horse continued to plague his conscience.

The horse selected for the first experiment was a thin brown mare which had been dyed white to show up better in the water and to match the younger horse which had been acquired for Donna to ride in earlier sequences of the film. Its spotless, powdered coat looked completely artificial, inconsistent with the protruding ribs and swayback. A tall Negro in a straw hat led it across the island to the ferry landing. Unprotesting, the horse followed along, stopping every few minutes to munch the new green leaves of bamboo trees.

"Get along, there!" the handler shouted. "Get along!" But he did not jerk at the halter rope, and his hand was gentle as he stroked the animal's flank.

"Move him along faster!" Nort said, pulling up in his jeep with Ben and Nancy. "I don't want to keep the men in those cages out there waiting!"

Slapping the old horse with the end of the halter rope, the Negro gave a gruff "Gid-ap!" and the animal broke into a disheartened, shambling trot.

When they got to the ferry, Ben was surprised to find that the landing craft was as crowded as a Hudson River excursion boat on a Sunday afternoon. Word of the spectacle had spread fast, and almost everyone on the island apparently wanted to see it. Donna Drake and her husband were standing in the pilothouse. At least a dozen old people from the retirement colony were there, picnic hampers in hand, and a half-dozen children of both races frolicked on the upper deck. Perching on a comfortable chair on the stern, Nancy smoked imperturbably. What with the camera crew, fifteen divers, and many technicians, the boat was so crowded that there was little room for the horse.

"All right — everybody off, except those who have my specific permission for this trip!" Nort barked in his deep voice.

An old lady who looked like a sweet old grandmother in a gingham dress and floppy hat pleaded with Nort tearfully for permission to stay. She had a new camera, she said, with color film, and had promised her grandchildren pictures.

"No!" Nort said sternly. "Everybody ashore except those who have my specific permission. Move! You're holding us up. There are men in cages out there waiting. Do you think they have air enough for the whole day?"

Muttering sullenly, about half the people straggled ashore.

"All right!" Nort shouted. "Now bring that horse aboard!"

The horse started to amble after the handler, but at the ramp it balked.

"Come on!" Nort said. "It's getting late!"

"Come on, baby!" the handler said, stroking the horse's neck. "Just a few more steps."

But the horse would not take them. The handler tugged at the rope, and the divers slapped its flanks and pushed, but the old horse just stood there, letting its nose sink almost to the beach.

"Goddammit!" Nort said, glaring at his wristwatch. "Give me a piece of line!"

Someone handed him a heavy manila mooring line. Knotting the end of it, he went up to the horse and with all his strength delivered a tremendous blow on the horse's right haunch. Stung, the horse lurched forward, panicked and reared like a young stallion in the center of the ferry, tearing the lead rope from his handler. Divers and cameramen scattered in every direction. Trying to avoid the flying hooves, Ben was almost knocked to his feet by three fleeing octogenarians who had ignored Nort's order to get ashore.

"Hold his head!" Nort shouted. "Get his head!"

Following Ben, three young divers sprang forward. It took only a few minutes to subdue the animal. With its sides heaving, it stood by the rail, its breath making a horrible rasping sound.

"There, there!" its handler said, stroking its neck. "It's all right, everything is fine now, you just quiet down."

"Let's get out of here!" Nort shouted. "Navy, you know where to go."

Navy put the big diesel engine into reverse. At the

unfamiliar sound of the gears, the horse threw its head up and its ears went back, but it did not rear again — instead, it stood stock-still, the muscles of its thin haunches and forelegs trembling.

The landing barge headed for a spot off the end of the jetty where the yawl was kept. There the two cruisers which had carried the divers and the cameramen were circling slowly. Coming alongside the ferry, the operator of the camera boat shouted through an electric microphone, "Everything's set, Mr. Clay! We've been towing hogs around here for two hours, and the men in the cages say there's everything down there from a sixteen-foot hammerhead on down to a million sand sharks."

"Fine!" Nort said. "Navy, anchor by that buoy, the way I showed you."

Working with the divers, Navy dropped heavy anchors from both the bow and stern of the ferry, paying out chain to keep the heavy craft by a small white buoy.

"Come on!" Nort kept shouting. "We're running behind schedule!"

"All set now!" Navy finally replied. "We're right on the spot."

"Get the horse to the edge of the bow ramp!" Nort said.

Once more the horse balked, but the divers were more careful this time and did not let it rear. Surrounded by a dozen athletic young men, the horse allowed itself to be pushed to the end of the ramp, where it stood trembling, its nostrils foaming slightly.

"You men get back!" Nort said, taking a heavy rifle from the pilothouse. "Get back!"

The divers and the handler sprang back, but before Nort could shoot, the panic-stricken horse, feeling itself freed, reared up on its hind legs again, slipped on the hard steel deck and fell heavily sideways into the sea, causing an enormous splash. Wild-eyed, the animal began to swim in frantic circles, turning first one way and then the other. Glancing at Nort, Ben saw that he was still holding the rifle to his cheek, aiming at the erratically turning head.

"Why don't you shoot?" Ben asked, wanting the horse out of its misery as soon as possible.

"Not in the water," Nort replied. "There are men down there. This is a damn powerful gun."

"I don't think you're going to have to bother," Dick Drake said. "Look!"

From three different directions black fins cut through the water toward the struggling horse, and under the clear surface of the sea, dozens of dark shadows became visible.

"Nort, you can hit the horse's head!" Ben said. "There's no danger."

"Why take a chance?" Nort replied with a smile, and lowered the rifle.

For a moment Ben considered the possibility of grabbing the gun from him.

"Look!" Donna shrieked. "God, look!"

The horse suddenly threw its head up, its mouth open in a silent shriek. There was a violent boiling of water, almost like the explosion of a depth charge, a cauldron of white foam which turned suddenly red. There was no sound at all — in its silence the horse's head with its open mouth and crazed eyes gave a strange dignity to terror and to death, Ben thought. For a split second the head and neck of the horse seemed to be growing larger as it thrashed, panic-stricken, and rose from the water. Then it collapsed, sliding sideways into the red foam, and slowly disappeared. The boiling foam turned to swirling eddies as the horse sank, carrying its great struggling knot of sharks after it, and the round little stain of red in the sea spread. Only about a minute had elapsed since the horse had fallen into the

355

water — the sharks had at least provided the mercy of speed.

"Is that all there is to it?" Donna asked, sounding disappointed.

"It's just beginning for the boys down below!" Nort said. He was standing with a telephone which had been plugged into the buoy. "Has it started?" he shouted. "Are there enough sharks to make it an orgy yet? Great! That's the stuff!"

Cradling the telephone to his ear with satisfaction, Nort said to Drake, "We're going fine. The sharks are starting in on each other now. My boys down there blooded a few with a speargun to get them going."

Imagining the ferocity of the scene below, Ben stared at the opaque surface of the swirling red sea surrounding the ferry. How curiously discreet nature was, he thought — the sea covered the killing orgy like a blanket, and if it weren't for the prying cameras of the men below, the savage drama would have remained private.

Glancing around the ferry, Ben saw that all the people aboard stood silently looking down at the water, giving the curious appearance that they were deep in prayer. Not a sound was to be heard, while the spreading island of blood gradually turned first to brown, then to gray, and finally a deep blue which became indistinguishable from the rest of the sea.

"It's over," Nort said with a sigh. Brightening, he added, "I guess that'll give the movie people what they want. Now we can concentrate on more important matters."

"Let's go ashore," Ben said.

He was, he found, filled with the most violent agitation, which seemed to be getting worse second by second. It was similar to but worse than the remorse he had experienced when leaving the bullfights in Mexico a few months before.

"When you leave the bullfights, there is nothing to do

but make love," a Mexican prostitute in a bar had said to him.

At the time he had fled back to his room to drink alone, but now he felt the most urgent need for Penny, for a whole day and night alone with her in their private ruin at the end of the island. Closing his eyes, he imagined running with her again through the warm shallows of the tidal basins. If they floated there in the basin filled by clean surf from the open sea, he thought, he might eventually begin to feel clean himself again.

"After seeing that, I don't think I ever want to wet a foot outside of a swimming pool," Donna said, and giggled.

CHAPTER 22

BEN's first real confrontation with Nort came only a few days later. The incident occurred when Nancy was serving a buffet supper to the divers on the terrace, which she had surrounded with kerosene flares to keep the mosquitoes away, and to give light. For a week Nort had not been eating his meals with the others, and Ben was surprised to see him come walking through the smoke created by the flares, his white duck trousers immaculate.

"Ben," he said pleasantly. "I want to talk to you — alone."

Penny had gone to get plates of food, and most of the divers were still gathered around the bar in the living room. Ben followed Nort to the garden. From the careful way Nort spoke, Ben guessed he had been drinking heavily.

"I've been doing some thinking about those cannon," Nort said. "I may have been working on some false assumptions. You've always been a pretty good sailor, Ben. Let me try something out on you."

"What?"

"Let's say you're a Spanish admiral in the year 1680. You'd still be a pretty good sailor, wouldn't you?"

"The best."

"Your flagship carries millions of dollars' worth of gold, including the gold cannon you're going to try to smuggle past the king's men for yourself. You get somewhere just off this island, and it looks as though a hurricane is coming. Remember, you're an old sailor who has sailed these waters for years. You know all the signs."

"I'd try to find myself plenty of sea room."

"You can't. Remember, there is always a calm before a storm. You're lying off these islands with the glass falling and not a breath of air in your sails."

"I guess I'd just set out all my anchors and pray."

"Wouldn't you try to make port?" Nort asked, his voice lowered conspiratorially. "Wouldn't you put out your longboats with every man you had and tow your flagship in?"

"I'd know there was no good port close enough to here. The Spaniards knew the Keys are a hurricane trap."

"No port good enough to save a ship, but how about the gold? How about the gold cannon? Wouldn't you row them ashore and bury them before you lost your ship?"

"I very well might," Ben said.

"That's what happened!" Nort said with triumph. "I'm sure of it. That old bastard had the gold put in longboats and rowed ashore, or maybe he beached his ship. He had his men bury the gold, and then he may have shot them, or maybe the hurricane killed them all, smashed the whole convoy without a trace."

"You may be right. It sounds plausible."

"You're damn right I'm right! That's why you can find every relic of Spanish wrecks around here, but never any gold! It's ashore, all buried ashore! The divers are looking in the wrong place!"

"Have you got the metal detectors for a beach hunt?"

"The best will be flown in tomorrow, and I'm not going to leave one grain of sand on this island unchecked!"

At this point Penny, who had been looking for Ben, came up to him with his plate. Nort was angry at the interruption.

"I guess what we need around here is some busboys," he said, slurring the words a little, perhaps as much from an excess of emotion as from drink.

"What?" Penny asked, wide-eyed.

"Busboys, we need busboys. For you. Isn't that what you like? Then you wouldn't have to carry the plates yourself."

Brushing a lock of hair from her eyes, Penny looked white. There was a pause before she said, "Can I get you coffee, Ben?"

"A little privacy is what we need," Nort said. "I'm talking business with Ben."

"Privacy, Nort?" Ben asked, his voice deadly calm.

Nort glanced up and their eyes met, and suddenly Ben knew — and he knew Nort knew that he knew all about the ubiquitous listening devices.

"I heard that you like to play cat-and-mouse games," Ben said.

Penny stepped back, turned to go, but sensing trouble, stayed.

"You're crazy if you start anything with me now," Nort said. "We're on the eve of the big find."

"Maybe. But if you're bugging my property . . ."

"Your property! Until the government puts it up for a tax sale?"

"That may be, but . . ."

"You're crazy if you pull out now!"

There was a tone of desperation in Nort's voice that made Ben keep silent.

"Listen!" Nort continued. "I'll double your share! Don't walk out on me now. The cannon are here! I know it!"

He stamped his foot.

"I won't leave you now," Ben said. "But Penny's not your mouse and neither am I. Do you think you can remember that?"

"I'd never play cat-and-mouse with you, Ben! You know you can trust me! I've always trusted you, haven't I? Haven't I, Ben?"

"Yes," Ben said.

"I plan to go on trusting you. I never learned anything about you that weakened my confidence in you. You're the only friend I have in the world, Ben!"

"I know."

"You wouldn't let a girl get between us, would you?"

"Get off her back, Nort. I'm going to marry her."

"Oh, you're crazy, Ben. You yourself don't trust her, or you wouldn't be afraid to read my dossier on her."

"What do you mean?" Penny said, stepping forward.

"I'm talking to Ben!" Nort said.

"A *dossier* on me?"

"I keep a dossier on everyone connected with my business, however remote that connection may be."

"I want to see it," Penny said. "That's my right."

"Penny, forget it," Ben said. "It doesn't . . ."

"I demand it!" Penny said. "There's been all this talk — detectives interviewing everyone I ever knew. For some reason, Nort, you've put me on trial. I want to know who my accusers are. I want to read the accusation."

"I'll let you see it sometime if you want," Nort said. "I doubt you'll find it very pleasant reading."

"I want to see it now," Penny said. "Where is it?"

"Please, Penny, don't get caught up in this!" Ben said.

"I am caught up in it already, Ben, and so are you. Nort, where is this famous dossier?"

"I believe it's in Nancy's room. She's been going over it."

Whirling, Penny ran toward the house. On the flagstone terrace ringed by kerosene flares Ben caught up with her.

"Penny!" he said, putting both arms around her shoulders. "Wait!"

"Let me go, Ben," she said quietly. "I have some rights in this matter."

"I don't want to see you hurt."

"Ben, I'm not afraid of my past. You know most of it anyway. I'm only afraid of what the details may do to you, but already there is no reality which could possibly be worse than what Nort is building up in your mind."

"There is nothing in my mind but love for you."

"But always there would be the dossier for you to wonder about. Wait here, Ben! I insist that you see it."

"I'll go with you."

"No! I want to get this from Nancy myself. She can give you a hard time, but not me. I want to confront her myself. Can you understand that?"

"Yes," Ben said, and let her go.

"Ben?"

Nort had followed him.

"What do you want now?"

"Ben, I'm sorry if I've caused you pain, but goddammit, I don't create the facts, I just gather them. If . . ."

"Shut up, Nort."

"Ben! Please don't ——"

"Get away from me!"

"Ben, don't take it so hard. Christ, we don't need anybody else, you and I . . ."

"Nort, I'm getting out of here."

"Ben, for Christ's sake, realize that everything I have done I have done as your friend. Don't cop out on me now. Christ, tomorrow we might find thirty million dollars . . ."

"Jesus!"

"Make fun of it if you like, but . . ."

"Nort, I don't want to hear anything more about your millions of dollars. I want no more from you, Nort! I want no more of your suspicions. I'll help you make no more seas of blood. Screw your gold cannon."

"But Ben, goddammit, you can't just run off like this after forty years of friendship! Who will I have, Ben? You may think you don't need me now, but . . ."

In the darkness by Ben's side Penny suddenly reappeared. Quietly she stepped up and handed him a large manila envelope.

"Here, Ben," she said calmly. "Here I am."

"This is not you," Ben said running his fingers over the envelope. "And I know what to do with it."

Taking one of the kerosene flares, Ben opened the stopper and poured kerosene over the envelope. Dropping it on the flagstone terrace, he tossed the lighted flare on top of it. In the flicker of firelight Nort's face looked the color of tallow.

For an instant the three of them stood staring at yellow flame.

"Ben?" Nort said suddenly. "Are you going to leave me, Ben?"

"I don't think I have to now."

The flames began to die down, shrinking around the charred paper. In the shadows Ben could no longer see Nort's face. There was only the blur of his shirt as he walked silently away in the darkness. Penny too made no sound. Turning from the dying flames, she pressed her head against his chest, and a small patch of his shirt grew wet with her tears.

CHAPTER 23

When Ben went to breakfast the next morning a truck was already unloading crates of electronic equipment which had come from the airstrip, and technicians flown in with it were busily putting together many devices which looked to Ben like the equipment used to locate mines during the war.

Dressed in spotless white ducks and a blue shirt open to the navel, Nort was sitting at the head of a long table, finishing his breakfast.

"Grab a tray and come up to my office, Ben," he said, as though the events of the previous night had never happened. "I want to ask your advice."

"I'll just take a cup of coffee," Ben said. Fortified with this, he followed Nort through the living room and up a winding flight of stairs, at the head of which was a big locked door, much like the one in Long Island. The office, too, proved to be almost a duplicate of the one in Huntington. One wall was devoted to racks of dumbbells and other exercising paraphernalia and another was lined with workbenches full of radio sets, guns, and disassembled electronic equipment. One wall was plastered with enlarged pictures of Nort's children, whom Ben had not seen for years in the flesh, and another was full of charts of Janus Island, with one big enlargement of an ancient map. It was to this that Nort led him.

"Now study that," Nort said. "That's a Spanish chart, drawn about 1602. You can see that the island hasn't changed much."

"The south end has eroded," Ben said.

"A little, and the reef has extended itself about a mile, if the old chart was accurate. Now the point is, Ben, where would you land a cargo of gold if you knew a hurricane was imminent?"

"A longboat could pull in almost anywhere."

"I'm going to start with the supposition that he beached his flagship. That gold was heavy, Ben — it would take a long while to transport it in small boats. The poor bastard probably waited as long as he could, hoping the hurricane would bypass him. The odds are he was in a hell of a hurry."

"How much did those ships draw?"

"A big galleon loaded down took more than twenty feet."

"Then there are only a few places he could come in. The

366

south channel would be his best bet. Even if he wasn't familiar with it, he could find it by the color of the water."

"That's what I think. He'd come in just about where we built the jetty. That's a natural landing place."

"Or he could come around the point into the bay, if he was looking for quiet water."

"Remember, it was a calm — that glassy day just before the hurricane hits. It was somewhere around the jetty, I think, and he wouldn't have moved the gold far. It was too heavy and he was too pressed for time."

"Sounds reasonable, if it was this island at all. I suppose it could have been any one of the keys, according to where he was when the calm hit him."

"It was here," Nort said positively. "He gave a description, Ben. There was one survivor who wrote it down."

"You're sure of that?"

"I have photostats of the old letters. They cost me plenty. Someday I'll show them to you."

"I'd like to see them."

"But first the gold! We'll start searching all around the old jetty. If there's nothing there, we've got to reckon with the possibility that the Gulf Stream was pushing him north all the time he was trying to tow his ship in. He might have been pushed down to the north end of the reef. I'm almost sure it's one end of the island or the other. Hell, he couldn't have come in right over the middle of the reef!"

"That's true."

"Of course, his crew might have survived the hurricane here on shore, and he could have had them bury the stuff anywhere at their leisure. What spot would you pick if you had unlimited time and manpower?"

"I suppose, high ground. I'd be afraid another hurricane would wipe out landmarks."

"Exactly. So we start with the south end of the island. If we find nothing, we go to the north end, and if nothing's there, we comb the ridge. If that's a bust I'm just going to make a systematic sweep from one end to the other. We really can't tell how the geography has changed."

"What if, after all that, you find nothing, Nort?"

"I'm going to find those cannon, Ben! I'm going to find them. I know damn well they're here!"

Moving with the suppressed energy of a boxer just before a fight, Nort ushered Ben out the door, which he locked carefully behind them.

"The men are ready," he said quietly. "Stick with me, Ben. You're going to see something fantastic."

And fantastic it was, Ben thought, as Nort led a long procession of people from the trucks which brought the men and equipment to the jetty. At the head of the procession with Nort was a white-faced technician who was pushing a device that looked something like an old-fashioned vacuum cleaner without the bag. Behind him marched a dozen young men who had been diving, but who were now armed with picks and shovels. In the main body of the procession were about fifty people of the island who had shown up simply out of curiosity. Minnie Lee was there with her baby in her arms, and Navy, the ferryboatman, was there with the little boy who helped him. Dick Drake stood sipping from a beer can. Donna, beside him, buffed her nails. Bringing up the rear were a dozen very old people from the retirement colony, their tanned faces wizened, their eyes bright with excitement. To Ben the long line of people walking slowly along the beach looked like a religious procession, with Nort some odd kind of perverse priest, his face rapt as he fondled his magic device which could probe the secrets of the earth.

"Something here," the technician said, studying a dial on the metal detector.

The long line of people suddenly transformed itself into a circle. In the center of it the young men with picks and

368

shovels started to dig furiously. There was no sound but the *chunk* of spades, and even the baby in Minnie Lee's arms seemed to hold his breath.

The shoveling ceased abruptly, and the men all bent over to examine the earth.

"What is it?" an old lady asked in a quavering voice.

"A pile of beer cans!" the technician said in disgust. "Damn all Boy Scouts who bury trash!"

"Let's keep going," Nort said, and the circle became a line again.

Every few minutes after that some form of metal was discovered and the men with the shovels went to work, only to discover some piece of junk. Within an hour they had located a length of rusty chain, an old hoe, a bag of nails rusted into a crumbling ball, an old stove and many more beer cans. Behind them the marching line of people left a series of holes — like graves, Ben thought: the religious procession was obviously funereal, some grotesque ceremony for mass burial, leaving open graves because of the mysterious need to hurry on and dig more.

"All right, move on!" Nort said impatiently every time a piece of scrap metal was discovered.

There were a lot of sand fleas on the beach that day, and it was hot. Before long Minnie Lee's baby began to wail, and she wandered off with it. One by one the old people dropped out of the procession. Within a couple of hours only those who were actually under Nort's direction were left.

Starting at the edge of the bay, Nort searched systematically up and down the beach all around the cove. When he got to the dunes, the technician let out a yell.

"There's a lot of stuff somewhere in here!" he said. "This thing is going crazy."

Moving his big machine with surprising speed, the pale-faced little man climbed up the face of the biggest dune.

"It's all around here," he said, circling. "I think this is

369

about the center of it, but you should find something anywhere within thirty feet."

"Wait!" Nort said. "Don't dig till I get back."

At top speed he ran to his jeep and roared away.

"Where the hell is he going?" the technician asked.

"I don't know," one of the diggers said, "but I could sure use a cold beer."

"They probably have some on the yawl," Ben said, and with Penny went to get a case of ale which Flint had on ice.

Twenty minutes later the men were sitting on the dune drinking ale and slapping mosquitoes when they heard the roar of a diesel engine up the road. They looked up and saw Nort coming around a bend with the bulldozer.

"For Christ's sake," one of the divers said. "He shouldn't use that! We might find something of historic value, and he'll bust it all up."

"Get out of the way!" Nort yelled. Lowering the big blade of the bulldozer, he headed straight for the dune.

The men scattered, leaving their shovels behind them.

Nort looked happier than Ben could ever remember as the bulldozer tore into the edge of the dune, sending up great sprays of sand. Driving in a circle around the base of the highest dune, he began to cut it down. In the white sand he left behind Ben saw flakes of red rust.

"Hold on!" he shouted. "You've found something!"

Cutting the engine, Nort jumped from his seat. The men recovered their shovels and started to dig frantically. The first thing they uncovered was the timber of an old ship, and then the end of a rusty boiler.

"Crap," one of the divers said. "This is a fairly modern wreck."

"Uncover it anyway," Nort said.

Working more slowly, the men shoveled away enough

sand to see that a section of a small steamer had been blown ashore in a hurricane and buried in sand.

"We'll just have to keep going," Nort said. A muscle in his cheek twitched.

"It's getting kind of late, isn't it?" the technician asked.

"We'll keep going till dark," Nort said. "Ben, go back and tell them to hold dinner."

Getting into the jeep with Penny, Ben drove slowly back to the house.

"What's going to happen if he tears up the whole island and still finds nothing?" Penny asked.

"That's the moment I've been dreading."

In the living room they found Nancy arranging flowers.

"Nort wants me to tell you they're going to work until dark," Ben said.

"I assumed that," she replied. "Are they finding anything?"

"Nothing of value yet."

"Stay with him, Ben," Nancy said. "These next few days, especially."

"I'll do my best," Ben said, and returned to the jeep.

As they passed the church on the way back, Penny said, "Could we be married there?"

"I don't see why not."

"Can we go in for a second? I'd love to see it again."

"I guess Nort can get along without me for another ten minutes."

Together they went into the church and Penny knelt while Ben, more moved than ever, stared at the compassionate face of the muscular Christ his mother had carved.

"Will you mind, Ben, getting married here a second time?" Penny whispered.

"No. I don't think I have any bitterness left. Perhaps

this is where I should make my resolves to do better a second time."

"Will you ask your daughter and her husband?"

"Yes. I hope both my children will come."

There was a moment of quiet.

"It's good to sit here," she said. "The silence is healing."

"There's something nerve-shattering about the sound of that dozer," he said, "but I guess we'd better get back."

Outside the church he hesitated, then walked back to the cemetery to look at his father's grave once more. Someone had placed fresh pansies around it, he saw. Was it Minnie Lee, or some other person he had never met? Somehow the grave looked different, now he knew more about his father, and there was pathos in the mental picture he had of his mother carving that inscription, preserving her own dream of her husband to the end.

That afternoon Nort did not justify the fears that Ben, Penny and Nancy had about him. In a workmanlike way, he continued his search pattern to the southern tip of the island. As the sun set, he turned off the engine of the bulldozer and grinned.

"I have a feeling that tomorrow's going to be the day," he said.

Early the next morning Nort organized additional crews to search other parts of the island simultaneously with new equipment which had just arrived.

"Ben," he said, "do you mind if we check out the place where your father's house used to be? I mean, it's a nice piece of high ground that might be a natural."

Ben hesitated. The remaining portion of chimney, the fireplace, the hearth and the makeshift shelter which he and Penny had built there — he disliked the thought of the bulldozer ripping it all apart. But wasn't there some millionth part of a chance that gold was there? How strange it would be to find that his parents had been living on top of a fabulous treasure the whole time they were so worried about money!

"I guess there's no reason not to check it out," he said, "but please don't use the bulldozer unless you have to. I like my ruin the way it is."

The metal detector showed a lot of activity all around the old fireplace, however, and the crew of diggers moved in. As they tore down the driftwood fence and the tarpaulin fell, Ben felt a curious sense of desecration. Then the shovels started to bite into the sand. The first thing they found was an old enameled sink, and many lengths of pipe. There was also a plate with a pattern of cloverleaves which Ben remembered from his childhood, one plate miraculously intact after so many hurricanes. Taking it from the hand of the man who had unearthed it, Ben felt deeply moved.

"Save this for our child," he said, giving it to Penny. "It's a very old plate. I think my mother's people brought it from England."

"My baby's first gift!" Penny said, and she kissed the plate.

"Hell, there's nothing here," the technician said. Picking up their shovels, the diggers moved on.

Nort kept four crews digging all that day and spent his own time speeding from one to another in the jeep. Whenever a big deposit of metal was indicated, he brought in the bulldozer, loading it aboard a big truck if it was at the wrong end of the island. More than fifty men were working, and they found some interesting objects: a handful of lead musketballs, an old pewter spoon, a cutlass rusted almost completely away, a powderhorn, and a pathetic little collection of dimes, nickels and pennies in a child's bank about fifty years old. None of these objects interested

373

Nort in the least. As the day wore on, lines of bitterness were etched deeply into his face, and the mannerisms Ben had noticed earlier were intensified. Unable to stick with any one crew for long, Nort drove his jeep headlong from one end of the island to the other and back again. He began to drink from a silver flask even while he was driving the bulldozer.

"Don't you think that's kind of dangerous?" Ben asked him.

"Have you ever seen me when I couldn't hold my liquor?" Nort demanded indignantly.

That seemed a question best not answered, and Ben said nothing.

"Damn it, quit trying to be my father, Ben!" Nort said, and took one more defiant swig from his flask before roaring off.

As the day wore on, Nort began to use the bulldozer more and more recklessly. When metal was detected under the dirt floor of an abandoned shack, he simply charged the big machine into the structure, careless of the splintered boards and broken glass that scattered all around his head. The act of destruction seemed to please him, and even before digging to see what metal was there, he turned the bulldozer around to return and crush the last wall left standing. After all that, nothing was found but some rusty tools. Apparently undismayed, Nort wheeled the big machine around and charged down on an abandoned chicken coop a few yards away.

There was nothing Ben could do to calm him down, and he was afraid that a cautionary word or two would make Nort worse. With a feeling of helplessness, he stood by and watched. By nightfall four fairly large sections of the island were so torn up that they looked like the sites of major battles.

When it was dark, Nort switched on the headlights of

the bulldozer and drove it toward the big house. Following him in the jeep, Ben had the nightmare thought that he might just keep on going and wreck the whole mansion with everyone in it, but a few hundred yards away Nort stopped and shut off the engine.

"Tomorrow we'll work the ridge," he said, climbing down. "I'm sure tomorrow will be it, Ben! I really am!"

But the conviction had gone out of his voice, and his whole body expressed dejection as he walked slowly toward his office, where he ate his dinner alone.

Everyone was jumpy at dinner that night. Digging did not hold the fascination for most of the men that diving did, and there was a lot of grumbling about being asked to do a different job from the one they had signed on for. Nancy, dressed in tailored pink slacks and a white lace blouse, paced restlessly around the room, unable to sit still long enough to finish her meal. Her constant movement made Ben fidget. As soon as they finished their cold roast beef, Ben and Penny went to their rooms.

Almost as soon as they got there, Ben heard a gentle tapping at their door. It was Minnie Lee.

"Ben," she said without preamble. "I think I know where the gold is. If I tell you, will you make sure I get a cut?"

He wanted to tell her to say nothing she didn't want Nort to overhear, but it was already too late for that.

"Come in and sit down, Minnie," Ben said.

The big woman sank heavily into an armchair and looked doubtfully at Penny, who was standing in the bedroom door.

"You don't mind if she hears?" Minnie Lee asked.

"We have no secrets. What do you know, Minnie?"

"First of all, will you make sure I get a cut if I'm right?"

"How much do you want?"

"I'd like half. Not just for myself, for the people of the island. I figure that much at least belongs to us."

"I'll have to talk to Mr. Clay about it."

"I'll trust you to do your best. We were always able to trust your father."

"What do you know?"

"I'm not *sure*," she said. "Leastways, I'm not sure how much is there."

"Where?"

"Do you remember that story of big Sam, the one who found the gold and all he got was killed for it?"

"Yes."

"Well, I think that was more than just a story. And the place he found the gold, he wasn't just afraid to tell anybody, he was ashamed."

"Ashamed?"

"It was the cemetery. He found it while he was digging a grave a long while ago, and he kept on digging around to find more."

"Who told you this?"

"My mother. She didn't want me to tell no one. There's more to the story."

"What?"

"About thirty years ago, more gold was found, nobody would say where, and quite a few of the people brought it to your father to get it sold. He took it into Miami and brought them cash. He gave some of his share to my mother, and you know what he told her?"

"What?"

"He told her not to put it in the bank. Banks were failing at that time, and anyway, if a colored woman went to a bank a lot, people started asking her where she got her money. A colored woman could get in a lot of trouble that way."

"I understand."

"So your father told her to keep it in the cemetery, because that's one place people don't dig. He told her to keep it on the grave of her child, and when she go to plant flowers, she can get what she needs. But my mother wouldn't do it. She said money from a grave would be jinxed, and that's when your father said he thought that that's where all the gold on the island came from anyhow. He said that old Indian mound might not be an Indian mound, there might be some of the old Spanish people buried there with all kinds of gold."

"The Indian mound!" Ben said.

"You know, it's part of the cemetery, it's holy ground. For years it's been a place people would never go digging — they even walk around it. When he died, your father was trying to figure out a way to find out what was there. He was working on old Mr. Corny Clay, trying to get him interested in some kind of digging for museums."

"I see," Ben said.

"George Grey knew about it, and so did I. George has been digging up there a long time, but he can't do too much, or people would see."

"Did he find anything?"

"I don't know. One man with a shovel can't do much. That's a pretty big old hill."

"We'll check into it," Ben said. "I'll do my best to get you your half if they find anything."

"I wanted to tell you when you first came, but George said not to trust nobody. He's crazy scared now that they'll find it anyway."

"I'll make sure you'll get something," Ben said.

"We'd all appreciate that," Minnie Lee said, and with a dignified nod to them both she left, her white dress fading into the darkness like a ghost.

"Do you think she's right?" Penny asked.

"I don't know. There's a certain plausibility to it all. For centuries the Indian mound was one place the natives didn't go near. It's a big hill rising out of flat land. For all I know, a whole ship could be buried there."

377

"Are you going to tell Nort tonight?"

"I'd rather wait till he's sober. But with all this bugging business, maybe he already knows."

"Does he listen to people directly, or to recordings?"

As though in answer there came the deep cough of the bulldozer engine starting.

"Jesus Christ, he's going to plow up that whole graveyard tonight!" Ben said, and ran outside. Dashing to the front of the house, he saw the yellow bulldozer lumbering toward the church, its yellow paint glistening with dew in the moonlight. High up on its iron saddle, Nort sat enthroned, with a bottle in his left hand, his right hand caressing one of the long control levers. Jumping into the jeep, Ben drove past him, circled and parked the jeep with its headlights blazing in a narrow part of the road between the corner of the house and a grove of royal palm trees. Standing up, he waved his arms as the bulldozer approached.

"Nort!" he shouted. "I want to talk to you!"

The big machine lurched to a halt, and Nort cut the engine. In a surprisingly controlled voice he said, "What do you want, Ben?"

"Wait until morning! Do this in a sane, sensible way!"

"Do you think I'm crazy, Ben?"

"I think you're tired and I think you've been drinking. Wait until morning, I say!"

"The only thing crazy about me is that I didn't know where to look in the first place. Of course it's the graveyard! Those cannon are lying right at the bottom of the mound, protected all these years by skeletons."

"Maybe, but wait till you have a crew. If you charge around with that thing now, you won't even know what you've found!"

"I'll know when I hit those cannon. I want to find them alone, Ben. Get that jeep out of my way."

378

"Nort, please! For me!"

The only reply was the bark of the big engine coming to life again, and the huge machine rolled forward. Ben leapt from the jeep. There was a crash of metal and splintered glass as the huge machine pushed the jeep aside, turning it on end. With his throttle wide open, Nort roared toward the cemetery without a backward glance.

"Ben, are you all right?" Penny called, her voice full of panic.

"I'm all right."

The front door of the house flew open, and Nancy came running out.

"Can you stop him?" Her face was ashen. She *does* love him, Ben thought with wonder.

"Call some of the divers. We can try."

Alarmed by the sound of the bulldozer and the grating of metal on metal, a dozen young men were already pouring out of the house. They went running after the bulldozer, catching up with it just as it approached the churchyard. But having caught it, they didn't know what to do with it, for Nort did not slacken his speed. One of the young divers crouched as though he were going to try to leap to the driver's seat, but the sight of the great caterpillar treads churning almost at the level of his eyes dissuaded him even before he saw that Nort had thrown away the bottle in his right hand and was brandishing a revolver. With its big engine roaring, the bulldozer veered around the wall of the cemetery and headed toward the high mound behind it. There was a clang as the huge curved blade came down, and a cloud of sand rose like a wave.

"All we can do is keep out of his way," Ben said, but some of the divers didn't hear him. They kept running after the bulldozer shouting and waving their arms. Turning sharply when he got to the end of the mound, Nort charged straight at them. As they leapt aside they resembled bullfighters panic-stricken by a beast twelve times the normal size. Scattering, the divers gathered in a clump near Ben, breathing heavily.

There was nothing they could do but watch. Circling erratically, Nort charged around the base of the mound, whittling it down. In the moonlight the sand was yellow, and if there were bones, they were invisible in the shadows of the irregular terrain. In a surprisingly short time Nort made the seaward side of the mound so steep that Ben thought it was going to cave in on him, but then he began circling the whole mound, cutting into the other sides. After about twenty minutes, the mound had become a narrow rectangle, and Nort began chopping off the ends.

"He's not going to find anything," Ben said to Penny with sudden conviction.

The remaining part of the mound got smaller and smaller, until the whole thing suddenly collapsed in a sea of sand crossed and recrossed by the bulldozer. As though the machine itself were demented, it scattered the sand farther and farther, and then began digging a deep valley where the mound had been. There was a splash as the deepest part filled with water. Lumbering out of the hole, the machine paused, and Ben could see Nort stand on the iron saddle to look around, his eyes probing the sand for some telltale glint of gold. The divers ran toward him, but before they got near, Nort raced the engine, manipulated the levers, and charged toward the cemetery, ripping through the fence. The huge blade clanged against row after row of marble tombstones, scattering them in every direction. Methodically as a reaper, Nort mowed down row after row of gravestones, tossing coffin boards high into the air. A scattering of bones glimmered eerily in the moonlight. One skull gleamed on the sand.

It took only a few minutes to wreck the little graveyard. When every headstone had been leveled, Nort started crisscrossing it again, digging long trenches that immediately filled with water. When there were no graves left, he stopped and stood again, looking all around him, but before anyone could get near him, he started the bulldozer at top speed and headed toward the church.

"Oh, God!" Penny cried.

It will kill him, Ben thought — it will collapse on him and kill him, but that did not happen. Nort attacked one corner of the building at a time, knocking it off its foundations. High in the little steeple, the old ship's bell clanged twice, before that end of the building collapsed, and the bell came tumbling down in its little wooden tower, missing Nort's head by a few feet. After knocking one end off the church, Nort attacked the walls, bursting through them in a shower of splintered wood. The windshield of the bulldozer was cracked in so many places that it was opaque, but it was shatterproof, and crouched behind it, Nort was unscathed. Circling back and forth, he scattered the timbers of the church and dug a hole where the foundation had been. Only when he hit water again did he stop, and this time he cut the engine. The sudden silence was shocking. Climbing on top of the hood of the bulldozer, Nort stared around at the scene of complete destruction he had created, the sandy pools gleaming in the moonlight, the long trenches littered with bones.

"There is nothing!" he said, his voice shrill. "There is nothing! There is nothing at all!"

He suddenly jumped to the ground, and without a glance in any direction stalked past the divers toward the house. Unsure what to do, everyone followed, walking together in an awkward silence. At the front door of the house Nancy met them.

"What happened?" she asked.

"*Nothing!*" Nort replied.

Striding to the bar in the living room, Nort poured himself a quarter-tumbler of scotch.

"Did you find anything?" Nancy asked.

"*Nothing!* There is nothing to find!"

"How can you be sure so soon?"

"There is nothing!"

"But you were sure."

"Bitch, be still!"

Nancy turned to Ben.

"What did he do? What did he do down there with the bulldozer?"

"Get out of here, Ben!" Nort said. "All of you, get out! I want to talk to this woman, if that's what she is."

"You'd better go," Nancy said.

Through the still air of the island that night came shrieks and howls so animal-like that it was impossible to say whether they were uttered by a man or a woman.

"I think I ought to go up there," Ben said.

"No! I'm afraid, Ben!"

A moment later there was a loud knock on the door, and Nancy was standing there, looking surprisingly composed.

"He wants to see you," she said. "I think you should just let him talk."

Resignedly, Ben followed her up the stairs.

"He's in my room," Nancy said, leading the way to a large suite on the other side of the house from Nort's office. "I can't get him out."

In the middle of a huge double bed with a canopy, Nort lay fully dressed, a glass in his hand.

"Ben, Ben, Ben!" he said. "Did you know all along there was nothing?"

"No," Ben said.

"Have a drink, Ben! That black bitch lied when she came to your room tonight, didn't she?"

"I don't know. You might have scattered gold ingots all over the place."

"But no cannon, Ben. No gold cannon. Do you think those bastards in Spain were lying to me?"

"I don't know."

"Lies!" Nort said. "Deceit, hatred, immorality — I've been surrounded by them all my life. That's all there is, Ben. Nothing but shit . . ."

His voice fell to a mumble studded with obscenities, oddly in the tone of a prayer. Thinking he was only half conscious, Ben got up to go, but Nort immediately said, "Stay, Ben! I want you to hear this!"

There was more mumbling, incoherent, obscene, self-pitying, bitter toward Nancy, bitter toward everyone. At times Nort's voice fell so low that it was little more than a hoarse whisper.

"Go to sleep, Nort," Ben said. "Go to sleep. Everything's going to be all right."

"You believe that, Ben?"

This sentence was asked in a voice strong and clear.

"Sometimes."

"Then you're a fool! Do you still believe in anything?"

"I believe in a great deal."

"Fool. Poor, stupid, fucking fool!"

The incoherent mumbling began again.

Patiently, Ben settled back in his chair for a long vigil. Every once in a while the door opened and Nancy looked in, saying nothing.

A little after three in the morning, Nort fell asleep. Nancy tiptoed in and covered him up like a child, taking the empty glass out of his hand.

"Would you like a nightcap, Ben?" she whispered as they went down the stairs.

"I'm too tired."

"I know. But please see me in the morning. I think the time has come. We have a tough decision to make. Meet me here at nine."

CHAPTER 24

WHEN Ben got back to his rooms he found Penny lying on the bed wrapped up in a blanket, despite the fact that the room was hot.

"Hold me, Ben," she said. "I'm frightened."

"Nothing's going to hurt us."

"I'll never forget the way he said it."

"What?" he asked, although he knew.

"*There is nothing,*" she said. "A friend of mine has been

scaring hell out of me by telling me just that the last two weeks."

"Who?"

"I didn't tell you. It was too complicated. But I have this friend, a man I've known since I was sixteen. I can't explain it. He's a man I've never really been in love with, but I could always count on him. I could go to him when things got really bad. Anyway, I wrote him about you and he told me I was crazy and getting crazier all the time. He said all my talk of finding love and kindness was a delusion. He said I had just gone down to Florida with some television writer and was trying to build it up into a great romance. There's nothing like that, he said, *nothing*. There is only trying to live sanely. Common sense."

"That's up to us."

"I can't stand the thought of that. Let's get out of here, Ben! I can't live with people who think there is *nothing*. When I was in Miami I found I could get a job at the hospital, and there's all kinds of work for you if you want it. Miami is getting to be a big television town."

"We'll go soon."

"When?" she demanded.

"A few days, probably. How can I explain? If I go now, I'd feel I was deserting my post under fire."

"All right," she said after a long pause. "But tell me there is not *nothing*, Ben!"

"There is anything we want to make."

"And we can make kindness and love into something more than a delusion?"

"If we work overtime."

"Yes," she said, and came to rest in his arms.

Ben himself did not sleep at all until almost dawn, but he awoke at eight-thirty as though an alarm clock had gone off, remembering that Nancy had wanted to see him at nine. She was in the dining room, and handed him a cup of black coffee.

"Where's your girl?" she asked.

"Still asleep."

"Good. Let's go up to Nort's study. He's still asleep in my room."

"Where are the divers?" he asked.

"Working over the cemetery with the metal detectors. They've been at it since dawn, and I understand that they've already found quite a few coins."

Nancy led the way up the stairs to Nort's study and took a key from her handbag.

"Nort doesn't know I have this key," she said. "I took his to have it copied one night when he was drunk."

Ben said nothing.

"You don't approve?"

He shrugged.

"If you live with a madman, you get a little mad yourself. Come on in."

Leading the way to the corner behind Nort's desk, Nancy pushed at the wall on which the big chart of the island hung. A door cut to the shape of the chart opened.

"Secret doors and everything," she said cheerfully.

Stepping into the room, Ben found himself in what looked like a compact communications center aboard a ship. Everywhere there were microphones and radios, with row upon row of switches.

"Nort showed me this one night himself," Nancy said, sinking down in a swivel chair and picking up a pair of earphones. "It's quite fascinating. I don't quite know how to work it myself, but Nort can sit here and tune in on almost any conversation on the island. I think this one is your room." She flicked a switch. From the amplifier came the sound of Penny's breathing.

"Please turn it off," Ben said.

"Want to try my room? He even had videotape in there."

"No," Ben said.

"So you agree with me that he is mad?"

"Of course."

"Do you know how hard it is going to be to commit him?"

"I can guess."

"But we have to," she said. "For his own good, if nothing else. We have to get him under a doctor's care before he kills himself or somebody else."

"Is there any chance he'd go voluntarily?"

"None in the world. But last night gives us our chance. Desecrating a graveyard, destroying a church — any court in the world would judge that mad."

"Yes."

"But you've got to help me, Ben. Lawyers can't do it alone. And he's got me powerless. Look."

Opening the drawer of a big filing cabinet, she showed him many thick folders.

"We're all here, on paper and on tape," she said. "He got a lot on me before I knew what he was doing. Want to see your file? Want to see a carbon of Penny's? You didn't really think burning those papers was more than a gesture, did you? He has copies of everything kept in safe deposit boxes."

"Does he have a microphone hidden in your room?"

"Of course," she said.

"Do you know where?"

"In the bedside lamp. And there's a camera in the air-conditioner. I've learned how to trace these things."

"Was it going last night?"

"Of course. If I tamper with them, he just finds new hiding places."

"I'll talk to him when he wakes up," Ben said.

"Do you want a couple of men to wait outside the door?"

"I don't think he'll be in a mood for any rough stuff."

"Where can I find you?"

"I'm going over to the cemetery now. I'll be back in about an hour."

At the wreckage of the cemetery Ben found every man on the island following four men with the metal detectors and sifting loose dirt through screens wrapped around barrel hoops. Perspiring freely, his face covered with grime, Richard Drake was presiding over a large box in which the finds were being collected.

"My God, Ben," he said jovially. "We've found three gold ingots so far, and a hatful of coins. I don't think there's anything tremendous, but it's not nothing by a long sight!"

"I'm glad," Ben said, and returned to the big house. Penny was still asleep. Too keyed up to sleep himself, Ben lay down beside her, taking comfort in the regular sound of her breathing.

In about an hour there was a tap on his door.

"He's up," Nancy said. "He wants to see you."

Nort was sitting on the edge of Nancy's bed, a cup of coffee cradled in both his hands.

"Christ, I'm glad to see you, Ben!" Nort said. "What the hell happened last night?"

"You went kind of wild with the bulldozer."

"Did I hurt anyone?"

Nort sounded terrified.

"No, Nort," Ben said. "You were lucky."

"Thank God! But I didn't find anything, did I? I remember that. There are no gold cannon, are there? There's nothing to find at all."

"I wouldn't say that. The boys are raking the site now.

Already they've found three gold ingots and a hatful of coins."

"That's nothing, Ben. That wouldn't pay for a hundredth of what I've spent."

"But it's interesting, isn't it? Can't you afford to give yourself a little fun?"

"I wanted to find them," Nort said. "The cannon. Do you think they might be on some other island?"

"I don't know. Nort, do you want me to level with you?"

"I always want that from you, Ben."

"I think you need help, Nort. From doctors. Before you feel worse."

"Still that, Ben?"

"Well, crashing that bulldozer around . . . You wrecked the church."

"That was my land, Ben. I own most of this island. The church was mine. I can destroy what I own."

"It's still not healthy."

"You say they're finding gold, don't you? That proves I wasn't crazy!"

"It doesn't prove you don't need help. Wrecking the church isn't the only thing, Nort. All this bugging business. You know damn well it isn't sane."

"Then my own government isn't sane! What do you think the Internal Revenue boys do? How about the CIA?"

"Governments can get away with a lot of things an individual can't."

"On this island, *I* am the government!"

"Perhaps, but only a very small government. Only the big ones can get away with going completely wild."

"Why is it crazy to listen in on people, Ben? Is knowledge crazy? Shouldn't I learn all I can about the people with whom I have to deal?"

"No."

"You'd be a lot wiser if you checked up on that girl of yours, Ben. She's immoral, has been for years. You should read the report."

"We're not talking about her now, Nort. Do you trust me?"

"God knows I do!"

"I'm telling you, for your own good, go to the Mayo Clinic and check yourself in. If you don't, I honestly think you'll be dead within a year, and you'll probably take quite a few people with you."

"What right have you got to say that, Ben? The bugging isn't evidence of any madness! I knocked over the church, but the boys are finding money. So I'm reckless sometimes, but I never hurt anybody. What proof do you have that I'm not sane?"

"Did you have this room bugged last night?"

"I have the whole island bugged. So what?"

"Was everything said in this room last night taped?"

"You're damn right it was."

"Play it back. Play it back for me now."

"Oh come on, Ben. I feel lousy."

"I want to hear it! How do you turn it on?"

"We'll have to go up to my office."

"Let's go."

"Not now!"

"If you won't listen to that tape now, I'm leaving the island this morning!"

"All right, Ben, hold on. Christ, my head aches."

Staggering a little, Nort led the way to his office.

"I have kind of a headquarters here," he said, pushing the chart on the wall.

"So I see."

Nort sank down in the swivel chair and cradled his head in his hands.

"Let me hear what went on in Nancy's room last night," Ben said.

"Why do you want to hear that?"

"You've taped all the rest of us, and now you've taped yourself. I want you to hear it."

"Christ, Ben! What are you trying to do?"

"You know the truth about everyone else. It's time you learned it about yourself. Turn the tape on."

Nort flicked a switch, and suddenly his own voice flooded the room, drunken, mumbling, repetitive, obscene.

"I was drunk!" he cried violently and turned the switch off.

"Listen to it!"

Reaching over Nort's shoulder, Ben flicked the switch on, and again there was the terrible mumbling, the cursing, the incoherent, paranoid accusations. Covering his face with his hands, Nort slumped over his knees.

"Do you have videotape in that room?" Ben asked remorselessly.

"I had to. Nance learned she couldn't talk. I was afraid she would take men there silently, just for spite."

"Play it back."

Nort flipped some more switches, and suddenly on a television screen, there was the image of himself slumped on the big bed, his tie askew, mumbling. The torrent of obscenities was unintelligible until, half sitting up on the bed, the figure of Nort on the television screen shouted, "Kill the yellow bastards! For Christ's sake, Jesus, why not drop the big bombs and wipe out this whole stinking mess of a human race? Pissing, shitting, fucking hairless monkeys! Even you, Ben, Christ you're only happy when you have your filthy hand in a woman's crotch. Wipe us all out, I say! We should all burn! Nancy fucks the goddam tennis instructor and Judy fucks the Dartmouth boys, and we're all one big happy family! I tell you, boy, I've got it on tape! I can let you hear it and I can show it to you! We're a race of monsters, and the only clean thing in the world is *death!*"

"Christ, Ben! Do I have to take this?" Nort moaned.

"I did."

Nort flicked the machine off.

"Why are you doing this to me?"

"To prove to you that you need help."

"Do I do this kind of thing often?" The question was piteous, but Ben refused to give in to the stab of compassion he felt.

"Yes, and it's getting worse."

"You're not lying to me?"

"Do tapes lie?"

"No, the tapes never lie, Ben. And neither do you."

"Will you let me make arrangements to check you into the Mayo Clinic?"

"Sure, Ben. Sure. Now, on the strength of that, let's have one good drink."

Opening a drawer, Nort took out a bottle of scotch and two glasses. Pouring each of them a quarter full, he handed one to Ben.

"No water, no ice," he said with a crooked smile. "Just the essentials. Let's drink a toast, Ben. To health and happiness!"

"To health and happiness!" Ben repeated and taking a sip of the whiskey, shuddered.

"You can make your arrangements, Ben. Charter a plane to take me where I have to go. My jet has a busted wing."

"I admire you for this, Nort."

"Do you?"

There was that old boyish grin Ben hadn't seen in a long while, the longing to be liked.

"Yes, I do. Facing the truth takes guts."

"I've faced it with everyone else, so why not me? Do you know how full of evil the world is, Ben?"

"And also good."

"Go through my files. Play some of the tapes I've got on my own family, my best friends. Then see if you can tell me that! Do you know what it's like to hear your own wife making love with one of your own employees?"

"I don't think I'd want to listen."

"Why not? Is truth something you can't face? Why don't you go through the file on your girl and look at the list of her lovers?"

"There are different kinds of truth."

"You're a damn ostrich, Ben! That I've never been. I know what the world is. I know about you and her and Nancy and now, I admit, myself."

"But you make everything so — terrible. Anything can be fixed, Nort!"

"That is a lie!"

"Superficially, it may be. But the impact of anything can be healed. The impact on your own soul."

"Do you believe in souls, Ben?"

"After my fashion."

"You think I'm insane. You even proved it, to *my* satisfaction. What do you think I think of your passionate mumblings with that much-used little broad? Do you want me to play some of *those* back to *you?*"

"No."

"You're not so much better off than I am, are you?"

"Look, Nort ——"

"But to health!" Nort interrupted, picking up his glass again. "To health and happiness."

"To health and happiness," Ben muttered.

"To the beauty of dreams and the horror of truth!"

"To our own ability to make the world what we want it!" Ben said, wanting to mean it.

"Have you made it what you want, Ben?"

"Sometimes. For a little while."

"To health and happiness," Nort repeated. "Is your world full of health and happiness?"

"At the moment."

"You're a sly dog, Ben! You made me listen to a tape of me. Why won't you listen to a tape of you?"

"I trust my memory. It's not as pitiless as tape."

"But you are pitiless with me. Have you *ever* liked me, Ben?"

"Often."

"Thank you for that. In one more minute, go call the funny farm, Ben. After one more toast, I'll throw the bottle away."

Refilling both glasses, Nort clinked his against Ben's.

"To the gold cannon," he said. "To the gold cannon, wherever they are. Even if the bastards never existed!"

"To the gold cannon," Ben intoned.

"Now get the hell out of here," Nort said gently. "Before your men in white come, I have a few things to do."

"There don't have to be men in white. I'll go with you."

"You'll stay with me, Ben?"

"I can't stay, but I'll take you there."

"That is, so to speak, white of you. Will your girl come?"

"I hope so."

"It could be a kind of wedding trip for you."

"We're trying to help you, Nort."

"Of course you are! So you really still have hope?"

"I do."

"You don't realize that hope becomes a delusion as you grow older?"

"It depends what you hope for."

"What do you hope for?"

"A few good years for both of us, for everyone I love."

"I always wanted more than that. Get out of here, Ben. Go make your — arrangements."

"Don't worry," Ben said, sounding to himself like his own lawyer. "There's nothing to worry about!"

"I won't worry. I promise you that."

With another boyish grin, Nort finished his whiskey. Wondering who he should call, Ben started downstairs.

He hadn't reached the hall before he heard the shot.

CHAPTER 25

Nᴀɴᴄʏ reached the door of Nort's communications center almost as soon as Ben did. They found Nort lying
slumped over his files, anointing all those many folders of
papers and tapes with his blood. His face was calm, almost
as though he were reading, and there was no mark on it.
He had shot himself through the heart.

As though she were stroking the face of a sleeping child,
Nancy smoothed back her husband's hair.

"Now, Ben, there is no one listening," she said.

"No."

Still Nancy smoothed her husband's hair, her hands more affectionate than Ben had ever seen them when Nort was alive.

"For fifteen years, Ben, I always knew he was listening," she continued. "Sometimes I thought it would drive me crazy, but it's terrible to know that no one cares enough to listen any more. We can do anything, Ben, and no one will know, no one will care. It is as though God were dead."

Giving her husband a kiss on the forehead, Nancy left the room and Ben followed her. Looking at Ben's stricken face, Nancy said, "You think you killed him."

"Yes."

"Do you think he would have lived long if you hadn't been here?"

"No."

"I don't know if this will give you comfort or pain, but he wanted you to kill him."

"What do you mean?"

"He said to me not long ago, 'I like Ben, but someday he will kill me. Ben is my executioner, and I am glad, because it is best to die at the hands of a friend.' "

"I didn't want to kill him."

"What difference does that make, Ben? Nort always got what he wanted, didn't he?"

"He didn't get his gold cannon."

"What would have happened if he had? Would they have made any difference?"

"No."

"He got what he wanted, Ben. Now it's time for us. Please call the sheriff and make all the necessary arrangements. I guess we'll have to bury him in Huntington, since we don't have a cemetery here any more."

"I'll see to it," Ben said.

"I'll leave for New York tonight," Nancy continued. "I suppose there's no chance of your going with me?"

"No, Nancy."

She nodded. "I wonder," she said musingly, "if I would want you if you were eager to come?"

"Then you would distrust me."

"Yes. Then you would be like all the rest."

There was a pause before she added, "What are you going to do, Ben?"

"Get married, I guess."

"And live on love?"

"We'll get along."

"I'm not going to make any great gesture to help you. Did you think I would?"

"No."

"Money is all I've got, and I don't plan to give it away."

"I can't say I blame you."

"I'll make a deal with you, though. Stay and manage my island. Make it profitable for me."

"I don't know much about real estate."

"No, but I can trust you. Sell the island for me, Ben. Make whatever deals have to be made so that I never have to hear the name of this place again. I'll give you whatever percentages are usual."

"All right."

"Tell me when and where to show up for the funeral. You can get me in Huntington."

"I will."

"I want to be free, Ben, free of all of it."

"I'll see to that."

"Thank you, Ben."

Putting her small dry hand on his face, Nancy caressed his cheek, running her fingers lightly over his mouth, almost as though she were blind and were trying to recognize him. Then she turned and almost ran to her private suite.

Ben called the sheriff, and then slowly walked back to his rooms. Penny was still sleeping, a slender young woman with one hand thrown over her head. Once again Ben lay down beside her.

"Ben?" she murmured.

"Yes."

"Are you all right?"

"Yes."

"What time is it?"

"Early."

"Good." Drowsily, she snuggled against him. "I love you."

"I love you, too."

She smiled, and the smile remained as she slept.